Where No Shadows Fall

PETER RITCHIE

BLACK & WHITE PUBLISHING

First published in 2019 by
Black & White Publishing Ltd
Nautical House, 104 Commercial Street
Edinburgh EH6 6NF

1 3 5 7 9 10 8 6 4 2   19 20 21 22

ISBN: 978 1 78530 196 4

A CIP catalogue record for this book is available
from the British Library.

Typeset by Iolaire, Newtonmore
Printed and bound by CPI Group (UK) Ltd, Croydon, CR0 4YY

*I'd like to dedicate this book to my granddaughter Nancy,
or Dublin Nancy as I call her. She's an absolute character
and I hope the world is ready for her.*

'We all have a dark side. Most of us go through life avoiding direct confrontation with that aspect of ourselves, which I call the shadow self. There's a reason why. It carries a great deal of energy.'

LORRAINE TOUSSAINT, quoted in *The Daily Beast*

'Can a woman forget her nursing child, that she should have no compassion on the son of her womb? Even these may forget, yet I will not forget you.'

ISAIAH 49.15 (ENGLISH STANDARD VERSION)

PROLOGUE

It was 11 p.m. on Christmas Eve and Bing Crosby sang 'Rudolph the Red-Nosed Reindeer' on the car radio behind him as he stared across the dark waters of the Clyde, trying to hold back the swirling emotions that threatened to choke him. The odd fat snowflake landed on his shoulders and hair, looked pretty for a moment, then disappeared forever. The poor little bastard he'd thrown into the river wrapped up in a filthy towel had never had a chance since conception, and he kept repeating the word 'sorry' over and over again, as if it made a difference. It was an unusual event in every way because he wasn't brought up to say sorry to anyone. He'd got rid of the evidence and watched the child disappear under the lapping waters of the great river. What could be worse than what he'd done that night? If he'd had any humanity left it had sunk into the depths of the Clyde with an innocent child.

'What the fuck have I done?' He looked up to the cloud-filled heavens, as if God would forgive him, before stumbling off into the night. The lights sparkled on the cold water that covered a son who would never know his father or mother. Some might have said the child was lucky, but then who else knew? He growled in the back of his throat as he headed back to the car and switched off Bing Crosby.

The evidence might have gone but some crimes can never be completely washed away.

1

Late 2008
Tommy McMartin shivered in the cold air of the Glasgow night. His jacket was fashionable but not worth a toss for keeping him warm. The boy cared more about impressing the 'talent' than his body temperature, and that was what being twenty-five and living in the city was all about in his world. He was a good-looking boy: something positive had passed through from his parents and gifted him, along with other features, straight white teeth that looked like he'd paid a fortune to a top dentist, but it all came packaged up in the genes. He was on the short side, but a ringer for Tom Cruise apart from his hair colour, so he played that for all it was worth and had perfected the little actor's eye and mouth movements. That natural gift gave him all the sexual attraction he needed, and more. He was lucky, because although he was a violent bastard when it came to the day job, otherwise he was great company and people gravitated towards him. Not all the sentiments he attracted were heartfelt and genuine, though, because he was the possible heir to a well-known family business.

The McMartin clan controlled a lot of people plus a shit-load of illegal cash that they washed with the assistance of bent lawyers, a couple of local politicians and some friendly accountants, who were all happy to fill their boots for the family. They provided their professional services regardless of the butcher's bill paid by the addicts so dependent on the product that saw them through their miserable lives. The business was mainly drugs, but also prostitutes or anything that could be turned into a profit. If there was a problem that stood in their way they maimed or killed it at birth, and after a few turf wars they'd come out as one of the leading crime families in the West Central Belt of Scotland. Nobody but nobody fucked with a McMartin. They bred like rabbits on Viagra and it gave them an edge. There were simply more of them than anyone else, so killing one or two did nothing but bring the whole nation down on your head. It was like killing a couple of Mongol soldiers when Genghis Khan was running the show. Tommy McMartin's father and uncles had done the fighting then built up the business to what it was. They made old Arthur Thompson's gangsters look like a bunch of well-intentioned social workers.

Tommy's uncle, and the man who'd led them to glory, was Benny 'Slab' McMartin, who'd earned his handle not through a trade in the building industry but because of an incident at the height of a gang feud. The story was that he'd used a concrete slab to flatten the nappers of two captured hard men who'd tried to take him when he was at his front door one night. Unfortunately for the two would-be assassins, Slab was harder, faster and possessed the instincts of a sewer rat when there was a threat coming at him. He sensed them before he saw them hiding in his prized herbaceous border, and that was the last mistake they ever made. He took pictures of the finished job and sent copies to their employers, who presumed that like their recently departed colleagues

4

they were probably fucked. That presumption proved on the money over the following weeks, and the carnage continued till the opposition ran out of fight, pulled up the white flag and buried their leaders.

Slab was a legend, and even though he was part of a family largely made up of part-time psychopaths, they all looked to him for leadership because he could think as well as act. Without him the family empire would have crumbled into civil war and their enemies would have picked them off a piece at a time. The CID and crime squads used to call him Tito after the famous Yugosla-vian Marshal who managed through sheer force of will to keep the warring tribes in the Balkans under one flag, at least as long as he lived.

The problem for Slab was that it turned out he was mortal like everyone else. Long years of hyper-stress, gang feuds and a passion for treble rum and Coke with the powdered version on the side had stressed his heart once too often. He collapsed in a heap one night as he beat the soul out of a low-level drug courier who'd lost a big consignment to the law. The poor bastard – through no fault of his own – had lost the H when he ran straight into a waiting police operation set up by his ex-girlfriend. It was the oldest story in the world: he'd been caught playing away with his fiancée's best friend and she had her revenge. Slab told the terrified courier that there was no excuse for blabbing details of the job to the cow and there had to be penalties for failure. Especially when failure cost Slab the best part of eighty grand. 'It's no' the social work department, son. I mean, do I look like a fuckin' social worker?'

Slab's team laughed because it was in their interest to join in the fun. The courier just couldn't do humour with four of his teeth already scattered on the muck-stained garage floor. Fortunately for the victim, who was already

5

saying his final prayer, the heart attack intervened just as Slab was getting bored, wanting to head home for his evening meal and thinking it was time to finish what he'd started. It was a bad one and Slab only survived thanks to the paramedics. In fact his team nearly killed him before the ambulance arrived by moving him away from the scene of the beating in case the medics were offended by what was lying bleeding all over the floor. The courier for his part could certainly have used their expertise at the same time, but at least he was able to stagger away into the darkness and, a couple of days later, head for London to start a new life as a homeless jakey.

Slab was finished with leading from the front, and he accepted that he'd have to delegate the violent jobs to the men and family in his team because his damaged heart couldn't be present at another torture session. The emotion generated at these gatherings might just stop his ticker completely the next time. He was still the one with the brain, but all his weakened heart would allow was to give orders and direction.

The McMartins were bred for aggression, committed violence with extra toppings and never quite got the concept of diplomacy or compromise. Only Slab knew how to parley with the other main men who controlled their own part of the west Scotland market. He knew that if he snuffed it the family would break into factions eventually, and he worried there was no way to stop that happening. His siblings were just as damaged as he was – too knackered or too old to think of taking the top job. The man he'd been closest to when he was younger, his cousin, the elder Tommy McMartin, had already gone to meet his ancestors. Slab had another problem: although he had a son and daughter of his own, they were hundred per cent bams and he knew that giving either of them control would be a disaster. Their nicknames said it all: his son was Bobby 'Crazy Horse' McMartin and his daughter was Brenda, sometimes known as 'The Bitch', and in a less enlightened age they would probably have been locked away safely in an institution. Even among the clan they were regarded as plain fucking mental and therefore incapable of ever running the business. They just created enemies through dead or badly injured competitors. But they thought they had what it took, although they were under no illusions that their old man felt anything for them other than a sense of genetic failure.

Slab thanked his God most days that his poor devout wife had died screaming giving birth to Big Brenda, because the result of their union would have broken her heart anyway. The family and foot soldiers saw the contempt between Slab and his offspring, took it as a bad omen and shook their heads when they contemplated the future stability of the team. His siblings had produced little McMartins as if they were coming off a conveyer belt, and every one of them sniffed the air like the predators they were when the king was struck down and weak.

Tommy McMartin junior was one of these heirs and just as greedy for the top seat as the rest of his cousins. His old man had been stabbed to death in a drunken brawl when Tommy was still on his mother's breast, and all he knew was that his father had been Slab's closest friend, and according to the legend, every bit his equal. The old-timers said that he would have led the family team if a twelve-inch meat knife hadn't entered his chest just below the breastbone and then pushed upwards, cutting through all the plumbing that mattered.

Tommy was his father's son in every way and in due course had developed the big advantage that he was mostly liked and had proved himself a smart operator who might just have his Uncle Benny's business nous.

Most of the other McMartins barged through life under the impression that just being violent was enough to succeed in the business. Unfortunately for the other contenders, Tommy's good looks were another big plus; he was a one-off because almost all of the clan were born ugly bastards, and particularly the women. All in all, his appearance, together with his violent disposition and abundant grey matter, made him the man to beat for the top job. What gave Tommy this advantage while also making him vulnerable was that Slab thought the sun shone out of his arse, and he wished he could have been the boy's father. Although Tommy had always regarded him as Uncle Benny, Slab's obvious preference made Crazy Horse seethe at the injustice, and like his sister he hoped his old man's trip to heaven wouldn't be too far off.

Tommy tried to put the dynastical problems to the back of his mind as he headed for the city and a night away from the business. It had been a tough couple of days. He'd travelled to Liverpool with a couple of gorillas to take a consignment of H from a new source, some Pakistani boys, and it turned out not to be the start of a long-term relationship. The suppliers had badly underestimated the Glasgow men they were dealing with and tried to rip them off with moody gear. It could have been a disaster; Tommy had tested a sample when they picked it up, and it had passed, but something hadn't felt right, and he'd thought the Asian boys were a bit amateur in their attitude. Amateurs were always dangerous in the business and invariably caused unnecessary headaches. You knew where you were with an out-and-out bad bastard, but when it was some fucking wannabe who'd learned his trade from watching *The Wire* on the telly, there were going to be problems. He'd tested another sample halfway to Glasgow and cursed the stupidity of anyone trying to rip them off; the gear was rat-shit quality.

'Fuckin' wankers.' Tommy had been disgusted and gobbed on the pavement at the affront. He'd said it several times more on the way back to Merseyside, and again when he was checking the sawn-off just before he blasted the Asian boys, who by then had been begging for their lives. 'No can do, Abdul. Say hi to Osama for me,' he'd said as he pulled the trigger, shaking his head at what had been a needless development.

He'd done a good job, and the deceased had a fridge full of cash that more than made up for the inconvenience. It was the sort of job that had come just at the right time for his profile, and the men who worked for the McMartins nodded to each other over their drinks that young Tommy was the future. But while it might have impressed most of the neutrals, it pissed off the other family contenders who had an eye on Slab's legacy.

If Tommy had a weak spot that made him vulnerable it was that he was bisexual and right into men at the time. He headed for the club and the guy he'd only known for a few weeks, but who pushed all the right buttons in all the right places. They just couldn't get enough of each other, and he could barely suppress the grin of anticipation when he saw the lights of the club bouncing off the shaved heads of the two bouncers protecting the door. The boy he was involved with was called Mickey Dalton, and the big plus was that he wasn't from Tommy's world. He seemed a completely straight peg, at least in his day job, and worked in banking. Tall, slim and definitely non-scene, he was educated and just great to be around. He'd travelled, done all the things that Tommy regarded as a bit glam and that were missing from his own world, where two weeks in Ibiza was all you were going to get, and all the human body could stand. Right out of the blue,

Mickey pulled Tommy one night. He'd just appeared at his arm when he was having a quiet drink after the big game. It had never worked that way in the past – Tommy did the pulling – but he was hooked from the start. The guy had blue eyes that just said come to bed, and that's exactly what he did. It was fun, nothing to do with the hard men who tended to be limited in their experience of the world beyond the business. It made him think about life outside the team, and he imagined maybe a bit of travel with Mickey in the future. He told him he was involved in the family haulage business and hoped he could keep it that way for the time being, but he would have to tell him the truth at some point if the relationship developed. The thought that Mickey could be frightened off by the McMartin reputation gnawed at his guts, but he was where he was, and all he could do was run with the cover story for the time being. Mickey had to have seen stories about the McMartins in the *Herald* or *Record* but fortunately hadn't tied Tommy to the infamous crime family.

Tommy put the worries over his sexuality to one side; he needed a night off just to relax and be young. Those worries hung about the back of his brain every day – in his family being gay was still regarded as a sickness and a mortal sin by the parts of their souls that still believed in the validity of the Catholic faith.

Another flaw in his personality that went virtually unnoticed in a land where half the population regarded getting rat-arsed as normal was that he worked hard for the family business and never touched the bevvy during office hours. However, on his rare days off he didn't know when to stop and just couldn't hold it like the professional drinkers he kept trying to match. Occasionally when he really wanted to unwind he'd add lines of coke, just to make sure the next day was really fucked up.

He always convinced himself that he deserved it, but for an ambitious young man it meant he was exposed and vulnerable, although he never saw it through the blindness of youth.

The doormen nodded him in without checking because McMartins didn't line up in the pissing rain with ordinary mortals. When Mickey quizzed him about the A-list treatment he said his uncle was a friend of the owner. It was almost true.

As soon as Tommy was inside, one of the bouncers made an excuse that he needed the bog and slipped into the lane at the side of the boozer. He made the call and hoped to God it never came back to him, but felt he had no choice. He'd run up a sack full of gambling debts to the wrong type of lender: the type who offered only a terminal solution unless the liability was not only paid in full but accompanied by enough interest to pay off the national debt.

Tommy staggered out of the club four hours later with Mickey and could hardly bite his fingers or feel them for that matter. He was vaguely aware of the taxi ride back to the flat and snorting a line of powder off Mickey's pectorals when he got there. Somewhere along the line the lights went out and his memory was just a big black fucking hole.

2

When the bizzies broke the door down in the early hours of the morning he never stirred, his brain still closed for business as it tried to cope with the toxins that had flooded his system to the point of near coma. The local CID had taken the original anonymous call that there was a violent row in the flat. They arrived after the uniforms had broken in and all they could do was sneer at the carnage. It was a fucking result and a half. A near-disembowelled shirtlifter and a McMartin covered in the deceased's blood and gore. Fresh dabs all over the murder weapon meant it should be an open-and-shut case, so they could have a right piss-up on the back of this result. Unless the fingerprints turned out to be Lord Lucan's, the job would only need the minimum of work to see the bastard locked up for the best part of his natural.

When Tommy came round he just couldn't work it out. He'd finally sobered up in a damp cell that was clean enough, but the smell of disinfectant made him gag and didn't quite conceal the odour of piss it was trying hard, but failing, to disguise. A detective with an extra-wide sneer told him he was the accused and why.

Tommy threw up all over the cop's shoes, which really made sure he was getting no favours on that particular night. He knew he'd been legless and, going by his past record, couldn't light a fag when he was like that, never mind carve up an unwilling victim. Then there was the real dilemma as his mind cleared and grappled with the reality of his situation. He'd been crazy about Mickey, who was just about as gentle a soul as he'd ever met in the dysfunctional world he inhabited. To be fair, he rarely met gentle souls in his particular trade.

As reality made the toxic sweat pop out of his skin like dewdrops, he struggled to breathe at the trap he'd landed in. Mickey didn't have a violent side to him or do angry; nothing made sense.

He got up from his mattress again and caught the reek of stale sweat from inside the paper suit they'd given him when they'd seized the gear he'd been wearing. Apparently, stained wasn't quite the adjective for what was on his clothes when the police had found him. According to the grinning suit his gear was soaked with what had geysered from the deceased when his throat had been cut.

'What the fuck?!' he shouted, hitting the cell wall with the side of his closed fist, which amused the bored uniform who was tasked with watching him in case he topped himself before the law took its course.

3

Danny Goldstein was the McMartins' lawyer of choice and had saved a few of them over the years from serious time in the Big Hoose and other institutions around the country. He was sharp, ruthless and the best at what he did, which was to get it right up the police and prosecution at every opportunity. He never lost a wink of sleep over his lack of morals and always had a ready smile and a politically incorrect joke (especially about Jews) for whoever would listen. That included the cops and prosecutors, who couldn't help liking the man, although his mother despaired of his lack of respect for the Jewish faith that meant so much to her. Goldstein never took life too seriously – and why would he when the money poured in faster than he could spend it? He loved his wife first, blonde women who weren't his wife second, good whisky next, and he also enjoyed his profession because it revealed something new to him every day. He never tired of the problems that his clients created, and it played to his ego that some of the hardest and most ruthless men and women in the city would come to him in the hope of salvation.

They'd brought Tommy from his cell to the interview room, where he could have a legal briefing with his lawyer before the detectives got wired in about his mince. Goldstein thought about how times had changed: the suspects rarely had a mark on them nowadays, at least not inflicted by the arresting officers. In the early part of his career it was accepted that a number of prisoners seemed to accidentally fall somewhere or were badly injured when they resisted arrest. It was just part of the game in those days, and everyone expected it. He remembered one client who was a nervous wreck because the detectives who'd arrested him hadn't given him a tanking. The poor bastard was convinced his team would think he'd turned grass green if he stepped out onto the pavement without a mark on his face.

'You know the drill, Tommy. When they interview you, say nothing unless I okay it. You hear me?' He was shocked at the state of the young man who'd been the rising star and a shoo-in for the top seat when the time came. The face that normally looked polished and tight seemed to have aged ten years in no time. What was more shocking was seeing something rare in the company of a McMartin ... fear. Goldstein told the uniform as politely as possible to give them a bit of privacy. The old constable was only too pleased to go and relieve his bladder, which was swollen to bursting point with a coffee overdose.

'What the hell happened last night, son?' he asked. 'Hell' was about the strongest language Goldstein ever used unless he was really infuriated; he believed that a real expletive only had value if it was used sparingly. He wasn't angry at Tommy, at least not yet, and Slab had told him to 'do whatever the fuck is necessary and get me answers'. Slab McMartin was as confused as everyone else about what had put his favourite in the pokey. Tommy told the lawyer all he could remember, which was next to hee-haw after he left the club. Then it was just a haze, but he was sure that there'd been no problem with him and Mickey up to that point. Goldstein accepted that nearly everyone he dealt with was an incurable liar, but the boy was either the best he'd ever seen or genuinely just couldn't remember. The problem was that if he was genuine, it kind of defied logic. The crime didn't really fit, but that wouldn't stop the detectives on the case.

Goldstein left Tommy in the interview room and went to 'have a word with the locals'.

When he came back he stared at his client and tried to hide what he was feeling. Tommy saw it clear enough. He knew the old lawyer could have acted for a living, but there was no gushing reassurance – the man was trying to find the right words when none would fit.

'Come on, Danny, I'm a big boy. Just tell me,' Tommy said.

'It's sewn up – unless there's a miracle or some police fit-up to rival the Birmingham Six. Your clothes are covered in whatever pumped out of that young man just before he died. In all probability your prints are on the knife, and there are signs of a struggle in the bedroom. There's CCTV footage from the street near the flat of you and the other young man going through the front gates of the complex and no sign of anyone else entering or leaving the premises until the cavalry arrive. It doesn't look good, son – not good at all.'

Goldstein stared at Tommy, and although he knew the boy could dish it out, the detectives had described a slaughter. That didn't fit. Tommy had always been described as someone who was violent when it was necessary but nothing more. The victim had a cut throat that was closer to a decapitation and a slash across the abdomen that had almost eviscerated him. Goldstein was a smart lawyer, had seen it all in his time and tried to keep an open mind, but this one made no sense to him at all. What he did know was that for whatever reason the heir to the director's chair had just lost everything. A thought passed through his mind about who was left to step into Slab's shoes, and it made him wonder about the McMartins' future prospects.

Tommy's complexion matched the colour of the walls and he was sick to his bones. For a young man with so much life in him he looked beaten already. He just couldn't make sense of it. His head ached as his body tried vainly to detox, and it had drained the fight from him. The problem was that he couldn't remember *not* doing it, so maybe, just maybe, something *had* gone wrong. It was the doubt that frightened him. The Tommy McMartin with balls who'd blown away the Asian boys in Liverpool was struggling to show up. It was game, set and match to the bizzies for the time being and there didn't seem anywhere to go.

Normally for a McMartin, and certainly one near the top of the tree, there was always a way out. Brown envelope to a detective, turn the screw on a few jurors or fit up some twat for the job were all options. Unfortunately, this was clusterfuck territory, and the only blessing was that capital punishment had been abolished a long time ago or the boy would have been a swinger of the dead rather than the sexual variety.

He sat with his head in his hands and stayed motionless for what seemed like minutes. Goldstein knew to let him be, take it all in, swallow it and then they could talk about the options, which at that point in time were all bad. The lawyer waited patiently till Tommy lifted his head. Some of the colour flowed back into his face as his jaw tightened, and he looked a bit more like the young hard man he knew. He had to hand it to the boy as he watched him get it together like a real pro – he was a tough little bastard. Tommy tried something like a grin then, which didn't quite work but was a great effort given the circumstances.

'Okay. Sounds like I'm fucked but, honest to God, I can't remember a thing apart from the fact we were having a good time. Jesus, he was just the best guy and nothing to do with the business. I don't get any of this.' He stood up, pulled back his shoulders and ran the fingers of both hands through his thick auburn hair. 'What happens now then?' He kept hoping Goldstein would give him just something to hold on to, though he knew there were no rabbits that could be pulled out of a hat for this particular situation.

'The suits don't need to interview you at any length as they have all the evidence they need, and my guess is they'll want to get away early to celebrate a good result. That result, my young friend, is you.'

Goldstein knew all the detectives who counted in the city, drank with them and, importantly, understood how they operated; and more importantly, how they thought. It was good business to keep them onside and got him the occasional favour that just might turn a case his way. Goldstein was one of the few people who understood that the McMartins got more breaks than was either normal or just good luck. No one, and certainly not Slab, had ever suggested it to him, but he was sure that when they needed a favour or break from the law they got it. Whether it was bent detectives or one or two of the McMartins having signed on as confidential sources he didn't know, but the police were usually missing in action if there was a chance to arrest one of Slab's top team. Of course, the troops at the working end of the operation just had to take their chances with the law, and if Goldstein couldn't get them a deal then they had to do the time and say fuck all that would get them a close look at the inside of the incinerator or dinner time at the pig farm. It wasn't much of a choice. For Slab's top team, though, there would be the occasional arrest for appearances' sake, but in most cases, it was minor stuff – at least minor in comparison to what they actually did in the course of their business. Goldstein was convinced that at some level deals were done between the family and senior detectives. It might be corruption or just tossing each other favours, but nobody was going to tell him which it was.

Something, however, was puzzling Goldstein this time. When he had spoken to the detectives working the murder case it was like they were celebrating Christmas. Why were the same guys who normally went AWOL when an executive-level McMartin was in the frame so happy about taking out the heir to the throne? It seemed that they'd scored all round. No one could point fingers after arresting a top man, but Goldstein thought that if he was a cynic he might suspect that the detectives had had the nod from somewhere in Slab's team, if not from the chief hooligan himself. It was confusing, but the day the bad men and detectives started acting rationally was the day they could do away with solicitors like him.

Goldstein's life was about tidying up clutter, and here he was, standing in an interview room full of it and with a situation that was going to test him to the limit. He just knew it, shook his head and decided that it had to be his imagination running away too far from the facts. He knew that wouldn't stop the 'puzzle worm', as he liked to call the sensation chewing the back of his brain and telling him he was missing something. The confusion he was experiencing meant he was working on automatic lawyer-speak, and for the first time in his life he couldn't come up with an original line. Normally his whole act was based on displaying an air of confidence, which he just couldn't apply in this case.

'They'll probably ask you a few questions, you'll make no comment and they'll go straight to charge. There is no chance of bail, you do know that?' He waited till Tommy nodded. 'I'm going to get on with this immediately and see what I can do, but this is a tough one, son.' He didn't want to say what came next, but Tommy needed to think about it. 'The papers are already all over this and apparently your friend was openly gay. And I don't know how to put this or whether you even knew ... Mickey Dalton was an escort worker, a rent boy – call it what you like – but at the class end of the business.'

'No way! Fuck that!' Tommy flared, his cheeks flushing red, and for a moment Goldstein thought he was in serious trouble. However, Tommy just didn't have the energy reserves in the tank, and he crashed again as quickly as he'd fired up. There was simply too much that he didn't know or hadn't considered. It was time to think. He was a professional criminal, trained since birth by the best in the business, and he didn't need a shit-hot lawyer to tell him when he was the fuckwit in the middle of someone else's little game. He shivered at the thought that he'd imagined sharing his life with Mickey Dalton while all the time he was being played. He was finally getting the message that he'd been guilty of arrogance and still had a lot to learn. The question was whether it might be too late to apply the lessons to his future. Did he still have a future?

Goldstein waited again, hoping that the boy would give some kind of explanation that would satisfy his uncle and the less-enlightened members of his family. All he got back was a look that said it all. Tommy was in a bad place, and he knew exactly what the reaction was going to be when it all came out. At least the one person who wouldn't judge him was the little Jewish lawyer in the room.

Tommy drew in a large breath of air, then sighed like a man who saw the future and exactly what it would hold for him. He was smart, and as soon as he thought about it, he saw exactly what had happened. Not the fine detail but the broad picture. It was enough to make the bile rise in his throat. 'We'd been sleeping together for a few weeks,' he told Goldstein. 'What else can I say?'

The lawyer stepped forward, put his hand on Tommy's shoulder and shook his head. 'I'll see what I can do. Benny is going to struggle with this, but then you know that already.' He turned and pressed the bell to bring the uniform back into the room. 'Tell the CID that we're ready for the interview.'

Tommy McMartin nodded in agreement, swearing to himself that he wouldn't let the bastards see his fear. The revelation that Mickey was on the game had thrown him, but not for long. He was a street animal, and it took no time to accept that he'd been fucked – the only question was who by? He knew a stitch-up when he saw one. He gritted his teeth, thinking how Mickey had played him like a kid and he'd fallen for it all. Christ, the guy could have won an Oscar for his performance if he hadn't been dead. He'd walked into the trap like an amateur and forgotten every lesson he'd ever learned.

4

Goldstein was right on the money – Slab McMartin nearly
choked at the news his nephew was gay, and he raged
more than was good for a man with a seriously dodgy
ticker. For him it was betrayal by his favourite, and he
knew that his enemies would take the piss and a great deal
of delight in the story. The fact that Tommy was bisexual
made no difference; it was the same as gay: a poof, a form
of perversion. And he'd wasted years treating him like a
son. 'It's a total embarrassment, Danny; the boy's sick.
Needs treatment, castration, whatever the fuck.'

Goldstein kept quiet, never mentioning the fact that
his own daughter was gay and living happily with her
partner. He loved and was proud of her – why wouldn't
he be? – and he'd said as much a hundred times over the
years to his friends and family. In a way he pitied the
man raging at Tommy's sexual orientation, unable to
put it in context with his own worthless existence. Slab
couldn't understand that the only value in his own life
was built on the misery of others. Despite his tolerance
of the subject, Goldstein wasn't going to argue with the
man, sick or not. Slab washed his hands of his nephew.

He warned Goldstein not to spend too much time or his money fighting what for him was a deservedly lost cause.

When the lawyer got home to his wife that night he was dejected and she'd never seen him so low. Every case tended to get his juices going, but this one troubled him. Logic said that it was straightforward: a young man who'd proven he was capable of extreme violence had killed his lover. It had all been done before, and what was new under the sun? It wasn't enough though; despite having nothing to go on he knew there was something wrong with the whole story. It was like a vague pain in his backside that he couldn't quite explain.

His wife poured him a shot of his favourite brandy and told him he was getting old. He sipped the drink quietly and decided she must be right.

5

When it came to the court case it was almost no contest. Tommy McMartin pled not guilty and went to trial without a snowball's chance in hell. Goldstein did his best, got a decent QC, but the man seemed to become exasperated when he couldn't convince the accused to plead guilty. Despite the trial being a waste of everyone's time the papers loved every gory minute. There was a feeding frenzy on the sexual angle that a prince in the top crime family was gay and involved with an escort, or 'rent boy' as the red tops preferred to describe the deceased.

When they squeezed Tommy into the transporter for the trip from court to the prison it was as if a massive download of negative energy surged through his body and he was racked with the shakes. While he'd been on remand in Barlinnie, or Bar-L as it was better known to its clients, it was almost as if he'd gone onto autopilot and the days waiting had turned into a blurred dream. Goldstein had done his best not to build any false hope, because none existed. It was bad enough already, though the screws had been fair, and no one had laid a finger on him. There was, of course, a good reason for that. The other remand prisoners had their own hopes for a not guilty or not proven come the day of their appearance, so he was more or less left alone apart from the odd warning of what was waiting for him. No one wanted to fuck up their chance of walking away from court because they'd done the business with Tommy McMartin. There would be plenty time for that if and when they were convicted, and an attack wouldn't make that much difference to them then.

Two of the Gilroy brothers were on the remand wing at the same time as Tommy, waiting for their own trial for an armed robbery. They had their own reasons to hate the McMartins: one of the men who'd planned to kill Slab at his home and ended up with his nut flattened was their uncle. The brothers were a couple of years apart in age, but there was no mistaking their relationship – they could almost have been twins. That was unfortunate because they were horrible bastards – one would have been more than enough, but two was an affront to humanity. And in addition to their almost matching features, even from a hundred yards away only a blind man could have missed the fact that they were both as thick as shit. They were a couple of gingers with hairlines far too close to their eyebrows, which were one continuous straight line, and pulped noses that had been squashed by too many second prizes. Although they were both short-arses, they were pit bulls with tempers to match; they only had two moods – occasionally extremely happy or, most of the time, completely pissed off. There was no such thing as a centre ground. Every time they saw Tommy McMartin they grinned as if they were starving and looking at a nicely cooked dinner. As confirmed thickos they pissed themselves endlessly when they saw him, making cut-throat signs, and sometimes the two of them would do a kind of simulated man-humps-man impression as either mockery of what Tommy was or what was coming to him.

Tommy had managed to get a line of some prescription tabs that helped take the edge off the mess he was in, and like with alcohol he didn't have a great tolerance for dope of any kind. At least the tabs numbed him enough to keep him away from the reality of his position. Spending his days shit-faced meant he could ignore the fact that, barring a miracle, he was destined for years behind the doors with people like the Gilroys waiting for any chance to break off a piece of a McMartin. Goldstein kept warning him to try and hold it together, and he'd promised he'd clean up once the trial was over, but they both knew that would only happen with a not-guilty verdict. Tommy clung to the dope-assisted fantasy that something or someone would come to his rescue.

When the trial was over and he stared at the man on the bench handing down a lifer, he smiled. The judge took this as confirmation that the accused was a thug getting justice, when in fact for Tommy it was a nervous reaction that was nothing to do with defiance in the face of the law. What terrified him most was the bewilderment, the fact that he was about to rot away his youth in Bar-L without knowing what or why it had happened. He couldn't handle the incomprehensible, and although he was almost sure he hadn't killed Mickey, he just couldn't be certain. If it was a fit-up there were always a million reasons why in his game. His business was inhabited by rats – big ones and small ones scuttling around in every dark corner, all looking to survive and, if possible, prosper. It never mattered if it was at someone else's expense. Slab had said it himself often enough. 'This game is dog eat dog, son, and the only lesson you ever need to know is this: eat the other fucker before he even considers doing it to you.'

Tommy had run a hundred scenarios through his head of why he might have been played and who might be responsible – the problem was that they all worked. The most likely was one of the family, because they were all candidates and being Slab's favourite had come at a price. His money was on Crazy Horse and Big Brenda, because Slab barely looked at them unless it was business, and they had to be pissed off that Tommy had almost taken their place in Slab's family. He was everything they weren't, and he saw it in the way they looked at him on the rare occasions they were in the same room. They ran their own teams within the organisation, and Slab seemed to intentionally keep him well away from the others. Unfortunately he couldn't prove it because he had no one on the outside who could dig into what had happened. If anyone from the family business came to see him, Slab would know before the visit was over, and that person would be lucky to escape with a Glasgow smile, which had always been one of Slab's favourite punishments.

In his game, prison was always a reality, and although Goldstein was a magician, everyone accepted that there were times when it was just your turn, things went wrong and you did your time behind the doors. Tommy, like almost everyone he knew, had thought about it, and there was a general belief that a few years away could add to the credibility of someone in the business. If you faced up to it like a man, took shit from no one and refused to grass, then friends and opponents gave you just that bit more respect, even if they wanted you dead. The point was that you had the family, organisation and other people who cared about you, and who you knew you could count on to still be there on the day of your release, to get you through the long hard days. All that had been stripped from Tommy McMartin. He had enemies outside and, for too many years to come, enemies squeezed in beside him who'd been told that a McMartin was there on his own – anyone with a grudge just had to wait for their shot. There would be a queue waiting for their turn, and the Gilroys would be right at the front.

6

When Tommy arrived back from the court it was a weird experience because it was almost as if he was going into Bar-L for the first time. Hope was gone, and all that he had was endless days in the halls. The prescription tabs he'd managed to buy were wearing off, and he felt sick when they stuck him in the dog boxes in reception, waiting for his turn to see the doc and get fed into whichever hall he was heading for. He started to hyperventilate in the confined space till eventually a screw helped him out and waited till he'd calmed down.

'It happens all the time here. Take it easy – the first night's always the worst.' The man's kindness threw Tommy and added to his confusion. The truth was that the first night wasn't the worst; it was each night as it came. They were all the worst.

When they walked to his cell in A Hall he was shocked by the silence; he'd expected something else, not this. The screw walking him through saw his expression, knew exactly what it meant and went through the same line he did with so many. 'It's always like this, son. Dead quiet and has to be. We control it and that's why. Most of the day you're all behind the doors, and unless you go for a bit of exercise or work that's where you stay.'

The screw sighed and wished it was time to go off his shift and watch the big game. He felt weary in his bones watching another young man destined for fuck all but wasted years. He remembered the days when he was all for locking all the bastards up and thought hanging was too good for them. It just tired him now, and he'd forgotten how to hate the endless lines of wasted lives. They just made the screw feel sad, and mostly for himself.

'You'll get used to it, son,' he added. 'Tell you the truth, there's no choice. Just keep your head down and watch your back.'

Tommy looked up to the top of the four landings and saw there wasn't another soul there. The place might have been empty, but it wasn't. Behind every door two grown men survived in cells hardly bigger than most people's bathrooms. The place was sterile and freshly painted with just a trace of cooking smells over the ever-present kick of disinfectant.

The screw walked him up to the second floor, the only sound the rap of their footsteps on the old walkways.

It was strange, because when the door opened in front of him, he found the cell was almost identical to the one on remand, but he still took a half-step back when he saw it. It was a shock to his overloaded defence instincts. His new co-pilot didn't even get off the bottom bunk to say hello but stared at the bottom of the mattress above him as if the door had never opened. He'd been told all about Tommy and what was coming to him. He didn't want any part of it and certainly didn't want to become his mate.

When the door closed behind him Tommy wanted to

crawl into a corner, but there were no corners available in a cell that didn't have a spare inch of space, and the quiet man in the bottom bunk obviously didn't give a shit about keeping it tidy. To add to it all the quiet man he was sharing his new life with had a serious problem with BO, and it just added to the sense of hopelessness that seemed to be weighing Tommy down. He tried anyway, although with little enthusiasm.

'How's it goin', mate?'

'I'm alright.' The man swung his legs over the edge of the bed, stood up and took two steps forward, which left about a six-inch gap between their faces. 'Just so we're clear, I'm not much of a talker, and that's the way I like it. Your bed's up there and that's all we need to know. You got a big fuckin' target on your back, pal, so stay clear of me.' It was on the word 'pal' that he started jabbing his forefinger into Tommy's chest.

He was a tall man, mid-thirties and far too skinny to be a battler. Tommy realised that the word had already gone out that he was in for a hard time, but this clown had taken that to mean that anyone could piss on Tommy with impunity. The mistake he'd made was that they hadn't quite reached that stage yet.

Tommy grabbed the finger in mid-jab, bent it backwards and, grabbing the man's balls with his other hand, squeezed just hard enough while leaving something in reserve. The clown gasped out all the air in his lungs and seemed to lift up to his tiptoes with the pressure Tommy was applying. His mouth was a big round 'O' as he tried to cope with the pain.

'That's fine then ... pal.' Tommy felt some of the old fire burn in his belly as he said it. 'Just so you don't get any ideas – I'll rip them off the next time and flush them in the lavy. We clear ... pal?'

His reluctant co-pilot got the message but swore he'd

run to the Gilroys anytime he could to help do Tommy McMartin's legs.

The world and his family all forgot about Tommy, apart from Goldstein, who made the occasional visit for what seemed to him to be incomprehensible reasons. He watched Tommy shrink and age, saw the occasional bruise and barely got a word out of him. He could only imagine what a friendless lifer with the name McMartin would be enduring inside. The big bonus for the predators was that when they came and took turns at holding him down, they could enjoy that rare treat of watching one of Slab's own cry like a baby. Goldstein tried not to think too much about that particular nightmare, but it kept coming back to him whether he wanted it or not.

He kept Tommy's file in his desk at home, pulled it out after each visit and stared at the pages, which just confirmed that there was no possible explanation other than that the boy had committed the murder. Every time he put the file back in his desk he gazed at the bookshelf opposite for a few moments, shook his head and knew that sleep would evade him yet again.

7

The governor had done Tommy a big and intentional favour when he'd moved him in with old Andy Holden after his first few months inside, which had been nothing short of a nightmare. Tommy had struggled to remain sane, and his bastard of a co-pilot had barely spoken to him – just lapped it up as he watched Tommy lose strength and will every day that passed. The memory that always raised his blood pressure was of being a front-row witness in the showers, leering at the Gilroys and a couple of stooges holding Tommy down. What they did got him off every time it came back to him.

It was probably a practical as well as a humanitarian move by the governor, because there was a danger that Tommy was going to be killed during the repeated 'incidents' that were never officially reported despite being picked up by the screws. They were tuned into even the faintest vibrations in the pokey, and a good officer knew what was going on without ever being told. They knew exactly what the bruises and discomfort meant when Tommy was asked to sit down.

Tommy tried to convince them that it was his 'ceramics',

but his refusal to be examined told them all they needed to know. Despite everything he'd suffered, he still had that tough core, refusing to go into protection with the beasts, even though the staff tried their best to convince him that it was in his best interests. Tommy knew that once he went in with the pervs he might be safe from animals like the Gilroys, but he would be finished with the world of real men. That would be the final ignominy, and he was determined to fight that one.

The Shawshank Redemption was one of Tommy's favourite films, and he always thought of Andy as Bar-L's very own incarnation of Morgan's Freeman's character Red. Before prison, and with the exception of a few fines for being drunk and disorderly, Holden had led a pretty ordinary life at the bottom end of the food chain. His great mistake, when he was still in his teens, had been to marry a woman who had almost no redeeming features apart from giving any of the local boys whatever they wanted whenever they wanted.

He was pretty naive in those days, mistaking lust for love, and when his future wife realised she was pregnant she picked Holden as the least bad option of all the boys who'd been there already. Her old man was a local hooligan who gave him two choices, the second of which meant no future, so he'd married a woman who spent her days nagging him into actually looking for work so he could get away from her for at least part of the day.

Three useless children and twenty years later he'd walked into the house early one day when he'd called off sick and found the woman who made every day a trial in a compromising position. Not quite as soon as he'd walked in. What he saw first were the Doc Martin boots just inside the front door, then the heavy black trousers, but what had made his heart race was the utility belt with all the gear a modern beat cop needs to keep himself safe on the job. This particular community cop was right on the job that day, and all his efforts were concentrated on Holden's wife. The coco was concentrating so hard he never heard the front door open or Holden go into the kitchen, drink a glass of water and rummage through the drawer for the biggest knife he could find. Much later he wondered why he hadn't just taken the incident as all the reason he needed to walk out of a waste of a marriage. What had blown his fuse was the lightning flash of realisation that he'd wasted twenty years he'd never get back and that his three children all looked remarkably like close friends.

His wife's special friend nearly fell off the bed when Andy appeared in the doorway with the bread knife hanging loosely by his side. The PC was a tough bastard, but what he saw in Holden's eyes told him that he'd be lucky just to lose his career. He was already on a final warning with the police, having been shown a yellow card for getting too close to the married ladies of the community he was supposed to serve and protect.

'You seem to enjoy the serve bit, son, but as far as public confidence goes you're fucking useless,' his inspector had told him, adding that the next scandal would be his last. This one looked like it was shaping up to have bells on.

Holden had the rage – he needed to hurt someone, and the PC was lucky only to get a shallow twelve-inch slash across his left buttock as he scrambled through the window onto the kitchen roof. He'd yelped like an injured dog (or pig in his case) as the warm blood trailed down the back of his leg, then dropped from the kitchen roof onto the damp grass, swivelling his head through 180 degrees as he looked for witnesses to his awful humiliation. He'd made that natural but futile gesture to cover his embarrassment – as if it would have made any difference. The cut on his arse hurt like a bitch, but his first priority had been to put some distance between the bread knife and his right buttock, just in case Andy wanted to carve a matching pair. As for protecting the woman he'd just been in bed with and promised that what they had was special . . . well he'd forgotten her already.

The local police were alerted by some terrified housewives reporting a naked man prowling about in the gardens. The last one was an old woman who'd said that the madman had stolen one of her nightdresses from the washing line. She was even more horrified when the pervert squeezed into the thing. Fortunately for him it had been made with larger ladies in mind.

'I've been wearin' that goonie for years and the bastard's away wi' it. My Henry, God bless him, bought it for our last anniversary and it always got him goin' if you know what I mean. What's wrong wi' the world?' She'd said it in all innocence to the police telephone operator, who knew a beauty of a quote when he heard one and had already filed it for the next piss-up with his mates.

When the patrol cars responded and the bleeding victim was discovered hiding behind a garden shed wearing the stolen goonie and blubbing like an infant, the officers had stared at each other in disbelief. Meanwhile the man's uniform was still in the same house where Holden was at that moment stabbing his wife to death. By the time the errant, and soon to be ex, PC had given the story to his grinning colleagues, she had twitched for the last time, and Holden had watched the light drain from her eyes.

'Cheery bye then, hen,' he'd said before he got back to his feet, breathing deeply after the effort of stabbing her seventeen times. It was harder work than he could ever have imagined but job done. The last one had gone deep into the soft flesh between her neck and shoulder. He'd struggled to pull the knife out again and decided that was enough for one murder.

He'd known it would be a long time before he would manage a wee drink again so he'd left the knife beside his wife and washed the blood from his hands, not to avoid detection, just to enjoy the short time he had left at home. He'd then gone back to the kitchen, poured a ridiculous measure of whisky into his favourite glass, opened a beer to chase it, lit a cigarette and settled into the old leather chair that he'd rested his arse on for so many years. 'Well shit happens, Andy,' he'd muttered to himself with a shrug, marvelling that whisky and a smoke had never tasted better. 'Funny that!' Then he'd closed his eyes and felt relaxed for the first time in years.

When the police stampeded through the door he'd asked them if the PC was alright.

'You've made him a fuckin' legend, pal, and put it this way: he's unlikely to make Chief Constable. Is your wife okay?'

Holden had grinned. 'Never better, officer. Why don't you go up and ask her?'

When he'd heard the sound of one of the uniforms spewing upstairs he'd thrown back the last of the whisky and stuck his hands out for the handcuffs.

'It was a moment of madness,' he used to tell Tommy and always seemed slightly amused by the whole thing.

Tommy never saw bitterness in his co-pilot and found it hard to believe that the wise old friend he'd shared a cell with over the years was a killer, but then he'd never been married.

Seven Years Later

8

Grace Macallan stared at the clock again; it had become part of her daily ritual as the minute hand struggled to reach 4 p.m. and her official finishing time. She could have started at any time of the day but liked to get in by 8 a.m. so she could escape by 4 p.m. without anyone thinking she was taking the piss. That last hour of the day had become a daily trial with the agony of watching the wall clock refuse to move any faster. It was an endless Groundhog Day, and the office was beginning to feel more like a room in the pokey. She sighed, realising that she was even arranging her pens into straight lines in her desk tidy. Her in tray was nearly empty, and what reports there were had been read and then stacked neatly with the edges in line. She shook her head at the bare, lifeless office they'd given her in Fettes; it seemed a reflection of her dull, meaningless job. 'Jesus, what's happening to me?' She said the same thing every day at about 3.45 p.m.

For the first time in her life she was suffering the trials of endless routine, but it was what she'd elected in an attempt to get a *normal* life. She'd been on the point of giving up her career until she and her fiancé Jack Fraser had talked it over and decided it would be too much like a junkie going cold turkey – too much room for failure. The result was that she'd sat down for a discussion with her bosses and opted for a uniform after years of taking on terrorists and criminals who were worse than the stuff of nightmares. It seemed to be a suitable compromise as she struggled to contemplate life without the job that had nearly driven her crazy and scarred her faith in human nature but which was where she felt she had to be. She was still trying and failing to answer those questions that had no answers.

When she'd been told that her boss would be Chief Superintendent Elaine Tenant she'd felt like doing a runner, but they'd surprised each other by finding a way to get along, despite their previous problems. Tenant was, and always would be, a minor politician who would live for the next rank up, retire unfulfilled, buy a cat then stare into the quiet spaces of a perfect house that had never felt like a home and wonder what it had all been about.

In fact, having quickly come to recognise each other's strengths and failings, Macallan and Tenant decided they could forgive, or at least make the situation work to their mutual benefit. There was a time when Macallan would have found it hard to believe that Tenant had any strengths at all, but she'd come to realise that although her former adversary was a bureaucrat, she was a very good one. In a force hamstrung with bureaucracy she was as well to have one of the best onside. Macallan was the first to admit that administration had never been her strong point, so they found a way to survive with each other. It was a strange alliance, and a grudging respect was forming on both sides.

Instead of putting Macallan out to a division, or 'the land of dog shit and broken windows' as it was affectionately known by the troops, they'd handed her a project to improve intelligence development with other forces and agencies. Her background in covert operations made it appear like the job from heaven and so she'd poured herself into it for the first few weeks until she'd realised that in actual fact no one was really interested.

The project had been the result of criticism by the Inspectorate after a review of the service had shown up weaknesses that hadn't been addressed in the early development of Police Scotland. As happens so often, it was set up to be quietly forgotten among all the problems that bombarded the police from politicians and a public who expected them to perform miracles and never ever get it wrong – in other words to achieve the impossible. When Macallan started to gripe she was met by genuine surprise that she could take issue with a nice cushy number where she could hide for months then write a report that would go straight in the basket marked 'who gives a shit?'. In fact, she was told more than once that she could carve out a nice career producing reports that were hardly worth the paper they were written on. She could churn them out almost stress free and probably get a promotion out of it. It was at that point that she started to watch the clock, and it was like a slow-growing form of madness.

On the domestic front, it had worked perfectly at first, and she was home every night on time, which was something that had never happened earlier in her career. Jack had given up law to write full-time, and the books were selling to a public who wanted more. It meant they could live in Edinburgh and keep their beloved cottage on the Antrim coast of Northern Ireland where they'd spent the happiest times of their lives with their two young children.

She'd surprised herself initially by enjoying a break

from the strain of hunting the savages who were always there, lying in wait. It looked like they could have a normal life, and she could hang on to the job that meant so much to her. She might be away from the action but was still involved enough in ways that might just help the men and women who risked it all in the shadows of covert policing.

Jack had seen the warning signs quite early on in the project but had tried to act as if it wasn't happening. They'd kept it going till their time together had become a strained act, at which point it broke and she'd poured all her frustration out to him.

'I'm so sorry, Jack, I just can't pretend. This job is shutting my brain down bit by bit. You've no idea what it's like.' That was the wrong choice of words, and she realised it as soon as she'd uttered them.

'I don't know what it's like? You should hear yourself – sometimes you just get it so wrong. I watched you lying in a hospital bed after nearly dying in that fucking bomb blast with our baby inside you. You slept with your demons, Grace. Christ, you know that better than I do. And on how many nights have I had to calm you down from nightmares? Think, for God's sake, about the other people who might, just might, actually be affected as well.' He'd hit the tabletop a little too hard with the wine glass, prompting her to sit back and acknowledge she was acting like a spoilt brat.

'You're right. Sorry. I just needed to unload, and you're the one that gets it. It's going to be in the contract, remember: for better or for worse, or words to that effect.' She'd smiled and gripped his big hand over the table. 'I'm a twat, will that do it for you?'

'Okay, admitting you're a twat will do. By the way, it's a humanist wedding we're having, so no for better or for worse stuff. That's what we agreed, right?' He'd walked round the table, pulled her up and held her close enough to show her that he was there and cared. She needed that every so often, and he always read the signs exceptionally well.

'So what does the famous writer and barrister think?' She'd pulled back and stared up at the face covered in at least three days' growth, which had become the norm since he'd given up court work.

'I think you were asked to do something that someone thought had meaning. You seemed to believe it had meaning ... So if it walks like a duck and quacks like a duck then the answer is obvious.'

'Sorry, can you explain the duck thing? I'm a simple cop.'

'Do the job you were asked to do and do it well. Make a noise. And for someone trained in Northern Ireland you should know about subterfuge. We're in the age of terrorist threats; if they ignore your recommendations, get your friends in the press to quote sources inside the police. They'll know it was you, but if your work is on the money they'll have to grin and bear it. What's new?'

'I always said you lawyers are a devious bunch, but nice one, and I've just stopped feeling sorry for myself.' She'd kissed him and hadn't wanted to be with anyone else that night.

9

Sometimes he couldn't quite work out how he'd got to where he was, weeks before his sixty-third birthday. He'd never stopped to think before, having always rolled on or over whatever was in his path. In most ways his life could be described as a success, at least up until his downfall. Maybe not in marriage, but in his professional life he was a ruthless bastard who could cut through the opposition like an acetylene burner. He'd never bothered to stop long enough to gloat – there was always another obstacle in the way that had to be challenged or dealt with. He couldn't remember what he would have called pleasure from his days in the sun, just a few hours' satisfaction before it was time to steam ahead again. An awareness that most of the people he'd worked with hated the ground he walked on never really troubled him. As far as he was concerned they were right to feel that way, and the sycophants who told him what he wanted to hear fed him all the fake respect he could deal with. They were necessary only in the respect that they could act as Judas where there was dissent. He always knew that the day would come when that life would end and the scavengers who fed in his wake would disappear in the direction of the next big beast who might influence their stupid lives.

His personal life was another matter. When he was young he'd made the mistake of believing that he needed the social decoration of an attractive wife with breeding to provide the right image in his professional world and that this was simply something that had to be tolerated on the way up. People told him she was a beauty, and although that was partly why he'd married her, he'd felt little in the way of affection. He was, however, blessed as an actor and gave her enough evidence to believe that he cared. At least initially. Although it didn't take her long to see the glaring truth.

Soon she was carrying their first child. Sex was what they did to prove how much they detested each other. The pregnancy was a surprise to him but not to his wife, who'd decided that conception was a nice form of revenge for what she had come to realise had always been a loveless marriage on his part. The birth of his son meant that two people could hate him instead of his wife doing it on her own. The birth of their second child, a daughter, brought that number up to three, but sterilisation prevented more of the same. They were in agreement that two unhappy children would be enough for one lifetime, even if they never actually discussed the matter.

That his marriage had gone cold became pretty obvious to the rest of the family when his daughter was born and he opted for a conference in London as being more deserving of his presence – or (in truth) more stimulating – than the arrival of their offspring. The standard of escort service he could use in London was always worth the trip, and he knew a night or two in such company would bring a smile to his face, whereas childbirth would be met with indifference.

By that time, he'd realised he didn't need decorations or a trophy wife to enhance his professional life. He was up there with the best, and there was no further need to impress anyone. Increasingly, being on his own at social occasions was the preferred option, although, to be fair, when they needed to put on a show his wife was there by his side and they lived out the lie. That was where her breeding, her ability to suffer for appearance's sake, proved its worth. If he needed a woman for anything else then he could pay for the best and get rid of them without pretending he cared. There was the odd brief relationship with colleagues or clients, but they rarely lasted beyond exposure to the morning light.

None of it mattered, and even after his downfall he accepted what was left of his life and decided that he could get all the comfort he needed from a bottle. His son was a dribbling idiot, locked away for life, but as there had never been anything but contempt between them he rarely lost any sleep over what had happened to the young man. He'd hardly seen or talked to his daughter in years because she'd moved away from home as soon as she could put distance between her and the cold war that had existed between her parents ever since she could remember. She'd kept in touch with her mother, who despite her faults had never deserved her father. The redeeming feature as far as she was concerned was that her mother had seen it as a duty to keep the house together, foolish as that might have been.

The news came as he slumped half-drunk into his chair after a day quietly trying to forget in the drab boozer that had become his local. One minute he was fumbling with the remote control to watch a programme that he wouldn't be able to remember in the morning, the next he was taking the call: his daughter dead by her own hand ... Or was it his? She had been all that seemed to have survived the collapse of their lives and now she was dead. Far from home, the shame and horror of what her brother and father had done was still too much. He wondered if she'd believed she was tainted by the same poison that ran through all their veins. An inexplicable feeling of loss almost overwhelmed him as he tried to come to terms with his complete failure to care for someone who might have had a happy life despite her roots. He'd never blamed anyone but himself, but now he felt nothing but rage and a need to release what gripped him. How strange was that?

10

Holden had looked after Tommy as best he could, sometimes talked to him all night, particularly on those days when he came back from the showers hardly able to walk. He would sit quietly as Tommy curled up in a ball and ground his teeth in rage and pain. He was the boy's only real friend inside. Holden was one of those rare men who seemed to be able to get things and favours that were unavailable to others. He'd supplied Tommy with the prescription drugs he craved, realising too late that they did nothing for the boy but make his life even more miserable. When he tried to get him off the tabs Tommy pleaded like a child till the old boy gave in, against his better judgement.

Holden tried his best to talk to the hard men whose word counted inside and get the attacks on Tommy stopped. A couple did it for Holden, but the rest told him there was no deal, that Tommy was fair game and they didn't want a crisis with the Gilroys, who were doing eight each. The attacks on Tommy had tailed off, but every so often bams like the Gilroys would get bored and rerun them just for laughs.

Over the years Tommy thought again and again about the life of crime that he'd been introduced to as a child. There had never been any doubt that he'd follow the family trade, but life inside had been even worse than he'd imagined, and now he wished he could have taken a different route. He started to read, and apart from Holden's friendship that was his only saviour. The books were all that kept him sane and took him away from the reality of what he suffered most days. There were books he'd never have thought of reading before. He began to learn about a world that actually existed – all you had to do was book the flight or buy the train ticket. There was freedom of choice, but he'd never realised it, and of course no one had told him. Apart from Andy Holden of course, who'd had almost the same thoughts about what life might have been for him with a different turn of events. Holden tried so hard to convince his young friend that there was still hope, because every day he sensed that the boy might not make it and was falling a long way compared to most of the population inside. In Holden's case life had been shite and was still shite, so no change there. He coped okay with that, but for Tommy McMartin ... well he was the equivalent of the guy who'd won the lottery then blown the whole wad with nothing to show for it but memories.

'You'll have lost a few years, Tommy, but you can still make something good. Just do what you want to do and go an' have a look at the world. It might surprise you.'

The thing about Holden was that he might be a wife murderer, but he meant every word of what he said. It was as if he might still live, or at least keep his dreams going, through Tommy. There were long dark nights where Holden talked endlessly to his young friend, who seemed at times to lose his train of thought, and it didn't take someone with a medical degree to realise that the combination of drugs, abuse and hard time behind the doors was wearing the boy down. The physical changes were there for all to see: the dramatic weight loss plus lack of sunshine added an extra ten years to the looks that had once been such an attraction to so many women and quite a few men. Holden came to rely on the boy, and for all his problems almost saw Tommy as family. After several years of watching his decline, however, Holden gave in to his own instincts and pleaded with the boy to protect himself. He didn't want to lose his company but knew if Tommy stayed in A Hall he wouldn't make it to the end of his sentence.

'You need to go into protection; there's no other way. Listen to your old pal ... Eh?'

Tommy's response was always the same: 'Christ, Andy. You want me in there with the fuckin' beasts! Behave yourself. Once in you never come out – you know that as well as I do. Is that what you want?'

Until one morning he came back to the cell and flopped onto the bunk, turning his back on Holden and curling up, which usually meant something bad had happened. When Holden saw the red stain on the back of the boy's shorts he cursed and felt nothing but self-loathing that there was nothing he could do to protect the boy.

That was the day Tommy finally cracked and admitted that there was no other option but the protection wing, or E Hall as it was known officially. He was under no illusions about what it meant. Holden had talked to the screws, who it turned out had been about to take matters into their own hands and move him before they were wiping up the pieces.

Tommy barely spoke when he left Holden and shook his hand for the last time. But later the same night Holden opened the drawer of his cabinet and found the expensive watch his friend seemed to treasure – it was the last vestige of the material wealth he'd once had. There was a note beside the watch: 'Thanks, Andy. See you later.'

Tommy was casting what passed for his life into a complete wilderness. He wouldn't see Holden again on the inside, and given the length of their respective sentences and Holden's age it was probably unlikely even on the day they stepped back through the gates and onto the streets of Glasgow. They'd both been convicted of horrendously violent murders, and neither was likely to get an early release. When – and if – the day came, the only thing he could hope for was that he'd be a forgotten man and he could hide in some miserable bedsit for the rest of his life.

11

Tommy McMartin opened his eyes and even after three weeks in E Hall he still expected to hear Andy Holden snoring gently in the bunk below him. Tommy should have thanked the old boy for always keeping the noise level down during those long nights they'd spent together in the cell. He'd been quite a contrast to the rest of the population in A Hall, who seemed to be competing for who could snore the loudest.

Unfortunately, although the move kept Tommy away from the Gilroys and the other animals in A Hall, the sense of isolation crushed him from the first day. The majority of the prisoners in E Hall were sex offenders, but there were a few like Tommy who had been under serious threat in the general population and had been moved or asked for the move. Even in E Hall they knew that it was healthier to stay away from the McMartin boy; they all had enough problems without adding more. For his part, Tommy wanted nothing to do with the beasts, and it sickened him that even among the lowest of the low there was a pecking order. The rapists were top of the pile and looked down on the paedos.

In fact, half of the rapists thought they'd done nothing wrong.

It took only days for Tommy to realise that he'd moved from one end of hell to the other. When the screw came into his cell to tell him that Holden had taken a beating, it nearly broke what was left of his spirit. 'What happened?' he asked, staring up at the screw from his bunk. He hoped it wasn't what he thought it was, but he felt the answer before the man spoke.

'They found him in the showers, son. Story is your uncle wanted payback for him being your mate all this time. Andy wants you to know he's okay though. He's worried about you.'

Once Tommy came to accept there was no way to see his sentence through it was a weight off his shoulders. He wanted out of it all. Simple really, and almost a relief when he acknowledged the option.

Tommy pulled his legs over the edge of the bed and rubbed some life back into the tired skin round his eyes. It had been so hard doing the time; if it hadn't been for Goldstein and Holden he couldn't have made it this far. He rubbed his thighs; they felt sore, and his body seemed to ache all the time, as if he had some kind of bug. He wondered if what had happened to him time and time again in the early days had passed on the virus. He thought his Uncle Benny would have loved that one as a fitting punishment for the McMartin who'd let the good family name down for loving the person rather than the gender. It felt like old age had arrived thirty years too early. Tommy was thin, and the hard muscle that he'd built on a combination of youth plus years in the gym was wasted – it only existed in the photos he never looked at now. Tommy had a bastard of a toothache on top of everything else, but at least he wouldn't have to worry about the dentist.

He stood on the pipes and gazed out of the small window with the view to the outside world, or at least the small part of it that was visible. The three slats were angled upwards so all he could see was the dark sky. It was enough that night. There was nothing to see, but he heard a couple of cons shouting to each other and laughing as if they were leaning against a bar, enjoying a beer and sharing a great joke. Tommy felt his heart stutter, and there was a moment of panic as he wondered if it would be too painful or if he'd fuck the whole thing up. It had to work – there was no other option, and his only regret was that he couldn't have one last talk to Holden to explain why. It would hurt his friend, although he was sure he'd understand in time. Holden always understood and had never judged him, no matter what he'd told him in those dark moments when he felt like something was eating his brain.

It was a bit awkward getting the shirt looped round his neck, and he realised he was going to die in just a few more minutes. He worried again that he might make so much noise that it attracted the attention of the screws, but two or three guys managed it every year in Bar-L so it could be done. Tommy blinked a couple of times and asked himself again if there was any other way – but the answer was easy and always the same. He let his weight drop slowly onto the knotted material; he'd measured it so the tips of his toes could just make the floor. He'd heard that was the way to do it – apparently the auto-erotic freaks did it this way and that's what got them off.

As the air cut off his breathing he struggled just a little, putting both hands to the tightening shirt sleeve, but he was strong in his mind, and then it was like crossing a bridge. He was halfway when the image of Holden and the cell that had been home for so long turned a grey-blue colour and started to lose definition. Any sensation

55

of panic and fear soon passed and then it was like falling asleep. Tommy McMartin went still; no one could hurt him anymore.

At the same time that Tommy was leaving this world, Holden's eyes flickered, and as he drifted up out of a warm dream about a beach on the Med under a blazing sun, he could actually feel the heat on his back. Consciousness kicked in and he realised he was waking up. 'Bastard,' was all he said, the same as every other morning at about 3 a.m. He cursed the ageing bladder that wouldn't let him do a full night with his dreams. He loved his bed and slept like a child who had all his life stretched out in front of him.

He said 'bastard' again and swung his feet onto the cold floor, shook himself, stuck on his specs and took two steps towards the cludgie before he paused and wished Tommy was still in beside him. He missed the boy. He said 'Tommy' into the empty cell and grimaced.

The screw on night duty had been worried about Tommy and when he was finishing his round thought he'd give him a quick check. He peered into the cell. 'Jesus.' His training took over from there, though Tommy's face and colour told him that the boy was already gone. Tommy had broken out of the Big Hoose in the only way possible for him.

The prison officer did his level best, as they always did with the poor bastards who'd just had enough. He opened the crash bag, took out the hook designed for the job and worked on the knot around Tommy's neck. As soon as he'd released Tommy's body and lowered him to the floor he attempted mouth-to-mouth – you had to try even if you knew it was hopeless. He'd called in a code blue, which meant there was an emergency but no blood to deal with, and the backup started to arrive, prepared to take over what was already a lost cause. The calls were made to the people who needed to be there.

Later the same day the deputy governor called Danny Goldstein, who said very little, sat down after the call and stared at the books in his study till his wife came in with his morning coffee. She'd heard the phone and only picked up a few words of what little he'd said in reply, but for some reason she could never have explained, she knew exactly what it was about. She laid the tray on his desk, wrapped her arms round him from behind and kissed the top of his nearly bald head. Only a woman who loved him could have done that.

'Drink the coffee. It's not your fault.' She left the study and closed the door quietly as if he'd been asleep.

Goldstein pulled out Tommy's file again, even though he knew that no matter how many times he looked at it the answer wasn't there.

12

Macallan had grafted, annoyed the right people and proved there were serious flaws in the system that needed more than taping over. It would require money, resources and some retraining in a force that had none of the above. Police Scotland was still trying to pretend that there wasn't a shambles under the surface of the spin machine's rosy picture.

When her report landed on executive desks there was a collective groan, but back-door warnings had been handed down to put a face on it in case the failings in the intelligence systems leaked out to the public, who didn't need any more negative stories about the force. They were a public already cynical about police performance and the never-ending scandals from the past such as Hillsborough. Then there were the fools who sold information to the red tops, forgetting about the laws of privacy. Lack of action against Jimmy Savile and the parade of well-placed child groomers had left the top brass terrified of the next problem that might tie up more and more resources they didn't have.

Macallan, together with Tenant as her line manager,

received her summons to discuss the report with an executive team meeting in the police college. She guessed there might be another reason that Tenant would be there – to give her an arse-kicking for allowing Macallan to do a good job and cornering them on the project. They couldn't kick Macallan's arse because she'd earned her spurs in the Troubles in Northern Ireland, and they knew that if they kicked her, she'd kick them back, with interest. So Tenant was selected to take the verbal beating in her place, because she would. Like the true bureaucrat she was she would take it on the chin, salute her tormentors then thank them for the privilege – because all that mattered was her next promotion. She was fine with it and actually wanted to take the flak for Macallan. It had surprised her that she felt that way because, at least up to that point, her life had never been about friendship and sacrifice. But Macallan knew exactly why her boss had done it, and it was as much of a surprise to her as it was to the woman throwing a protective cloak around her. She realised Tenant was discovering something new in herself, and if Macallan had learned anything in the past it was that people could change. She was a perfect example herself.

When they got back to Edinburgh Macallan asked for five minutes in private with her boss, who was looking slightly shell-shocked after the experience of having offered herself up as the sacrificial lamb.

'I know you took it in the neck for me. I'm sorry about that – you didn't deserve it.' There was nothing else to say.

'It's fine,' Tenant replied. 'You did the job and they have to go with it; that's the important thing. We can't afford to get it wrong in this day and age. Anyway, I'm your boss so I'll take some of the plaudits when it starts to produce results.' She almost smiled, but maybe that was a step too far.

Tenant might not always do things for reasons she'd

agree with, but Macallan was sure that her boss would at least always do what she thought was the right thing by the book. Even though the woman wasn't flexible, she could at least be relied on never to stray too far from what she believed were her standards.

'Suppose the big question is what do I do next? Do I stay on the project and see it put into operation?' Macallan asked. She would prefer there to be something else in the pipeline but she wasn't holding out much hope.

'No, they want you to hand it over to an implementation team; I think you've caused them enough of a headache on this one. There is something else I've been asked to sound you out about, though, which comes from on high. I appreciate you gave up on investigation, but there's a job that needs an SIO that should be straightforward and is really more of a review than anything else.'

Macallan tried to keep her expression neutral. The letters SIO should have been enough to persuade her to say no, but she ached for an enquiry, routine or not. She thought about the pens lined up neatly in her tray and that last hour of the day spent staring at the clock that refused to move. She waited to hear what was on offer.

'You'd have very little in the way of assistance, and the fact is that senior investigators are tied up all over the country, but this doesn't need a high level of detective ability. Would you like to hear about it? If you don't, just say and we'll get someone else. To be honest, a competent senior uniformed officer could do this.'

Macallan knew the alternative would be another project that would probably drive her over the edge; the nerves in her stomach rattled with anticipation. 'Okay. Run it past me and we can see.' She was glad Jack wasn't in the room with her as she put out the feelers. There was a brief twinge of guilt about what they'd agreed, but that feeling only lasted for a moment.

Tenant gestured towards the seat opposite and told her the story. Tommy McMartin had committed suicide by hanging himself in his Barlinnie cell. That should have been straightforward, nobody cared, and Macallan hadn't even heard the name – she'd been otherwise engaged with the paramilitaries in Northern Ireland when Tommy had been convicted of cutting up Mickey Dalton.

'The problem is that he'd enough prescription drugs in his system and cell to keep Boots going for a week. Everyone knows that drugs get into jails, this isn't the first problem they've had there, and there have been all sorts of allegations about staff selling this stuff to the guests. God knows we're not going to sort that particular problem out. Just stick to the bare facts of McMartin's suicide and leave it at that. We'll make sure the remit is as tight as we can get it. If they want to look at the other issues in the prison service they can set up a public enquiry … that isn't going to happen.' She paused for a moment and looked at her paperwork. 'The potential issue with this one is that the post-mortem threw up some problems.'

The word problem always stimulated Macallan's interest in a briefing. It was the unknown; it always meant discovering something new – a twist in the normal strands of life. She sat forward in her chair.

Tenant saw it and knew that Macallan had no way of resisting the offer. She'd noticed this trait over the months and had come to like her for it. It was a flaw in Macallan's character, yet she never tried to hide it too far away. She wore her flaws all along her sleeve.

'Apparently Tommy McMartin had some injuries, which, although they were healing, indicated serious abuse.'

'Was he in a cell with another prisoner?' Macallan

61

had asked the obvious question. If he was on his own it couldn't be murder, and if he was with someone there was only one suspect if it wasn't suicide. She wondered what the problem could be: suicides happened from time to time inside and you normally would expect the local team to look at it.

'It's slightly complicated. He was on his own so it wasn't murder. However, they found that he'd suffered serious sexual assaults, probably on a number of occasions, and there was significant evidence of that.' Tenant squirmed; she'd never been involved in investigation and had never been hardened by exposure to years of attending crime scenes. 'To cap it all, the senior detective who attended was lifted after being caught up in a sting run by Europol's child-porn operation. Can you believe it?'

Macallan could believe it. The capacity for men and women who should know better to completely screw up their lives was endless.

'Jacquie Bell seems to have latched on to the story and has claimed there was an organised conspiracy against McMartin and that he was driven to suicide. She's running some campaign through her column about suicides in custody. So this needs to be done right.'

Tenant sat back and waited for a reaction. Macallan took a moment before treading the next few steps carefully. Jacquie Bell was a reporter who tended to frighten whichever part of the establishment she was after, but she was also a close friend of Macallan, and relationships with the press were a minefield for senior cops.

'Who would I see as the next of kin?' Macallan's mind was already moving into gear and it would have been impossible to row back. This was what she had wanted. As Tenant filled her in with some background, she tried to bury the thought that she would later have to face up to the problem of what this meant for the future, not least what Jack would say.

'Tommy's father was a well-known Glasgow villain who died years ago, so I understand his closest relative is his Uncle Benny, otherwise known as "Slab" McMartin. I say uncle, but according to the files his father was actually Slab's cousin. As a boy Tommy was always treated like a nephew and was apparently his favourite. Old Slab has been bed-bound for some time now, and we've been told he's not long for this world. He was it as far as next of kin was concerned because the boy's mother died years ago and there were no siblings. It's all in the intelligence brief I have for you.' She pushed the file, marked 'Secret', over the table to Macallan – who immediately realised that secret meant some of the intel must have come from a sensitive source.

The penny didn't just drop for Macallan, it clattered. The name McMartin should have rung the alarm at first mention. 'Is this Big Brenda McMartin's tribe?' She didn't know whether to laugh or run from the room to the nearest boozer at the name of the woman who bulldozed into her thoughts and dreams every so often.

'I'm aware you had dealings with her on the Handyside case. She's an unpleasant character, Grace.'

Macallan wanted to say, 'Unpleasant? You haven't met the woman!' but let Tenant continue as the image of Big Brenda re-formed in her imagination.

'I've read the file and you have my assurance that if you don't want this it goes to someone else. Bad as the McMartins are, they appear to have washed their hands of the deceased when it was disclosed that he was bisexual. The family aren't going to shed many tears. Anyway, from what's in the intel brief they're in terminal decline as a business and some of their competitors smell blood.'

Macallan sat back in her chair, took a moment to

gather her thoughts and let her pulse rate calm down a few notches. She had indeed come across Big Brenda – aka The Bitch – during what had been her last major case before Kate was born, although it seemed like something that had happened a long time ago. A walking, breathing nightmare who looked like she'd been crafted to appear as the monster in an old Hammer horror film, Brenda was Slab McMartin's only daughter, although the intelligence was that they barely communicated. Her brother, Crazy Horse McMartin, had been killed in Edinburgh on the same night and in the same place that the Fleming twins from Leith had met their maker. It had gone down in police legend as the Gunfight at Ricky's Corral because it had all taken place in and near Ricky Swan's front garden. He was a pimp and sauna owner who'd scandalised the good people in the Ravelston area of Edinburgh, firstly by moving in and then by showing his lack of class by calling his smart five-bedroomed house 'The Corral' from his love of western movies. That small part of Edinburgh had then turned into the Wild West, and there had been chaos all over the city on that fateful night. At about the same time, Big Brenda had been seriously injured in a brawl in Leith, and Macallan had had her one and only meeting with her at that time. It was fair to say they hadn't got along.

'Okay, I'll do it,' Macallan said. 'I'll need someone to work with me on it though.' She felt a slight tremor in her hands as an adrenalin surge began to waken her senses, dulled by days of watching that clock in her office. She'd surprised herself by taking the job without too much convincing and she felt a tingle of anticipation at getting somewhere near the real game again. She could dress it up to Jack as not much more than routine (which was, after all, pretty much how Tenant had described it), an interlude before the next miserable project or divisional

64

post. He was no fool though, and she knew she'd have to put on a performance to convince him. She didn't want to deceive him; she just didn't want to worry him.

'We're struggling to find enough detectives to cover the cases we have at the moment, but Jimmy McGovern has put a request in to go back on the front line, although I was minded to talk him out of that if possible. But this should keep him happy for a bit and he's not far off retirement. There shouldn't be too much stress, and I know you're friends.'

'Jimmy would be perfect. When do I start?' Macallan said it in too much of a rush and wondered again what Jack's reaction would be if he was in the room with them. She wanted to run from the office and be anywhere but staring at the clock on her wall.

'Now's as good a time as any, and you can work from the office you have. Although, having said that, Glasgow should give you full cooperation because it's on what was their patch originally.'

Twenty minutes later Macallan walked out of the front door of Fettes and stood for a moment in the glow of the public entrance. The city was dark, cold and the lights flickered off the damp streets around Comely Bank. She took a deep breath and held it for a moment. She felt a lightness in spirit and realised that the time spent grinding through the intelligence project had weighed her down. A traffic patrol car burst out of the main gates with its blues and twos warning the good citizens of Edinburgh that the police were on their way to some new drama.

'I just love this job,' Macallan said to herself, wondering where the emergency was and what it would involve. She always wanted to be there; it would always be that way. It was a moment of truth at last after the weeks of denial. She'd tried for Jack and the children to prove that there was another way to have a police career, without being a detective. Jack would understand; he always did and she loved him for that – for putting up with a woman who didn't always deserve what he gave her. He was over in Antrim at the cottage with the children and dog for a couple of weeks, making sure the builders were on the job with their extension. She would join them for the weekend.

She ached at the thought of them, that physical contact like a warm blanket, protecting her from the demons that would lie dormant deep inside her then slither into her mind and remind her that they'd always be there ... waiting.

Fumbling around in her pocket she pulled out her iPhone, tapped in a quick 'I love you' to Jack and added a smiley just to prove to him it was true. She grinned at the small, insignificant act that made her feel close to them at least for a moment.

Fat raindrops started to pat her shoulders and head, but she hardly noticed and couldn't stop thinking about the job she'd been given. Routine or not (she thought probably not), she couldn't wait – and working with Jimmy would be a bonus. She wasn't sure that he should be anywhere near the front line again, but this case shouldn't be a problem. Routine. She thought about that description over and over again and stood it alongside the picture of Big Brenda she had in her imagination.

'How can something anywhere near that woman be routine?'

The couple who walked past her when she mumbled the question decided she must be pissed and disappeared into the night.

13

Macallan stepped down the old worn stairs to the Bailie and felt the rush of warm beer-scented air envelop her as she opened the door. Mick Harkins was at the bar arguing with one of the punters about independence and why Joe Public had got it absolutely fucking wrong in the referendum. She hadn't seen him for weeks but shook her head and thanked God that some things, and especially her friend Harkins, never changed, including his topics for arguments. She could see that he was on the verge of headbutting the pinstriped suit who was trying vainly to defend the Unionist position. She put her hand on his shoulder. 'Let's find a seat, Mick, before you get us barred from the place. I like it here.'

He turned and smiled when he heard her voice. Mick looked well, and life away from the job seemed to be agreeing with him. More likely it was the fact that Felicity Young lived with him now and kept at least a partial rein on the man who'd made a career out of refusing good advice. Felicity, a senior analyst and a friend of Macallan's, was the complete opposite of the man, but for better or worse she seemed to care deeply about Harkins, who'd had his share of problems and had nearly died at the hands – or, rather, under the wheels – of a serial killer. Against the odds he'd lived but his career was over.

She saw the pinstripe breathe a sigh of relief that he'd survived the encounter with Harkins, who he'd initially taken for some loser and made the terrible mistake of trying to show him how clever he was. Harkins loved it when tossers did that, unleashing all his best lines and watching their expression turn from superior being to nervous wanker in a matter of minutes.

She got the drinks in. A pint and a nip brought a smile to his face and they settled in for the catch-up. 'How's you then?' she asked him.

'Tell you the truth – I'm bored to the tits and need to get a job or a hobby. My life is becoming the same story every day and I'm even getting pissed off with the bookies.' He slugged back a third of the pint and pulled off his damp jacket, which meant they were in for a session.

'I wish you wouldn't use the word tits like that. Makes you sound like a sexist.' She said it with a grin because she knew he did it just to wind her up. He was playing his favourite role and they ran the same script every time.

'You know I'm a sexist and proud, Grace. Men were put on this earth to hunt and drink, and women are here to gather twigs for the fire and serve our every whim.' They clinked glasses. The piss-take formalities were past and they held up their drinks to the barman to get the tab building.

She told him about the project and the job looking into McMartin's suicide. Harkins went from slugging the drinks to sipping, a sure sign he was interested. Macallan saw there was more in his expression than passing curiosity. 'You're giving me the look. What does that mean? It's the "I know stuff because I'm Mick Harkins" look.'

'The McMartins are bad news. But then you know that.

Thing is that when I was in the major crime team before they decided to let Strathclyde swallow the rest of the country and call it Police Scotland, I had some dealings with that family of fucking pond life. They're the worst of the worst – but then you've met Big Brenda so you've had a taste.' He gulped another third of his pint in one go and Macallan marvelled at his ability to slug booze like that.

'You could say that. If you remember, even with cracked ribs and enough injuries to kill a normal human being she wanted to get out of her hospital bed and do me.' She shook her head at the memory and couldn't hide her smile when she remembered Brenda McMartin getting so angry she managed to tip herself out of the bed. Macallan had enjoyed winding her up to the point where she'd lost it completely and lay cursing on the hospital floor.

'Listen. The problem is that old Slab has been dying for years, and from what I've heard his one-way ticket might be needed quite soon. I was involved in the investigation into the death of the boy Tommy McMartin carved up. We were roped in because the victim travelled through to Edinburgh a couple of times a month to put a smile on the faces of a few very well-connected people here. Needless to say, there were denials all round and a few top lawyers shouting about harassment of their clients. To be fair, it was a side issue to the murder itself and wouldn't have made a difference to the verdict, so it slipped off the radar. We just had more important things to do. A couple of married politicians paying for a man romance wasn't going to be anything that new even back then. And any leak to the press would have been blamed on us so it wasn't worth the hassle of an internal investigation.'

Macallan nodded slowly and waited for the punchline but Harkins just stared across his drink at her till she gave

69

in to impatience. He did it all the time but didn't seem to be enjoying this one. 'Okay, that's all very interesting,' she said, 'but it makes no difference to anything – and you still have that all-knowing look on your face. Give.'

'Let's put it this way: I wasn't at the heart of the investigation, but the vibes and rumours were that they didn't exactly break a leg with this one. Okay, Tommy was bang to rights, but it was all closed off just too quickly. What I heard was that there were DOs in the McMartins' pocket, but don't ask me who was who; I just don't know any more than that. The strange thing is there were standard lines of investigation that were never followed, and again I wasn't close to the gaffers so I don't know more than that ... Look, I was involved with one of the female Weegie detectives on the case and this came out on the pillow if you know what I mean?'

He shuffled uncomfortably and Macallan noted that even a man who'd committed as many sins as Harkins could still be slightly embarrassed. It was a rare occasion and she couldn't hide her grin. But then who was she to judge?

Harkins nodded to the barman for refills and she took the opening he'd left her. 'You don't have to explain it was a female. But naturally, if it was one of the men then that's okay as well.'

Harkins narrowed his eyes for a moment before recognising the piss-take and putting his hands palms out in submission. 'Very clever ... for a wee girlie.' He lifted his glass, grinned back and continued with the serious business. 'None of that made sense. Given that young Tommy was fucked anyway, why not do it properly so nothing could be pointed at them if there were questions asked later? What didn't they want to find?'

'I'm sorry? As usual you're way ahead of me and I'm still not getting it.'

Harkins shook his head and waited till the barman put the fresh drinks on the table. 'Call yourself a detective? The thing is that the McMartins are a big gang of fucking nutters, right?'

She nodded and ignored the dig.

'Slab was the man who held them together as a force. Everyone – and certainly every detective in Scotland – knew that. He was in decline even back then, and although he's managed to hang on, the last I heard he's nearing the root-vegetable stage.' He saw the lines crinkle on Macallan's forehead – she was still struggling and getting fed up waiting for the pay-off.

'Tommy was the red-hot favourite to take over. When he was done for murder the field opened up to the rest of the lunatics in the family who might want the top job.' He saw her finally get it. 'Look, the evidence was more than enough to convict. Tommy boy couldn't remember a thing, and there wasn't a shred to say that the verdict wasn't the right one. Thing is, it was all just too safe. No loose ends. Most importantly . . . and you know what I'm going to say . . . the lower-rank detectives on the team, including the girl I was involved with, picked up a bad smell the way it was run and closed off so quickly. It's always the same – the bent bastards always give off signals. They can hide it from most but not from their own. That's it. There was nothing to go on and no more than that. I may be completely wrong or was blinded by love at the time, but I've told you what I know. Thing is that if someone wanted their hands on the crown, old Slab has fucked it up for them by refusing to die.' He paused for a moment. 'Just one more thing . . .'

'Okay. I'm all ears.'

'Slab has taken years to get to death's door. He'd no time for Crazy Horse, but I heard the shock that his boy had been snuffed just about killed him, and he's been a broken man since then. Sees all he built up going to rat shit. You'll know as well as I do that the McMartins are falling apart as a team, and it's only a matter of time before people make a move on them, if it's not happening already. Collapsing empires generate chaos, it's always the way. Last I heard Big Brenda is running what's left of the show and it's a shambles. So you've got people who you might have to go to for help who are up to their armpits, and then there's Big Brenda, who won't give you a hug if and when you start knocking on their doors.' He sat back and sighed before picking up his beer and drinking as he waited for Macallan to digest what he'd said.

'How in the name of God do you always know so much?' Macallan said it with a smile but knew he could only know some of the stuff he did because he got it from inside the job. It was sad but all too familiar, and like the common cold would always be there. Some retired and near-retired detectives (and especially the fanatics like Mick who'd lived for the job) would keep in touch and rerun the old days, forgetting that the world had changed, and they'd feed out intelligence to men like Harkins. They just couldn't let it go, and there was a legend that old detectives were condemned to have three dreams a week where they were in their mid-thirties, wearing the sharp suits again and putting the neds away. It was their curse to be reminded of what they'd once had – the cross they'd bear till the grave.

'It was my business. It's what made me what I am; and if you remember, it brought about my spectacular downfall.' He held up the glass. 'Here's to us.'

'Wish me luck, then. I think I might need it.' She took a long pull on the drink. 'No more talk about this job. Tell me some war stories.'

Harkins smiled wickedly. 'Did I ever tell you about meeting Jimmy Savile?'

'Christ, no!' She sat back, amazed at what her friend knew about the human race. It was just what Macallan needed: a night chewing the fat with Harkins, who always kept her entertained till she realised she was on the verge of pissed.

For the first time, though, they both decided it would be a good idea not to travel the whole journey to a hangover, and Macallan wanted to get started the next day with a clear head. They left the bar before closing, stood outside in a clear cold night and made a deal to meet again the following week.

Harkins stepped into the road and hailed a taxi – he was one of those blessed creatures who just needed to stick his hand in the air and a fast black appeared from nowhere – but he turned to Macallan before he climbed in. 'Be careful. Stay inside the remit and remember that's a rat's nest you're looking at through there.' He had the taxi door half-open but closed it again, telling the driver to wait.

She was surprised to see that pensive look on his face again; it was unlike Harkins to take anything so seriously after a few drinks. 'What's wrong?' she asked. 'I'm a big girl, remember.'

'Look, there's a lot of paedo stuff coming back to haunt us, and there's so many of these investigations into historical abuse in high places that it's going to swallow a few careers over the next few years. You start biting the wrong people and they'll bite back. These crimes leave a worse smell than the majority of murders. It goes back a long way. Before I was even in the job there were all sorts of allegations about "magic circles" in high places, but it came to nothing at the time. Then there was the break-in at Fettes back in the nineties when a shitload of confidential documents were stolen by an informant. The press thought it was all connected and a lot of good cops took a fall for that particular fucking mess.'

'The meter's running on the taxi and you're a pensioner. I still don't know what you're trying to tell me.' She pecked him on the cheek to annoy him, remind him that she cared about him and to tell him to stop worrying.

'I'm telling you that a lot of people still in office have questions to answer, and let's not call it a cover-up but the next best thing. You push too hard and they're going to react. One bit of advice: speak to Tommy's lawyer at the time, Danny Goldstein. You will anyway, but I know him well. Did a lot of defence work over the years all over Scotland but mainly Glasgow. Quite a character and been on the McMartins' books for years. If you can forgive him that, he's worth speaking to.'

Macallan gave Harkins another squeeze and told him out loud not to worry. She watched his face behind the taxi window as it drew away and had never seen him show so much concern for her. She thought how strange it was that all his warnings did was excite her; in a way, she wanted the investigation to be something more than routine. It made her feel alive, the idea of a challenge, facing something that might hurt her, cause her pain and even loss. She knew she wouldn't sleep that night.

14

The next morning, bang on time, Jimmy McGovern breezed through her door looking a stone lighter and a few years younger than when he'd suffered what appeared to be a mild heart attack. They'd remained as close as ever since Jimmy's illness and Macallan was delighted they would be working together again.

She stood up, gave him a hug and asked how he was. His beam lit up the room. He seemed to have recovered well from his heart problem and had been working in Criminal Intelligence since returning to work. He had missed being at the front end every day, and the chance to sidekick for Macallan on what seemed a routine enquiry was too good to miss. His wife had her doubts, but he'd convinced her it would be no more than a walk in the park.

'Don't know if I could step into the ring again but feeling good, thanks. Just needed a break, and as far as the quacks are concerned the ticker thing was at the mild end of turns. Tell you the truth, I think this driving a desk is more damaging than anything.'

Macallan nodded towards a chair and poured him

some coffee. He saw her shake her head before she turned and handed him the mug. 'I had a drink with Mick last night and maybe this doesn't completely fit in the "routine" folder after all. The remit is straightforward enough, and if we stick to it there shouldn't be any problems; however, he did flag up a few things from the past.'

'Well, Mick has a habit of doing that – he's the all-seeing eye.' McGovern had straightened up by the time she'd got to the end of the sentence and was looking at her keenly. Macallan hadn't expected any other reaction from a man as addicted as she was to the game.

'How much do you know about Tommy McMartin's conviction?'

'I remember it okay. It was big news at the time, and I know the major crime team were doing some enquiries for the Weegies through our way. I mean, you're talking about the McMartins... Well, everyone knows that particular team because they were Public Enemy No. 1 at the time.' McGovern's face was lighting up even more. 'I was told that this job we're going to do is a tidy-up exercise, but from your hints it looks like that might not be the case. You know what though? It's good for me, whatever it is.'

'One thing, Jimmy.' She said it with full eye contact. 'You feel any reaction to this then own up and get back behind the desk, tedious as that may be. I need to know you'll be honest with me?'

He gave her the promise, but they both knew he would struggle to stick to it.

She told him as much as she knew and handed over some intelligence reports that they both scanned over their coffee. It was hard to believe what they saw in the documents, which had come from a number of sources, including informants. The McMartin business empire was coming apart, the predators saw it, detected the stink of blood in their nostrils and had started to circle, looking for the weak points opening up. Slab was on his last legs, Crazy Horse was long gone and Big Brenda had grabbed the reins. This meant some of her cousins had decided that they weren't going to die all guns blazing, although she probably would. There seemed to have been a collective 'fuck her' from the family, followed by her relations making their own deals with the opposition or deciding on early retirement on the Med. The income from their illegal businesses was falling off as customers realised they might get away with not paying. Others syphoned off from the money streams while they were still running and the whole enterprise was collapsing in on itself like a black hole in space. Brenda, like most nutjobs, didn't react with a new business plan; instead, she raged against fortune and couldn't see that she might bear some responsibility.

There was some intelligence that she might be responsible for some rip-offs from other organisations that were guaranteed to piss off the wrong people – in other words, those who already wanted to see her head on a stick. Brenda and what was left of her team were fleecing or taxing dealers and couriers working for other organisations. It was as if she had a death wish, and everything she did made sure that day was coming. Most of the real pros in her inner circle had either already deserted or were actively planning their departure, and to make the situation all the more bizarre, she was recruiting halfwits who didn't have the nous to work out they were joining a suicide mission. If McGovern and Macallan needed any convincing, they saw it in a line at the bottom of the last report in their file. Bobo McCartney, possibly the dumbest bank robber in Scotland, had just been released from prison and signed up with Brenda.

'McCartney? Jesus Christ! That means Big Brenda's

lost it completely. Why would anyone in their right mind take on McCartney?' McGovern and Macallan looked at each other in disbelief.

'She's not in her right mind, Jimmy. That's something that hasn't changed.'

When they'd read the reports, they agreed to kick the investigation off the next morning. They would need a day to read through the statements and documents from the prison relating to Tommy McMartin's suicide.

When they split up outside Fettes, McGovern turned, smiling. 'Routine.'

'You and me aren't meant to do routine. All we have to do is convince our respective partners that it's a paper-shuffling exercise and get on with it. It's a tight remit though, and if we stay inside the lines there shouldn't be too much aggravation. It'll just be nice to be away from the ranch.'

'Do you think we'll get to meet Brenda?'

'I think we will. And I wonder how she'll react to me after the last time? Somehow I don't think I'm her favourite copper,' she said with a shrug before she headed towards home.

15

Big Brenda McMartin drew on what was left of her cigarette and blew out a line of smoke that added to a smog of pollutants in the car. She was in the back seat and glared at the necks of the two fucking idiots in the front. The driver was Bobo McCartney, who, being a tobacco addict, could tolerate the fug and was helping it along with his fourth smoke since they'd parked up in Market Street, Edinburgh. They were facing downhill, which allowed them to watch the front of Waverley Station, and were oblivious to the grand view of the east end of Princes Street gardens and the Scott Monument to their left. The aesthetics of that particular sight meant nothing to any of the Glasgow team.

The man in the front passenger seat was Gordon 'Goggsy' Woods, who'd never smoked in his life and felt like he was going to throw up if he didn't get some fresh air into the car. It was second time around for him with the McMartins, having taken up the job again after doing an eighteen-month stretch in Bar-L.

The pigs had stopped Woods on the M74 after a run down to Liverpool to pick up a few ounces of charlie.

It had been a blatant set-up and he knew it. The cops just loved that stretch of road to intercept the runners in what was always passed off later as a routine stop and search by the uniforms. Fat fucking chance. If nothing else he was a born pragmatist, a man who accepted jail as an occupational hazard and took it on the chin, which hadn't stopped him wondering at the time why he was running south for such a small amount of gear. When he was lifted he knew the tip-off must have come from inside their own team, and quite possibly from one of the McMartins themselves; it happened. He knew as well as every other small-time criminal that most of the top men were involved in a bit of quid pro quo with the forces of law and order. They were all bastards, like bosses every-where, and it was just the way the world spun. Someone was throwing the suits a bone and he happened to be the handiest length of calcium on that occasion.

During his stretch he'd heard stories that things were on the slide since Brenda's brother had been wiped in a shooting in Edinburgh. Even though Crazy Horse McMartin had been incapable of organising a piss-up in a proverbial brewery, he'd been totemic in a business that maintained an old-fashioned respect for the male gangster. This meant that despite Brenda being a walking nightmare, it was her departed sibling who'd put the fear of God in their rivals. Bad as she was, the opposition still saw her as a woman who could be taken without the threat of revenge from the other parts of the family. Brenda had taken a severe tanking in Edinburgh around the same time that Crazy Horse had been dispatched courtesy of the working end of a sawn-off, when she'd been ripped up by a short-arsed but extremely violent Edinburgh criminal called Andy 'Cue Ball' Ross. He'd left her a hospital case, and from that day on, stripped of her mad brother and fearsome reputation, the enemy realised she was as vulnerable as anyone else. Perceptions were everything.

For part of the time that Woods had been inside he'd been on the same wing as Tommy McMartin. Although they hadn't been close friends, having been on different teams with the McMartins, they'd liked each other and had been known to share a few drinks or the occasional line of charlie after Saturday matches. Woods knew that the very mention of his name could send Crazy Horse and The Bitch loopy on a bad day. Everyone knew what it was about: Tommy was the future and, for whatever reason, Slab treated his own flesh and blood like vermin. In any other world Woods would have caught up with Tommy, but the problem was that he'd worked for Crazy Horse, Brenda was his gaffer now and the word had come down to the Big Hoose that Tommy McMartin was a dead man walking. It came straight from Slab and that meant what it said on the tin: the official McMartin policy was that Tommy was out and no one connected with Slab's organisation could lift a finger to help him.

Woods, however, wasn't that strong a character, and when he'd seen Tommy on the wing one freezing January morning his instincts had overruled his head. He liked the guy so what harm could a quick hello do? He'd walked up behind Tommy and put his hand on his shoulder.

'Tommy, boy. How's things, pal?'

Tommy had spun round quicker than Woods could react and grabbed him by the throat.

'For fuck's sake, Tommy; it's me, Goggsy.' He'd winced at more than the crushing pain on his windpipe. From a distance Tommy had been recognisable, but close up it was obvious his time inside had dried the skin that had gleamed with health only a few years earlier. Tommy was still a young man, but grey hair had made an appearance, and what had once been small laughter lines now looked like they'd been slashed round his eyes with a Stanley knife. Woods saw the fear and anger all mixed up in his eyes and then recognition that this wasn't someone about to slip a blade into his kidney.

'What the fuck, Goggsy? Sneakin' up like that.'

'Christ, Tommy, was only wantin' a wee blether.' He'd shifted nervously from one foot to the other, and when Tommy let him go it had dawned on him that the other man must have been living every day waiting for the next attack. He'd heard what the Gilroys had been doing. They were scum but Woods was no match and didn't want to end up on their fuck list as well.

It must have been the shock of a friend reappearing from the past that lit Tommy's eyes for a moment, and he'd managed a half-smile remembering the days when they'd discuss the big games for hours in the pub after the final whistle. They were both big hoops fans and the old club's woes were a constant source of anxiety for them.

Then, as quickly as it came, the smile had dropped away again and Tommy had put his hand on Woods' shoulder. 'Stay away, man. You know the score in here – you'll end up wi' the fuckin' Gilroys followin' you into the shower.'

He'd then shaken Woods' hand, because he was one of the few people who hadn't turned his back on him. Whenever he saw Woods after that he blanked him completely because it was the right thing to do. That was the last contact Woods had had with Tommy before he was released.

When he'd walked through the exit gate from Bar-L onto the street the second thing that had entered Woods' mind (after how to find some female company) was money. He had no choice, he needed readies – what else mattered?

82

Without it you were just another zero doomed to watch every other fucker snuffle in the trough while you stood in line at the food banks. That wasn't for him, and whatever the risk, the fact was that crime was all he knew, all he'd trained for since he was old enough to be ignored by his parents. What had surprised him was just how far and fast the McMartins' organisation had gone downhill. They wouldn't have touched the job they were about to pull before he'd gone inside, and now they were up to their arses in the rip-off business. It was death-warrant territory. There was no problem robbing the arseholes who couriered the gear; ultimately, though, it belonged to people who mattered.

This was the third turn he'd been on in a month and people were getting seriously pissed off. It was one thing losing gear to the pigs, but having some fucker inside the business disrupting trade every other week was a declaration of serious hostilities.

The turn was to hit two couriers who were running gear from London to Edinburgh and then on to Glasgow. What set Woods' nerves on edge was that the consignment of charlie had been bought and paid for by the Logans. Just thinking about the Logans was bad enough; stealing their gear was an idea dreamt up by someone with several screws missing. That person was sitting in the back of the car, and he was regretting ever signing up with Big Brenda. The woman had been aptly named The Bitch, but the nutter behind him had lost it completely. The McMartins, always aware that she was a loose cannon, had kept a measure of control over her in the past; now, however, that was gone and with her new-found freedom she acted like someone who just didn't care anymore. It was as if she wanted to bring the killers to the gates. She worried him big time, and the mere thought of ripping off the Logans was a major problem, and more. They were in the process of taking over as top dogs in the west, and if the job she was planning went wrong then her team were as good as dead, no doubt about it.

Questioning her was always a risk, and at the moment she was even more unpredictable than usual. It was catch-22 for Woods – whatever he did would be wrong – but the urge to speak out was too much to resist. 'Look, Brenda,' he said, 'are we sure about this turn – I mean, robbing the Logans' gear? Everyone's trying to figure out who's doing these turns and it's only a matter of time before they work it out. Can we take on the Logans just now?'

He sat back and closed his eyes, unsure what would happen next. Brenda hated even perfectly reasonable questions, especially when they were raised by some fucking loser making out they were on the wrong track. Sure enough, as soon as he closed his mouth he regretted what he'd said – but it was too late. There was a moment's pause as she scrunched up the cheese-and-onion crisp packet she'd just emptied. Woods heard her open another packet of fags and flick the lighter a couple of times to get her smoke going. The atmosphere in the car had tensed up and he wished he was home in bed or watching the game with a can of lager. He silently cursed his decision to ignore the rumours about the collapse of the McMartins' business and rush back into a life of crime without thinking it all through. He'd walked straight into a kamikaze unit.

'Right, Bobo.' She surprised everyone in the car by saying it quietly and without a hint of tension before continuing: 'Tell us again what the info is so that Goggsy can be clear on the plan.'

Woods had heard it half a dozen times but being 'clear' wasn't why she was doing it. He knew that much. McCartney was maybe a bit of a halfwit but endlessly enthusiastic and happy to tell it all as many times as they wanted. He loved the sound of his own voice. Woods winced at the thought of hearing his partner in crime running through it all again. He just knew in his bones that the useless twat wasn't telling the full story.

'Right. My half-sister is gettin' humped by one of the Logans' crew.' McCartney said it with the accompanying smile of a confident man. He was ever confident. 'Thing is that he's a radge, right, and she wants away, but he says he'll fuckin' top her and the wean. So, she hates the boy, right?' He paused, waiting for an enthusiastic response from the audience, but there was just stone-cold silence in the car. He told it as if it was the first time.

Woods screwed up his eyes and said a silent prayer because he was in a car with three people who nobody in their right mind would want to work for in a million years. First there was Brenda, who was a lunatic; enough said. Next to her was Jimmy 'Fanny' Adams, a broken-down gangster who was past it and normally did most of the driving. He'd been with the McMartins all his life in crime, and at one time during the glory days he'd been Slab's wingman. Now he was just the old man Brenda loved to humiliate. Most of his friends called him Jimmy, but Brenda, and those desperate to curry favour with her and look bigger than they were, called him Fanny. Then there was the icing on the horseshit cake: Bobo fucking McCartney, the most useless robber in the West.

McCartney carried on; he was enjoying the spotlight because he was the one person who just couldn't work out the risks. He was over the moon that he was able to put red-hot info to Big Brenda that would bring them in a mint, at least in his dreams.

'So she wants to stick it to the bastard. I tell her to keep her ears open and see what comes. The man's a pish-heid and talks for Scotland. Anyway, right, to cut a long story short, he's one of the gadgies that's runnin' this gear up tonight. There's two – him and this other numpty, Deeko. It's a big deal: twelve fuckin' kilos. They stop in Edinburgh first, go to a hotel in Waterloo Place just up from the station; they drop off three Ks to a local team from The Inch – fuck knows who they are, but anyway. Once that's done, they kip in the hotel then back to Glasgow in the mornin' an' take the rest of the gear back to the Logans. Plan is, right, we go in hard in Waterloo Place, rob the bastards and Bob's your auntie! Waterloo Place is close to the town centre but dark and quiet at this time of night. It's pishin' rain so even better.' He wanted to carry on but waited for Brenda to speak. She blew a line of smoke towards the back of Woods' head.

'Sounds like a plan to me, McCartney. Sound like a plan to you, Fanny?'

Adams grunted something like agreement. The truth was he hated the sight of Brenda but had nowhere else to go for work, and his pension plan had never existed.

'So, Goggsy … Tell me – sound like a plan to you? If not then get the fuck out of the car and I'll see you later.'

The reason McCartney was behind the wheel and not Adams was that he'd taken on the job of lifting a car and putting a set of number plates on it for the rip-off. That was something else that worried Woods: anything that McCartney touched was a concern and tended to turn into rat shit at some stage of the plan.

Woods knew exactly what her question meant. She wouldn't let him survive if he disagreed in case he grassed them up looking for a favour from the opposition. He was caught hard and fast in a place he didn't want to be, but there was nowhere to go if he was going to survive. He made up his mind in that moment that if he got the chance, he'd rip off gear or money from Brenda and head south to the smoke.

'I'm in, Brenda. Just want to be sure this is right; twelve Ks is a lot of money so a good score and worth the risk.' He said it, not believing a word; apart from McCartney, neither did anyone else in the car.

Brenda McMartin didn't like anyone that much, but she certainly didn't like Woods. If she actually made up her mind she didn't like someone, it quickly became apparent they had a serious problem. But she was running out of troops, and almost all of the good men on their team had disappeared or gone over to other outfits. It was a fucking scandal, but she never blamed herself or tried to analyse what had gone wrong. The truth was that Brenda McMartin didn't seem to give a shit anymore. She wasn't frightened – she'd just decided to play up to the final whistle and go wherever it went. The robberies were crazy, she knew that, but the business was collapsing and this was the only action she could get. It was that or sit in a dark room till a man with a gun or a knife came for her. She was going to upset as many of the bastards as she could before that time came. They deserved at least that from her.

'Let's do this then. Bobo: you and Goggsy get ready. Fanny: you take over the wheel – the train should be in anytime now. You definitely know this guy by sight, and he doesn't know you even though he's podgerin' that cow of a sister?'

'Half-sister, Brenda,' McCartney corrected her, because the man he called their father was hers but definitely not his. His real old man was someone he'd never met and his mother had only known for a couple of hours, including the act of conception. As they sat in the car planning an armed robbery, that man was dying of liver cancer in a Belfast hospice. McCartney and his biological father had never known each other and never would.

He moved on with a smile. 'The gadgies won't know

me. Anyway, we'll have the balaclavas on.' He was high on his dreams of greatness.

Woods felt as if his stomach was melting into his colon. By nature, he was Mr Laid Back but he shuddered at the thought that he was about to rob a couple of crooks, partnered by the one and only Bobo McCartney – a walking, talking, absolute calamity on legs. If any of his mates knew they'd laugh out loud and think it was a wind-up. Before he went inside, the McMartins had a team of professionals – okay, some were lunatics running the asylum, but nevertheless they were La Liga, Real Madrid and simply the best. He looked at McCartney, who seemed as happy as a pig in shit, and he heard the contents of his gut gurgle in alarm.

'We'll eat these fuckers, Goggsy. Take no shit – that's always been my motto.' McCartney said it as if they were going to take some kid's ball away as he checked the rucksack for the umpteenth time to make sure his butcher's knife and balaclava were there. Woods was carrying the sawn-off in his bag.

'Get out of the car, and try not to fuck it up. I'd do this one myself but a six-foot robber with tits would probably give the game away, if you know what I mean?' Brenda shook her head, knowing she should have given this one a body swerve, but they were talking big numbers if it came off, which might, just might, put her back on the road to recovery. Her life was shit, though, so why should it change now?

16

Woods headed down into the station while McCartney waited near the old Waverley Steps exit on Princes Street in case the couriers were missed in the crowds who poured off the new arrivals. He had a description from McCartney of the radge who lived with his half-sister and apparently it was impossible to miss the guy: six-inch scar running from the left-hand side of his gob and a rock-and-roll haircut complete with full sideburns. According to McCartney, the rock-and-roll theme extended as far as his dress sense and he tended to go for the aviator look. The six-inch scar and don't-give-a-fuck attitude to dress sense rang alarm bells with Woods – combat scars could mean the guy was a battler. His stomach gurgled in alarm again.

'Jesus Christ. Get a grip, boy.' He said it out loud, trying to divert his attention enough to steady his nerves, and felt a little moment of panic when two uniformed pigs seemed to give him too much eye contact. He was a mass of nerves. The joys of working the job with McCartney and having the uniforms giving him evils were too much. He had five minutes before the train arrived and sprinted for the bogs.

Woods had calmed a bit by the time the train heaved alongside the platform, and he prayed that it wasn't so busy he might miss the targets. It seemed unlikely if McCartney's description was anywhere near right, and in any case the halfwit with the eyeball on the Waverley Steps would give him a shout if there was a problem. Brenda and Adams were going to park well away and do the pick-up when the job was done and dusted.

The queue of passengers waiting inside the carriages started to stream off onto the platform but Woods had a good position on the walkway above the main concourse, which meant that if the couriers took the natural route up the escalator he would get behind them in seconds.

The crowd started to thin out and his heart started to thump again, although he hoped something had gone wrong and they weren't on the train after all. McCartney would take any flak going from Big Brenda, and at least he could go home and dream about quietly pissing off down south.

When he saw the two men with the rucksacks it took only a moment to match the taller of the couriers to McCartney's description. His heart sank because the fucking idiot who was the other half of the robbery squad had left something out. No doubt about it, the boy had a rock-era fetish and the scar was right where it should be, but what McCartney had decided wasn't worth mentioning was that Mr Rock and Roll was a big fucker. And there was something else. He had that thing – the hard-man thing – the look that said 'don't fuck with me unless you have a death wish'. It might as well have been stamped on his big wide forehead above his big Arnold Schwarzenegger shoulders. Woods froze for a moment while he tried to make up his mind whether to run for it and take the consequences, almost forgetting to send the prepared text to McCartney and Brenda that the targets were on their way up. Any potential getaway scheme he might have was hindered by the fact that he was in Edinburgh and everything he owned was in the room in his old lady's place. Woods needed money, only had thirty quid in his wallet, knew full well that Brenda might get to his mother's before he could and that, unfortunately, the old bat who'd given him life would set him up for a bottle of gin and a few cans of Carly.

'Fuck it,' he spat, deciding that if he got his hands on any of the gear, he'd leg it and take his chances. As soon as he'd done that he'd call the Logans and rat The Bitch out.

Woods sent the text and got his arse into gear behind the couriers, who looked like they might be a bit pissed, which might prove to be an advantage. If they'd had a few they wouldn't be aware of a follow. The burst of action got his mind off the negatives. He'd stick the sawn-off right in the rocker's puss because staring into the wrong end of a shooter took care of the best of them. It would be done in seconds, and he could decide at that point whether or not to leg it as far away from the crazy gang as possible.

The two couriers seemed more interested in whatever they were discussing and weren't taking any of the normal precautions Woods would have expected or carried out himself. They'd had a few drinks, no doubt about it, and they were just too casual. Every courier knew you had to be alert when you stepped off a train, because if there was a police operation on the case then the chances were that you'd end up kissing the concourse floor and making a mental note to cancel all holidays for the time being. The station was busy enough, and Woods kept close enough behind them, mixed in with the weary travellers on their way to their hotels or homes. They stepped onto the escalator that had been installed to ease the lung-bursting climb up to Princes Street. Woods had to stay close because although Waterloo Place was quiet compared with Princes Street, there was always the chance that a bunch of Yank or Japanese tourists would walk over the top of them and cause all sorts of mayhem. They had to be close, go in hard, grab the gear and be back with the wheels in under two minutes: that was the only way to rob someone on the street. If there was any snash from the two couriers, Woods would give them a kick in the shins with the steel toecaps he always wore for this type of occasion.

When they got to the top of the Waverley Steps and turned right past the grand facade of the Balmoral Hotel, he saw McCartney straighten up and fall in behind them but on the outside edge of the pavement. Woods bit his lip because he could see that despite all the talk in the car McCartney was twitching with nerves and so self-aware that he was walking as if he had some neurological disorder.

'For fuck's sake, Bobo, hold it together,' he said under his breath, sensing once again that the job was doomed; it had to be when McCartney was the prime architect.

He was parallel to McCartney but on the inside edge of the pavement, as close to the hotel walls as he could get. It was a relief to see that at least the couriers were relaxed, and Woods sucked in deep breaths to steady his breathing for what was to come. His thoughts were clear: quick in and out, take no shit and it's a nice little earner. If only he could believe it.

The couriers stopped on the edge of the pavement at the foot of North Bridge, waiting for the lights to change as a stream of traffic drifted past. Woods leaned against the corner of the hotel and pretended to make a call on his phone. He tried not to but looked again at McCartney, who seemed to be bouncing from one foot to the other, and it was clear his nerves were stretched to the limit. He kept rubbing his chin furiously as if something had bitten him.

The lights changed, and as the couriers walked casually across the junction they burst into laughter, digging each other in the ribs. Woods could hear enough to make out that it was about their performance with a couple of hookers when they'd arrived in London to pick up the gear. When they walked into Waterloo Place the rain started to piss down with force, and Woods made a quick call to Brenda saying nothing more than, 'We'll be with you in a minute.'

Brenda McMartin nodded to Adams, who started up the car and drove the short distance to Waterloo Place, pulling in about fifty yards behind McCartney and Woods, who they could see trailing the couriers. Adams pulled the car round in a U-turn and parked at the junction facing Princes Street, ready for a super quick offski. When the boys had the gear, it would only be a short sprint to the car, and in no time they'd be heading west, away from the couriers. By that time, they should have been heavily traumatised with a good old dose of shock and awe that even George W. Bush would have been proud of.

Woods saw the targets slow as if to cross the road to the hotel side. They were still pissing themselves. There wasn't another soul near them and they wouldn't get a better chance. He nodded to McCartney and they pulled the balaclavas down over their faces and moved in.

'Fuckin' hold it right there, sunshine.' He jabbed the working end of the sawn-off into the spine of the shorter man, who looked about half the size and weight of Rock and Roll.

The couriers now morphed into victims and turned slowly to the problem that had appeared to their rear.

The sight of the big fucker close up was dramatic. He was definitely a scary monster and should have had 'handle with care' stamped on his forehead.

'You are havin' a laugh ... right?' Rock and Roll shook his head as he said it and there wasn't a trace of panic or fear in his voice.

Woods lifted the sawn-off higher, so it was pointed at the shorter man's head. He wasn't going to be any problem as he was already shaking like a junkie in rehab. McCartney had pulled out the butcher's knife and was waving it about in front of the couriers like a kid with a pretend lightsaber. Woods wanted to tell him to calm the fuck down but it would have sent completely the wrong message to the two victims in front of them. It made no difference; Rock and Roll had seen it, digested it and knew that at least half the team trying to rob them was a complete idiot.

'Right, no fuckin' around: toss the rucksacks on the ground.' Woods barked the order, but his frayed nerve ends meant there wasn't quite the conviction and aggression he wanted in the delivery. He waited. The short-arsed courier was already taking his pack off and just wanted the fuck out of it. But Rock and Roll didn't move – he just stared at Woods and McCartney as if he was deciding what was the best way to absolutely ruin their day. He put a bigger than normal hand on his partner's forearm and stopped him throwing his pack on the ground.

'Hold it there, Deeko.'

Deeko was the top man Frankie Logan's nephew. Unfortunately, he was a spineless waste of space, but they were trying to give him the odd job to make him feel wanted and part of things. Carrying a bag alongside a pro like the big man seemed safe enough even for a twat like Deeko.

'I'm no' happy with this nonsense. When I get paid for a job, the job gets done. Know what I mean?' Rock and Roll kept staring straight at Woods, who realised the bastard wasn't even blinking. In that moment he knew his instincts had been on the money. It was bad, all bad and they hadn't even got to the bad bit yet.

'So, tell me, pal. If we don't hand over, what happens next? I reckon you're no killer, my friend, are you?' The end of the gun was picking up the tremor from Woods' hands. They all saw it. 'You're no' goin' to shoot that fuckin' thing, are you?' Rock and Roll wasn't even flustered. That didn't make any sense, because the *Final Destination* end of a sawn-off should have had him begging for his mammy.

'For fuck's sake, Psycho, do we need this shit?' It was obvious that Deeko, for one, was happy to hand over the goods without a battle.

Psycho. The guy called him Psycho. Woods twitched at the words going around his brain. The big guy was a bear, had facial scars and a handle that was a bit of a clue. In that moment he knew that they were careering towards clusterfuck territory. The choices were that he could either shoot the bastard – and by the look of the man he might survive that then rip his eyes out – or just leg it as far away as possible from the world of radges he seemed to inhabit.

The sheer nerve of the man he now knew as Psycho was too much for McCartney. His own nerves were stretched too far and too tight; they snapped and he made a terrible mistake. Wound up to screaming point, he needed an energy release and the only thing he could think of doing was waggling the butcher's knife in front of the man's coupon. Deeko had given in at the first sign of danger, and as far as McCartney was concerned Woods was acting the fucking pussy. He decided they needed to add some Tarantino-style aggression to the robbery and it was time to escalate the threat level.

'Get the fuckin' bag on the deck now!' McCartney almost screamed it – it was loud enough to wake up the residents of Calton cemetery just behind them. He was out of control, and Woods winced at the sight of his partner dancing around like Muhammad Ali in his prime. The problem was that Psycho still didn't seem impressed, and apart from putting a steadying hand on Deeko's forearm had hardly moved a muscle. Woods could have put money on that being only temporary. The question was, would he crack and hand over the goods or do something else?

Psycho opted for doing something else. He was quick for a big man who'd had a bevvy. McCartney was far too close and, like the liability he'd proved himself to be in the past, managed to get himself between the targets and Woods' sawn-off. Psycho was a born fighter: big, hard and one of those rare creatures who just didn't frighten. When it was time to get physical neither emotion nor nerves ever got in the way. He just picked the spot he was going to hurt and went for it with two hundred and thirty pounds of good old Glaswegian aggression. He swung his leg upwards with all the power he could muster and drove the toe of his shoe into McCartney's groin. Luckily for the boy's goolies he was a few inches off and the force of the blow was delivered to the inside leg, but there was just enough contact with McCartney's favourite part to drive the air out of his lungs. Woods heard the whoosh of escaping breath and watched as McCartney almost lifted off the deck and fell to his knees beside him. Psycho grinned in triumph and it just added to the package of shit Woods had been handed by Big Brenda. They were trying to rob a fucking radge and unless Woods shot him they'd probably die. He grabbed McCartney by the arm

96

and dragged him back a couple of paces, keeping the sawn-off pointed somewhere between the two couriers.

'Like that, fucko?' Psycho – real name Stuart McManus – was enjoying himself and it had rubbed off on Deeko, who'd rediscovered his balls and realised they might just come out of this covered in glory. McManus was mad but definitely not stupid. Still facing the wrong end of the gun, he knew full well that rushing the man just might cause a nervous reaction and discharge in his general direction. He was pretty sure the boy wasn't going to squeeze the trigger so he would just keep enough pressure on them to make sure they backed off and the gear stayed with the men who'd paid for it. McManus had a reputation to keep up and he was fucked if he was going to lose it to a couple of comedy robbers.

'If I was you, pal, I'd get that boy some ice for his knackers.' To prove he was cool *and* rock and roll, McManus pulled out his Lucky Strike cigarettes and lit one up. He loved the emblematic American smoke and blew a couple of rings into the damp air as if he was trying to impress a couple of children.

Woods had pulled McCartney up on his feet and started to back up another few paces. Deeko sniggered as if he'd driven them off on his own and was really starting to enjoy the show. McCartney was still gasping, although the initial pain from the assault on his jewels had eased. If McManus had been sober and hit the spot correctly, he would have been at least a hospital job and highly unlikely to father wee McCartneys. Woods kept one eye on the enemy and shoved his mouth close to McCartney's ear. 'Get fuckin' ready to leg it. Do it or I'll leave you with these fuckin' radges. Hear me?'

They turned and started to jog as fast as McCartney could manage towards the waiting car about a hundred yards away. Woods tore off the balaclava, not wanting any concerned citizens reporting that a couple of ISIS jihadists were on the loose in the capital – that would have brought down heavy teams from all over the Central Belt. He said the word 'fuck' over and over again.

McCartney's fear had given him some new energy and he pounded the road unsteadily alongside Woods, wincing with the pain in his groin and yet another terrible blow to his ego. He pulled off his balaclava and wiped the dribble from his mouth. Woods was trotting just ahead of McCartney when some deep survival instinct told him to check one hundred and eighty degrees. Looking over his shoulder as he ran he could see that their troubles were far from over, and he nearly fell on his face with the added shock to his system: Psycho was jogging about thirty yards behind them. He was a smart bastard even if he did look like a relic from the fifties, carefully maintaining a safe distance out of range in case Woods decided to go for the glory shot.

'Fuckin' hell! Move it, he's still behind us.'

McCartney didn't need to look. They both started to sprint.

'I see you.' McManus was laughing as if it was some quality joke. Deeko was just behind him so he could take a leading role when he told the story.

Adams had been standing outside with a smoke, so he saw them running and what was behind them. He was a veteran gangster, well past his sell-by date, but he'd seen his share of fuck-ups and was smart enough to jump in the car and gun the engine, ready for a quick exit. McCartney and Woods got to the car heaving in lungfuls of the wet Edinburgh air and both made a bad mistake – they looked round, heedless of the fact that Adams had parked in a well-lit part of the street. McManus got all the look at their faces he needed for future reference. He'd stopped a safe distance from the sawn-off, and although

Woods pointed it at him again, it made no difference to a man who'd already proved he wasn't easily impressed.

'I'll be seein' you boys. Two or three days max.' McManus pulled out another Lucky and flipped it into his mouth.

'Get in the fuckin' car!' Brenda screamed from behind the privacy glass. McManus heard enough to know the voice was female and knew exactly what that meant. He was about to become the star witness in the case against Big Brenda McMartin.

In the moment McCartney and Woods had locked eyes with McManus they'd realised that it was as bad as it could be. He'd clocked them, and it wouldn't take Sherlock Holmes to track them down.

The sound of Big Brenda screaming abuse brought them back to earth with an almighty hard landing. They threw their rucksacks in the back and each still had a leg dangling out of a rear door when Adams put his foot to the floor and threw the car forward, away from what were supposed to be the victims. Adams shook his head just enough to satisfy his instincts but not enough for The Bitch to notice. He'd seen the whole McMartin operation slide down the swanny over the previous months, and if he'd needed proof that it was all over then the attempted robbery sealed the deal. It was goodnight Vienna, and they were risking their necks letting halfwits like McCartney go on the front line. He thought Woods was a decent spud, but he wasn't really hard; there was no killer in the boy, and in Adams' day Woods would have been running errands and making tea for the men who mattered.

He wheeled the car hard left at what was almost a red light and burned some rubber heading up the Bridges to get as far away as possible from what had just happened – or *not* happened, according to the original plan.

'Slow the fuck down, Fanny, or we'll have the highway patrol behind us.' Brenda turned and stared at Woods and McCartney, who were trying to control their breathing and come to terms with the shambles in Waterloo Place. 'What the fuck happened out there? It'd better make sense or I'll bury you before we get back to the city.'

Woods tried to work out what to say, knowing that it probably wouldn't make any difference; in fact, it might be simpler to stick the sawn-off in his gob and take the quick way out. If that big fucker Psycho tracked him down (and he would), then he might possibly survive – but the minimum injury he could expect from a man like him meant he'd be damaged for life. That was a pointless train of thought and he knew it. They'd knowingly tried to rip off the Logan family. No grey area there as the street law was clear on that one: torture then a painful exit card.

He looked round at McCartney, who was hyperventilating and seemed to be having something like a seizure. Woods was in extreme danger after what had happened, but there was an immediate threat sitting in the front seat just looking for an excuse to do him on the way back to Glasgow. It was every man for himself. He tried his best to keep hold of the tremors ticking the muscles in his face and jabbed his thumb towards McCartney, whose eyes were bulging unnaturally. The boy's standard-issue pale complexion had been further drained of colour, leaving only the odd red splash to highlight the location of his facial plouks.

'Well, this daft bastard forgot to mention somethin' that might have been handy to know before we moved in. The big man is called Psycho.' Woods shrugged. 'I mean: Psycho. It's a fuckin' clue, Brenda. Know what I mean? He looks like a rock 'n' roll legend and he's built like a wardrobe. Did you get a look at him?'

100

'Oh, I got a look at him alright. Never met the man but the description's enough for me. There's only one model fits the bill, and it's news to me that he works for that bastard Logan. Psycho McManus, that's who that was. Fuckin' mental, complete bad news and now he's right on our case. Brilliant work boys!' She of course forgot that Woods had questioned the job; someone like Brenda never liked taking the blame, especially when there were twats around.

On another day Woods might have smiled at Big Brenda describing someone else as bad news. If she paid that compliment to another gangster then they were in big trouble. When he heard it, the bells started to ring and he remembered a story he'd heard going around about some mad fucker from the Govan area that matched McManus's description perfectly. There just couldn't be two like that. If it really turned out the bastard was a criminal legend and they'd just tried to stick him up ... well, he'd had better news in his time. Woods felt all the energy drain from him as if there was a leak somewhere in his system. He wanted to stick the nut on McCartney, but he guessed whatever Big Brenda would do would be a bigger problem for the boy. The mood she was in he knew she might just waste the two of them, because the chances were they'd all be tracked down. Frankie Logan had been just waiting for an excuse to finish off the McMartins and now it had been presented to him free of charge.

17

They were just passing the Braid Hills on the way out of the city and would be on the bypass in minutes. Brenda reached over and grabbed McCartney by the shirt front, pulled him close in, almost over the back of the seat. He started to sob and moan at the same time.

'Take the next left, Fanny. There's a car park below those hills.' They all knew what that meant: McCartney wasn't going back to Glasgow. Woods wondered if the same rule applied to him.

They pulled into the dark area under the Braids, whose rocky outcrops formed part of the seven hills that had been moulded by volcanic and glacial activity and had watched over the old city since its earliest days. Brenda kept a grip on McCartney, staring into the terrified boy's eyes, watching the fear almost pop the veins in his neck. Adams was manoeuvring for a spot in the darkest corner when McCartney failed to suppress an involuntary act that saved his skin for the time being. He couldn't hold it in and heaved all over Big Brenda, who cursed like a trooper but let go.

'For fuck's sake!' Adams almost retched himself with

the stench in the car. He banged on the brakes and forgot that Brenda had taken off her seat belt to grab McCartney. She lurched back and cracked the base of her skull on the dashboard.

If she was pissed before she was fucking raging now. All the doors flew open at the same time and she staggered about in the darkness of the car park, trying to wipe away the warm puke that had been in McCartney's gut just a minute before. It was on her face, arms and front. She thrashed about and cursed till the heavy rain helped free her from the stink. When she felt she'd cleared herself as much as she could for the time being, she looked round and growled into the darkness.

Adams was gagging near the car, trying to get the smell of the poisonous vapour out of his nose, but Woods and McCartney were gone; they'd fucked off and legged it into the trees.

Brenda McMartin was a violent, treacherous nutjob, but she knew she was going to be lucky to find them in the dark. Luck wasn't something she was carrying about in a bag at that time, though, and she knew the odds were against her. She screamed towards the dramatic outlines of the Braids, which were unmoved by a mere human's little difficulties.

She turned to Adams, who was now lighting up a cigarette in response to the reek that had pervaded the car.

He leaned on the roof and stared at the woman whose eyes had never shown a glint of respect in the years since Slab had ended up on his back and unable to work the front end anymore. He truly hated her, and all that had kept him on the team was that he was fucked for a bit of work without her. He was too old and too well connected with Slab's past to get a favour from any of the other gangsters who were worth working for. He'd been with Slab when they'd put a lot of men and a couple of women in hospital or the ground. Adams had been like most young tearaways in his day and thought the money and jobs would keep coming. He'd been a guy people respected and feared in the day, and now he was reduced to driving a mad woman and a couple of robbers who could have been a hit as a comedy double act.

Big Brenda pulled out the hunting knife she was carrying under her jacket and was on the verge of saying something to Adams when she saw the look – it hadn't been there for a long time, but she knew what it meant. What she had to say could wait till later. She'd had about enough of the old bastard; every time she looked at him he reminded her of what the McMartins had once been and how without Slab at the helm they were a lost cause. There were scores to settle, but she wanted to take care of McCartney and Woods first. Chances were that they were breaking the sound barrier in the other direction, but she had to give it a go.

As she disappeared into the darkness, Adams climbed back into the car and wiped the rain from his eyes. The whiff of McCartney's accident had reduced (luckily most of it had been deposited on Big Brenda), although some had spilled onto the back seat. He pulled out a box of tissues and wet wipes from the glove compartment and cleaned the seat down till it was more or less free of McCartney's last meal, which seemed to have included chips. He shivered, in part from the chilled damp air but more with the final acceptance that his glory days were over. If he was lucky he might walk away from the calamity they'd been involved in that night. He had a widowed sister in Fife who still cared about her errant wee brother and would welcome him into her home, where he thought he might at least get some peace. The world that he'd once lapped up was now full of monsters who didn't understand the old rules.

He started the engine, put the heaters on then lit up another smoke, trying to work out what he would say when Brenda reappeared. In the same way he was always Fanny Adams to her, she would always be The Bitch to him. He hoped to God she didn't find Woods or McCartney: they were losers but just kids in the wrong game at the wrong time who didn't deserve what she'd do to them.

Adams didn't have too long to wait for her to reappear from the dark shadows under the ancient hills. He knew by her expression that she hadn't found them and he almost smiled. She would be seriously pissed and about to take the whole fucking mess out on him – that's what she always did, and for too long that's what he'd been around for – but he was ready this time. He decided that particular problem was over; he was Jimmy fucking Adams and had been breaking legs and arms when she was still on her mother's pap.

'Is there any fresh gear in the boot?' She stooped down and glared at Adams through the open passenger door. 'I need to get this stuff off me, it's fuckin' howlin' an' right through. I'll skin that wee bastard Bobo when he turns up.'

Adams noted that the big fuck-off knife with its serrated edge was still in her hand, which confirmed what he already knew: the venom she wanted to use on the two escaped robbers was about to come his way. He'd worked all that out before she ran into the darkness and had taken out the insurance policy that he was now clutching in his own right hand where she couldn't see it. The tyre wrench felt almost comforting given that he knew a homicidal maniac with a giant blade was coming his way. He still remembered how to take part in a bit of action, but Brenda was so used to taking the piss out of her old man's one-time right hand that she'd forgotten that and taken none of her usual precautions.

While she stomped round the passenger side to the boot, Adams unlocked it from under the dash and slid out of the car to join her. He wasn't going to be a sitting duck. Each intended to malky the other, but while Adams knew what she was up to, Brenda thought he would just stand there and let it happen.

Having the element of surprise, he let fly at her right arm with the wrench. It did the trick: she groaned and the hot currents of pain shooting from the site of the blow made her drop the knife. Knowing from experience that you had to follow up the first blow to ensure the job was finished, Adams kicked her flush on the knee with the toe of his boot. This invariably hurt like a bastard and sucked the strength out of the recipient for the moments required to do whatever came next. He didn't need a murder squad on his back so he wasn't going to kill her – someone else would do that as sure as God made little green apples.

She toppled onto her side, cursing and trying to cope with twin pains as she watched Adams calmly lift the boot lid and pull out the bag containing a change of clothes they always carried. He dropped it on the ground next to her. 'I'm off, Brenda. I'd like to say it's been a pleasure but that would be an exaggeration. In another time you'd probably look for me and find me, and we know what comes next. Waste of time now. There's men comin' for you, girl, an' I reckon you're done, but guess you know that already.'

Adams climbed back in the car and started the wipers before spinning it round and halting right next to Brenda, who was recovering and up on her good arm. He opened the driver's window. 'I feel sorry for you, hen. I know somethin' happened way back then, but you're a fuckin' disgrace.'

He closed the window and headed off to whatever

came next. One way or another he wasn't too bothered, as long as it didn't involve a visit in the night from Psycho McManus.

Brenda was hurt but no bones were broken and most of the damage was unseen. Her self-esteem, or what was left of it if it had ever existed, was what had taken the real hit. Getting back to Glasgow was going to be a bastard, but that was the least of her problems now that she'd realised it was time to take care of all the business she'd left unsettled over the years. She began limping off towards the street lights at about the same time as McCartney and Woods managed to steal the car that would get them back to their city and to temporary safety.

As Brenda headed back towards Edinburgh and transport, a flash of lightning tore across the sky, briefly turning the old hills into black silhouettes and ripping open the heavens to trigger a spectacular two-minute shower. The injured woman hardly noticed either the painful throbbing in her limbs or nature's great display of power. She trudged through the swirling water and thought about Adams' words. He'd said she was a disgrace. She wondered what he would think if he knew the truth.

A few minutes' drive across the city and not too far away from the scene of the failed robbery, McManus sat in his bedroom watching the downpour and playing some favourite Jerry Lee Lewis tracks on his iPhone. He was high on a mixture of adrenalin, expensive train booze and the whisky he'd ordered for the room. The pished grin plastered across his coupon was down to the thought of what had happened earlier. The Logans would see him as the bollocks, no doubt about it, and with a bit of luck he'd get the job of tracking down the calamity twins to give them a bit of rough justice – and he knew how to do that with bells on.

There was a knock at the door and, if anything, his grin widened. That was not the reaction of the escort on the landing, though, who had to try to conceal her absolute dismay when he opened the door and she realised what was about to crawl all over her.

'Hi, I'm Angel.' She tried her best to construct a smile that conveyed warmth and desire, but she shouldn't have bothered because McManus really didn't give a fuck.

'An' I'm fuckin' gaggin', darlin'.' He grabbed her by the wrist and dragged her inside.

18

Wilma Paterson tried to light a cigarette but her hands were shaking so badly she couldn't hold the smoke still. Her brother, Bobo McCartney, had called her in a complete meltdown. Up to that point everything had been fine and she'd taken the opportunity to down a bottle of B on Psycho's last night away. She almost wished her brother would blow the bastard away and be done with it. Psycho didn't like her getting pissed, but the strain of living with him was taking its toll and a wee drink helped unwind the knots in her brain. She'd dumped the infant on her mother for the night then settled down happily chain-smoking and drinking till she was in that delusional state where everything was going to be alright. She imagined a big pay-off for the gear from the robbery and maybe her ticket out of the life she was leading. She'd smoked some Denis Law as well, just to add to the sense of temporary elation, but the mood was short-lived because Bobo had called and he'd been so hyper she could hardly make out what he was saying.

'Calm the fuck down, Pat.' She never used anyone's nickname. 'What's the problem?' She had still been parked somewhere near never-never land and it had taken a couple of minutes for the message to sink in and kill the pleasant couple of hours she'd just spent away from reality. When she really got it she'd almost thrown up on the brand-new hall carpet that still hadn't been hoovered since they'd bought it the month before. Housework was never Paterson's strong point, and to be fair, her mother hadn't been much of an example or teacher.

When McCartney had managed to stop gibbering long enough to give her a rough outline of the debacle in Edinburgh she'd put her hand to her mouth and said 'fuck' in a whispered voice straight into her palm.

'What the fuck, Wilma? That mad bastard saw me full on. Fuck's sake.' McCartney paused and said 'Fuck's sake' again because he had no idea what else to say or do next. When they'd got back to Glasgow with the stolen wheels Woods had told him to piss off and stay clear of him.

'Wilma?' He said it because there had been a long silence on the line and he needed direction. She'd managed to light her cigarette now and kept imagining McManus when he was on the piss. That was when he liked to give her a hard time, and if he figured this one out he'd cut her throat.

'I never should've got you involved. You're a fuckin' eejit.'

'Wilma?' McCartney said again. It was a question and a plea to come up with an answer he was incapable of forming himself.

'Where the fuck are you?'

He told her. She stuck her fags, lighter and what was left of the draw in her coat and two minutes later was pulling the door closed behind her.

Half an hour later Paterson walked into the boozer just off Buchanan Street, saw McCartney sitting in the farthest corner and was surprised they hadn't asked him to leave already. She'd been brought up rough but even to her McCartney looked like a fucking junkie trying to control the shakes. He was just coming apart – and with good reason. If McManus worked this one out, the best she could hope for was to leave Glasgow. Even then she wondered where she could go because everything she was and all that remained of her miserable family were in the city. Apart from a couple of piss-ups in Blackpool and some better-forgotten trips to Magaluf, the city was all she knew. Where could she go and survive without ending up on the game? She'd calmed down since her initial panic during the phone call with McCartney, but the sight of her brother twitching like a chimp on speed made her reach for the fag packet before she remembered the no-smoking rules.

When McCartney saw his sister, he rose halfway off the leather seat in the booth, but he didn't know what to do or think next so sat down again. He locked his hands together to stop his own version of the shakes and almost looked like he was at prayer.

Paterson had always been the stronger of the two, which wasn't too hard a call. The strange thing was that, for all his problems, she cared about McCartney – she knew that all he'd ever wanted was to be somebody and had never been able to accept that just wasn't going to happen. The sight of him made her think maybe he'd finally reached the point where he would have to admit it to himself as a fact of life. Then again, knowing him as she did that was probably a bit optimistic.

Paterson went to the bar first and bought a double vodka and Coke. She wasn't a big spirit drinker but the occasion did call for a real stiffener. She sat opposite him and saw that even by his standards McCartney looked like warmed-up shit. 'Jesus! What the fuck

111

happened?' she said. 'Tell me exactly.' She slugged back half the drink and felt the warm rush as the alcohol did its thing.

McCartney's face looked weary and there were some tracks where tears had streamed through the grime and worked clean patterns down his coupon. 'It went tits up, sis. Woods fucked it up. Lost his bottle when it counted and we had to leg it, right. No fuckin' gear.'

When he'd finished completely distorting the truth he tried to drink the half-empty glass of flat beer sitting in front of him. It was as if his throat had been closed off and he struggled to swallow it down.

'So what's the problem? Thought you were masked up for the turn.' She hoped that all they'd lost was the gear, but from what he'd said on the phone something seemed to have gone very badly wrong and she needed to know what this meant for herself, never mind the wreck sitting opposite.

'We took them off when we got back to the car but he was right behind us. He's a fuckin' radge.'

She closed her eyes and sank the rest of her drink. She had to find something in the story that meant it wasn't as bad as she imagined. 'He doesn't know you, Pat. Don't lose it for fuck's sake and it'll pass.' She knew it just wasn't that easy, but there was nothing else she could say or think of at the time. She had to keep McCartney on his feet till they worked something out or they were both toast.

Something flared in McCartney's eyes and it was a reaction to the futility of what she'd just said. He needed a bit of anger to release the tension that was threatening to pop something in his head.

'Get a fuckin' grip! Brenda's been robbin' everybody for weeks and they're lookin' at her as the number-one suspect. They'll get to us eventually. Have to ... Jesus

112

Christ, what a fuckin' mess.' He shook his head and stared at the table.

Paterson looked up at the barman and thought about ordering another drink, but he looked like he was getting uncomfortable with McCartney, who had all the appearance of someone about to have a seizure. She walked over to the bar and did her best to look sincere.

'Just lost his ma. He's okay, honestly. Any chance of a refill?'

The barman took a moment as he thought about refusing but found a compromise. 'Okay, honey, but nothing for the boy, right?'

She smiled again and grabbed the glass as soon as it hit the bar. The first drink had eased her and she pulled back in opposite McCartney. They'd almost no options so she had to try and ride it out for the time being.

'You get the head down and I'll work somethin' out.'

It was almost no plan, but it was all they had and he lifted his head at the slightly positive note in her voice.

'What about you though, Wilma?' He said it weakly and as if he cared.

'I'll find out what he's doin' an' see where it goes. He'll be on the sauce in Edinburgh the night so we're fine for now.'

They parted and McCartney went off to his old lady's place in Easterhouse; for all she was she'd still put him up for a couple of days – and, more importantly, keep her gob shut. His father, or rather the man who'd thought he was his father, had died of lung cancer when his lifetime fifty-a-day habit had finally taken its revenge. McCartney had been easy-oasy about his old man and only felt a bit down for a couple of days before the grieving had worn off. They agreed that McCartney would keep a low profile till Paterson had spoken to McManus and let him know how much damage had been done. It looked like his only option would be to head for London and see if he could make it in the big smoke. McCartney still hadn't learned, even sitting in the biggest hole he'd ever managed to dig himself into.

Paterson headed home and, on the way, stopped off for another bottle of B. Normally what she'd had already would have done the business, along with the draw, but the shock of what they were facing had sobered her up and left her with some terrifying possibilities. If there was any chance of sleep she'd need something to help her on the way.

In the end she went for a nice New Zealand white rather than create the hangover from hell with another bottle of Buckie, and one more stop, this time at her dealer's, got her enough draw to see her through the night.

As soon as she got home she called her mother, told her that McCartney was on the way and that she would need to take care of her grandchild for another couple of days or so.

Her mother didn't make too much of a fuss, and the aching loneliness of widowhood meant that looking after her grandchild had become a bonus rather than a burden. She wasn't sure about having McCartney though – there was enough in the tone of Paterson's voice to tell her there was a problem. She worried about her daughter having a partner like McManus. The girl hadn't had a lot of luck with men and her previous marriage had been nothing short of a disaster; she'd still retained the name Paterson even though the man was an out and out bastard. Her mother had seen a few like him in her time, and even her late husband had blackened her eyes a few times over the years, although nothing too serious by the standards of her community. That was the life she'd been born into and she'd never made too much of it.

She looked in on her grandson and wondered what the

future would mean for him. Maybe he would break away from his family and do something with the all too short years he'd be given.

She closed the door to the bedroom and wiped a tear away from her eye.

Once the bottle of white was arsed the rest of the night went from a dreamy haze to a complete blank for Paterson, which was exactly what she was aiming for. About 3 a.m. she woke up in the chair and shivered from the cold air drifting in through the gap in the window. She'd opened it to let out the fug and drifted into sleep before she could close it again. Her eyes almost refused to open and seemed stuck together with adhesive. It took about five seconds for her body to react to the alcohol, smokes and dope she'd consumed. She tried to get some saliva going to relieve the dry rag that seemed to be inhabiting her mouth, gave up and tottered through to the kitchen for the pint of cold water she needed to cool her parched throat.

'For fuck's sake.' It all came flooding back: the complete fuck-up that had suddenly become her life. McManus would be back later in the day, and the only saving grace was that he'd probably have been on the piss in Edinburgh the previous night. If past performances were anything to go by he'd have a few in Glasgow too, after meeting Frankie Logan. That meant she'd probably have till late afternoon to swallow some aspirin, slap on a thick coat of make-up to hide the truth and hope McManus was pissed enough to talk and say what the score was.

The water did the trick with her throat and she filled the glass again before heading through to her bed, where she drifted in and out of a half sleep that did nothing to rest her mind or body.

Paterson finally mustered enough energy to drag herself out of her pit in the middle of the morning, and she tried some toast and jam but it wouldn't stay down. She felt like shit and making herself look half presentable for McManus was going to be an ordeal. Her hands shook like an old man with Parkinson's, and the more she shook the more she panicked that he would see right through her lies. He had the instincts of a sewer rat and could smell trouble a mile off.

McCartney called in the middle of her second black coffee, talking endless shite, which meant he was probably high on something plus stretched to the limit. There was nothing to add to what she'd said to him already in the bar. Eventually she cut him off and told him to stay where he was till she got back to him.

'An' for fuck's sake, stay off the bevvy and dope.'

19

Frankie Logan sucked hard on the first cigarette he'd put to his lips in a week. It was the end of another failed attempt to give up the evil weed, but the news he'd just had meant he needed something to soothe his nerves. His moderate intake of illegal substances had stopped a long time ago, and he was even canny with the booze now. He was first to admit that he'd been a bit of a mad bastard in his youth, but the day he'd found his younger sister lying dead in a pool of mixed vomit and blood with a needle in the mess was the day he'd given the poisons up for good. He'd adored Jeanette, and she'd been the only female member of the family left after his mother had died in a road accident as a young woman. He barely remembered his mother and so his baby sister became about the one and only person he really loved. He'd been close enough to his old man but they kept a stiff Presbyterian space between each other; physical contact was strictly for the women in their world.

His father had been an old-school gangster who believed he had principles and claimed he never hurt anyone who didn't deserve it. To an outside observer that might have been a claim open to debate, but that's what old Frankie had firmly believed. The Logans had cleared out of Belfast in the seventies during loyalist in-fighting that ended in Frankie senior accepting that he would get wiped out if he stayed in the Shankill any longer. He'd moved to Glasgow and went to work as a heavy for a local Govan crew who'd supported the loyalist cause over the water. He made his name as Mr Reliable. You gave Frankie Logan a job, he did it with as little mess as possible. Over the years he'd climbed through the ranks and ended up heading a team of his own who stuck firmly to their own territory and wherever possible avoided conflict with other gangs, because he'd seen what that meant in Belfast. He taught his firstborn, Frankie junior, the right way to do business – to earn respect so that people knew exactly what his word meant.

'There's enough for us all, son,' he'd always said, 'so don't get greedy. Build the business like a good football team. That means getting a good basic structure in place with players you can trust. But play to win – what's the point of being in this game to come second best?' He was a big fan of Sir Alex Ferguson and liked to use and quote his philosophies for success.

Old Frankie had made sure that his eldest son and the two younger boys, Abe and Alan, were well trained by the time the shock of his daughter's death, compounding the loss of his wife, became too much to bear. He'd basically given up and drank himself to death. It was a clear choice he'd made, satisfied that his boys could carry on without him.

Young Frankie took another long, satisfying draw on the cigarette and looked across at McManus, who was lighting up his own smoke after giving them the story about events in Edinburgh. Frankie had asked him to go over it twice to make sure they hadn't missed anything.

Some bastard had been hitting various businesses and it was an outrage. Although they seemed to be disappearing down the tubes, the main suspects had to be the McMartins. Frankie always remembered his old man's words about needing proof before acting, and it sounded like they had got it – or nearly got it. He wanted proof because if the McMartins' business empire was about to disintegrate then it meant there would be a feeding frenzy over the dying corpse. That was bad for business and Frankie Logan needed it to be done in an orderly fashion. His team were top of the gangster's premier league and he wanted it to stay that way. Being the one man in Glasgow who had lines open to them all, he'd already made contact with the men who mattered in the other crime families and organisations. It had to be him because everyone else tended to be in a constant state of tension, if not open war.

McManus was clear about what he'd seen and heard. Logan had no reason to doubt him – although the man was mad, it meant he never panicked, and unlike so many in the game he also stuck to the facts when it was business. That's why he'd hired him a couple of months before. McManus was a pure Glasgow hard man through to the empty space where his soul should have existed. He'd been in Liverpool for nearly six years working for a gang who did a lot of business with the Logans and Frankie had realised there was a place in his team for a man with some special talents.

McManus had already been a bit of a legend when he left Glasgow. His critics only spoke at a safe distance, never to the man's face, and they said that he must have gone to the ten o'clock school as a kid because he was a daft bastard. That was fair enough, but only up to a point; he claimed proudly that he'd been more of a radge than stupid as a boy, so the authorities had tried to keep him away from the mainstream and sent him to a special school. He always maintained he'd got into crime as soon as he could take his old man in a square go and had then made his name as part of an outfit who specialised in breaking into top-end business premises.

Unfortunately, on one of the jobs a security guard had got in the way, displaying balls well above his pay scale. His bravery left him brain-damaged, and although McManus was pulled in, there hadn't been enough evidence to hold him. The problem was that the old security guard was an ex-marine who'd fought and been decorated for an action in the Falklands War. Even for a heartless bastard like McManus it was a PR disaster. He'd walked free but decided to take a break from his native city till the tag that he'd brained the old hero on minimum wage was washed away by the passage of time. He'd known that the detectives working the case had sworn they would put him away eventually, so it had been time for pastures new.

He'd enjoyed his time on Merseyside, and after a few years became the muscle for a few runs up to Scotland with gear for the Logans, which reminded him how much he missed his home city. Eventually Frankie made him a good offer to come home, and seeing as the detectives who'd wanted his skin had retired to their holiday homes in Florida, it had seemed a suitable time to get back north of the Rio Grande. With the money he'd made over the years he managed to buy himself a decent flat in the centre of Glasgow, and the real icing on the cake was pulling Wilma Paterson. She had fuck-all brains but very tasty looks; in other words, his kind of woman. She was the perfect fit for McManus, and although she was a bit of an arse when she had a few wines in her, she did what she was told, and if she overstepped his red lines a bit a slap in the puss usually did the trick. She'd hinted at a trial separation a couple of times but that wasn't going to happen. If there was any walking out it would be when he decided it was game over.

The truth was that he knew little about Paterson and wasn't that interested anyway. He just liked the idea of having a female there to fulfil his needs or to hang off his arm when they went out to the boozer. He'd told her straight that if she tried to walk he'd stab her, and she could take that offer or leave it.

'You reckon you'd know these clowns again then, Stuart – no doubts?' Logan asked. He could see a chance opening up to finish off the McMartins once and for all. Slab was on his last legs, Crazy Horse was manure and all that was left was the mental daughter.

'No fuckin' doubt about it, Frankie; gimme the turn and I'll bring them in for questioning in a couple of days. It was definitely a female in the car so it has to be The Bitch. Case closed.'

Frankie turned to his idiot nephew and asked a question he already knew the answer to. 'What about you? Get a good look at them?' He studied the weak link in the Logan dynasty and hoped to God the reins were never in his useless hands.

Deeko shifted uncomfortably and after a silence that was almost an answer he decided to come clean to his uncle, who expected absolutely nothing. 'You know I'm short-sighted, Uncle Frankie. No glasses on. Saw them close up with the balaclavas but I couldn't ID the bastards when we chased them.'

McManus looked round at Deeko as soon as he suggested he was due equal glory for terrorising the would-be drug robbers.

'No problem, son.' Frankie had only asked the question because he had to and was happier that Deeko did not need to have any further involvement.

121

McManus was feeling pleased with himself, having proved his worth facing off a couple of highwaymen armed with a sawn-off. That took balls, and Frankie knew that Deeko couldn't have handled it without the big man. Few men could look at the wrong end of a gun and win the day; in fact you had to be a twenty-four-carat nutter. McManus ticked all the boxes for that.

'Bring these boys in first before we move on her. One of them will do if you can't manage them both. I want to hear it from them. Let's keep it quiet for the time being, and if we can close them down I'll decide what to take off the McMartins before the vultures start circling. You okay with that, big man?' Logan asked, though he knew McManus would lap it up.

'Fuckin' right I'm okay with it. I'll have them nailed to a door for you in a couple of days maximum. Personally, I'd set fire to the cunts.'

'Alive – I need them able to talk. Keep that at the front of your mind. Got it? The driver has to be Fanny Adams, but he must be due for a bus pass so we can think about him later, alright? I mean we're no' the Glasgow branch of fuckin' Islamic State, Stuart.' Logan shoved his palms out and looked at his minders, who nodded, but then there was no way they were going to disagree.

McManus was mad but he knew who the boss was. He blew a succession of smoke rings as a kind of confirmation that Logan's will would be carried out.

When McManus left the room a few minutes later, Logan leaned back in his leather office chair and closed his eyes for a moment. He ran it all through his head and was sure everything was in its place. Once they had worked on the two robbers they could make their move and get this business over and done with. If it was the McMartins then what they'd been up to was messy, and he didn't like messy. It was a sure sign that their business

122

was falling apart and their income streams must have dried up. That meant an opportunity to move in. Timing was everything. He couldn't believe how quickly the McMartins had car crashed after Crazy Horse was done in Edinburgh.

Frankie's old man had trained him well, and he'd become as much a businessman as a gangster. His younger brothers still liked to get a bit of blood on their knuckles, but Frankie knew that his place was on the business side with strategic planning and always an eye to the future. Things were good and he wanted to keep them that way. He wanted his boys to go to uni, into nice professions away from crime, and by then maybe the business would be mostly legit. Worth going for.

He pulled a long Cuban cigar from a wooden box in his top drawer. He kept them for special occasions and this felt like as good an excuse as any to indulge himself. There was a chance to wipe out the McMartins, who'd pissed on the Logans a few times in the past when their league positions were reversed. He puffed the thing alight and savoured the rich, almost wine-flavoured smoke. He looked across and caught his reflection in the mirror opposite the desk.

Frankie Logan was overweight. Not grossly but he was definitely a bit on the heavy side. Like his brothers, his skin had an olive tone and his hair was so dark as to be almost black. There must have been something in their genes that had once developed under the Mediterranean sun. In his youth, Frankie had actually been a decent midfielder, and if he hadn't had a taste for beer and charlie, he might have made the grade. Once he'd stopped kicking a ball though and started keeping clean after his sister's death, he'd piled on the pounds and barely kept control over it. But for a man in such a serious business he also smiled a lot, and the small lines he had around his eyes gave him an almost mischievous look. That, coupled with the extra pounds, made him look more like a celebrity chef than a bad boy, or so his brothers said, and he found he liked that idea. He didn't fancy the stereotypical gangster look that had turned ninety per cent of the men in the business into clones.

He looked at the framed picture of his family on the desk and blew a satisfied stream of cigar smoke into the air. Things were good, no doubt about it. His two kids went to a great school, he lived in an attractive area of the city and the neighbours thought he was just another successful business man. Of course, they were spot on. In addition, his wife was a stunner he'd picked up on a stag night in Budapest. She had poise and had learned to speak English with almost no accent – just enough to make her sound exotic. She had a degree in law from the Hungarian Republic and was smart enough to figure out that the man she'd married and his brothers worked both sides of the law. He never brought work home and he was good enough for her. Her family had been poor but struggled to put her through her degree, and the life he'd given her provided opportunities she'd only dreamed of when he'd bought her that first drink in Budapest.

Frankie Logan was a careful man and his father had taught him caution. Some said there was no place for caution in his business, but he'd seen what had happened to the other clans when greed had taken hold. In a way, what bothered him most was that despite his nature, they'd climbed to the top of the pile, and he worried the other competitors would watch the Logans' seat on the pinnacle and fancy it themselves. It was what it was, he knew that, and as long as he could control his wilder younger brothers they'd be okay. If this thing with the McMartins needed doing then so be it. He never shirked from an order to dish out violence – that was just how the game was played. But Frankie was unusual in the business because he never let emotion come into his decision-making. He weighed all the angles, and like all good managing directors he was a strategic thinker. The McMartins were fatally wounded and it would almost be a kindness to deliver the coup de grâce to Brenda and what was left of their team. She was a puzzle: brutish, violent, with barely a feminine attribute apart from the obvious ones God had given her, or so it seemed.

'How in the name of the wee man did she end up like that?' he said into a cloud of fragrant smoke.

It was a question so many had asked but no one could ever have imagined the truth.

20

After he left the meet with Frankie Logan, McManus decided to stop off and get a few on the way back to his flat in Charing Cross. He called Paterson and told her he'd be back in an hour, which was never going to happen when he was on the piss and high from success in Edinburgh.

'Once we've some scran down us we're out on the town, darlin'. Frankie gave us a nice wee fuckin' bonus.' He waited for enthusiasm but it didn't come, because Paterson knew that he was in 'let's get pished' mode and they'd never get past the door that night. He'd be out of his skull and unconscious by the time the evening news came on the telly. The other problem was that she was cracking up because she already knew that the robbery plan had all gone to rat shit and she was barely keeping it together.

'Try not to get over fuckin' excited, doll,' he said when she didn't reply, then shook his head, wondering if it was time to get rid of the cow.

'Okay, Stuart. Just had a shit day wi' the bairn.'

McManus grunted down the line, which was the

nearest he could get to interested, and put the phone down before she could say anything else. He shouted to the barman to do him a treble and started annoying every other punter in the bar. But no one was ever going to tell McManus that he was a boring bastard. The more whisky he drank, the more annoying he got, but in his mind he was the man everyone wanted to listen to. And could he talk when he was on the juice!

McManus eventually managed to tear himself away from the bar and onto the street, leaving the customers who had managed to survive listening to him to roll their eyes and get back to enjoying themselves. He blinked into the sunshine and hoped Paterson had something on the go for eating.

He stopped off on the short walk back to the flat and bought a bottle of cheap whisky to go with whatever she would have cooked for him. He preferred cheap whisky, always maintaining that 'malt was for poofs'. He sniggered when he put the words Wilma and cook together.

'Cooked. I should say fuckin' warmed up in the microwave ... Cow!' He laughed at his own joke and saw the passing shoppers try to speed up a bit to get past the bam talking to himself. Best avoided, especially when they were the size of a garden shed and dressed like a World War Two Yank pilot.

'What the fuck you lookin' at?' He directed the question at a frail old woman, who grasped her equally frail husband's arm. He quite rightly gave it the welly and steered her away from the nutjob while avoiding all eye contact.

McManus loved winding up the elderly; it always gave him a good laugh.

When Paterson took the call from McManus she still felt ill and it had turned out to be one of those all-day-plus-probably-the-next-day hangovers. He was high and full of it after saving the Logans' gear, and he'd filled up on whisky, which he always did when he was pleased with himself.

'Bastard.' She said it at the phone when she'd finished the call from him. Paterson wanted and needed something to calm her down, but any alcohol or dope so early in the day would just make her more ill than she was already. Her worry was how to stop her hands shaking, and she just hoped he'd be that pissed he wouldn't notice. If he did, she'd have to say she'd done some wine and a curry that had kept her up all night.

Paterson sat in her favourite chair, working her way through another packet of smokes, her back stiff with tension. For the rest of the day she stared at the phone and waited. At some point McManus might or might not call and tell her he was on the way back from the boozer. How could she lie and get away with it to a man with his instincts, and why the fuck had she got involved with him in the first place?

She remembered the night she'd first met him. As usual she'd been pissed enough to be interested when everyone said what a big noise he was – a real gangster, not just some wanker who liked to talk a good game. Women like Paterson always had limited choices in men, but this time it was as bad a choice as she'd ever made (and she'd been with a few wasters in her time). McManus was good to her for about a fortnight, which was par for the course, but then when she saw him doing his Jerry Lee Lewis impression in the local boozer the warning lights had started to flash. He played rock and roll music from morning till night and basically ignored her and the kid unless he wanted her to go to the pub. Then there were the rough fumblings she had to endure after his sessions in the boozer. She tried as far as possible not to think about

128

that. He snored like a gorilla, and her nights were spent staring up at the stupid rock-star posters he insisted on hanging on the bedroom walls. She'd never even heard of Bill Haley and the fucking Comets till she first saw their ugly coupons on the poster opposite the bed.

Paterson had only taken McManus to meet her mother once, which had been enough for the two of them to decide they couldn't stand being in the same room. So that was that for happy families. She'd lost touch with Bobo McCartney some years earlier, and anyway, he'd been inside for most of the time she and McManus had been together. They'd only got in touch again because of their old man's death and funeral and discovered that they actually liked each other. It was fair to say that as far as possible she kept her family out of conversations with McManus, who didn't really give a fuck anyway.

When she'd talked to Bobo it hadn't been long before she'd mentioned McManus's association with the Logans and that she'd like to get as far away as possible from the bastard. For his part, McCartney had ignored the man's CV and dreamed up an idea to make some money.

Life had become a complete bore for Paterson, and to make it worse McManus didn't like her going out on her own. He seemed to be convinced that she was shoving it about with other men – as if anyone would have been crazy enough to stamp her card while she was involved with him.

'See, yer a nice lookin' burd, Wilma, an' some prick might try an' take advantage when yer pished. Know what I mean, hen?' He'd actually looked sincere when he'd said it.

Chance would be a fine fuckin' thing, she thought. She'd tried to talk about splitting up, but that wasn't up for negotiation. He usually turned up the volume on the sound system when she started to bore him, to show her that the conversation was over. If she left it would be on McManus's terms – and he'd promised her more than the stoat in the puss that he liked to dish out every now and again if she dared to make decisions or think independently.

Paterson was checking herself in the mirror for the umpteenth time when she heard the key scrabbling to penetrate the lock. That meant he was well pissed. She felt her shoulders slacken off a bit as it probably meant he'd be asleep in a couple of hours, max. With a bit of luck, he'd have stopped at the offy on the way back to top up whatever he'd had already.

'Hi, darlin', any kisses for the boy?' He laid the bottle and fag packet on the hall table then grabbed her round the waist. She was tiny in his arms and tried not to wince at the reek of his breath. He hadn't shaved, and by the look and smell of him he hadn't bothered to shower that morning either. That was par for the course when he was on the pop.

'Miss me, hen?' He started to nuzzle her ear, and she wondered if he could feel her heart thrashing against her breastbone. She bit her lip and did the best she could with her lines.

'Course I did. It's no' the same when you're away on a job. How did it go? You said Frankie was pleased wi' somethin'.' She pushed her face into his shoulder to avoid his eyes.

'Fuckin' right he was pleased.' McManus's mind was concentrating elsewhere, and that was on food. 'I could murder a pizza, honey. Nuke a pepperoni. I'll go an' have a wee wash and you open that bottle at the same time. Good times are here again.' He grabbed the remote and got Little Richard blasting from the sound system before heading for the bathroom.

Paterson cringed at the noise but so far so good. When McManus disappeared into the bathroom she whacked on the pizza and opened the bottle, pouring a king-size shot into the glass to make sure he packed in as much booze as possible. The idea was to get him talking then comatose so as to buy her another night to think it all through.

When he came out of the bathroom he was showered and wearing a clean vest that showed off huge arms and his tattoo – the word 'kill' above a bleeding dagger, and when she put the pizza on the table in front of him he wolfed it down as if he hadn't eaten for a week. She knew that wouldn't be the case – he was just a greedy bastard. He threw back the whisky in one go and pulled open an extra strong lager he'd taken from the fridge.

'So how did it go then?' She tried a smile and stuck her hands in the pockets of her zip top to hide the shakes, which had steadied slightly. In some ways it was easier having him there: at least she might be able to find out what the score was and how much danger they were in.

'Sweet, honey. Two fuckin' cowboys tried to rob us in Edinburgh.' He was slurring his words, and she filled his glass again, leaving it neat. 'No problem though an' they legged it once I made it clear what the score was. Know what I mean?' He leaned over the table and squeezed her breast in what he must have seen as a sign of affection. The word gentle didn't mean much to him. It hurt, but she tried not to show it.

'So the gear was okay then?' Paterson tried to sound matter of fact, but she had to be careful and was asking questions she normally left alone. She just hoped he was pissed enough not to see anything in it.

'Saved the gear and chased the bastards. Kicked one o' them in the chuckies an' actually got a look at them wi' the balaclavas off. Can you believe it?' He snorted a laugh as he finished the lager and crumpled the can before throwing it at the rubbish bin, missing by a mile. A trickle of lager dribbled from the can and across the floor. It didn't make too much of a difference because the floor, like the hall carpet, hadn't been cleaned for a while. It sounded like everyone had Velcro on the soles of their shoes when they walked across the kitchen floor.

'Frankie Logan was just a wee bit pleased. Big bonus and we're on the town tomorrow so I need a good night's kip – though after we've had a wee drink.' He sank the second whisky and his drinking followed a familiar pattern – when he was so far gone, he drank to go lights out. He stopped tasting the stuff and just poured it over his throat as fast as he could.

'What about those boys then? Logan after them?' She felt her stomach squeeze into knots waiting on the answer.

'I've got the job an' tell you what ... when I find them they'll regret ever seein' me. Chances are it's The Bitch an' her team, but we'll soon find out.'

Paterson felt the nerves in her face twitch and one minute later she threw up in the toilet as quietly as possible. She splashed some cold water on her face and squirmed when she looked at the haggard woman staring right back at her in the mirror. She dried herself and drank some water from her cupped hands. When she went back into the kitchen McManus was on his feet with the bottle in one hand, his glass in the other and was dancing, or what he thought was dancing, to Ben E. King's version of 'Stand by Me'. He started drinking straight from the bottle and when the recording finished he grabbed her by the wrist and pulled her towards the bedroom. The temptation to scream was almost irresistible but she knew he would pass out before anything actually happened. She was barely managing to keep it together but succeeded in manufacturing an expression that just passed for pleased.

Half an hour later Paterson managed to disentangle herself from McManus – he was completely out for the count. It crossed her mind that she could have stabbed him there and then but there was no way she'd get away with it. The cocos would have her dubbed up in a day, and apart from one conviction for shoplifting she had limited experience in lying to the police.

She stared down at the snoring heap and shook her head. 'Pity,' she said, knowing that if there was a way to escape from McManus she'd need to figure it out as soon as. When he was sobering he'd smell her fear, and he would have to make the connection between McCartney and her eventually. They already thought it was Big Brenda, so they'd soon tie the whole team down and figure out who was who. McManus was pissed and intended having a day off, so that meant another day of him being on the bevvy, which gave her some room to manoeuvre. She pulled on her coat, took the lift to the ground floor and called McCartney. 'We need to meet now, Pat.'

McCartney had fallen asleep watching big Arnie take on the Predator for the umpteenth time. He was in his old room and wished he was back with the gang he'd had before he'd decided to rob that fucking bank in Edinburgh. Life had been good then. He surfaced in response to the jangling tune on his mobile and didn't want to hear the grim reality of his situation. 'Jesus. Can it no' wait till the mornin'?'

'Are you fuckin' serious? We're in the shit, brother, an' you're dead meat if we sit and wait. Move your arse an' I'll come over to you.'

McCartney heard the tension and fear in her voice and

he got it. He switched off the film, which wasn't real, and remembered that McManus was very real and hurt people for business and pleasure.

'What do we do, sis?' His voice trembled with the question.

'We have to waste the bastard.'

'Eh?'

21

Early the following morning Macallan and McGovern were on the road to Glasgow. They'd hardly spoken a word since leaving Edinburgh, but it was that comfortable situation where old friends could sit and take care of their own thoughts without feeling the need to say something just to fill the gaps. Neither had imagined they would get to work together again. For McGovern, his heart problems had forced him behind a desk, and he had only a short time left before retirement; he just needed another shot of something near the real thing. Perhaps this job would be no big deal, but it was out there and investigating so probably the best he could hope for. The bonus was working with Macallan again, and he knew she was in the same place as him, although for different reasons.

Macallan smiled as they passed Harthill services, that cluster of eyesore constructions that marked the logical halfway mark on the road to and from Edinburgh. She closed her eyes for a second and spoke. 'So, how's it for you, Jimmy?'

'It's just good to be away from the office, but on the

other hand ... are we just delaying the inevitable? I'm retiring soon enough, but what about you? How will Jack see this one?' McGovern frowned when he said it – they were both on sensitive territory.

'I'm going over to Antrim this weekend. He's there with the bairns and making sure the builders have made a job of the extension. I've told him a bit, and to be honest he sounded sceptical – but then he's a lawyer and knows how I operate.' She tried to put any explanation to Jack to the back of her mind for the time being and they both drifted back into their own thoughts.

McGovern eventually broke the silence again. 'Well I think in this case his suspicions will be right on the money.'

When they pulled into the small car park in front of the old prison there was the evidence for all to see that there was never enough public money to go around. The main entrance was relatively new in comparison to the prison itself, but what should have been 'Barlinnie' in giant letters above the entrance had been reduced to 'B L NI' through the ravages of weather, time and cheap workmanship. Macallan experienced the same feeling that she'd had every time she'd gone to a prison to interview a prisoner or speak to an informant: as soon as she walked over the threshold it was like entering an alien environment. Like every detective, she'd only ever dealt with one or a few villains at a time, but here they were all stuffed into the one tinderbox. The men and women who worked in these places were never seen in the same light as the glamorous beings depicted in a thousand detective stories, where troubled investigators tore themselves apart but almost single-handedly brought down the worst of the worst. In this world they dealt with cold, unpleasant reality, and it took a special kind of person to spend all their working hours inside and, in most cases, watch a hopeless parade of wasted lives walk past them several times in a career.

Like everyone who'd served in Northern Ireland, Macallan had watched the demented lunacy of the Maze prison turn into a theatrical farce in front of the public's eyes. What had started off as a place to hold and control many of the world's most experienced and dedicated terrorists had been crippled by political expediency. The prisoners watched the other side weaken in the face of what the world saw as over-harsh treatment. The hunger strikes and dirty protests had proved that they were strong, and gradually they had gnawed at the prison regime till they virtually ran everything inside the walls. It was a victory for the men behind bars and a nightmare existence for the men and women who worked there and pretended that they were still in control. The lesson Macallan had learned from this was that she could never work in those conditions. Being a detective had given her a form of freedom that most prison officers only dreamt of having, and she thanked her stars for that one. It was one of those jobs that no one wanted to do but, miraculously, some people were prepared to take up the challenge.

This was someone else's world, and the detectives were under control as much as the prisoners when they walked within the walls of Bar-L. The very name conjured up images of a Glasgow world past and present that represented all the old stereotypes. Hard men and hard time. Battlers who wore their facial scars like badges of honour. But if you had a lie-down in Bar-L you never forgot what that could do to the toughest men, and the reality was that in the dead of night, generations of screws had walked quietly past the doors and heard the sounds of hard men sobbing quietly. In the day they could act the part and say 'fuck you' to the world, but in those quiet dead hours when all they could imagine were years of isolation, there was nothing but despair. Some famous killers had taken their last walk to the gallows within those dull grey walls, and there were screws and inmates who swore blind they could still hear those men with their entourage of guards and ministers take those last steps to the execution chamber.

The detectives passed through the security checks, and stuffed coats and electrical equipment into plastic boxes for the security scans that were obligatory even for lawyers and police. The days when they were seen as being on the same side were long gone, and no one was trusted as safe anymore.

They sat down and waited with their coats over their laps, stripped of much of the power they carried in their everyday lives. They both stared at the wooden plaque with the names and dates of service of all the old governors and conjured up images of the men who'd played God in Bar-L down through the years.

They were to meet the deputy governor, Bertie Stanton, who was standing in for his boss, who was off with a long-term illness. When he arrived to greet them, he seemed to squeeze through the door rather than just pass normally. Macallan had been told that his nickname was The Bear, and the title was well chosen. He looked like two people had been stuffed into the one skin. Years of playing rugby beyond his time, including six caps for Scotland, were cut into his ears and eyebrows, which were thick with a build-up of scar tissue. His red hair formed part of a mop that seemed to have ignored any attempt at brushing and was closer in form to wire than anything of human origin. Macallan thought Jack was a big man, but Stanton was something else, and she wondered what it must have been like on the playing field, watching this man bear down on you.

His smile was immediate and broad, as if he was seeing

old friends for the first time in ages. According to his reputation, he was a good man to have on your side and a complete bastard if you wanted him as an enemy. The background they had on him was that he was respected from floor to ceiling and had earned his spurs inside some of the toughest prisons in the country. He'd done a two-year secondment in the Maze during a difficult period and SB intelligence was that if the peace process hadn't been on the table, the paramilitaries would have had him near the top of their target list. Macallan knew the very fact he'd volunteered to serve there made him special.

Stanton shook Macallan's hand first and she was sure half her arm disappeared into his paw. It was that gesture that convinced her she could like the man. For all his size and obvious strength, the handshake was as gentle as a child – he didn't do the inadequate-man thing of trying to crush her hand to show what a big guy he was. He grabbed Jimmy's hand next and just gave equal pressure. The two men looked into each other's eyes and liked what they saw.

'I hope you like builder's tea, Superintendent; it's the only way I serve it.'

Macallan smiled and started to relax. 'Please call me Grace. And we're polis, Mr Stanton; a brew keeps us going through the long dark days until the pub opens.'

The governor laughed warmly and the sound he made reminded her of Brian Blessed going full tilt at an audience. They became even more at ease when Stanton went through his acquaintances in the police and it turned out that Macallan had known and worked with the SB liaison officer who was based in the Maze when he was there.

'Tough times then, Grace. Some of those paramilitaries really didn't like me too much.'

'I think you should take that as an inverted compliment.

They tended not to like it when you did your job.' She sipped her tea. He'd been right that it was brewed builder's strength – it almost drew her cheeks together. Somehow, she couldn't quite imagine him doing a fruit tea.

Stanton leaned forward, rested his Popeye forearms on his desk and got down to business. 'You know you'll get every cooperation from me and this establishment, but I'm still not entirely sure what the issues are and why they've brought in yourselves from the Far East.' The question was reasonable and there was no hint that he had taken the hump at the development.

'I'm not sure how much you know about the McMartin case, Bertie, but we want to be as open about this as possible. I'm sure you know about Jacquie Bell's campaign, and that must be causing you enough problems on its own.' She waited for a response because anytime the papers got on the case in public life, it tended to swamp normal business.

'I've met Jacquie Bell a few times.' He stopped for a moment and picked his words. 'She's obviously a talented reporter but she's causing senior management heart attacks at the moment.' He spread his hands. 'Having said that, I'm big enough, ugly enough and paid a lot of money to handle it, so we'll see where it goes and what you have to tell me.'

'Do you know what the results of the PM were?' McGovern stepped in, which was how they'd planned it in the car. They'd worked together in the past and trusted each other's ability.

Stanton said he'd heard there were problems at the post-mortem, but the CID who were involved had been tight-lipped, and he couldn't get a hold of the senior detective who'd run the investigation. Stanton was clearly in the dark and struggling for answers to a problem that he didn't quite understand.

McGovern explained what had happened and that the detective in charge was unlikely to answer any more calls, at least in an official line.

'You've more chance of seeing him in here as a customer the way things seem to be going,' Macallan said with no more than a trace of a smile. She pulled out a briefing note they'd prepared and gave it to Stanton. 'Everything that's an issue is there on paper. We're not CID or major-crime-team officers so the powers that be aren't treating it as a crisis.' Macallan said it in as businesslike a way as possible, but before she'd finished Stanton had put his palm up for a pause in the conversation.

'Look, cards on the table. Neither you nor Jimmy are traditional desk jockeys, so I don't think that the fact you're not with the celebrity detectives means this is half-hearted. That's not the reputation we've heard about in here, so I'm confident you'll do what you need to do.' For a moment he looked like his shoulders had sagged and Macallan wondered at the strain that must have been on this man's back for so many years.

'We really just want to go through the witnesses here again, and there might be nothing to add to what they've told the police already.' McGovern looked Stanton straight in the eye when he delivered his next line. 'This is definitely no witch-hunt, and as far as I can gather, his family – God bless them – are not setting up any protest movements claiming it's all the authorities' fault.'

Macallan picked up the next lines. 'The Jacquie Bell thing is something else, but I guess we'll see her at some stage.'

'Good luck; she's definitely a one-off.'

'Ah, Jacquie's an old sparring partner and I know how she operates. Anyway . . . who do you suggest we see first?'

'His co-pilot and friend, Andy Holden. If there's anything to find out, he's the man for you.'

'And when will we be able to see him?'

'Now. I've already set it up.' Stanton looked pleased with himself, and the detectives both felt confident with a man like The Bear onside. 'He's in for murder, no question he did it, and to use the cliché: it was brutal. But Andy's well liked in here, and you'll get your answers if you take it easy.'

Stanton clearly meant what he said, and Macallan thought it was another credit to the man after all his years working inside.

22

Andy Holden shuffled into the interview room and for a moment looked like a rabbit caught in headlights. Macallan and McGovern were standing when he came in and planned to take the governor's advice to go easy on the old con, who'd taken the news of Tommy's suicide so badly that there were fears for *him* now.

The screw who'd brought Holden from his cell stayed in the room, but when he nodded it meant it was over to them until the interview was finished. Holden stood quietly waiting for the next order; he'd been inside for so long he wouldn't make a move without being told.

'Please sit down, Andy. You don't mind if we call you Andy?' Macallan smiled across the room but he still waited. Sitting before the law sat down didn't compute – McGovern had seen it a hundred times. He sat down first to give him the okay signal. Holden sat and looked at the tabletop, waiting for another instruction. McGovern looked at Macallan and raised his eyebrows in a non-verbal 'this is like pulling teeth' gesture. They'd agreed, based on the governor's assessment, that McGovern would probably make more progress than Macallan. Apparently Holden was a football fanatic and, unusually for a Glasgow man, like McGovern he was a Jambos supporter.

'How did that come about then, Andy?' McGovern asked. The governor had already told them, but it was a made-to-measure icebreaker and no football man could resist the tug.

'Everybody thinks I'm a Weegie but I was brought up in Gorgie Road. Old man was a fanatic, and I was goin' to the matches as soon as I was old enough to abuse the referee.' Holden spoke nervously at first, but Macallan marvelled once again at how the game could unite the strangest bedfellows. She'd seen it in Belfast where the hardest men who wouldn't unlock their mouths to save their lives would suddenly open up when last week's football controversy was dropped into the conversation. 'I still remember the great Hearts team, son. They were the days: open terraces an' freezin' yer knackers off in the winter.' He smiled apologetically at Macallan for the slip, which brought it home to her that the governor had it right about Holden – he'd committed a terrible crime, but other than that he was just an ordinary man.

'It's okay, Andy, I've heard worse.' She grinned at his embarrassment and all the ice was broken.

They did the official requirements and explained that they wanted nothing more than to go over what he'd said to the police who'd attended Tommy's suicide. McGovern was running over Holden's initial statement to the police when Holden half raised his hand. McGovern stopped mid-sentence and realised just how institutionalised the man had become.

'What is it?' McGovern said it gently, understanding that they were dealing with a fragile soul who perhaps had something more to tell them. The statement that had been taken initially was brief, obviously rushed and to use the technical term ... crap.

'Why are you here? I thought this had all been closed down? Tommy was on his own.'

Macallan had intended keeping their side of the issue under wraps as much as possible but she'd seen enough of Holden to know that the governor was right again. If anyone could give them something from inside the prison, it was the man on the other side of the table. She took her chance, after giving the screw that was in the room with them a quick glance; he might be staring at the wall, but his ears would be in record mode and anything said would go back to Stanton. She wouldn't have expected anything else. 'Andy, I know you were close to Tommy.' He nodded and lowered his eyes to the tabletop as Macallan took her gamble. 'There was a post-mortem and it's clear Tommy suffered a number of serious assaults at some stage. He had several injuries and must have been hurt pretty badly.' She leaned forward and put her forearms on the table, trying to make eye contact. 'Andy.' She let it hang there and watched the muscles in his face twitch with emotion.

There was a long silence; McGovern and Macallan gave each other a quick look, recognising it to be what they knew in the trade as a 'buy sign'. Holden was ready to say something. When he broke down and sobbed like a child it was sudden and not quite what the detectives had expected, but then they didn't really know Andy Holden.

'Would you like a couple of minutes on your own?' McGovern stood up and put his hand on the man's shoulder, and the gesture seemed to break Holden even further. McGovern nodded to the screw, who opened the door and they left Holden to recover.

Macallan leaned back against the corridor wall and stretched her arms out in front of her to undo the knots in her shoulders. 'What do you think?'

'I think the old boy in there is going to tell us what he knows. I'm still not sure why it matters. People get hurt in prison, so what's new?'

'It's a different world, and everyone's afraid of what might be thrown at them nowadays. Jacquie Bell has this campaign going, and I suppose the fear is that if Tommy was driven to his suicide she will hunt them for failure in their duty of care. She'll say that serious abuse is a crime wherever it happens and someone is responsible. It's the new world we live in, Jimmy.'

They opened the door, at which Holden stood up and apologised.

'Nothing to apologise for, Andy; he was your friend. It's natural.' Macallan looked straight into his eyes as she said it.

'What do you want to know, miss? Only thing is I could get the same treatment for telling you this. Christ. I'll have to go to E Hall.'

'Everything,' Macallan said, and Holden told them as much as he knew. He told them how he'd watched his young friend decay and die in the years inside and there was nothing that could stop it. Slab McMartin had basically declared open season on the boy and it had turned out to be a death sentence. He told them about the Gilroys and the other men who'd ambushed Tommy every chance they'd got. 'They're fuckin' animals. Know what I mean?'

'What about the prison officers, Andy? Could they have done more to protect him?' McGovern looked up at the screw as he said it but the guy never moved a muscle.

'There's nothin' these boys could have done. They asked Tommy a dozen times if he was havin' a problem, but he was a stubborn wee laddie. Know what I mean? Truth is Tommy was a tough bastard, but he couldn't do his time. It wouldn't have mattered where they'd put the boy in the end.'

McGovern wrote down Andy's statement. It seemed like a weight had lifted from the man's shoulders.

Macallan started to wind it up and assured Holden she'd speak to the governor to make sure he was protected if any of his information came out.

'What about the drugs he was taking? We know he was shot full of stuff. You must have known about that.'

He looked at the screw and told them he didn't want to discuss any of that. The look was enough. Drugs came into prison – that was a given – and at least somewhere in the equation there would be low-level corruption. If Holden started mentioning bent screws then that might just make his life a bit harder, and it was only his occasional use of dope that got him through his own days. Macallan decided to leave that one for the meantime.

'Anything else, Andy, before we go?'

'Aye, the most important bit.'

'What's that?' McGovern stopped packing his briefcase – this was one of those moments that come and jab you in the eye on some cases.

'Tommy was innocent. Fitted up. No doubt about it.'

The detectives – like every other detective – had heard it all before. The prisons according to their guests were full of innocent men and women who'd been fitted or wrongly convicted. McGovern snorted and continued stuffing his papers into the briefcase. 'Come on, Andy. The case was tighter than a duck's arse.' McGovern didn't even look at Holden when he said it, but Macallan watched the old con's eyes burn with conviction.

'We can't reopen a case with such a weight of evidence. After all, how could you know?'

'I'm as guilty as sin, never denied it an' never tried. I killed my wife, and you know what? I would do it again. I spent years listening to that boy. He was a nippy bastard, and if he hadn't ended up in here he would have hurt a lot of people in his business. All I can tell you is that he never did it. He didn't know why it happened, but his best guess was it was in the family.' Holden stood up, looked at the screw and nodded a signal that meant the meeting was over. He left without another word and Macallan sat at the table for a minute as McGovern got ready to go. He looked at her and saw her working some idea.

'Don't go there.'

She looked up and smiled at her friend. 'Would I do that?' But she said it with an expression that worried him.

They managed to find time to see the pathologist who'd carried out the PM on Tommy McMartin. They weren't expecting anything from him other than what they'd seen in the report and knew that pathologists tended to be rigorous in the extreme in what they committed to paper. They had to be, as errors would come at a heavy cost.

'It's all there in the report, Superintendent. The boy had suffered a couple of fractures that hadn't been reported. God knows why, but he must have been in pain so one wonders why he wouldn't have sought help. He was using a variety of drugs, but we're still waiting on the results before we can issue a final report. There was no doubt in my mind that he'd suffered serious sexual assaults, and I can spell it out, but it's all there.' He was impatient, as they always were, and Macallan knew they would gain nothing else, though she told him they might need to see him again.

When they left the mortuary Macallan and McGovern dropped into the first coffee shop they could find to chew the fat. The sludge served up by the waitress, who looked like she might have anger-management issues, was almost undrinkable and unrecognisable as having come from a coffee bean.

'What do you think, Jimmy?'

148

'Well . . . no one wants us to go near the drugs-in-prison thing. It's there in the toxicology reports, or will be, so it's just a factor that no one will give a toss about. The biggie is – did the assaults contribute to his death? Nothing new there either, but who knows?'

'We need to see Tommy's lawyer, this Danny Goldstein. He was one of the only people to visit Tommy, so let's see what he's got to say. Try and get it fixed up for the morning. Meanwhile, I need to talk to the SIO who ran Tommy's case when he was lifted for the murder.'

'Anything else?'

'Yes. Jacquie Bell, but I'll do that one. Think we'll try and get a look at the HOLMES system for Tommy's original case, but we'll leave that till next week. After tomorrow I'm off to the cottage for the weekend and then coming back on Monday. That suit you okay?'

'This is easy stuff, but who's complaining?' McGovern took out his phone and called Goldstein, who sounded pleased that he was going to get a visit and they arranged it for the following morning.

23

Danny Goldstein had dipped his toe into retirement and didn't really like the feel of it. He missed the pressure, the days when there were never enough hours to cope with all the dramas he had to unpick or argue in court. He missed leaning on the bars of half the boozers in Scotland listening to confessions and the inside gossip on who was doing what to who. Goldstein knew enough to fill the front pages of the scandal sheets for a month, and some of it would have been written off as fiction, it was just that bizarre.

At one time he'd represented a sauna owner called Big Pam Costello, and when he managed to get her a not guilty for a cast-iron case of serious assault on a twat of a customer, she'd become his pal for life. Big Pam had seen it all and had the evidence for a rainy day. She was gay, so never got down and dirty with the customers herself, just watched them come and go, take her allegedly free drink and spill their guts. They came in all shapes, sizes and professions. Once they'd told Pam what they wanted to pay for then there was nothing else to hide, so the regulars thought of her as an old friend. She played the part for all it was worth and was an excellent listener. To be fair, she'd never intended using her knowledge unless she needed to, but in the same way her customers opened up to her, she opened up to Danny Goldstein. He was an excellent listener as well, and they loved each other's company.

Big Pam had died of breast cancer only a few days before, and it was as if another part of those glory days was gone and soon to be forgotten. Danny missed them, and increasingly poor health meant there was probably no way back, so he tended his garden while waiting for the phone to ring. That was happening less and less, and his wife had never been happier because at long last she had him at home to herself. She'd always accepted that he played away – that particular sideshow had run without any major damage to their marriage, but she was relieved it seemed to be at an end. She was a devout woman and just wanted them to get over the line together. Every night she prayed for Danny, because she suspected his entry into heaven might take a bit more understanding than hers.

When the doorbell rang, Danny's wife answered and smiled at the two police officers like old friends; that was her way. By the time they'd reached his study she'd talked them into accepting some food and drink they could have done without, but that was her way as well.

'Come in, please.' Goldstein waved them to a couple of chairs in front of his old and battered but much-loved desk. 'I hope you don't count the calories, because my wife thinks that's all nonsense and she'll be offended if you don't eat every crumb.'

Macallan liked the old lawyer and remembered that Mick Harkins had said she'd need to forgive him for some of the people he'd represented and saved from hard time. She never let that bother her and rarely judged people in that way. In his day Jack had done defence work but, to be fair, he always claimed he liked 'putting the bastards away' better than shaking their hands after an undeserved not guilty. McGovern had more of a problem with defence lawyers, but he hid it well when it was in the interests of the job. Macallan had never seen a man love his food like Jimmy, which meant old Mrs Goldstein had already found the way to his heart. In between mouthfuls of the most delicious meats and bread they'd tasted during working hours in a long time, they talked about everything apart from the reason they were there.

'Mick Harkins told me to look you up, Mr Goldstein. Remember him?'

Goldstein's eyes lit up and he slapped the desktop with the palm of his hand. 'Mick Harkins! My God, I thought his liver would have packed up by now. Seriously old school and the only man I remember who could drink me under the table. Mick was like me: spent his life connecting with people and never had to go far to find the man that knows. It still works best, you know. Tell him I asked for him and that he still owes me twenty quid.'

'You'll never get it back. This is Mick we're talking about.' Macallan swigged back the last of her strong black coffee and got to the business end of the day. She explained what they were doing, left very little out and, true to form, Goldstein stayed quiet but listened intently. He nodded occasionally, and at one point when she was describing the injuries Tommy had suffered, she was sure she saw his eyes well up. He was old, though, so maybe it was nothing.

When she'd finished, Goldstein took out an old file stuffed with paper and tied round with ribbon that had seen better days. He dropped it on the desktop and there was a pause as he tried to gather his thoughts.

'This is Tommy's file, which I've kept since his arrest and conviction.' He touched it for a moment as if there was something precious inside. 'It's a while since I saw Tommy, but every time I came back from the prison after a visit I'd take this out and go through it again because I was convinced he was innocent. So was he, even though he was completely out of it the night Mickey Dalton was killed.' He sighed and put the file back in his desk. 'Like you I've spent my life listening to people lie, including a lot of detectives giving evidence in court. You get to know, don't you?'

'Have you any hard evidence? You know the problem – we're only investigating the circumstances of his suicide, and even if we thought there was something wrong . . . well who's going to look at it now on a hunch?' McGovern said it with some conviction and Goldstein nodded in acceptance of the argument.

'I know, and that's what I'm telling you. I have no evidence, only that I know he didn't do it. And as far as I'm concerned he's dead because of that injustice. Most people, and I suspect most of your colleagues, will think that's a good thing. I, of course, knew the boy and see it in a different context.'

Goldstein called through to his wife for more coffee.

'Is there anything you think we need to look at that might help?' McGovern had warmed to the man and lightened the tone again.

'I've spent so much time on it that I can only come to one possible conclusion. No one expected Benny McMartin, or Slab as you would know him, to last as long as he has. When this all happened, Tommy was the man who was destined to take over. Benny despised his offspring, and little wonder. Crazy Horse and Big Brenda! Now there's a combination that would disappoint any father. My guess is the answer lay somewhere in the family dynamics, but

153

will we ever know?' Goldstein shrugged; he seemed to have aged a little more even in the short time they'd spent with him.

'Is there any possibility we can look through your file? It might help.'

Goldstein took it back out of the desk and paused for a moment before speaking. 'You're welcome, but I suspect there's nothing you don't know already. The only thing is I have to make a confession. There are sheets of phone billing in there that . . . let's say I got from a contact in the phone companies. It's the phone calls made by Tommy and Mickey Dalton in the couple of months prior to the murder. I was going to get subscribers from the same contact, but unfortunately the poor soul was arrested before he could get them for me. I wanted to see if there was anything in there that might give us some leads. To be fair, the engineer in the phone company never named me and I represented him free of charge.' He opened his palms up and waited on their judgement.

'It's in the past, Danny, and I'm positive the phone work was all done. It's usually the first priority nowadays, as I'm sure you know. We'll look through the file in confidence and you'll get it back when we finish.'

Goldstein's wife came in with fresh coffee and cake, refusing to let them leave till they'd sampled it. Goldstein shrugged and patted her back. 'What can you do with such a woman?'

When Macallan's phone rang, saving her from the last piece of cake, she discovered it was Jacquie Bell, whose voice was crackling with energy as usual, and even though it had been months since they'd last spoken, it was as if they'd just parted company that morning.

'How's business, honey? My impeccable sources tell me you're sniffing around Bar-L and Tommy McMartin's death. I'm on the case with overcrowding and associated shit in the prison service so I think we should meet. Thought you weren't a grim-faced detective anymore?'

There was no way Macallan was going to resist the invitation from her friend, who was a force of nature and capable of making even the strongest men nervous in her presence. She'd pulled down a few big careers in her time, and the legend was that she had Mick Harkins' knack of knowing where all the dark secrets and bodies were buried in public life in Scotland.

'Tomorrow morning for breakfast. I'm going over to Northern Ireland to be with my man and bairns for the weekend. How's that?'

'Done. Usual place in George Street?'

'Sure.'

When she was done, Macallan slipped the phone back in her pocket, made her excuses to Goldstein and picked up the file. When they stepped outside they turned to say goodbye, but he spoke before they had time.

'I failed Tommy. I really did. He was the first innocent man I ever represented and I couldn't do it for him.'

His wife bit her lip and put her hand on his shoulder before closing the door.

They got in the car. McGovern turned on the ignition and looked at his friend, who was deep in her own thoughts. 'If it makes any difference, my gut tells me the same thing – but who's going to give one about it?'

Macallan stared straight ahead and nodded but didn't speak till they were on the M8 heading for Edinburgh.

24

Woods sucked the foam off his fifth pint. The first four had hit the spot and Christ did he need that calming effect. Since the disaster in Edinburgh he'd hardly slept, apart from having the odd half hour when he'd dozed off through sheer exhaustion. Even that gave him no respite, though, because no sooner had he dropped into deep snooze mode than McManus and Big Brenda would stride side by side into his unconscious mind and scare the living shit out of him. It was always the same dream: McManus would grin, and it was as if his face opened up in two halves with a gaping mouth that exposed several rows of huge white teeth. Nightmare McManus was always dressed in a white boiler suit splattered with wet bloodstains, and slung over his shoulder were the chewed-up remains of Bobo McCartney. Just before Woods woke up screaming, Brenda would piss herself laughing, stand over him and raise the biggest fuck-off mash hammer imaginable. He would watch, unable to move a muscle, his mouth screaming without sound, as the hammer was lifted and then swung towards his face in a huge arc.

He gulped the top quarter of the pint and closed his eyes as he savoured the drink. It had been three days since they'd fucked up the robbery and if he could just get through this night, then he was away on the 10 a.m. to London the next day. After making it back to his old lady's he'd stuffed what cash and possessions he had into a case to get somewhere Big Brenda or McManus couldn't find him. His mother was pissed as usual, so he'd gone into her bedroom and found the old leather bag she kept her cash in. She'd done next to nothing for him, which meant he didn't feel he owed her anything back. Feeling generous, he took most of her stash but left a tenner so she could get fags and a drink in the morning.

Woods bunked up with a close mate, told him he needed to keep the head down for a bit and made the excuse that he'd had a falling-out with his old lady; it seemed wiser not to mention the fact that the Logans were looking for his scalp. He needed more money than he had at that moment and his plan was to borrow whatever he could from whoever he could without actually mentioning that the minute he'd mustered what he needed, he was out of the city and they'd never see a penny back. He didn't like doing it, but needs must and this was definitely life or death. If he'd had enough dosh available he would have pissed off to London without waiting, but he needed a stake. He was fucked if he was going to live in a cardboard box at the side of the Thames. There were a couple of old mates down there working for London teams and they'd get him involved. All he had to do was survive one more night in Glasgow then he could stop dreaming about McManus or Brenda visiting him in the night, but unfortunately neither McManus nor Brenda had read that particular script. Sometimes people are in the right place at the right time; for Woods the opposite was true that night and just sheer bad luck. Shit happens.

The pub he was in was a decent boozer, out of the way and as far as anyone knew it didn't attract any of the city's gangsters. That was almost true until fate played its hand and dealt Woods a bummer in the form of one of the Logans' team, Sammy Kerr, who was playing away from home. It just so happened that Kerr's bit on the side stayed in a nice part of town and about two hundred yards from the pub. He'd had an afternoon session with the part-time stripper, who was giving him what his wife didn't and definitely putting the fizz back into his sex life. He was grinning from ear to ear as he left her flat, and the thought that his exertions deserved a beer had only just entered his head when the warm boozy smell leaking out of the pub doorway acted as a direct invitation. He sauntered in, ordered up and took a seat in one of the booths, still glowing from his success with the stripper. An abandoned copy of the *Record* lay on the table so he checked it out, although he knew there would be nothing in it apart from bad news front to back. Politics meant almost nothing to him, so he turned to the sports pages while sipping the top of his beer and intermittently looking around the bar. Luck played its shit hand to Woods by having stuck Kerr in Bar-L's A Hall for a couple of months when he was inside. They'd only spoken a couple of times but Kerr had picked up that Woods had worked for the McMartins before he was dubbed up. So when he spotted him at the far end of the bar the lights started flashing in his head that the Logans were looking for anyone with the McMartin stamp on them; in other words, he might be about to turn a good day into a great one. Kerr had only worked for the Logans since he'd been released and was barely above the cleaner in rank, which meant there was almost no chance Woods would have known that.

'How's it goin', Goggsy?'

Woods was half-pissed but still nearly fell off the stool at the sound of his name, a reaction that told Kerr he might be on to something. After a few moments, when Woods realised there wasn't a knife going in his back, he struggled to remember Kerr's first name. It came to him and he smiled nervously, taking it as just a chance meet. 'Hey, Sammy! How long you been out?' He stuck out his hand. Some company would take his mind off things. Kerr had always seemed like a sound guy inside, and he had a good reputation as a thief.

They got up a round and Kerr told Woods in graphic detail what he'd been up to with the stripper so they both fed on their favourite subject. Woods had been so wrapped up and stressed working for Big Brenda that he'd hardly been near a woman in the weeks since his release. To make things worse, he'd paid a hooker to revitalise his fantasies and failed miserably. Chewing the fat with Kerr, combined with pint number six, made him feel like his old self again; he'd reached that point on the alcohol scale where it was pish-up time and fuck the consequences. After all, he thought, it was his last night in the city, he was out of the road and he'd met Kerr, who seemed like his best mate. If Woods had kept his head on he'd have remembered rule number one – the most basic lesson of being a professional criminal – trust no one, and especially not the guy who turns up like your long-lost brother.

'What you up to then, Goggsy?'

Woods's vision was beginning to blur, like his defence mechanisms, and he knew, just absolutely knew, that he could trust Kerr. He leaned in close like a co-conspirator, instantly confirming Kerr's rat instincts that he was on to something, and gave away some gold nuggets to his new best pal.

'Tell you the truth, Sammy boy: I'm fuckin' off in the

mornin' and ta-ta to this dump. Headin' down to the smoke, my friend. Bit of a fuck-up involved. Know what I mean?' He winked at Kerr, who smiled back as if he was watching someone standing on the scaffold and tying the rope round their own neck.

'How's that, pal?'

Kerr was playing with someone asking to be caught. 'Went back and did some work wi' Big Brenda. Fuckin' disaster, Sammy, so it's time to go south. That fuckin' woman'll get us all malkied. Know what I mean?'

Kerr ordered another drink plus goldies and headed for the toilet, where he dialled Frankie Logan's younger brother Abe, because pond life like him wouldn't dare go straight to the man at the top.

Abe Logan had matured over the years but still had hot-headed tendencies at times, and it pissed him off that he always had to defer to Frankie on the big occasions. As far as he was concerned he wasn't getting the respect he deserved, was often treated like the office junior and it was a fucking scandal. And he thought Frankie had turned into a pussy. He'd made up his mind that if Frankie kept acting like royalty then he'd take a fall eventually. In the meantime, he pretended to give him all the respect he needed, and occasionally his older brother would reward him by allowing him to get his knuckles skint on some poor bastard's face. Apart from telling Alan, who heard his gripes over and over again, he kept his thoughts to himself. Although Abe loved his younger brother, in his opinion Alan was all brawn and no brain and would never be a threat in the way he planned to be to Frankie. Alan was known as the Quiet Man, and when he was pointed in the right direction he could do the business – as long as someone else was doing the thinking for him.

What Kerr told him set Abe's engine going and his

first instinct was to grab his younger brother and do the necessary. The problem was that he knew a lot rested on what happened with the McMartins' collapse, so he resisted his first impulse, called Frankie and told him the story.

'Listen, get a hold of Psycho first – that's what we pay the bastard for – and the two of you can get your hands dirty on this boy. You call the mad bastard and let me know he's on the case, okay, brother?' Frankie was easy with it and lifting someone then screwing the truth out of them was usually straightforward enough. They were criminals – it was what they did for a living.

'I'll do it now, Frankie, but get a couple of the boys to cover the door of that boozer in case Sammy loses this character.'

'Good call; go for it. This punter: what's his name again?'

'Goggsy, or some fuckin' thing like that. Might know hee-haw but could take us to the boys we want.'

25

Abe Logan called McManus's number and fate played another card into the situation. According to the team's rules it should never have happened and only McManus should have answered, but Paterson picked up his phone. This threw Logan for a moment.

'Where's Stuart?' He ground the words out through clenched teeth and unlike his older, wiser brother he thought McManus was good at what he did but that his relationship with the sauce made him a giant fucking liability.

'He's . . .' Paterson hesitated because she knew it had to be one of the Logans and she tried to think of how to explain to McManus's employers that he was shit-faced again. 'He's sleepin', been a bit ill – must be this bug that's on the go.' It was the best she could do, but Abe Logan's impulsive streak took over, concerned that they might miss the chance to clear up what had happened in Edinburgh and elsewhere. He wasn't taking it in the neck for getting this one wrong.

'What's the fuckin' score here? Is he pished? An' who the fuck are you?'

'I'm his partner. Who the fuck was it supposed to be?' Paterson's temper flared – she was pissed off that some guy who'd never even met her was treating her like a fucking idiot.

Abe Logan told her to get McManus, pished or not, and put him on the end of the phone.

'No arguments, sweetheart, this is his fuckin' employer – you hear me?'

It was said with enough venom to make sure she got the message. She told Logan to hang on and padded through to the bedroom where McManus was snoring for Scotland. Although she'd laid the phone on the hall table, Abe Logan could hear the snoring as soon as she opened the bedroom door. He cursed, shook his head and promised himself to argue it out with Frankie that this mad bastard was more bother than he was worth.

Paterson grabbed McManus by the shoulders and tried to shake him, although their size difference meant she could hardly move the dead weight of a drunk man. She said his name over and over again, but there was no reaction. She padded back to the phone and had given up trying to pretend to someone who obviously knew what the problem was. 'Can't wake him. Sorry.' She lit a smoke and saw the tremor had returned to her hand.

'Right, listen to me, hen. Go through there and throw some water on him if you have to, but get him to the phone. Do it now or I'll come round there and open your puss.' Abe Logan was acting the brave bastard because he was Frankie's brother, and McManus was some distance away and pissed. The truth was that he couldn't do McManus in a square go – or any other type of battle come to that. He knew it, but on this occasion he would take whatever it needed in men and weapons to get the bastard's attention.

'Hang on.' She was on the edge of panic when somehow

or other McManus's brain lit up again and he woke. He lifted his head painfully, trying to focus and make sense of where he was and what all the fucking racket was. It wasn't really a racket but felt like it in his fevered brain, and he knew someone was on the phone. He was suspicious of all phone calls, especially when Paterson was involved.

'Who the fuck is that?' He sat on the edge of the bed and rubbed his eyes, trying to clear the mess that was going on in his head.

Paterson breathed a sigh of relief and walked back through to the bedroom. 'It's for you.' She struggled to hide what she felt for him now; every time she looked at his face she wanted him dead.

'Get me a drink,' he snarled at her and took the phone from her outstretched hand. 'What?' McManus snapped down the phone. He'd never understood the concept of manners, especially when he was at the wrong end of a binge. He felt like shit and would share that with whoever crossed his path for the next few hours.

'What?' Abe Logan fired the question back. No one should have been able to talk to a Logan like that, and certainly not the paid staff. He knew that McManus was unfit for duty, and if he'd been anyone else he would have been on for a severe tanking from the management team. Logan had lost control of his anger and was at a safe-enough distance from the man on the other end of the blower to hand down some shit. 'I'll tell you what: we've got one of Brenda's team available for lifting ... Your job unless I'm mistaken. And maybe I'm gettin' this all wrong, Stuart, but you're fucked up wi' the bevvy. Tell me I'm wrong.'

McManus was always unpredictable and this time was no different. Logan expected the bastard to give him earache back because he was an arrogant shite, but McManus knew he depended on Frankie Logan big time. His claim to fame was that he was ready for any job anytime and now his drink problem had exposed him as just another fuckhead, great when he was sober but useless when he was pissed. Though nobody who knew him would ever have guessed it was possible, McManus was embarrassed. It was always the same: he'd done a great job in Edinburgh then believed he could do exactly as he liked, and the bevvy had made him forget he was an employee in a game where you were only as good as the last fuck-up.

'Sorry, Abe, just a couple too many. Let me get my head together an' I'll be okay.' He ran his hand through his hair and was sobering up with every throbbing beat of pain in his head.

Logan told him to wait by the phone and he'd be back to him in a couple of minutes. He sent a text to Kerr and the two boys he'd dispatched to cover the pub door. They were five minutes away and Kerr texted back that Woods was shit-faced and close to lights out. Logan told them to wait and called his older brother to fill him in on the story so far.

'Fair enough.' Frankie Logan was easy; he was annoyed at McManus but relaxed as always. 'Might work out for the best. We lift this Woods, bed him down in the old garage for the night and when he wakes up in the mornin' he'll have the hangover from hell to deal with, which'll be the least of his problems once Psycho gets to work. You can take it from there and back him up in case there are any problems.'

Frankie knew that his younger brother was like a hunting dog who'd been restrained too much and needed to bite something, so he would let him back up McManus, who was unsurpassed at torture. 'Get back to him and tell him early doors at the garage and that if he's not there he can fuck off back to Scouseland.'

The chance to get involved in tormenting Woods brought a smile to Abe Logan's face and he felt better for being included. He was calmer when he called McManus back, who by this time was drinking black coffee with a whisky chaser. The hard man's thumping headache was bad, but his mind had cleared up enough to know he was close to a red line with the Logans. Paterson was in the next room and sat up when she heard his phone ring again. She heard enough to know that they'd come across some guy called Woods and McManus would have a job to do on him in the morning. She was under no illusions what McManus was capable of and he delighted in describing to her some of his successful 'interviews', as he liked to call them.

McManus drank two more shots of whisky then flopped back into bed and told Paterson to wake him at 7 a.m. 'Do not sleep in or we're both in the shite. You hear me?'

'I hear you. You got a job on?'

McManus looked at her sideways, and if he'd been anywhere near sober he would have seen the small twitches round her eyes and mouth. The fresh whisky was having an effect and his vision was blurring again. On the plus side, it had shaken off the painful rhythmic banging in his cranium.

He shook his head, trying to clear his thoughts, but tiredness was overwhelming him again and he just wanted to sleep. 'They've found one of the McMartins' boys. I'll be working on him in the mornin' and need to be up bright an' early, doll.' He didn't wait for an answer, lay back on the bed and was out for the count again before she left the room.

Paterson's gut was squirming because she was pretty certain Woods was the name of the person McCartney had mentioned as being with him on the failed Edinburgh job and, what was far worse, that it was him who knew she was the source of the information for that job. If it was him and he talked (and he would), they would have her relationship to McCartney sooner rather than later. The Logans would come for her eventually, and even though she probably wouldn't be their top priority, she would be McManus's. The fact that he'd been set up by his woman would do his head in, and the Logans would want payback for him compromising a big job, no matter that he'd ended up saving the day. His reputation wouldn't be worth a glove full of shit in the city and he'd have to kill her – there'd be no other way. Some gangsters would balk at killing their woman and would settle for a tanking, but not McManus. She lit up another smoke and ran down the stairs to the street to call McCartney.

26

Paterson chain-smoked and kept calling her brother, who didn't answer at first. She knew he'd be watching another horror film or be doped up, or more likely both.

'Yer a fuckin' fanny, Pat,' she said twice into the phone as she paced up and down the damp street, even though her brother wasn't on the other end. She fought the urge to throw the phone against a wall to help ease her anger and fear. He was a waste of space, and she promised never to go near him again if they managed to survive the next couple of days.

Paterson had been overdosing on coffee and nicotine, which combined with the stress of knowing that she might end up a murder victim made her hands shake uncontrollably. What made it worse was that she knew McCartney just wouldn't grasp it. For some reason she'd never understood he just never seemed to read the signs of impending danger. The other thing that always worried her was that you could never really predict where his search for the meaning of life would take him next.

The phone call they were about to have would prove that assessment correct beyond all reasonable doubt.

When he finally answered, she could hear Sigourney Weaver battling an alien in the background. 'Pat, where in the name of fuck have you been? Do you have any idea how much shit we're in?'

Any normal person would have wanted to know what the problem was, given who was likely to be involved, but not him – he changed the subject completely and his sister wanted to throw up at the change of direction.

After spending one night at his mother's, he thought it might be an idea to go somewhere less obvious and moved into the spare bedroom of a friend, Wee Peem Waddell, who he'd met in the Big Hoose. Wee Peem, as everyone knew him (physically he was weak and lightweight) was one of life's real losers, even compared to McCartney. He had only been in Bar-L because the system had nowhere else to put him, a petty criminal who got caught for everything he did because he was – as his grandmother always told people – 'a bit short in the brain-cell department'. He was so short of those important cells that he was actually impressed by McCartney and believed he'd become buddies with a big-time operator. Waddell had tried but failed every attempt as a shoplifter, and in more politically correct circles he would have been described as having learning difficulties. But his world was not politically correct so they just called him a bawbag. He couldn't hold down a job, and had neither the looks nor charm to pull a woman, so he lived his life through his fantasies. He'd watch endless films about square-jawed men who were invincible and killed with ease. He imagined and he dreamed (although nothing original), but that was all he could do. The thing he liked about McCartney was that he never took the piss, and it meant something when a class operator treated him like an equal. He would have done anything for McCartney and now did all he could for this friend who'd been the only person to have anything to do with him in Bar-L.

For McCartney it was a good deal because he could make up any old shite and the boy believed every word. They also shared a love of films, particularly ones where serial killers or creatures from another world were trying to destroy the human race. Since he'd arrived, McCartney had stayed behind the drawn curtains and consumed enough Carly to float an aircraft carrier, which he'd paired with any kind of dope Waddell could lay his hands on. McCartney told him he was preparing for a big job that meant he had to lie low till it was time to move; the boy loved it and would have given McCartney his last.

McCartney had run a hundred options and worries through his fevered mind and knew that his career in crime, at least in Glasgow, was over. He thought of endless mad ideas to make a new life and at one point was so fucked up on dope that he believed he'd just come up with an idea that would make him a millionaire: a mobile-phone ringtone with Jimmy Savile doing that strange undulating noise in his throat. He ran it past Waddell, whose face went blank for a few moments before he said, 'That's a shite idea.'

This assessment from someone with such limited intellectual capacity made McCartney sit back, blink, sober up and groan at the realisation that everything he touched or came up with was keech. After that he was filled by a wretched fear that he'd never be able to work out a plan for the future, and all he could imagine was Big Brenda or McManus putting him in the ground.

While his friend was out scavenging some weed to see him through the coming evening, McCartney paced around the flat, trying to unwind the knots cramping his muscles, and started to open drawers for no reason other than that he didn't know what else to do with his hands. That's when he opened the drawer in an old hall table and lifted the worn Bible out into the first light it had seen in years. A gaping hole in the curtains allowed sunlight to stream across the room and hit a spot on the wall just above the table. McCartney stared at the book as the sunbeam hit the cover fully. For McCartney it was one of those moments when the bells went off in his head and he believed that he'd been sent a message from above. He sank to his knees, and as he pored over the book, the stories and parts of stories he'd been told as a child took on new meaning for him. McCartney had seen the word of the Lord and it was good.

'Honestly, sis, I think I've found the answer at last. I've been reading the Good Book, right, and feel like I've been born again. I think I'll go and see a priest.'

'Born again? So does that include bein' up to the tits on dope? Get a fuckin' grip! God won't stop Stuart kickin' your brains out through your ears. We need to do somethin' before he finds out.' She lit the last smoke in the packet. 'By the way, when you go to confession remember to confess to bein' a fuckin' eejit! They've already got this Goggsy guy, or they're about to lift him, but either way Stuart's going to be workin' on him in the mornin'.'

McCartney's eyes widened. The dogs were coming for them, and his instinct was to run for cover. He knew he should have been out of the city, but he was boracic and as always had been burying his head in the sand. 'What should we do then?'

'Well first of all, if you have this guy's phone number get him to get the fuck out of wherever he is if they haven't got him yet.'

'Then what?' McCartney felt cold, was coming off the dope and, despite his new-found faith, wished his friend would come back so they could do a bit of weed just to take the edge off. He'd promised himself that he'd kick the dope later as part of his rebirth into the community of the church.

'Then what?' Paterson repeated it, barely suppressing the anger in her voice at the mess she was in. 'Then what is what I told you already. We need to put that fuck that I live with to sleep ... forever. Right?'

McCartney gulped several times, and his Adam's apple bounced up and down as if there was a small animal trying to escape from his throat. 'I can't do that, Wilma. Life is precious. "Thou shall not kill." I want to leave all that life behind me.' The truth was that McCartney had lost his bottle completely and finally accepted that there was no place in the underworld for him after his catalogue of failed criminal ventures. The thought that Big Brenda or McManus could come out of the shadows at any moment was simply more than he could cope with, and finding religion was a crutch to justify whatever his life might be. The problem was that they'd kill him at the altar and use a brass cross to do it, because his church didn't mean a thing to them. There was only one way out for McCartney – a thin blue lifeline. 'I'm goin' to the polis in the mornin',' he told her. He definitely needed to do the weed first before he became fully reborn.

'You're fuckin' what?' Paterson splattered saliva all over her mobile. 'What the fuck is wrong with you?'

McCartney's attention was diverted by the return of Waddell with enough weed to send him to heaven and back, which would take care of his last night as a criminal. Paterson had no idea where he was so she continued to rage at him, knowing he wasn't for moving and that she was on her own.

When he spoke again, McCartney was calm. 'I'll phone Goggsy though and warn him, right? It's the least I can do.'

Paterson screamed down the phone once more but McCartney had already clicked the off button. He hand-signalled his friend to roll a couple of joints and tapped in Woods' number.

27

Woods was as happy as the proverbial pig – meeting Kerr had been a real bonus and had taken his mind off what had been a fucked-up week. He was so cheerfully pissed that even though he heard his phone bark like a dog he ignored it, because he was deep in conversation with a guy at the bar on how far the new manager could take the national team. Kerr was outside for a smoke and he was just coming back in the door when Woods pulled out the phone, screwed his eyes up and tried to focus on the screen. It was a voicemail, and when he tried to listen to it there was just too much noise in the pub to get it. He grinned as he passed his new best friend on his way back in. 'Just be a minute, Sammy.'

He stepped out into the cool evening air and shook his head as he tried to open up his thought processes. He called up the voicemail. When he heard it was McCartney, his first instinct was to cut off the message, but his curiosity held for a moment, then pissed or not the message hit his survival circuits and the smile dropped from his face. It was the usual garbled delivery from McCartney but the message was clear: the Logans were

174

on to him and if he hadn't been lifted already 'get the fuck away from wherever you are, mate!'

He tried to convince himself that it was only McCartney and the daft twat was probably high as a kite, but these were special circumstances, and his gut told him he couldn't afford to get it wrong. He looked round instinctively to see if there was anything out of place on the street. It seemed clear, but he was pissed and knew his street senses were running at only seventy-five per cent capacity.

Woods looked round again and noted a few parked cars but nothing obvious. He called McCartney, lit a smoke and despite the cargo he'd put away, he was sobering up – he couldn't make any mistakes with the people who were after him. The phone rang on and there was no voicemail. Woods cursed and was about to give up and write it off as McCartney on a bad trip when it was picked up at the other end.

'What the fuck, Bobo?' he asked. 'You takin' the piss or somethin'?'

McCartney spelled it out in clear detail and Woods already knew about Paterson's role in sourcing the information for the job in Edinburgh. There was too much detail and far too much at stake to ignore McCartney's warning. His face drained of what little colour he had, and his heart rate went up a good thirty beats a minute.

'Have you seen anythin' funny? Any wide boys hangin' around?' The young man was actually trying to be constructive, and despite what McCartney was, he wasn't guilty of taking the piss – especially when the stakes were this high.

'Nothin' unusual. Havin' a bevvy and takin' off in the mornin'. Just met up wi' a guy, Sammy Kerr, who was in A Hall at the same time as me.' Woods double drew on his fag and turned to look at the front door of the pub. He

175

said 'fuck' quietly enough but realised he'd just broken all the rules for someone in as much shit as he was.

'Don't know any Sammy Kerr. Is he sound?'

'Seemed okay but I'm not so sure now. He's asked a lot of questions now I think about it. And he knows I've worked for Big Brenda.'

'Leg it, Goggsy. Just leg it.' McCartney put the phone down and knew that a bad situation was deteriorating fast. Waddell handed him the biggest roach he'd ever seen in his life. 'Light me up for fuck's sake,' he urged his friend.

About fifty yards from Woods the two men sitting in a Freelander watched him take the call on the street. They were two of the Logans' best and every movement and gesture told them that whoever was on the other end of the line was spooking Woods. It might have been a coincidence, but they were pros and always put their money on the worst-case scenario. They called Abe Logan and told him what they'd seen.

'Okay. First chance you get, lift him if it's safe, and if he's been tippled how the fuck has that happened? If that's what the phone call is then I'm fucked if I know how that's happened. Don't lose him ... right?'

'We've got it covered, Abe, but maybe you can text Sammy just so he knows?'

'Doin' it now. Let me know as soon as you get him in the boot.'

Woods made an unnecessary mistake. His coat was still in the boozer and there was a quarter ounce in the lining. His diary with all his contacts, including the London boys, was there too, as well as the keys to the flat he was using. The guy he was bunking up with was away for a couple of days and he needed to get his stuff. It was a gamble, and the bevvy gave him the wrong dose of courage. He walked into the bar and smiled at Kerr, who was reading the text from Abe Logan. They made eye contact just long enough to realise that they both knew what was happening. 'Need to go, Sammy. A wee burd I've been seein' wants me back up there for a farewell performance. Has to be done, know what I mean?'

Kerr wasn't sure what to do. He couldn't attack Woods in the pub or the law might get involved, so he kept the pretence going as long as they were inside. 'Fair enough. Think I'll call it a day as well. Get you outside.'

The question for Woods was whether to run or brass it out. Were there reinforcements outside or was Kerr on his own? He'd no way of knowing, but he was sure he could take care of Kerr if it came to a knuckle debate.

They walked outside and Kerr asked him which way he was going. 'Want to share a taxi?'

'Naw, man, need tae walk off the bevvy before I meet the wee burd, know what I mean?' He winked as best he could.

They walked a few yards from the pub and Woods started to panic because it was a smart area and the street was dead quiet. He had no idea what the best option was so he'd have to gamble that Kerr was on his own and just keeping tabs on him. And, of course, McCartney might have been wrong, meaning that all this aggravation was for nothing. It made no difference – he was for the off in the morning and he couldn't take the chance on Kerr one way or the other. He had to temporarily take him out of the picture. He stuck out his hand. 'Thanks, Sammy, enjoyed that. Good to see you, mate.'

Kerr took his hand, and for a Glasgow man he should have seen it coming. He did, but just a fraction of a second too late. As soon as their palms gripped Woods took a half-step back and pulled Kerr just off balance then pushed his weight forward, at the same time cracking the nut on him. Luckily for Kerr, he was a few inches shorter than Woods, and although it hurt like a bastard, the blow was high on the forehead and didn't have maximum effect. Kerr's knees buckled, but he was hard and had enough left in the tank to grab hold of Woods' jacket and pull him down as well, so they both landed in a heap on the grass verge.

Woods struggled to get clear but Kerr knew he'd get solid shit if he lost the prize and just refused to let go, which meant that although Woods was doing his best to land a haymaker, they were too close to get the desired effect. He was so caught up in the struggle that he never heard Logan's men trot across the road, but he felt it when one of them drove the end of a pickaxe handle straight into his exposed back – clean on the kidney area. He groaned and almost slid off Kerr, who had a three-inch cut high on his forehead that was pissing blood. They gave him another shot with the pickaxe handle round the knee area, then one to the shoulders, and Woods curled up into a tight little ball. As if that would do him any good. Within one minute he was in the Freelander and told to swallow a couple of tablets or the knife they were holding at his throat would go all the way. Within a couple of minutes they were on the road and the drug was hitting his system. The pain and terror were fading and he felt like he was crawling into a warm clean bed for the night.

They headed for the old workshop near Bellshill where Slab had suffered his near-fatal heart attack. It was off the beaten track and at the bottom of a dead end. The Logans had used it for years to stash gear, and when it was required they used it to interview suspected touts or just anyone who'd pissed off the bosses. They stuck a syringe full of H into Woods' arm just to top up what was already in his system. He was comatose and wouldn't move a muscle till the morning, when they'd go to work on him.

The driver looked in the rear-view and grinned at his partner and Kerr. Woods was propped up between them, a line of dribble running down his chin and onto his neck. 'That poor bastard has a bad day coming. Christ, imagine coming off that much bevvy and dope and waking up with Psycho on the case. Fuck!' The driver chuckled at the prospect and hoped he could watch the action. 'By the way, is his phone in the jacket, Sammy? The boss'll want a look at that if there's a fucking grass.'

'It's there alright.'

They settled down, chuffed that Frankie and Abe Logan would be pleased.

Two hours after the abduction McCartney couldn't settle. After he'd put the phone down on Woods it suddenly came to him that both their fates were tied up. He needed to know what had happened to Woods, even if he'd managed to get out of the city, so he could make his own plans. McCartney imagined what might happen and the bottom line was that Woods would last about two minutes before telling them everything they needed to know. He should have made an arrangement with Woods to keep in touch to try and save both their skins. He pulled his phone out and called the number but it went straight to voicemail.

'Goggsy. Just wonderin' if you managed to get away from this Sammy character. Watch the back, pal, and let me know once you get the train. If I hear anything I'll bell straightaway.'

McCartney put the phone back in his pocket and realised that he should have said fuck all. He groaned and hoped to hell that Woods was okay.

When Woods' phone rang it was lying on a table next to Abe Logan while he was talking to the boys who'd lifted him. They all looked at the phone when it went off and did synchronised grins when the voicemail was played back. Abe Logan listened to it a second time before he played back the stored voicemails and heard the one Woods had received in the pub.

'What the fuck? Someone's been openin' their big fuckin' gob. It just gets better and better! I hope that fuckin' lunatic Psycho is the problem. He's a pish-heid an' they can never keep it zipped.'

Abe called his brother Frankie to let him know there might be a problem with a leak somewhere.

McCartney tried the number a couple more times round midnight but there was no reply. He withheld his number and kept it shut this time when the voicemail came on. The fact that he couldn't get through was enough to convince him that Woods was in deep shit and he might have already dropped his name to the Logans. The hard men could be out searching for him already, and that meant game over. He sent a text to his sister to let her know what had happened. Despite his fears McCartney felt exhausted; however, he also knew what he had to do and that for the time being he was safe at Waddell's. He managed to sleep, which was more than could be said for his sister, who spent the night hours chewing her knuckles and chain-smoking while trying to think of a way out.

If McCartney had been willing to help, Paterson would have killed McManus, but she realised that it was probably futile and either the CID or the Logans would get before they could make a new life. It was a mess, and it was time to do something or end up with McManus's hands round her throat. If the story about Woods was true and they had him, the Logans might already be working out what had led to the fuck-up in Edinburgh.

McManus could get the call anytime and then it would be her turn.

It was the early hours of the morning and the flat was cold. She started to shake uncontrollably. There was nothing left in her stomach – she'd retched up what little had been there already.

Gradually she calmed down and made a decision. McManus was old-fashioned and always kept a stash of money in the flat rather than at the bank. It was only a couple of grand but would keep her going for a while. There was no way she could take her kid so her mother would just have to get on with it. She'd never wanted the child anyway – it had been an unintended conception after a hen party in Blackpool.

When she checked the bedroom, Paterson was relieved to find McManus snoring quietly, and the room stank of stale whisky, so with any luck he wasn't going to wake up anytime soon. She hated the bastard and had to fight the urge to plunge into him with a bread knife. It was definitely time to pack up and go.

She kept some of her stuff in the spare room, which looked like an explosion in a charity shop but was safer to plunder for wearable clothes than the bedroom. Next she needed McManus's stash of money from the holdall in the hall cupboard. Unknowingly, he'd given her a small break by adding a bonus from the Logans for the Edinburgh turn to his stash and there was nearly three grand. She felt a slight lift – it was a fortune for someone like her – although she couldn't work out that it would only keep her safe for a few weeks at most. It didn't matter – she'd already decided that if she had to go on the game then so be it. At least she'd be alive.

Twenty minutes later she was on her way to the station. At 6 a.m. she called her mother to break the news and was surprised when the old woman didn't make any fuss.

The truth was that her mother felt like she'd been given a second chance and she was getting what she wanted: another child of her own so she had a reason to live.

After Paterson bought her ticket she stood for a moment while all her emotions seemed to be battling for supremacy. She had to leave all of her life behind, including her child, who she was fond of to some extent. There was no going back and she had no idea what future was lying in wait for her, but like her mother, she felt a moment of excitement that maybe, just maybe this could be the start of something better. She was tired, but cleaned up was a good-looking woman. If she went on the game then it would be escorting, and she'd take care to do it on her terms. She had pals who flogged it, so what was the problem? Delusion was the drug that would keep her going for the time being.

She pulled the mobile phone out of her bag, stared at it like a junkie looking at their last bit of dope, took the SIM card out and broke the phone up into pieces. She dropped the SIM in another waste bin and felt her old life drifting into the past. The train was already waiting at the platform by the time she'd bought an overpriced first-class ticket, and no more than a couple of minutes after she sat down it started to pull away, gradually picking up speed as it left the station and crossed the points. She closed her eyes and hoped she could make it alone.

28

McCartney was up early for the first time he could remember. It was a big day and probably the end of his aspirations to become a major criminal, but as everyone who ever knew him could bear witness, you just never knew with the boy. His head felt remarkably clear, and the combination of an imminent threat to his life and the imminent high of walking in the front door of a cop shop and grassing up some serious people had given him the most amazing buzz. The rush made him feel healthy, although when he stared in the bathroom mirror the guy staring back looked like a car crash.

'Weird,' McCartney said to his reflection as he attempted to make himself presentable for his trip to the local pig farm. He shaved the bum fluff from his coupon with a razor that was so old it hacked rather than glided and left him with several pieces of toilet paper glued to the nicks on his chin. He slapped some gel on his hair, combed it back, saw that his hairline was retreating and for the first time admitted to himself that he was balding. McCartney was still a young man, but the signs of age were showing already, and he felt a knot of fear that he was mortal, something that hadn't occurred to him before. At least he looked cleaner than normal after he'd squeezed out the contents of a couple of yellow-capped plouks and dabbed the red patches with some cheap aftershave. Although there wasn't much he could do about his clothes, he'd asked Waddell to buy him a couple of things, and the new sweater and jeans made him look almost respectable. They were a real change in style from his usual gear, which marked him out as a total chav.

He walked through to say his goodbyes to Waddell, who was still in bed and rubbed his face, trying to work out why McCartney would be up and about in what was still the middle of the night for him.

'That's me away. No' sure when I'll be back, pal, but big respect for letting me crash here.' He felt something unusual: gratitude. Waddell had done more for him in a couple of days than all his so-called mates in the past. The boy thought McCartney was the business and that was all he'd ever wanted in life.

'Let me know how it goes. Anytime you need me, pal, just shout.' The wee man smiled, and McCartney felt a lump swell in his throat and wished he could just stay there, watch shite movies, talk football and smoke a bit of dope. It would have been better if he'd never met a gangster, far less try to be one.

'Take care, Peem, and when the dust settles I'll see you.'

McCartney walked out into the street and Waddell thought he'd better follow the news for some big event coming off. McCartney hadn't told him what was going down but it had to be good.

At 7.45 a.m. McCartney walked in the front door of Helen Street police station, better known as Govan polis. It was the most secure station in the country and McCartney thought it was appropriate for what he was about to do.

'Can I help you … sir?' The receptionist wasn't quite sure whether McCartney deserved the salutation, but they were trained to be courteous to everyone, regardless.

McCartney explained that he had information for the CID and that it was 'big stuff'. The receptionist thought *that'll be shining bright* but told him to sit down and called up one of the local suits she was having a fling with.

The detective was busy: he was not only up to his eyes in paperwork, he was sitting with the rest of his team having his morning coffee and participating in the daily team rant about how one chief constable could manage to bring down so much crap and problems on the force. He didn't need the call, but the thing with the receptionist was in its first passionate weeks so he had to keep her sweet. 'What's his name, Beth?'

She told him and the detective shook his head. It meant nothing to him so he tried the name on his team.

His DS was sitting at his desk trying to ignore the criticism of the Chief and work out how he could shift his reports to the Fiscal before he was due to go on holiday. He was pissed off with the pressure of trying to meet his targets for the month and wondered if he could go off sick with stress, maybe get a couple of weeks at the police convalescent home then retire due to ill health. The job had changed out of all proportion and he just wanted out.

When the DC shouted out the name Pat McCartney it caught his attention and he looked up. It wasn't the most unusual name in Glasgow but rang a particular bell. 'Ask her for a rough description and date of birth.' He looked back at the memo that had come down from the area commander saying that everyone needed to push harder on housebreaking. 'Twat,' he said under his breath and wondered if he had a problem with blood pressure. He was drinking to calm down at night and eating shit. It had to be having an effect.

When the DC looked up from the phone, gave the date of birth and description, it made the DS perk up. 'Christ, it's Bobo McCartney. I was in the source-handling team and ran the tout that put that wee fucker away for the job in Edinburgh, remember?' A couple of the DCs nodded, though not too enthusiastically, in case the DS asked them to speak to him. No one needed another problem for their day. The DS couldn't face looking at his in tray any longer, decided it would be a distraction and said he would take care of it himself. The DCs breathed a collective sigh.

The DS went to the front desk, said nothing more than, 'Come with me,' and took McCartney to the only spare office he could find in the building. He recognised McCartney from the photographs when he'd got the original information from the tout for the failed bank job in Edinburgh. He knew the boy was regarded as a bit of an arse, but you never knew and lived in hope.

'Okay, son, talk to me. You walked in the door, I've just given you a nice coffee from the machine and I'm all ears. Don't waste my time because I'm always in a bad fuckin' mood, right?'

McCartney nodded and sipped the coffee. He struggled to find the first words but the DS had seen it all before and knew just to let him take his time. If it was shite he'd kick his arse, and if there was something in it, he'd get the credit.

McCartney scratched the site of one of the plouks he'd squished that morning and the DS screwed his face up until the young man started to talk, at which point he realised he needed to concentrate on McCartney's story instead. It was a bit garbled, because that's how his mind worked, but it was all there: working for Big Brenda, the attempted robbery in Edinburgh, the total fuck-up and everything that came after it. What really got the DS high was the possibility that someone called Goggsy Woods might at that moment be dead or about to die or could just be being tortured. McCartney had then thrown McManus's name into the pile and the DS knew all about that particular fruitcake. If there was an ounce of truth in the story and there really was an imminent threat to life then he needed to get his arse into gear. It was the kind of situation that could end your career if you dragged your feet and the subsequent enquiry found you hadn't acted properly. The media loved that stuff.

The DS changed colour slightly, called his office and told one of the DCs to quit scratching his arse and join him 'fuckin' pronto'. The detective was there in two minutes and the DS spoke to him outside the office. 'Do not let this wee fucker move till I get back.' He left to start making the calls.

The wheels started to turn almost immediately – the DS had a good reputation and people listened. The teams required for an intelligence/rescue operation started to mobilise, but the big problem was that McCartney hadn't a clue where they would have taken Woods. The first call went to the duty detective super, who recognised right away that this would have to have an SIO trained in kidnap management. He breathed a sigh of relief because he didn't have that expertise, but there was something else: one of his close friends was Superintendent Charlie MacKay, who was trained, had run a few of those jobs in the past and, more than that, had a special interest in the Logans.

Charlie MacKay was with the team about to run a surveillance job on a Somali gang who were on the point of taking delivery of a consignment of guns and drugs. When he took the call from the duty super he closed his eyes for a minute and his team saw that whatever he'd just been told was a problem. He made a couple of urgent calls and one of his DCIs took charge of the Somali job.

MacKay might have been a couple of ranks below executive level, but he was one of the most powerful men in the force because he'd almost grown up in special operations, knew more than almost anyone else about the subject and the executive were frightened to argue too hard with him because they hadn't a clue how the dark arts really worked. There was an exception – Macallan's experience in Northern Ireland gave her the edge, but they'd never met and only knew each other by name. That would change, because the events they were both involved in would draw them together in ways they could never have predicted or wished for.

The clock was ticking, but MacKay acted against his instincts. He didn't really want to intervene in anything the Logans were doing at that time because he was already running an eighteen-month intelligence operation that would be coming to fruition as soon as all the pieces were in place. It made no difference, because the report of an abduction had been made, and if they didn't act and there was a loss of life, he'd take the hit and far too many worms would crawl out into the light. The problem was that he was the authorising officer for a high-grade covert human intelligence source (CHIS) who was being controlled by his DCI, Tony Slaven, and handled by one of his DIs. The source, known as Jigsaw, was gold dust and right in the guts of the Logans' set-up. It all required careful balancing.

MacKay had already spent a lot of time dismantling the Slab McMartin team to the point it was almost no more than a memory. The abduction was a chronic pain in the arse and could tear up all he'd planned for. At least being able to take charge of it was a lucky break, and hopefully he could control some of what happened. He called in Slaven, filled him in on the developing situation and watched the DCI pull a couple of uncomfortable faces at the prospect. Slaven knew some of what was at stake – not as much as MacKay but enough to be concerned.

'I know it's not the arrangement we have with him, but we need to get a hold of him right now, find out whether he's involved and, if not, where the fuck they're holding this boy. Get to it and I'll start setting the teams up.'

There was nothing more to say and the DCI left the office.

Next, MacKay called the DS at Govan, got every detail he could and told him to go over it again with McCartney then bring him close to the team he was setting up in Pitt Street. This was the old Glasgow HQ for Strathclyde and had all the comms required for a hostage situation. 'We might need to pick his brains during the op. One of the handlers from the source-handling team will take over from you. Is he looking for a deal or something?'

'Just going to ask him, sir, and then get him over to your boys as soon as.' The DS knew the situation was growing arms and legs above his pay grade, and he was happy to unload the thing and take a bit of undeserved credit later on. He hurried back into the interview room and nodded to the DC to give them a moment.

When the door closed he looked at McCartney and hoped his story was on the money or he'd take some serious flak. 'Okay, son. This thing's moving. We're doing our best to track down this Goggsy, and fingers crossed this McManus character doesn't get too much of a start.'

'God willing!' McCartney said it straight-faced and he was serious, although his words threw the DS for a moment. He squinted at McCartney and looked for a half-smile that would signify the twat was delivering an inappropriate stab at satire.

189

'God willing?' The DS sent it back as a question that really asked: are you taking the piss on my territory?

'God willing.' McCartney batted it back and nodded sagely. The DS finally got it; McCartney wasn't taking the piss.

'Look, son. Nice that you've brought God into the room, but correct me if I'm wrong here ... You are admitting to being part of a gang that carried out armed robberies on other equally nasty bastards?' He raised his eyebrows to stress the question. He wished it was the old days and he could have given McCartney a knuckle sandwich just for the hell of it.

'I've done bad things, Sergeant, but I've found peace and want to start a new life with Jesus.' He did the wise nodding thing again, and the DS unconsciously mimicked McCartney till he caught himself at it and reverted to his normal persona of a cynical bastard.

'Look, son. Find Jesus once we've done the business, or rather when you've done the business and told us all about these robberies and anything else Big Brenda's been up to.' He slapped the palm of his hand on the table to reinforce the fact that God was off the agenda for the time being.

'I'll do whatever you need, Sergeant. And do I get witness protection?'

The DS told him he'd be handed over to another team who'd take care of all that side of the business.

'I was hoping to go to Australia, right, and start a new life.' McCartney still had that serious face and the DS sighed in exasperation.

'Look, son. This is Govan fuckin' polis, no Thomson's holidays. Now let's get to work.'

McCartney realised again that he was in a difficult position, but such was his life, and as long as he could keep clear of Brenda and McManus that would do for now.

29

The private detective was the best money could buy and he seemed to be just about as heartless a bastard as was possible. Ex-CID, sharp suit, sharp line in patter and utterly devoid of any principles, which was the clincher. He was paid over the odds and, in the best traditions of film noir, told there was a bonus for success. It seemed like the thing to do and the PI almost quivered at the figure, which would be kept well away from the Revenue's grasping reach. It would never be paid of course.

He was good and came back in no time with a nicely presented file containing more than enough about where Macallan lived. He'd included a report on her work, but that wasn't really necessary given the circumstances – although the PI didn't need to know that. The photographs were well-produced black and whites and his breath shortened at seeing her again. There was nothing about her private life and the PI said that would take time to build up. He didn't need that; her home was what he wanted to see. He never expected the bonus of her telephone number. The PI just leered, pleased with himself, and said he still had his contacts in the job. It was proof enough that the world stank and those sanctimonious bastards who hid behind their badge were no exception.

He spent two days before he got his break, waiting near the house while worrying that he would attract local attention and, worse still, the police. Fortunately, the townhouse was near Stockbridge in Edinburgh, which had become an upmarket hotspot over the years, and people swarmed around the area all day. The detective had told him that she left the house at almost the same time every day but there was no way of predicting when she would arrive back at night. No matter – he knew where her office was and there were options. The break came when he saw her leaving the house carrying luggage. It wasn't a big case but at least an overnighter. He was just taking the first sip of an overpriced takeaway coffee when she opened the door and stood on the steps for a moment as if she was testing the morning air. She still had that air of cool reserve – he'd never seen her smile – and seemed to keep so much back. He remembered that even when he was in the interview room with her and his life was imploding, he'd felt a pulse of attraction for her. But he could never have her, and she could never want him; that was the simple truth. However, for someone obsessed with control it mattered. More than that, she had style and his chest gripped with nervous tension. He blinked rapidly, feeling the rims of his eyes fill and sting, and confusion as he wondered what had taken hold of that empty place that had been his soul.

He watched her pull her hair back from her forehead and step into a taxi that had pulled into the kerb beside her. There was no point in following.

The previous evening he'd come back after dark and struggled over an old stone wall into the garden at the back of her home. That side of the house was still in darkness and he saw that the garden was carefully manicured, the borders and shrubs beautifully kept. Could she have done all this herself? He'd smiled and settled into the dark space between the shrubs, directly opposite what looked like the sitting-room window. It wasn't cold and he'd felt almost comfortable being so close to where she lived and dreamed. He wondered whether she ever thought about him.

When the lights clicked on he had seen her with a phone to her ear as she took off her jacket, gesturing as she spoke to whoever was on the other end of the line. He'd pulled further into the darkness as she stood at the window and stared out into the night, still talking, and imagined what it would have been like to be that close to her. He guessed her friends would be like her: talented and with everything to live for.

When she moved away from the window he'd had to resist the temptation to move closer, because he hadn't wanted to spoil what was to come.

After an hour, she'd come back into view wearing a bathrobe and drinking a glass of wine. She'd dimmed the lights, and although he couldn't see her he'd noticed the flickering shadows on the wall that meant she was watching the box. Another hour passed then the lights in the sitting room had gone out and what he guessed was her bedroom lit up. He'd imagined that in another life he could have been that person on the other end of the phone saying goodnight and that he was there for her anytime she needed him.

Time seemed to drift and then he'd realised the house was in darkness.

As he moved off into the shadow below the perimeter wall and then back into the street, he put his earlier thoughts out of his head, because he was there for his daughter and that was the least a loving father could do.

30

Macallan's taxi dropped her outside the bar in George Street and she struggled through the doors with her suitcase. She scanned the few early-morning feeders and saw Jacquie Bell sitting at the back of the restaurant. It was light, cool and one of Macallan's favourite stop-offs when she was shopping.

Bell saw Macallan approaching, got up, squeezed her and whispered in her ear, 'Want one on the lips?' It was the usual wind-up and related to the one-night stand they'd had not long after Macallan had joined Lothian and Borders after leaving the PSNI. Macallan had still been low at the time and had never been able to explain why it had happened. What had really confused her, and still did, was that it came back to her from time to time and brought a smile to her face. Bell looked like a star but was a hard case who could slug it out with the best of them. She'd been threatened by some serious criminals and high-profile public figures in her time but took it all in her stride. She loved Macallan, which was something she'd never told her because she knew it would have caused more problems than her friend deserved. 'Bit early for a drink but never mind, it'll soon be eleven o'clock and I can get my starters then.'

'How's life then, Jacquie? Still slaying the high and mighty?' Macallan waved to one of the girls serving, who was clearly rushed off her feet. She ordered poached eggs, fruit juice and toast, while Bell asked for black coffee and cursed the fact she couldn't have a smoke with it, which was her normal first meal of the day.

The bar had windows all round and in the ceiling, the light was clear and for a boozer there were few shadows. Macallan studied Bell and marvelled that someone who had the appearance of a Hollywood A-lister could keep her looks on a diet that consisted mainly of caffeine and alcohol. Despite a few grey strands and the finest of lines that seemed to have clustered around Bell's eyes since Macallan had last seen her, she was still a most striking woman – a younger Sophia Loren, who was just going to age like a fine wine.

'I'm meeting the Sturgeonator this afternoon. My God, that woman has turned from nippy sweetie to a political dragon slayer. She tramples all before her.'

'Don't try anything with her. I think she'd scratch your eyes out.'

'Not my type, honey. I like them obsessed with work and totally confused by their Presbyterian guilt.' She winked, grinned and enjoyed watching Macallan flush at the neck. 'Okay, let's get to work. What you up to? And I'll quote nothing unless you tell me to.'

Macallan told Bell exactly what she was doing because she knew the reporter would know anyway – she always did. She was bound to have one or two of her bosses in her pocket.

'That's interesting, Macallan,' she said and called to the waitress for more coffee.

'No, it's not. You know it already.' She raised her eyebrows and Bell shrugged as an admission. 'What about you? Anything I can do to help? Job is all routine so far.'

'This little crusade of mine about conditions in the prison service? It's really not an attack on the men and women who work in it – I'm sure they're having a hell of a time ... it's the lack of resources that's creating a dangerous situation inside that's concerning. And I'm sure I'm not the only person to be thinking this, but perhaps I'm the one who can give it more of an airing and bring it to more people's attention? Everybody knows there's chronic overcrowding but I don't think they really understand the implications.' Jacquie's sources had told her that the increasing numbers of ethnic prisoners and suspected terrorists being locked up, plus the drive against paedophiles that was filling up the protection units, meant that prisoners had to be kept behind the doors more than was healthy. The lid was kept firmly bolted down, but there were side effects. The last thing the prison authorities needed was a kicking from the press, but that's not what Bell was after.

'I've started to run stories about the problems, and at the moment I'm looking at different aspects from a number of angles. Tommy McMartin is a perfect case. I know he was getting a hard time in there so no wonder he committed suicide. Christ, I would. I'm putting something out tomorrow about suicides and just want to mention you're on this case. Nothing more, but you're a celeb and will put a little bit of sauce on the story. Other than that, I'll keep in touch and you let me know if you need anything.'

Macallan thought about it for a moment and decided it couldn't do any real harm. 'Will do. Anyway, I need to

196

go or I'll miss my flight.' They agreed to meet again, and when they stopped at the door after paying the bill, there was another squeeze.

'By the way ... the way I heard it, our boy Tommy never did it.'

'How?' was all Macallan got out before Bell stepped forward and jumped in a taxi.

Macallan was in her own taxi heading for the airport when she received a text. 'Nothing I can prove but police source told me original investigation was manipulated to cover lines of enquiry that were buried. That's all.' That was Jacquie Bell: the all-knowing reporter.

Macallan called up Jimmy McGovern, who was spending the day in the office putting what they had so far into statement form and dealing with some admin. That way he could get an early finish and prove to his ever-loving wife that the job was all routine and he didn't even have to work at the weekend. 'Jimmy, could you get a hold of the SIO on Tommy's case and make an appointment with him, for Monday if possible? The other thing is: find out what permission we need to look at the HOLMES system that was run at the time, or rather who we approach to get it.'

'No problem, and I know the SIO. Not that well but we were on the newly promoted inspectors course together. The most boring few weeks of my life, learning how to talk business speak.'

'What did you think of him?'

'Super smooth, sharp as a needle and big on ambition. Not liked by the pack, and to be honest he didn't give a toss. I'm told that our female colleagues and one of the guys on the course thought he was Scotland's answer to George Clooney. Not my type, mind you, and don't think I was his either.'

'Thanks, I get the picture. Seen that type a few times

in the job. Anyway, leave it after those calls and see you bright and early Monday.' She put down the phone, closed her eyes and thought about holding Jack and the kids tight in just a couple of hours.

31

Charlie MacKay followed the book and training for the situation. He knew it like the back of his hand, and as long as he followed the guidance on set-up then that was one less thing he could be criticised for in the aftermath if things went wrong on one of the most difficult types of operations to run. He got Tony Slaven and started the balls rolling into the correct pockets. The DCI had worked with MacKay for years, had his notepad ready and would follow his instructions to the letter. He already knew what they would be because, like his boss, he'd been there before.

MacKay told Slaven to get the green team in place. They were the dedicated intelligence outfit who'd be crucial to the outcome. 'This is a threat to life so it's grade one. First job is to get into the intel, and if we can track this Goggsy's phone we'll get authority to ping the thing and at least find out where it is.' Normally there would be a delay in processing a request to trace a phone, owing to the number of similar applications that were submitted every day on serious crime jobs. A clear threat to life, however, gave them almost immediate priority.

If they had the number, they'd locate the phone in short time. 'Get the blue team co-located with the intel boys and make sure they're the business.' The blue team were the surveillance unit, who would deploy as soon as the hostage's location was identified, and they would ensure they got eyes on the site.

There was a firearms team ready to go and MacKay put a hold on them so they were ready to move if and when the hostage was located. They wouldn't go in all guns blazing. The maxim was 'locate, contain and neutralise', which, unlike in popular fiction, did not mean blowing everyone away but controlling the situation to let negotiations take place if possible. They could only shoot where there was a clear and imminent threat and the firearms boys had no choice but kill or be killed. MacKay thought it was a travesty, but that was the modern force and modern thinking. If he could have got away with it he would have put a lid on the situation, but too many people knew he was running a source inside the Logans' team, and if it came out he'd compromised this job for a CHIS, he'd end up in the High Court as the accused.

The DCI came back into the office fifteen minutes later. 'Jigsaw's not involved so that's a break. Abe Logan is the "hands-on" man but reporting to Frankie. They use a workshop near Bellshill for "interviews" as they like to call them. It's not far from the built-up area but seems like a rural situation: three disused small farm/industrial buildings, dead end so only one way in and one way out by car. I've got one of the intelligence boys working on anything we have on layouts. It looks like they doped the guy up and Psycho McManus is going to work on him this morning.'

'Psycho? Jesus, that's just what we need in the mix. Get a team over to his place and see if there's any sign of him. If it's possible get the CROPs. I want an eyeball on this site now, so get the blue team leader to get his finger out and deploy as soon as possible. Right, let's see if we can get this place contained and take it from there. I don't know who this poor bastard Goggsy is but he'll last about thirty seconds if it's Psycho doing the necessary. Let's get moving.'

The last item on MacKay's immediate to-do list was to get the team leaders from the blue and green teams with the firearms team leader and warn them that he'd have them issuing parking tickets till they retired if there was any in-fighting. It tended to happen if there was a weak man in charge. He was the man in charge, and it wasn't going to happen on his watch.

32

McManus woke up slowly and thought that Paterson must be making him something to eat. He rolled over and noticed the time on the bedside clock about the same moment that his phone rang. He sat up and tried to figure out why the clock hands were at 8 a.m. He bawled through for Paterson and when he stood up he'd already decided to give her a pasting. This was the last fuck-up he needed. It was straightforward enough to guess who was on the blower.

'Where the fuck are you?' Abe Logan now had all the evidence he needed to get shot of McManus.

'That daft burd never woke me up, an' I'm still in the flat. Swear to God I'll fuckin' mark her this mornin'.'

'Well, mark her when this is done. Get a move on and I'll come in the car for you. You're a fuckin' waste of space, my friend. Frankie will crack up on this one.'

McManus put the phone down, lifted his leather belt and gave it a couple of turns around his hand, leaving the heavy buckle dangling by his side. He walked through the flat looking for Paterson. It was quiet with not a whiff of cigarette smoke, which meant only one thing – she was offski. He couldn't make any sense of it. About thirty seconds later the alarm bells went off in his brain and he checked his money stash. When he saw it was gone he grabbed the nearest chair and started to smash up the flat.

By the time he had himself under control again the flat looked like it had been the target of a drone strike. McManus dressed in his best gear and promised himself that he'd make the boy they'd lifted suffer. Someone had to, and he swore that if Abe Logan opened his sneering gob too wide he'd cut him a new smile. He'd spent his life barely controlling the rage that burned in the centre of his being and the situation with Paterson had forced it too close to the surface. If what she'd done got out into his world the humiliation would be too much, and there was always some smart bastard who just had to open their mouth. If they did, he'd be ready.

McManus was about to close the front door behind him when he stopped, turned back and rifled through his music collection for a particular CD. He stuck a portable player in his rucksack beside the cut-throat razors, and that meant he had everything he needed for the moment.

When he climbed into the car with Abe Logan he was calm again and imagined what he'd do to Paterson when he got his hands on her.

33

It was just starting to spit and the clouds seemed to drop just above the land when Abe Logan and McManus arrived at the site. As the light dulled under the cloud cover it seemed to affect McManus's mood and he struggled to straighten out the thoughts that lanced his mind like hot knives. He was having one of those headaches that could reduce him to tears with the mixture of confused emotions and physical pain. The headaches frightened him, and when they were at their worst he could spend days in bed curled up in a ball and wishing it was all over.

Logan had phoned ahead and told the boys who'd lifted Woods that they were almost there. They had a shooter inside and he didn't want to end his days as a victim of friendly fire. He knew they'd be nervous, and he didn't fancy being mistaken for the law coming through the door.

When he pushed back the rusted sliding doors he shivered – it was stone cold and stank of ammonia. The place had been overrun by vermin and pigeons over the years and the smell almost took his breath away. 'Fuck's sake, we need to clean this dump up when we get this done. You lot bring a hose first chance and wash the shit out of here before we all fuckin' die.'

Inside, he saw a hooded figure strapped firmly to a chair, his head at an angle that said he was still under the effects of the dope they'd stuck in him. 'How much gear did you shove in his arm, for Christ's sake? He should be screaming for his mammy by now.'

His team looked nervous, shagged out and he guessed, rightly, that it had been a long night. Sammy Kerr was the first to speak; he was still trying to make an impression with the bosses. 'He's okay, Abe – comin' round now.'

'He fuckin' better be, Sammy. This is a fucked-up day already because we have one man can't set the alarm and you geniuses nearly OD the poor bastard.' He stared them down and missed the look in McManus's eyes that should have told him to tread gently. 'I want to see you all in the shed through here.' He pushed open the side door, which gave access to a small corrugated workshop that had been added on to the main building at some point.

Once inside he pulled the door closed behind them and looked around at the men. 'Right, you three can go in a minute, but leave the shooter – it's good for scaring the shit out of the boy next door, and if things go wrong then we can give him a quick exit. As it stands, Frankie is happy to hurt him as much as possible but that'll do unless somethin' changes. The boy's probably just some fuckin' wanker anyway, so no need to get a murder squad on our arse if it's no' required. Okay?' They all nodded, but he noticed that McManus's eyes seemed to be hooded, as if he was on some trip. 'Anythin' else?'

Kerr spoke again, and the other two were relieved because in most cases when Abe was having a bad day it was better to keep it shut. 'That voicemail on Goggsy's phone. I was there in the boozer when he took it. Like I said, there's no doubt he was spooked an' knew somethin' was about to go tits up.'

Abe Logan smirked at the thought that the daft twat hadn't had the sense to put a security code into his phone. 'They never learn.' He found the voicemail recall and played the messages again. Someone inside the team was a rat or a twat; the failed rip-off didn't prove it beyond all reasonable doubt because there were other possibilities – like the Edinburgh buyers bringing in Brenda for a cut of the gear. These calls, though, proved they'd been grassed from the inside.

He listened to the voicemail again before putting it on loudspeaker, held it up and let them listen in, although McManus was the only one who hadn't heard it up to that point.

'Right, so this fuckin' guy knew what was comin'. How the fuck is that then?' He watched for any reaction, but apart from three frozen and very nervous expressions there was no answer.

McManus listened, still looking like he was having some out-of-body experience, and although it didn't press the nuclear button, something tingled across the wiring in his brain. He knew there was something seriously wrong on his part, but he couldn't join up the warning signals. What he could say was that Paterson had done a Dexy and now this. If there was a connection then he was fucked, because the other point he could prove with some certainty was that he'd said far too much to Paterson about the job, which was usual when he was on the bevvy, when he liked to shoot his mouth off.

'Let's get to work on the boy, Abe. We'll get all the answers we need from him.' McManus said it without looking at Logan, and the lids of his eyes still drooped as if they were trying to keep the light out of a dark room. He'd already decided that if things went wrong then he might need to do Logan as well as the boy they had trussed up like a pre-slaughter grunter. It would be as much pleasure as business getting rid of Logan, who loved to rub his face in it but wouldn't have the balls to hand it out if it hadn't been for his family name.

'Okay, you lot can go. But keep your phones on, no bevvy and be ready to move again if we call. Right?' Logan was wound up tight and something was gnawing at his gut. He didn't like any of it and he just wanted to get this job done then get the fuck away from McManus. If he'd really faced up to it, Logan would have realised that what he was feeling was as much fear as concern about the job.

His team nodded and left McManus and Logan facing each other. Logan looked again at McManus's dead eyes and wished he'd arranged for the rest of the team to arrive with him. It was a mistake, and he was regretting it already. He just wasn't equipped to handle Psycho if he went off script.

34

The land around the old buildings was flat and open so it would be almost impossible for the CROP and surveillance teams to get close in during the hours of daylight. They had arrived only twenty minutes after Abe Logan and McManus, and the surveillance team couldn't say whether there was anyone inside any of the cluster of buildings that included the disused workshop. What they did feed back was that there were three cars parked outside the largest of the three buildings, including a four-wheel drive. If their owners were there then they must all be inside. MacKay told them to hold their positions till they got a sighting or indication of who was there. McCartney had provided Woods' number and the intel team were working to locate its position.

MacKay got his first break when his DCI came into his office wearing a grin and told him that Woods' phone had been pinged and was smack-dab inside the buildings they had almost surrounded and contained.

'Thank fuck.' MacKay started to see mileage in the job; if he did what he was good at he could come out smelling of roses.

The CROPs officer was DC Pam Fitzgerald, who'd been doing the job for about two years and loved it. It was the hardest thing she'd ever done in her life, and it wasn't that long ago that the consensus had been that a female couldn't lie in a hole in the ground for days on end, wet, stinking and without a make-up bag. She was one of the women who had broken that particular prejudice. Now she was accepted as one of the best.

Aware that this particular job lacked preparation and planning, she accepted that sometimes that was how it was. This was a big turn, and the briefing warned them that the team they were after were heavy duty, and one in particular was a nutjob. The surveillance boys had dropped her a few hundred yards from the site, and she'd managed a good creep into a ditch with a load of old rusting corrugated sheets covering part of it. The hide gave her superb cover plus a perfect eyeball on the front of the main building. Although she wasn't in a position where she could see everything, she had a clear view of the road leading in, so if anyone moved in a vehicle she could call it. With her binoculars she could probably get the registered numbers with brief descriptions of any of the bandits. If anything happened in parts of the ground she couldn't see, another CROP was deploying behind the site to cover unforeseen problems there. The mobile surveillance teams were arriving and finding positions where they could move when required. The men in the building were being locked inside a human and technical trap that was closing all the time.

The ditch stank, and she tried her best to avoid thinking about it, which was part of the discipline. The worst thing for a CROPs officer was seeing and doing nothing for hours on end – it played havoc with your powers of concentration. On this occasion, though, she was barely settled in when she saw three targets leave the main building and get into a 4x4. They sat for a couple of minutes, which gave her more than enough time to give physical descriptions, and when the car started to manoeuvre slowly towards the road she clocked the number and called it in to the operational commander who was in the control van no more than two miles away.

That'll do nicely, Pam, she thought, moving her lips but not actually speaking it out loud, because part of the discipline was keeping it shut unless required. She just loved it – lying in that wet, stinking hole made her part of something that mattered, and she smiled as she imagined all the activity that was going on around the area, and those gangsters inside didn't have a scooby.

There had to be a decision on whether to follow the men leaving or stay covering the building where they believed the hostage was being held. They hadn't yet confirmed who was still in the building with the hostage; the intelligence had already found a phone number for Abe Logan but drawn a blank for McManus. They were close to getting permission to ping Logan's number. The operational commander on the ground had already agreed with MacKay that they'd get a team to follow the three men, but until they were sure about the situation inside and who was there, they'd hold back from making any arrests in case they set off a chain of events they couldn't control.

MacKay was in the Pitt Street centre with the intel team and had comms there that would keep him in touch with whoever he needed in a hurry. Despite the fact that it was going better than he could have expected, he knew these situations could turn into a calamity in a heartbeat. That, however, was what he was paid to do, and when it went right you were a star. Most men hated the risk; for MacKay that was the buzz, what did it for him. It was down to the gods now, and as soon as they had confirmation that Logan was in there with the hostage, he'd make the next move. The presumption was they wouldn't kill the boy, so the priority was negotiation. This was not the moment to go sending in the ninjas – the firearms team were there only if they were required, or if some cowboy came out of the building blasting away like a baddy in a Martin Scorsese film.

35

'You do what you need to do and I'll take over if he won't play.' Abe Logan watched McManus's face split into a gaping rictus grin under eyes that looked like they belonged to a three-day-old corpse. McManus's capped teeth seemed to have doubled in size and Logan watched a line of dribble wind down over his chin. He wanted to say *for the love of fuck* but didn't want to do anything to make the man even more unstable. He couldn't work out what was going on and wondered if it was the drink or drugs. He knew the guy was coming apart but couldn't understand why. If he had known then he would have had all the excuses he needed to pop the bastard and be done with it.

'He'll play alright.' McManus said it in almost a hissed whisper as he retrieved the portable CD player and razors from his rucksack.

'We havin' a fuckin' dance party here or what?' Logan tried to hide the tremor in his voice, although it made no difference to McManus, who basically didn't give a fuck anymore.

He turned his back on Logan and took the half dozen

steps towards Woods, who'd come around and had earwigged most of the conversation. He was hyperventilating and sick to his stomach, sucking air in through the hood then blowing it back out, and McManus leered as he watched the mouth area of the black hood pulse with the boy's heaving breath. That's what he wanted to feel and smell – human fear – something he could play with and control. He needed to make someone pay for Paterson's betrayal.

Putting his face close to the hood, he listened to the wheeze of Woods' breathing for a moment before standing erect and pulling it off. 'Well, I'll be fucked.' McManus took a step back and a spark seemed to return to his eyes. 'Just gets better and better.'

'What?' Logan almost felt he was no longer either part of or in control of events. He was starting to feel on the edge of panic.

'It's one of the desperadoes, the one with the sawn-off. Ya fuckin' beauty.' McManus walked over to the old table about six feet from Woods and set up the portable CD player. He laid out the cut-throat razors on the table and fed a disc into the machine. Logan and Woods were both mesmerised, trying to figure out what was going on. McManus pulled off his jacket and shirt, leaving only a vest that showed off the sheer hard bulk of the man.

'Would you mind telling me ...?'

McManus held up a finger to his lips and shut Logan up halfway through his question. Logan's eyes had become more round than oval, and he needed to call Frankie. What he watched unfolding proved he needed some guidance from his older and wiser brother.

McManus pushed the play button and Gerry Rafferty started to blast out those sweet sad tones that echoed Dylan and reflected his own brilliance and tragedy. 'I just love Rafferty. Play him all the time. This is a wee compilation I made up. You like him, son?' He towered over Woods, who stared up at huge pecs and arms that seemed to pulse and ripple with barely contained power. He glanced at Logan, wondering when and how the pain would come. McManus ripped the tape from his mouth. 'Now, son, we're here for a wee talk. So you're Goggsy, right?'

Woods nodded and whispered, 'Aye'. His throat felt like it had been treated with a blowtorch.

'Ever watch gangster films, Goggsy? Tarantino – that kind of thing?' McManus's face seemed a bit more human; it was obvious that he was in his glory and acting out some fantasy.

'Naw.' It was squeezed out again and Woods would have cashed in his old lady for some cool water. *Why the fuck is he asking me about gangster films?* Woods thought, and it only added to the panic that was nearly bursting his heart open. The combination of booze, H and fear had dehydrated him to a dangerous level. The question about gangster films meant nothing to Woods, which was just as well, and at least gave him a few more seconds hoping that it might all turn out okay. Whatever they wanted he'd give them. Logan on the other hand watched and loved gangster films and had learned a few tricks from them himself. He felt his throat tighten because the Gerry Rafferty music threw up an image he hoped was just his imagination running wild. It was time to call Frankie; he really didn't want to watch what was coming.

'I'm going out for a smoke and to check in with Frankie. Okay?'

'I'm fine, Abe, just fine.' McManus pushed the button to select the right track, turned up the volume and picked one of the razors.

Logan heard the first two lines of 'Stuck in the Middle with You', and as he closed the door behind him he watched McManus start to dance around Woods. He pulled out a cigarette and tried to light it but his hands were shaking so much he struggled to get the thing going. At that precise moment the intelligence team confirmed that Logan's phone had been pinged and was at the same site as Woods.

'That's a male matching the description of target one outside the main building. He's on the phone. I have a picture and it's on its way.' Fitzgerald cursed because the rain was steady now and she felt the chill try to work its way under her thermal clothing. It was fine, though, just part of the job and no more than a nuisance.

'That's the bastard.' MacKay knew all the Logans and had studied them top to bottom. Slaven was back in the room with him. 'No point in fannying around – get me an update on those three they're following and I'll open up a line to Logan.'

Back inside the old garage workshop Woods stared in horror at the cut-throat razor and the radge who was holding it as he bopped round him to the solid beat of the music. The rush of fear gave him just enough strength to plead hopelessly, and he began to sob as if his life depended on it, even though it made no difference to the madman who seemed lost in his own world.

'That's great, son.' McManus smiled as he moved towards Woods, always keeping in time with the tune. The first assault happened so quickly that Woods hadn't even realised that McManus had sliced off part of his left ear. Then he felt wetness and the pain kicked in. In case he needed confirmation, McManus dangled it in front of his face. All Woods' instincts told him to scream, but he was so weak that the only sound he made was a barely audible groan.

'See it's only a wee bit of ear, pal. No' the whole thing. I've done you a right favour, son. In fact I've cut it at an angle so it's like a wee Vulcan lug now. No' everyone that's got one o' them, son.' McManus put the song on repeat because he was far from finished. 'Now tell me about Edinburgh and how the fuck you knew so much.'

Logan heard the phone ring a few times before Frankie answered and his brother seemed as calm as ever. He realised that he lacked the minerals to deal with a crisis like this and it made him despise his older brother all the more. He told him what had happened so far and that Psycho thought he was the star in some fucking gangster movie. The information and image even threw Frankie Logan for a minute.

'He's doin' what?' He heard his brother the first time but just couldn't get his head round the image. 'It's Bellshill for fuck's sake. A wee bit away from California, know what I mean?' It was a real problem, and he didn't need his brother to tell him that they should never have brought McManus back from Liverpool. Being the main man meant that problems came up and it was his job to solve them. That's what real leaders did, though this was off the bizarre scale ... but then the world of criminals was never straightforward. He sighed, reached for a pen and started to doodle on his desk pad as he thought about their next move. 'Right, three of the boys left here about half an hour ago so should be with you as soon as. I'll ring them and tell them to put the foot down. We just need to hear it from this boy. Confirmation it's Big Brenda for all these jobs. Get me that and don't let him die. You hear me?'

No more than twenty-five feet from Abe Logan, McManus squatted in front of Woods and took his confession,

216

which was given up in no more than a whisper.

'Story... from your burd... Bobo's half-sister or somethin'.' Woods was weak but he was still able to see the effect of his words and the confusion in his tormentor's eyes. He was a young man, desperate to live, but sometimes suffering can become too much and holding on to life no longer seems like the best option. The fear dropped from Woods like a coat falling off his shoulders. Somehow he managed a grin and sniggered like a child. 'You've no fuckin' idea. Jesus, the big-time operator done up like a fuckin' turkey.' Woods' voice had gained a bit of strength.

McManus stood up and let it all sink in. He looked down at Woods, who was still sniggering, so he sliced off a piece of the other ear. Same angle so now Woods had a matching pair. The captive moaned and his head dropped as he drifted somewhere between conscious and unconscious.

The door ground open over the worn runners. Logan stood in the doorway and couldn't make the step inside. 'We need him alive. We want to find out how the Edinburgh thing happened.'

McManus had already found out that it was all down to his big fuckin' gob and couldn't let Abe Logan, of all people, know. He had to find this Bobo McCartney and take him out of the scene. But first he had to put this to sleep – including Logan.

He lifted Woods' head up by the hair and sliced the boy's neck open almost halfway through. Blood exploded from Woods' open throat, and McManus let it spray over him. He locked his stare into Logan's terrified eyes and held him like a frightened animal. That's when Logan's phone rang and saved his life.

'Is this Abe Logan?'

He said a dry yes and couldn't draw his gaze free of

McManus's. The lunatic's chest was heaving with the release of adrenalin after slaughtering Woods, whose head had tipped backwards with the weight, drawing open the massive, almost pornographic wound that was now exposed to the light.

'I'm Detective Superintendent Charlie MacKay. We met a few years ago. Don't know if you remember?'

Logan's mind was swamped with information overload and he couldn't quite cope. He said yes like a robot although he really couldn't remember MacKay at that moment. He had to keep his eyes on McManus to see what came next, because everything in the mad bastard's eyes said his throat was next for a bit of fresh air. McManus took six steps forward and was in striking distance of Logan, but he wanted to know what the call was before he made his next move.

'It's the polis.' Logan was drawing in deep breaths as he tried to control his fear but failed badly. He had a madman a few feet away from him with a cut-throat razor covered in blood and the bizzies on the blower. What he needed was help.

'What the fuck do they want then?' McManus dropped the hand gripping the razor to his side and waited for more information.

Logan asked MacKay what he wanted to talk about and the tremor in his voice was unmistakable. The detective wondered what was spooking a man who liked to project the image of top Glasgow hard man. MacKay explained in brief but clear detail what the situation was: the law was all around them, including firearms, and unless they could find a battle tank there was no way out. It was a complete lockdown.

'Gimme that fuckin' thing.' McManus grabbed the phone from Logan's shaking hand and turned his back on him. All his anger spilled out, all his intense sense of

218

betrayal, the grinding confusion trying to compute an idea to take him out of there. But McManus's mind was a small but intense electric storm, utter chaos, and all he wanted to do was scream and take on anyone who came near him.

'Who the fuck is this?' he screamed down the phone and MacKay pulled his phone away from his ear but kept his cool – that was the training. He knew this had to be McManus, and his gut told him it was not going to end well. *So be it*, he thought – if it was to be a bad ending then he would make fucking sure it was Psycho who was on the losing side.

He'd deployed a small army of firearms officers so they were covered if it needed some flying metal. Although at this point he had no indication there were firearms, with this mob it was a possibility.

Logan had already broken into a sprint away from the slaughterhouse – for the first time in his life he wanted to be in the arms of the law.

MacKay was starting to explain who he was and that there was no way out when McManus put the phone down and the only words the detective heard were, 'Fuck you. Come in and get me.'

McManus threw the phone on the floor and crushed it with the heel of his shoe. He sat down, fired up a Lucky Strike and got himself ready for whatever came next.

36

'That's target one away from the main building and trying to break the world speed record on two legs. He's coming straight up the road towards you so beware. I can't see any weapon in his hands.'

Logan ran as if he were being pursued by the hounds of hell until the firearms team appeared out of the hedgerow in front, behind and to the side, at which point he stopped dead. He put his hands up and, lungs burning with the effort, managed to say, 'Thank fuck for that.'

'He's done the boy in. Fuckin' mess, chief.' All he wanted was to please his rescuers and prove that he was cooperating all the way, and that the bleeding mess that used to be Gordon Woods was nothing to do with him.

The lead firearms officers tried to calm him down as they cuffed him but got the story that not only was McManus in there on his own with the recently departed but it seemed there was a fully loaded equaliser in the nutter's hands. This information was relayed back to MacKay and the team on the ground. The Ops Comm manoeuvred the teams in closer and made sure that if McManus showed his face there was nowhere for him to run.

'Keep it peaceful if possible.' That was MacKay's last instruction to the firearms team.

'As long as he does the same, boss,' was the reply, and that was fair enough.

The fact that it was the pigs who had penned him in only increased the urge in McManus to fight and fuck the consequences. He'd intended taking Abe Logan but hadn't even noticed the bastard legging it. It didn't really matter – he was calm now, and he grinned at the thought that people would be talking about this for years to come. The big Hollywood exit had always appealed to him, and dying peacefully as an old man surrounded by his loving family had never really been a likely option. *Anyway*, he thought, *where the fuck will I get a loving family?* Just in case it was some twat playing games, he picked up the shooter in one hand, stuck the clean razor in his pocket and went for a deek outside.

'That's target two from the description in the operational order. Standby.' Fitzgerald took a moment to be sure she was seeing what she thought she saw. 'It's him and beware, he's covered in what looks like blood, firearm in his right hand and a cigarette in the other. Picture on its way. He's looking around and seems to be shouting something. Wait one – I'll try and catch what he's saying.'

MacKay, like the Ops Comm and all the troops at the site, could hear every word the CROPs officer was saying. It went quiet, but they knew this was about to become headline news and for all the wrong reasons.

'To the Ops Comm, he's shouting "fuck you". Just saying it over and over again, then "I'll be back in a couple of minutes". He's back in the main building.'

The Ops Comm moved everyone in even closer but still far enough away to keep them safe. They'd hold it there for as long as it took to negotiate and he prayed that MacKay could talk the man out.

McManus sat down again and lit up another Lucky. He pulled off the soaked vest and wiped himself down as best he could, then pulled on his shirt and jacket and ran his hands through his hair, hoping he looked smart enough for the big finale. He enjoyed the cigarette and waited patiently till it was burned down to the point it was burning his fingers.

He stood up again and stared for a moment at what used to be Woods.

'Sorry, son. Pity you ever met me, eh?'

Woods didn't answer him back.

He picked up the shooter and threw the razor back on the table. There was an axe lying next to the door and he decided that really would give him the charisma required for the occasion.

He stepped outside again, looked up at the sky and felt the cool rain wash his face. He sucked a few deep lungfuls of air and smiled. 'I've been in worse situations.' He said it even though it wasn't quite the truth, but he felt like he was the anti-hero in the big climax of a violent gangster movie and he had to say something with a bit of grim irony wound into the scene.

'That's the target out, out, out. Shirt and jacket on now; firearm in right hand and an axe in the other. He's starting to jog up the road.'

MacKay swore at almost exactly the same time as the Ops Comm and firearms leader – they all knew where this was going.

'Come on, ya bastards!' McManus knew the pigs had to be close and it was just a case of finding some of them. He stopped every so often, went off the road then backtracked until he was about twenty-five yards from the firearms leader and one of his team, who were behind the remains of an old brick wall that had once formed the perimeter of the site. They saw McManus closing on their position and there seemed to be only two options. First, they could try and run to avoid conflict, but McManus would be at their backs with his firearm. Not an option then.

The firearms leader raised himself up to full height, aimed his weapon and called the official warning. The other officer followed his boss and within seconds the two weapons were ready to do whatever was required.

McManus stopped, took it all in and let both hands fall to his sides while still holding the weapons.

'Don't do it, pal. Lay the weapons down and we'll work this out. Okay?'

McManus was breathing heavily so he said and did nothing as he watched other firearms officers move into different positions near him where they could engage without hitting each other in crossfire. In the distance, he saw an unmarked car and van pull into view and halt. He turned round in a circle and took one last look at the world.

'The weather's shit anyway,' he shouted, and spat towards the firearms team leader. 'Fancy droppin' the shooters an' havin' a square go, pal?' He laughed quietly to himself.

The firearms officer heard it and handed out another warning that he knew the mad bastard was about to ignore.

McManus raised the axe and threw it for all he was worth but missed his target by a mile. 'Bastard.' He was genuinely disappointed by the effort and it would have been the 'bizo' if he could have landed the axe in the uniform's napper. *Ah well. Worth a try*, he thought.

He lifted the gun to a straight-arm position, and as he started to walk forward he opened fire. The first bullet hit him in the middle of his second step towards the cops. It was almost a perfect shot and took him in the centre of the breastbone, splintering bone and flesh. McManus felt like he'd been hit with a mash hammer, and all the breath seemed to disappear from his lungs. He was a powerful man though, and somehow managed to squeeze the trigger again – for the last time. As his legs wobbled into the third step the second bullet hit him near the abdomen. The firearms officers watched him half double up with the blow, his legs developing weird and separate lives of their own. He began to perform an almost clownish little dance, then his back arched in agony and he fell backwards. The police team moved in carefully, even though they knew he was a goner. They were trained to expect the unexpected, and there was ample history of apparently dead shooters getting off one last round.

But McManus was dead, and a man who'd caused nothing but pain in his years was just another very ex gangland legend. Few, if any, would mourn his passing, including his own side, and if he even had a family, no one knew who or where they were.

MacKay went out to the locus and although he would have preferred to catch McManus as a live specimen, it was fair enough, and at least the taxpayer wouldn't have to pay to keep the bastard inside for the rest of his natural. All in all, it was a good result. There wouldn't be too many problems with the shooting, though these events were normally a pain in the arse with the media inevitably finding something to criticise. He had also taken Frankie Logan's brother and second in command out of the game. That was hunky-dory because if he'd found himself having to take Frankie that would have wrecked his master plan. His fear at the start of this job was that it would take him right to the man at the top. So although there might be a few questions for the boss of the team, there was nothing he couldn't answer.

After he'd had a look at the site and screwed his face up at poor old Woods, he phoned his DCI. 'Call Jigsaw and tell him job well done. He's got nothing to worry about.'

MacKay had another detective superintendent take over the murder investigation and tidy up. He was too involved in what he liked to call criminal social engineering, and that was going pretty well: the bosses were happy, he was happy, Jigsaw was happy and everyone was a winner. He just had to figure out the best way to finish off Big Brenda... wherever she was. It wasn't much of a problem anymore and could wait because he was going to have a couple of days off for some serious R&R. He was just heading back to Pitt Street to tidy up when he got the call from McGovern.

'Hi, Jimmy. Thought you were retired – ticker problem or something.'

McGovern told him what he and Macallan wanted and that they'd like to do it on Monday. MacKay really couldn't be arsed with some half-baked review of a case that no one cared about. It confirmed in his mind that McGovern was just being handed errands to see out his time. He'd never liked the man because he remembered that on the course they'd both attended McGovern was the one person who was obviously not impressed with him. He'd hated that. All his life he'd needed to be openly admired and he'd come to expect it – anything less was an insult. Any other day he'd have made an excuse, but McGovern had told him Macallan was the lead on the review. She was someone he'd never met, a different deal, and he was curious to see how she matched up to

225

her billing: top-drawer career and a bigger celebrity than he was in police terms. He'd heard what she'd achieved and it bothered him, because she'd done things at the front end he could never duplicate. That meant she was well worth meeting. Even if she was back in uniform and by all accounts finished with investigation, apart from the nonsense they were involved with around Tommy McMartin.

'Monday morning it is,' he told McGovern. 'Be good to see you.'

37

Lying came easily enough to MacKay; indeed a lie detector would probably have failed in his case because they just rolled off his tongue, as his one and only long-term girlfriend had once remarked before she threw a cup of coffee in his face. That had taken place in a smart Edinburgh restaurant and he'd never forgotten the humiliation. It burned, and he'd never got close to a woman again. In fact, he'd never got that close to anyone again. Relationships, apart from the one he had with himself, just got in the way of his career. Even the odd good friend he made in the job was there because of what they might be able to do for him. Anyone who was a real pro could smell trouble where MacKay was concerned and stayed well back.

MacKay resented people like McGovern because they had the one attribute he could never have and that was raw physical guts. He was a bottler, though few people would ever have known it because he'd crafted a career and legend that was about ninety-five per cent true, five per cent smoke and mirrors. He'd carefully avoided the toughest challenges, but his CV showed the right ticks in the right boxes. When he was promoted to DCI in a tough division, in order to get the appropriate credibility, he managed to spend a large part of that time on the FBI course in Quantico. Over the years a few Scottish officers were gifted the chance to go to Quantico to polish up their CVs. His real forte was intelligence and managing covert operations. That was where he shone – pulling the strings and making other people dance to whatever tunes he had in mind. As long as the end result was to his advantage, he didn't worry too much about ethics. On the surface he was the walking, talking encyclopaedia of modern-day senior management bullshit. He rarely made a promotional interview or presentation to the public or the press without sprinkling the words transparency, accountability and partner organisations all through the text. He knew the executive liked to hear their rising stars talk that kind of mince, and the fact that he didn't believe a word of it never caused him a minute's concern.

He carried a degree of luck, no doubt about it, and when he came back from Quantico the Tommy McMartin thing had fallen right into his lap. He'd known there had to be a God when that one had come off, because he was in the right place at exactly the right time to make the moves that had put young Tommy away for life. The executive had loved him, another gold star was added to his CV and a few months later he was shoved up a rank and safely back into covert ops where he could do what he did best: fuck people without them ever realising what had happened.

He put the phone down after speaking to McGovern and turned on the news. The top and breaking story was that there had been a hostage situation near Bellshill and shots had been fired. There was no other information available according to the reporter, so he switched it over to his media player and nodded to the heavy beat of Prince giving it laldy to 'Purple Rain'. He just loved the wee genius.

38

MacKay was a razor-sharp operator but always concentrated far too much on his own priorities, and it was a weakness that was often enough a severe pain in the arse for some of his junior staff. Characters like McCartney meant almost nothing to him, and although for a short time he'd been an excellent means to an end, the situation at Bellshill was now over and it was a clean-up operation, with law enforcement getting a result that the public would like and sections of the press would slaver over. Dead bad guy dispatched by the police and another one slaughtered by his own kind. Two for the price of one – it really didn't get much better than that. They had complete cover on taking McManus out and procedures had been followed so the fall-out would be minimal and, most importantly, containable.

The problem for McCartney was that as the clouds of dust fell over the aftermath of the incident in Bellshill, MacKay forgot altogether that the boy who'd walked in off the street and gave them the turn was still sitting in a cramped office in Pitt Street. He was squeezed into what had once been a document store without windows or ventilation and in the company of a junior detective who'd been told to shut the fuck up and just keep an eye on the wee ned till someone with credibility came to relieve him. The junior detective had been identified as an arse, and his days in the department were numbered. Till the day they could hoof him out of the door he was the office gofer.

The long, almost lonely silence in that office became excruciating for both the DC and McCartney's bladder, which was swollen to combustion point with the coffee that had been piled into him earlier, when he'd been the main man for about half an hour. He started to shift uncomfortably on the old office chair and couldn't control the urge to fidget, which helped keep his mind off the need for a slash.

As the time crawled by McCartney's fingers crept over the levers at the side of the chair, and because he was who he was, he pulled on the handle without thinking. That was the story of his life. That chair had been retired into that small room for over a year because it was way past its sell-by date for a piece of cheap shite. As always in public service no one had the authority to dump it, so they stuck it in a room where it could serve no useful purpose whatsoever. It could have been described as broken, though the label 'death trap' might have done it justice as well. The back of the chair flapped backwards taking McCartney and the startled DC by complete surprise. McCartney's weight had been leaning back as the support disappeared and the result was that he flipped towards the floor and did a backwards somer-sault that most gymnasts would have been proud of – until the wall stopped him completing the move. It was all too much for the DC, who was already an angry man because no one liked him and he was stuck in a room with a halfwit who stank of cheap aftershave. He sprang to his feet in surprise then anger. All the frustration at being a wanker and unable to do anything about it welled up, and he screamed at McCartney and partly at himself. 'I've had enough . . . Bastard!'

The DC sank the boot into McCartney's abdomen, and to be fair he would never have planned it, but the inevitable happened because McCartney had just had the fright of his life and temporarily forgot that he was keeping iron control over his bladder. He pissed himself, and although the DC had been about to work him over he recoiled in horror as the dark stain spread over the front and legs of McCartney's new jeans and proceeded to creep menacingly across the surface of the old wooden floor towards his shoes. The DC cancelled the rest of the attack.

'Oh for fuck's sake,' the DC said in a strangled voice. He'd made a terrible mistake. He remembered that he was supposed to be a cop and put his hand to his mouth as a passing uniformed inspector heard the commotion, opened the door and looked back and forward between the victim, who was crying, and the DC who'd joined him.

'Jesus Christ. Who the fuck are you and who the fuck is that on the floor?'

MacKay got the call from Tony Slaven, who'd just had a rocket from a uniformed super. It was an assault on a witness on police premises so they needed a skull to crush. MacKay tried to get his head round the scene, but it was difficult. It was a minor glitch on what had been a big day, but he was an expert at covering his arse, and the fact that the DC was already marked out as a dead man walking was a good start. MacKay would shift the blame to the DS, who'd been McCartney's first point of contact, and blame him for putting a twat in to cover McCartney during the operation. MacKay could claim that they did have plans for McCartney and were going to get back to him. 'Let the uniforms get on with fixing the DC. Get a hold of McCartney and talk to him for a couple of hours then tell him to piss off.'

'He thinks he goin' into witness protection, boss – new life an' all that shite.'

'He's goin' nowhere, Tony. What can he give us now? Stories about robberies where we have no complaint from a victim. Kick his arse.'

Slaven didn't like it but broke the news to McCartney that there would be no new life courtesy of the taxpayer and that he'd need to take his chances back on the street.

'But Psycho'll kill me.' McCartney's brief dreams of a fresh start in some exotic spot were crumbling in front of his eyes.

'Well, he'll need to break out of the fuckin' fridge in the mortuary first, son.'

McCartney blinked and started rubbing his chin in a nervous reaction to the news. He tried to work out what it all meant. He asked about Woods, and Slaven spared him the details, just saying that he was dead as well and McManus had probably been responsible. It was still being investigated. 'You should be okay, son – as far as we know Big Brenda will just keep the head down and shouldn't worry you.'

McCartney just wasn't sure what the Logans would know or whether they would care about him. He'd called Woods and warned him but hadn't left his name, so maybe they knew nothing to connect him ... but maybe they did. Maybe Brenda would come after him regardless – but what good would it do her? The way she was going she'd never collect her old age pension. It was a lot to try and work out, and there was no answer that would let him sleep easy. It made no difference; he was shown the door in Pitt Street and given the less than reassuring advice that if there was any problem 'just call'.

He walked the streets in something close to a state of shock. He'd gone in to save Woods' life and done his best. The poor bastard was a goner, but that wasn't his fault.

It started to rain and his clothes were soon soaked, which added to the misery of pissing himself in the cop shop. Having lived his life among people who quite often suffered serious hygiene problems, it shouldn't have bothered him, but the jeans were beginning to stink, and, if anything, being drenched in the cold Glasgow rain made the problem even worse. He wandered into a coffee shop to warm up but a minute and a half later the manager ordered him out onto the street and rubbed even more misery into his wounded soul by calling him a 'durty bastard'. McCartney was pissed off, scared and lonely.

There was only one place he could rest his head for the night and be welcome and that was at Wee Peem's. As he trudged towards his friend's door, he knew there was something he needed to do, which went against the grain for him, and that was to tell the truth. Peem had trusted him, thought he was the dug's baws and liked being his friend. In his past, he would have just made up some new fantasy to cover his arse, but Peem deserved better than that. McCartney had admitted to himself that he wasn't and never would be a big-time operator, and Wee Peem was the true level of society he should be content with.

It was strange because it was almost like a great weight had been removed from his shoulders. The years spent trying to be something he could never achieve had done nothing but shatter his ego, and he'd rarely slept properly for worrying about his catastrophes. He began to imagine nothing more complicated than watching movies filled with explosions and shattered bodies, a few cans of beer and arguing about the state of Scottish football. That was enough, all he really wanted, and as the thought began to take real hold he straightened his back and quickened his step.

39

McCartney scratched his chin a few times as he explained exactly what had happened, and basically it was a confession to being a complete and utter lying bastard. Wee Peem never said a word during McCartney's long rambling disclosure, and when it was finished a knowing smile lit his face. Peem put the forefinger of his right hand under his eye and pulled downwards.

'Aye right then, Pat. I believe you.' He let the lower eyelid snap upwards again and winked. 'Stay here as long as you like, mate.'

Wee Peem had listened to McCartney tell the whole truth and nothing but the truth for the first time in his life and didn't believe a word.

McCartney wanted to say *for fuck's sake* but he was a born-again Christian and that was the language of his old life. He tried again and told his mate about his newly discovered faith.

Wee Peem listened again, then pulled his lower eyelid down again and followed it up with another wink. 'Whatever you say. Secret's safe wi' me, pal.'

McCartney stared at his friend. He couldn't even get

Wee Peem to believe him when he was telling the truth. He began to see the funny side of it and pulled his own eyelid down then winked back at his friend. 'Knew I could trust you, pal.'

They stuck on *Terminator 2*, and although McCartney was a Christian he thought that a few beers were permissible given the day he'd had.

They switched the box off at about 3 a.m. and McCartney was out of it about three seconds after his head hit the pillow. He'd decided that there was nothing he could do about Big Brenda, but everybody and their auntie wanted her as fuel for the crematorium so he would put his trust in God.

He woke up with a start about an hour later, having dreamt that she was at the window. Once he realised it was just a nightmare he relaxed again and slept soundly.

The next morning, McCartney decided that there was no way he was going to hide from the world till he could be sure he was off the wanted list, and when he left the flat around midday the sun was sparkling and there was real heat in the air. He caught a bus into the city centre, wandered round the shops and watched the world go by. He only had a few quid, but it was enough to enjoy the day, and when he looked into the windows of a couple of fast-food outlets he noticed signs saying they were looking for staff. McCartney hadn't worked a day in his short life but this was a new chapter and he thought, *Why not?*

He decided to enjoy a couple of hours, get a sandwich then try them for a job. The thought excited him, and he sensed that there were still possibilities in the world but now they wouldn't involve crime. He felt his pulse race with excitement and he headed towards a Costa for a blast of caffeine. That's when he picked up the sound of the music. In his old life, it would have washed over or past him, but this wasn't his old life. It took him two minutes to walk to the source of the music, and as he stood in front of the players something spoke to him.

A woman who was standing beside the players with a pile of leaflets in her hand noticed McCartney's expression and could see he might be a potential customer. They were rare enough now in this godless society. She stepped forward and McCartney had his first conversation with someone from the Salvation Army.

40

Macallan looked out of the window of the turboprop as it descended over Belfast Lough on its way to land at George Best Airport. She felt the nerves in her stomach rattle with anticipation, and she still found it hard to believe that it was only a few short years since she'd left Northern Ireland a lonely and exhausted woman after everything she'd believed in had conspired to destroy her career and what had been her personal life. She'd fought in the Dirty War and seen so many good men and women die or have their lives torn apart by injury and grief, but had ended up an outcast in the organisation that she'd loved and been proud to serve. On the day she'd sailed out of the Lough on board the Stena ferry to start a new life in Scotland, she'd sworn she would never set foot on Ulster's soil again.

In the intervening years, she'd rebuilt that career and surprisingly fallen in love again with the man who'd deserted her back then when she'd needed him most. That experience was perhaps the greatest lesson she'd ever had. Even though she'd turned her back on religion when she'd seen what it was responsible for in the Troubles, she'd forgiven Jack Fraser, saw what was so good in him, forgot his failure and in three weeks' time they would marry – a family, two children included. It was something she would never have believed possible in those dark days when she had begun to doubt there was a good human being, including herself, in this world. Now she was like a teenager again, excited by the prospect of the future, and the job was now simply a part of her life instead of all of it.

When she walked through the gates she immediately saw Jack with Adam and Kate, one in each arm; the three of them were grinning from ear to ear and both children had their arms outstretched. Macallan felt her nose run and a couple of fat tears bobbled down her cheeks. Adam struggled out of his father's arms and toddled towards Macallan with some thick coloured scribbles on a piece of paper.

'I think that might be a picture of you, Grace.' Jack said it with his deeply serious court face.

'Is that for me, Adam?' She tried to take the piece of artwork, but he wasn't for letting go, so she just swept the boy up for a cuddle. Kate was still grinning at her from her father's arms.

'God, I missed you lot. Let's get home.' Her voice choked, and she loved that feeling of belonging heart and soul to those three other human beings who cared what happened to her.

'I wish some of those hard men you used to chase about could see the real snivelling you.' Jack bent down a few inches to let her kiss him, and the four of them did a long, warm group hug.

Macallan felt pressure on her lower leg and realised she'd forgotten one of the family. She unlocked herself and crouched down to hold the dog behind both ears and laughed as he almost unbalanced through sheer excitement. When they'd inherited the dog from his original owner, who was a pimp jailed after the Pete Handyside case, it came with the unlikely handle of Gnasher, which was a bit of a stretch for a spoodle. Jack had demanded a name change, quite rightly pointing out that the dog wouldn't mind. So Gnasher became Gary, and to be fair the dog hadn't objected once.

The children were so excited that they managed to tire themselves out and, thankfully, Macallan was able to see them off to sleep without too much effort. The next day would be all for them, but what she wanted this evening was to sit with Jack talking rubbish. He was pro-union, and she was starting to admire wee Nicola, who'd now graduated to just needing her first name to be recognised as the one and only, so they'd made a pact over red wine to avoid politics.

There had been a system of freezing northerly air washing in from the Arctic and it gave them the perfect excuse to pile up the open fire and let the warmth of the flames soothe them into a contented peace with just some music to add to the feeling that they were completely away from all the troubles in the world. The dog took up his favourite position a few feet from the warm flames and settled down to his dreams, and Macallan did something she had never been capable of in the past – she completely forgot about the job she was doing and for a few hours didn't really care. That lasted until Jack finally asked the question that had been hanging in the air since she'd arrived. What he said took her by surprise and made her realise that after the disaster in Belfast, the loss of her best friend and bearing witness to too many horrors, she'd now been gifted more than she could ever have wanted.

'Look, before we put the lights out, I don't know what this is you're working on and I should be pissed off ...

but I'm not.' He leaned over, kissed her neck and made her meet his eyes. 'I know you can't really give this thing up. We made a deal, but it won't work, and I've heard so much about how good you are at it ... Just a couple of things though – I don't want to know what this is about so don't bring it home. We have these two people in our lives now and they matter the most. Okay?'

He waited but Macallan had no idea how to reply or what had made him say what he had. Instead she nodded and tried to think of something that would have meaning that he could accept.

'Don't bring it home.' He said it for the second time, and for a man like Jack Fraser that was proof enough that he meant it. 'In the past you've used the odd drink or bout of self-loathing as medicine for what you've had to do. Now you have all this and people who love you. That's the medicine now, so when you feel frightened, remember those demons can't get near you when you're with us.'

He kissed her again and she held him as tightly as she could. 'There's also the small matter of a wedding – and unless I'm mistaken you're an important part of the proceedings.' He held her face and she watched his face break into the broad smile that still made her chest tighten with emotion.

'You're the best, Jack. I don't want to be with anyone else. That's the truth.'

They both slept soundly, and the demons never came near Macallan that night.

41

Frankie Logan sipped the last of his coffee and wondered why he kept drinking the stuff. The taste was bitter and his breath stank after it, but it gave him the occasional lift when he was feeling a bit jaded. He was tired, and kept nipping the bridge of his nose and rubbing it as if it would make any difference. He was calm enough – his great gift was staying focused when things were rough, and the news from Bellshill meant things were definitely rough. He'd spent hours trying to make sense of what had happened and work the various options so that he was sure his response was the right one. In the first place, when his brother Abe had called him, he'd reported that it was all about McManus and that the big man had lost it with Woods. It had all been for nothing because the job was just to get the boy to pin the target on Big Brenda. Frankie had never been into killing nonentities like Woods unless it was completely necessary. A tanking and maybe a couple of facial scars usually got the same result.

Frankie's youngest brother, Alan, had been in the room with him for over an hour and had hardly spoken a word, letting his older brother think through their problems before he dished out the orders. He was watching the game on the telly in the corner with the sound down, and Frankie eventually got up from his chair, sat down in the one next to his brother and asked what the score was, although with all the other problems to sort it wasn't his top priority.

Alan knew his brother was ready to talk it through now and switched the box off.

'I never should have brought Psycho back, Alan. Big mistake and down to me.' He looked like making that call genuinely troubled him, but it was what it was. He shook his head a couple of times and got on with covering all bases.

'As far as I can see we should be able to dampen this down. Psycho's toast so that's sorted and saves us a job. The way Abe was talking on the blower he had nothing to do with slicing up the boy. Christ knows what that was all about. I've called our brief and he's on the case with Abe, but we don't know what they have on him so we'll have to wait and see.' He stopped for a moment and drifted off into his thoughts again.

'Need me to do anythin'?' Alan wanted to help his brother, who'd always treated him well and made allowances for his quiet nature.

'The number-one problem is that we're leaking somewhere. There was this message to the boy when our guys were about to lift him. I could live with that – it might just be a slip somewhere. Thing is, how did the fuckin' cavalry arrive at Bellshill? It means there's a rat, or we're bugged or whatever the fuck. Until we figure that out, we have to put everything on hold as far as possible. Okay?' Alan nodded and waited. 'We still need to finish this thing with Big Brenda though. We didn't get the story, but we go ahead anyway. Not how I wanted it but needs must.'

'Want me to do it?'

Frankie looked at his younger brother – the offer exposed the other man's lack of savvy when it came to these situations. 'No way, Al. There might be surveillance teams all over us at the moment. I want you to go down to our friends in Liverpool and contract the job out to them. We've done it for them, and Christ knows they've enough professionals on their books to do this one. Tell them we'll pay up front or whatever arrangement they fancy. Just get it done. We need to get this woman sorted and out of the road. Forget everything else at the moment and let me know the details when you've spoken to them.'

'You want me to go today?' Alan was happy with the idea of a trip away from the city and avoiding the next couple of days, which would be nothing but stress and trying to avoid the law crashing through the front door.

'I want you on the next train. Now stick some clean undies in a bag and get moving.'

At 2 a.m. on Sunday morning Tony Slaven was contacted by the CHIS codenamed Jigsaw who confirmed that the Logans were going to put a contract job on Big Brenda. A Scouse team of desperadoes would probably take it on and work out a plan. He said they wanted it done as soon as they could find her, which might still be a problem. Slaven cursed the news because there were protocols to follow when there was a threat to life, even if that life was Big Brenda McMartin. He called MacKay because he didn't really have a choice. MacKay knew there was a way out though, because the intelligence was that Brenda was keeping her head down. There was information that she had a safe house, but they had no idea where that might be. That would do nicely for the time being.

'Can't warn her if we can't find her, Tony.' MacKay didn't need the news but they'd have to appear to be trying to trace her. 'Put it on the system but leave it meantime. Other stuff to do.' He grimaced. 'Human rights – they'll be the fuckin' ruination of this country. Put a report in requesting any sightings of Brenda and make it look like we're trying to track her down. Get back to Jigsaw and tell him to keep in touch if there are any updates.'

Big Brenda McMartin was safely outside the city in a small two-bedroomed cottage she'd bought years before. It was somewhere she could be well away from all the people who she had to work with but couldn't really stand and was the one place she had any form of peace. It also had the benefit of being detached, which kept the nosey bastards around her out of sight. It had always been possible that it could be handy for a safe house; nevertheless, it was still a blow to her that at last this was what it had become.

She'd heard the reports on the Bellshill incident and knew too well that she was knee-deep in shit, and where could she go now? Woods was dead and must have talked first. McManus had joined him, which was the only good news. She had no reason to shed a tear for them, but the message was clear. This was the last line, and she knew that sometime in the next few days they'd find her and that then she could stop thinking about the past and those nightmares that made her whole body spasm in the night, leaving her weak and moaning into the pillow.

She'd hardly moved from her chair in hours. Every few minutes she glanced down at the sawn-off on the stool next to her. Within her reach but out of sight to anyone else who might come into the room, it was the only friend she had now.

She was stuffing her face with coffee, energy drinks and a bag of legal highs to keep her awake. The combination made her feel like shit, but then that was nothing new. And although she knew it wouldn't stop what was bound to happen in the end, she was determined to look the bastard in the face when the time came. Despite the poisons she was pouring into her bloodstream, she fell asleep and dreamt about her father, Slab McMartin. That hadn't happened for many years and she was shaking when she sat up and checked the shadows in the room. Nothing came at her, but she knew it was just a matter of time.

42

Sometimes he saw flashes, almost like subliminal messages crackling across a TV monitor. He was getting anxious now that, with the years, disease was taking hold and he'd google words like Alzheimer's, Parkinson's and neurological horrors that might leave him needing the support of other people for the first time in his life.

It was strange, because he couldn't remember the last time he'd felt so physically strong. Seeing Grace Macallan made his skin tingle with energy. It was as if all his years of success were just faded dreams where he struggled to remember what had happened. He couldn't recall the details, just that he'd conquered everything and everyone who'd stood in his way.

The next step was a risk, but he wanted to see her life up close, to touch the fabric on her favourite seat, the place where she read, watched her favourite soaps, where she talked to her friends on the phone and laughed or frowned at all the latest gossip. Her books would tell him what interested her, what stirred her emotions and perhaps made her cry. The problem of how to get into the house gnawed at his bones. In the end there looked to be only one possibility: a small window that looked old could be the weak point. There was no other way, and he thought it could probably be forced with the minimum of effort.

The window was tiny and about five feet above the roof of a ground-floor extension. It was all that was left of an original pantry, but he was so thin now that he thought it might just be possible. The thought of being inside her home almost made him sick with the thrill of discovering who she was in her private life and perhaps identifying where she was vulnerable. The waiting was over and it was time to move.

High walls enclosed the garden and protected it from prying eyes, and even in the dull morning light the man concealed in the shrub border could move with relative confidence that no one was going to see what he was doing. He struggled to climb onto the roof and felt his heart shudder when he tried to push the window up. The disappointment he experienced when he found the window was firmly closed was a physical ache. He'd come too far to retreat, and it needed a change of plan and nerve. Being an intelligent man with nothing to lose, he pulled the leather gloves tightly over his hands and carefully punched in the old glass. The window was ancient, and the small pane gave easily. He managed to push his arm through and push the catch over.

Getting through the narrow window drained what was left of his strength, so when he made it, he sat on the floor just inside the window and waited a full ten minutes till he felt like he could get to his feet without collapsing again. The rising excitement of what he'd managed to do brought him back to life and he opened the door into the hall, tipped his head back and pulled in the still air of the house through his nose. There was a very faint scent of perfume and flowers. The paintings in the hall were abstract and full of colour that seemed to almost ring from the canvas. The paintwork and carpets were subtle, letting the artwork catch the visitor's attention. He smiled at the thought that the woman who lived in this house had so much talent and an eye for decoration.

The sitting-room door was half open, and he paused before entering with one slow step at a time, making sure he disturbed as little as possible. The room was like the hall – spare, but every piece of furniture and the ornaments worked together as if they had been designed by a professional. It was strange and not what he'd expected of the woman he'd only known under the wrong circumstances.

He knew there was more to the house than the hand of a professional – it had someone's touch. It was in the small things: the pictures of other people, friends laughing, a bowl full of pine cones that he guessed had been gathered during a walk. The more he saw of her world, the less he understood. He'd expected the drab loneliness of someone who lived alone, discarded fast-food cartons or an unwashed wine glass with the dregs souring in the bottom. He recognised what must be her favourite seat, directly opposite the TV, a telephone on a small table next to the chair, accompanied by a couple of thumbed magazines and the previous day's *Herald*. There were shelves of books, and he could see that she loved history, though nothing too heavy, and there were enough travel books to fill a small shop. He knew she would be a traveller; it fitted with everything he'd seen so far – the modern professional woman who saw horizons as just something else to be crossed.

He sat back in the chair and felt close to her. There was a worn patch on the arm where she must have rested her hand and arm, night after night. He put his arm there, closed his eyes and imagined being there, that it was his home and his chair.

He stopped at the bedroom door but he had to see it: the place where she slept. Where she felt safe and warm.

The bedroom was as tidy as the rest of the house, and his heart thumped when he saw the two rag dolls in pride of place on a dressing table. The picture next to her bed, however, stopped him in his tracks. His skin froze at the sight of the man with his arm round her, their heads together. It made his throat close as if a ligature had been applied. A man in her life? Then he scanned round and saw the pictures of the children, and another of them with the children, and he started to heave in panic, dropping to his knees. It had never crossed his mind and it puzzled him. It was as if he'd discovered some foul little secret hidden there. A man in her life altered everything. What would it mean? The idea of sharing her was not what had kept him going as he'd shivered in the dark garden night after night. She had all the things his daughter could never have now and he realised how it had to play out.

He sat back down in the sitting room and looked up an emergency glazier. 'It's my daughter's house and she's going on holiday today so I need it done now. I'll pay whatever it takes.'

That offer was good enough for the glazier, who would have happily done it for the normal price. He knew the area and just wrote it off as some middle-class twat with more money than sense.

The guy did the job in an hour and tried to sell the client new windows. 'Not perfect, mate – those windows are Stone Age. I'll leave my card if your daughter fancies some new ones. A kid could break in through these.'

After the glazier left with the cash in his hand, he went through to the old pantry and cleaned it up as far as possible. There was a difference in the new glass but the old room seemed to be used as a glory hole so it might never be spotted.

He left through the front door half an hour later. Everything was going well, and having the balls to get someone to repair the window had given him a buzz and a half.

43

Macallan woke early with the sun streaming through the blinds, and she felt as if she'd slept for two days. The sleep had been a deep black world where there was no need to dream, only rest, and as soon as she opened her eyes, fresh energy started to flow – all she wanted to do was haul Jack out of bed to get the day going. Talking to him had made her feel a little guilty, because she'd been prepared to spin him a story, and all the time he'd been way ahead of her. She'd always known he was a formidable lawyer, and now she realised he would be a formidable husband. It worried her for a moment that she'd been prepared to deny him the truth to get what she wanted, and she wondered what that said about her.

But Macallan put the thoughts out of her mind and poked Jack in the ribs. It was a glorious Sunday morning, she could hear the kids were wide awake and she wasn't going to waste a second. It was the one morning of the week where all thoughts of their regular morning meal of porridge and fruit went out of the window, replaced by the famous but potentially fatal Ulster fry. She could almost smell the bacon before it was on.

Jack opened his eyes and pulled her in close, but she told him to wait and brought the children through so the four of them could start the day in a tangle of arms and legs. She wanted to put everything about work out of her head and concentrate on her family for the rest of the day. Macallan was due to meet McGovern at Glasgow Airport in the morning so they could see MacKay and, if it was possible, Slab McMartin – although whether the old gangster would speak to them was another matter.

At the same time Macallan and Fraser sat down at the ancient wooden table in the kitchen, Jimmy Adams stepped out of the bakers with his morning rolls and the Sunday papers. He was in St Monans, a picture-postcard fishing village on the East Neuk of Fife. It was part of that glorious trail of land between the little harbour at Elie running along the north corner of the Firth of Forth to the ancient university town of St Andrews, one of the oldest seats of learning on the British mainland. Good enough for royals to send their son and the place where Alex Salmond had proved he had a head for figures.

In one short week, life for Adams, or just Glasgow Jimmy as some of the locals had come to know him, had changed completely. He'd spent time at his sister's before, but the calm routine of ordinary lives had frightened him off and he'd always been convinced he couldn't live like a normal punter. Now there was nothing he wanted more. He wanted to be almost invisible, just a guy who'd come to live with his sister, liked the odd beer and was keen to take in whatever game was on at the boozer. His sister was over the moon that he was there, having been lonely since her husband had died suddenly a couple of years before. Her husband had been a deep-sea fisherman and had met her one day when he was in Glasgow to watch his beloved Dunfermline FC play Rangers. He'd ordered a fish supper after the game and she'd served him, he'd smiled at her with warm eyes and she'd smiled back. It had been that simple.

Adams and his sister had been brought up in a tough time but had parents who'd taught them to love each other, and even when Wee Jimmy, as they'd known him, had started to run with the gangs, they'd forgiven him, because they'd never seen what he was capable of. Their parents were long gone now, and his sister had never been able to have children, so he was all she had left.

Adams walked into the kitchen, laid the rolls down on the table and almost dribbled at the smell of bacon and eggs. For most of his adult years all he would eat in the morning was a jam sandwich, depending on how late he'd gone to bed. It occurred to him that so much of his life had been lived in the night and there was almost nothing he could remember that could be described as a good morning. In his glory days, if he wasn't working, he'd be out all night: booze, short meaningless relationships and talking crime with his mates. Whatever they wanted they took and, when Slab was top man, everywhere they went people stepped out of the way or served them whatever they wanted, and of course there had never been a charge. But that was gone now, as if it had all happened to someone else.

His sister told him to put the news on the telly, sit down and she'd bring his rolls to him so he could read the Sundays in peace.

Adams settled back into the comfortably upholstered settee, closed his eyes and enjoyed that wonderful moment when he thought that all he needed to do that day was whatever he wanted. It was that easy. His sister wanted him to cut the grass then he could have a wee snooze and walk down to the pub for the big game later in the afternoon. She was making a roast for dinner, and then they'd be glued to the box for a few hours.

He did the sports pages and avoided politics as far as possible, although it was hard not to shake his head in wonder that wee Nicola had managed to sink the boot into old Labour so thoroughly. In his family, if someone had suggested a vote other than for Labour they would have ordered the chuckle wagon, but times were changing fast, and the old world he'd inhabited was nearly gone. The gangsters were all bastards now – no shred of morality however skewed – and, like business empires, only driven by profit.

He turned over a couple of pages, barely reading what was in front of him because he didn't want to see any more bad news about floods of immigrants or terrorist attacks. He was a gangster who'd never been frightened of anyone, but the rolling depressing news from across the world did nothing but flatten him and was another reminder that so much that had been accepted as the norm when he was a young man was gone. He was glad he didn't have any children to worry about.

His eye caught Jacquie Bell's report on the problems in the prison service. With his career background this was something that interested him, so he settled back and read every word. The article included the information that Macallan was reviewing the circumstances of Tommy McMartin's death and that there were concerns over what had happened to him before his suicide. Adams was hardly aware of his sister coming in with a heaped plate of rolls that would have fed three men. The second time she said his name he broke out of his train of thought and looked up as if he was seeing her for the first time.

'You okay?' She put her hand on his shoulder; there was something in his eyes that worried her. She hadn't asked him why he'd suddenly arrived and stayed. She didn't want to know and just hoped his past life would stay where it was and leave them alone.

He nodded absently and was beginning to munch on the first of the rolls when the Scottish news came on the box, and he gradually stopped chewing when the Bellshill incident was reported. They'd released the victim's name and a picture of Woods flashed up on the screen. By the time the reporter had described McManus as having been shot dead by a police marksman, breakfast had been forgotten. One unnamed man had been arrested at the scene and the investigation was ongoing. It was too much for Adams to get his head round – there was so much he didn't know, and it was impossible to work out what it all meant for him.

He told his sister he was going out for a while and headed for the harbour, as it was a good place to think. She stood at the door and watched him walk away with the feeling that the past had come back to him again.

The newly retired gangster stared at the boats bouncing around on the fresh south-easterly wind blowing off the North Sea. The sun warmed his back and the breeze cooled his face. 'Christ, I'm an old man,' he said into the breeze and the words disappeared as they left his lips.

He hardly moved for a couple of hours then headed for the pub and ordered a beer. He didn't drink too much these days. Not because he wouldn't have liked to, but unfortunately his digestive system gave him hell if he overindulged.

He watched part of the early kick-off, but it hardly registered, and after about one mouthful of his second pint he nodded to the barman and headed back to his sister's.

When he opened the door, he stood motionless for a moment, and she did her best not to show concern even though it was there, burning in her stomach. Jimmy was all she had left. 'Will I make a pot, Jimmy?' She turned away from him and switched on the kettle without waiting for an answer. Jimmy never refused tea.

'We need to sit down, hen. Need to explain a couple of things to you.' Adams had already admitted that he was worth nothing and meant nothing. All the old glories were long gone. There was no ex like an ex-gangster, and the young climbers didn't give a fuck who could piss the furthest twenty years ago. He had no idea what the events at Bellshill would trigger in the way of a reaction from the Logans, Big Brenda or the law. McManus was off the pitch and one less problem to worry about, but he'd got to Woods, so what did that mean? It didn't really matter because all the options were bad if they came for him. Anywhere else, well he was almost past caring, but he was living in the home of the one person who still meant something to him and the one person who cared about him. He couldn't bring any of it to her door and knew he'd been kidding himself that it might all go away.

'I need to leave again, hen. Want to stay, believe me, but there might be a bit of trouble and I need to take care of it before it takes care of me, if you know what I mean.'

She pleaded with him, but he knew that she couldn't even imagine in her worst nightmares what the bad men might do – and if she was in the way then they'd just hurt her as well. No problem for them.

He did something he'd never done in their lives and put his arms round her as her shoulders shuddered with the grief of losing someone again.

He made her sit down and told her probably more than she needed to know so that she might understand, because he guessed he might be the next item on the Scottish news. There was more though, and it all came on top of Tommy McMartin's suicide and Jacquie Bell's story.

What had happened to Tommy, and what he knew about it, had gnawed at his gut like an ulcer for years, and he could never resolve why it had all panned out the way it had. Maybe it was time to make things right; maybe that was the only way he could survive and have a chance at that anonymous life he craved.

His sister listened and nodded occasionally. She took his hand. 'Go an' sort this out, Jimmy. Do whatever you need to do and your room'll be ready for you. Okay?'

He nodded, went to his room and called the police to try and get in touch with Superintendent Macallan.

It was one of those strange quirks of life that Adams was a nobody, and for the real players he would have been forgotten about, seeing as he was no threat to anyone anymore. The Logans had more to do than hunt down an old man, and while Brenda was a threat, her destiny was heading in another direction.

44

Later on that busy Sunday afternoon, at about the same time Adams took his decision, Alan Logan was sitting across the table from Terry Norman, a top man with his own organisation and a big player on Merseyside. His brother-in-law was the head of the team but never did face-to-face business because he knew he was a priority target for an NCA operation that had been trying for years to nail him down. They were allies of the Logans and had done a lot of business over the years; Frankie's nous for politics and strategy kept things sweet between them when most such arrangements tended to end up in blood feuds or at least in a severing of relationships. It was a truly free market they operated in, so competitors could go where they liked without a single lawful regulation holding them back. Somehow the Logans and Scousers made it work.

Norman was a bit of an enigma, and much of that was to do with his appearance. There was no doubting his skill as a gangster – he'd proved himself time and time again as a resourceful and clever operator who rarely put a foot wrong in the business – but when people met him for the first time they couldn't quite work out whether it was some stupid joke or piss-take. He dressed and spoke like the Scouse character Harry Enfield did so well and ticked every box in the Liverpool book of clichés. He had it all: the perm, the Freddie Mercury moustache and enough chunky jewellery to sink a small boat. It wasn't a joke though – he genuinely liked the look and saw it as part of his rich heritage. As far as he was concerned Liverpool was the centre of the world, and he had a particular hatred for 'southern poofs'. He normally refused to do business with anyone from 'that London' unless it was to rip the arse out of them.

That particular prejudice against East Enders came from a meeting they'd had a couple of years earlier where a Cockney wanker had pissed himself laughing when introduced to Terry for the first time. The Londoner had wanted access to the Scousers' connections in South America and ended up in intensive care with injuries the admitting doctor thought were the result of a bad car accident. No one from London ever laughed at Terry Norman again.

'Erm, what can I do for you, lad?' he asked Logan.

Logan explained exactly what the score was and that payment was not a problem. If they did it, Frankie would return the favour in full, though he explained that they might have some attention from the bizzies and needed to stay off the front line for a while till it settled down again.

'That's sound. These things happen in our business, and it's better to be careful, like. Leave the details with us and we'll see what we can do. Erm, I take it you know where we can find her?'

'Not yet, but our friends in the force will let us know as soon as they trace her. Might take a bit of time but you'll get it as soon as we have it.'

'No problem.' Norman thought for a minute and smiled broadly, showing the gold tooth that dominated the front of his mouth. 'We've got a Jock who works for us and is the absolute business. He looks like he's a fuckin' blert, like, but he's a Rottweiler when there's action. To tell you the truth, I wouldn't fancy the cunt meself.' He pissed himself laughing; the minders behind him performed their duty and laughed at the same time, although it wasn't even that funny.

'"Cue Ball" Ross. You might have heard of him? Got him working over in, erm, Holland at the moment, like, but I'll get him back. He'll enjoy a trip to the old country.'

Logan had heard the name but couldn't remember the story. If he had he would have recognised one of those coincidences that do happen in the strangest circumstances. Cue Ball had been an Edinburgh criminal with a flair for violence, had met Brenda McMartin before and had put her in the hospital after she'd tried to take the man Cue Ball was minding at the time. He'd made a mess of her, but the McMartins were still a power at that time so he'd done the wise thing and headed over the border. He'd doubted he'd ever be able to go back, because having the gall to reupholster a McMartin had been a capital offence at the time.

While a couple of his lads took Logan out on the town, Norman made the call to Amsterdam and got Cue Ball on the second ring. He was having a drink with his girlfriend near the red-light district at the time, and although he liked the life in Holland, he did miss Edinburgh and wished he could get back to see a bit of the old city. When Norman explained what the job was he nodded a few times, and then shook his head when he heard the name of the target.

'Well I'll be fucked.' He sat back and pictured the scene

when he'd lost part of his ear to the woman. 'Know her well, pal, and let's just say she needed a few repairs the last time we met. I'll do the job, no problem.'

Logan was sticking money into a pole dancer's only item of clothing when he got the call from Norman confirming that the man for the job would be in Glasgow as soon as he could get across. He'd wait till there was a confirmed location for the target and get the job done in no time.

'It'll be a pleasure to help you out with this, Al.'

Norman put the phone down and turned on 'Ferry Cross the Mersey'. He loved that song; it made him sure he was graced to be a Scouser.

45

Macallan was almost asleep when her phone drew her back from a long drift downwards into a peaceful darkness. She was annoyed because she and Jack had made a house rule that phones were switched off after eight, and she'd clearly forgotten to do the necessary.

She pushed the hair from her face, leaned on one elbow and watched the screen flash for her attention. It was McGovern, who'd eventually been contacted after a series of phone calls and told that Jimmy Adams wanted to speak to Macallan. She told him to hold on, stepped into the worn-out slippers she loved so much and went into the kitchen, where she could speak without disturbing the rest of the house. Jack managed to snore gently through the whole thing, and she envied the way he could switch off from the world and let it all be.

'Don't know what it's about, but we've done a few checks and you might remember that he goes a long way back with Slab McMartin and used to be his right hand. Been relegated through old age to Brenda's driver and he ended up in the ambulance with Brenda the night Cue Ball Ross decided to say hello.'

'Of course. Used to be quite a boy in his day. Does it sound urgent? Because we've made arrangements tomorrow.'

'All he would tell the operators was that it was about Tommy McMartin and so it must be something to do with Jacquie Bell's story. Who knows, could be just another old ned wanting to tell us what a star he was in the day. Intel is he was still Brenda's driver up to the last entry, so worth a go.'

Macallan chewed her lip and realised that she'd now be lucky to reach the level of sleep she'd been heading for just five minutes earlier. She asked McGovern to hang on while she flicked the switch on the kettle, even though she knew that coffee was probably all wrong at that time of night.

'Have you been following all this stuff at Bellshill? The man arrested at the locus was Abe Logan. The Logans are the ones trying to put an end to Brenda and what's left of the McMartins.'

'Violent times. Wonder if any of the dots join up to our thing?' Her mind clicked back to priorities. 'Did you manage to get permission to look at the HOLMES system for the Mickey Dalton murder?'

'Got it and we can do it at Pitt Street.'

'Tell you what: any chance you can get a hold of Felicity and the two of you have a look at the system to make sure there's nothing that might be worth looking at?'

Felicity Young had a brilliant mind and could cut through mountains of data without being overwhelmed by the task. She was ideal for this type of job.

'We might get flak for looking at the murder. I know a couple of people with not a shred of evidence have given us their theories, but it doesn't mean a thing. It's a bit outside the remit, and we might get some serious grief over it,' McGovern said, though he already knew what her reply would be.

264

'No stone unturned, Jimmy.' Her tone was too sharp for a man who was her friend and had a right to bring this up. She knew that, closed her eyes and tried to make amends. 'You know what I'm like. If there's a problem I'll take the blows, and anyway your retirement day is in sight. What are they going to do now ... arrest you for following an order?'

He caught the humour in her reply and threw it back. 'You were born to get up people's noses – it's what you do. Consider it done and I'll call Felicity now. She's a big mate of Elaine Tenant, isn't she, so I'm sure she can swing it for a couple of days. What are we looking for though? That's the first thing she'll ask.'

'What's not there that should be. Mick and Danny Goldstein have suggested problems in the investigation team. If there was something wrong and a fit-up then it's what's not there.'

'What about you?'

'I'll go and see Charlie MacKay on my own; I'll pick up a hirey. Set up a meet anywhere that suits Adams and I'll go and see him, or he can come to me. Whatever.'

'Charlie MacKay ran the Bellshill op from the back.'

'Those coincidences again. He runs the Dalton murder and here he is just when we're in the game.'

McGovern would have gone through a wall for Macallan, and she knew that. They were stepping into dark waters – they both knew that as well, although neither could have explained why. The gods were drawing a number of people together, because some crimes can never be washed away without retribution and atonement.

Macallan slipped back into bed, stared at the ceiling and tried to understand what was troubling her, but there was nothing apart from that deep instinct. There were people she'd never met who had to answer for their sins, and at some stage she'd face them and listen to their confessions. Macallan had rejected all forms of religion but wondered why there were forces that drew her to these people. Was it something unresolved in her own life, a recognition that she was no better than the men and women she accused?

Jack turned and threw his arm around her. 'Go to sleep.'

She kissed him, then put her legs back over the edge of the bed and sat there lost in her thoughts for a moment, unaware that Jack had propped his head back up on the pillow and was watching her without speaking. She padded through to the kids' bedroom and lowered herself into the wooden chair that had belonged to Jack's grandmother. As she stared at them, watching for the movements in their chests that proved they were okay, Jack came in behind her and put his hand on her shoulder.

'They're wonderful, and they're all ours. Imagine that?'

Jack always managed to say the right thing. She pulled the back of his hand to her lips and held it there long enough for him to recognise she was having all those doubts again. He knew how to see her through them now, and although he was still learning, they were getting stronger – it was just a case of hoping nothing came at her in those moments of weakness.

'Bed.' He took her arm and she followed him back to their room. She managed to sleep, which was its own form of miracle and the result of the comforting effect the old house had on her.

Across the Irish Sea Brenda McMartin's body ached for rest, but apart from occasional lapses into half sleep she forced herself to stay awake. The room was dark apart from the lamp behind her chair where she read Jacquie Bell's article for the third time. She'd never thought

Tommy McMartin's name would rise to the surface again, and it was another bad omen. Her world was full of bad omens, and on the same page there was another one to ponder: Macallan, the detective who'd visited her in hospital the night she was taken apart in Edinburgh. The same detective who'd got so far into her bones she'd tried to get to her with broken ribs and an A4 sheet of injuries. She'd been left moaning on the floor, cursing in frustration at this woman who looked down on her and sneered.

She kept snapping her head up at the slightest noise, waiting to identify the source then calming again. She eventually dozed and the paper slipped from her hands onto the floor.

She woke again with a start and although there was no sound she was sure an ice-cold hand had brushed her neck. She stood up and gripped the sawn-off, her chest heaving. There was no one there, and she would have believed it was just a draught, but everything was closed up tight and there was little or no wind outside. She never moved a muscle for a couple of minutes, but still nothing moved. She walked round the doors and windows and checked them all, but they were as she'd left them the last time. There was no one else in the house, only her nerves firing erratically.

A mug of black coffee and a couple of tabs later she sat back in the chair and tried to settle down till she felt it again – a cold rush of air, but this time running across the left side of her face.

'What the fuck?'

She stood up again, peering into the darkness, but once again there was nothing, and she wondered if she was becoming delirious with the pile of highs she was forcing into her system. She realised she had to get out of the house, even if only for a short time, or she'd end up howling at the moon. It was time to take care of one last piece of business, which she'd do in the morning, and then she hoped the man selected to come for her wouldn't hang around. She was exhausted and had carried her burden far too long.

46

Jack drove Macallan to the airport for her flight to Glasgow in the morning and she sat in the back with the little ones on either side of her. They were wide awake but subdued because they knew she was leaving them. When they said their goodbyes, Jack held her close. 'I love you, you know. We'll be over in a couple of days and then there's lots to do to get this wedding off the ground.'

'Can't wait,' she said. 'These two are going to steal the show, not their old mum and dad.' She leaned down and pulled the two small faces into her and breathed them in as if she needed it to live.

As the plane lifted off and bumped through the turbulence, Macallan peered out at the city fading below the spots of cloud and sighed as she thought what a long trail it had been to where she was now. The wedding was rushing towards her, and she wanted to put the Tommy McMartin thing to bed. She was confident that was possible because this wasn't a needle-in-the-haystack job. The players were all there, and somewhere in the evidence she might find the lies. All she had to do was keep pushing and something would give, she was sure of it. She yawned and managed to drop off for twenty minutes.

The appointment with Macallan was fixed for 10 a.m. so MacKay could take care of the morning nonsense and calls that had to be made to senior officers to make them feel wanted and important. Most of them were a complete waste of time, but he was a master at massaging the egos of nonentities and did it on autopilot. The call he received at 9.30 a.m., though, pissed him off, and he felt as if someone had reached around his guard and landed one.

'They're what?' he said back down the phone, though he'd heard it perfectly the first time.

Slaven knew what the effect of this news would be and was glad he wasn't in the office with MacKay. 'They've got permission to look at the HOLMES system for the Dalton murder, boss. Doing it this morning, and Jimmy McGovern has an analyst with him. Just thought you'd want to know.'

MacKay put the phone down, tried to keep it together and wasn't quite sure why he was so pissed off. He worked hard on the image of being super cool, but this manoeuvre had scratched some nerves. The woman hadn't even bothered to give him the courtesy of a personal call to look at the case he'd overseen. Not any case – the Tommy McMartin case. Getting McGovern to do it showed a lack of respect for the rank. It hadn't bothered him at the time, but the pressure was building and he was creating areas of blame.

He made a couple of calls to executive-level tossers who he could beat up because he had the goods on them. It was closed doors and bad excuses all the way, which meant she had at least as much clout as he did. He called Slaven back, told him to make sure they looked like they were giving every cooperation but that one of their own operators from the investigation was there to 'help' them look at the system. 'I want to know what they look at. Every detail. You hear me?'

Slaven put the phone down and had that gut feeling again that the more he saw of MacKay the more he saw too much ambition. He'd only worked for him for a while but had picked up whispers that there were a couple of rotting skeletons lurking in his particular cupboard. Not dirty money but favours for favours from all the wrong people. Slaven was a practical detective, quite happy to alter the facts where necessary, but there were boundaries, and he had no love for MacKay. If there was a sniff of anything approaching a train crash then he'd stick him in and watch him burn. As far as he was concerned it would create a vacancy at Super level; Slaven was every bit as ambitious as his boss and had his own career path to navigate.

It took the intervening period for MacKay to get a grip on himself, and he spent a few minutes in the washroom adjusting his tie, smoothing his hair, removing small imaginary flecks from his suit and applying just a splash too much of the expensive cologne he kept in the office for special visitors. When he got the message that she was waiting downstairs he called through to one of his DCs to bring her up.

MacKay changed his position a couple of times in the chair, trying to create as casual an impression as possible. He looked up at the knock on the door and hadn't really thought what to expect because he rarely considered that other people could match what he offered. He'd seen a couple of grainy shots of her plus a few where he'd googled her name to study her background but that was all. The woman who walked in the door and smiled looked a little plain at first glance, and that had been his impression from his research. When he stood up and walked round the desk to her he felt that knot in his stomach that tended to tighten when he was reminded that he was human and flawed. In his case the flaws were deep and poisoned.

MacKay realised that his initial impression of a plain woman could not have been more wrong. Certainly the clothes were more businesslike than plain, but not unattractive; the hair was short and the only style was an almost male side parting that looked like it required little maintenance. She even had the confidence to allow a few grey strands to stand out as proof that she didn't care what her appearance said to other people.

Close up he felt almost betrayed by what he saw in her face. The eyes sparkled sea green with an almost imperceptible slant upwards that must have been introduced to her genes from somewhere in the furthest eastern edges of Europe. Her skin was pale, almost cold looking, but the smile – the smile was that of a confident woman who knew exactly why she was there.

Before they'd even spoken a word to each other MacKay struggled to equate this woman, who looked like she would crumble if enough force was applied, with the stories of the SB officer who'd fought the paramilitaries during the dark days of the Troubles. She'd made high-profile arrests in Scotland, and he made up his mind that she must have achieved it all off other people's backs. After all, that's how he did it.

Macallan gave MacKay the benefit of the doubt, even though it was clear that McGovern had his concerns about the man – and he was usually a decent judge of these things, despite his tendency to look for straight lines. McGovern only saw good guys and bad guys, whereas she saw the world in more shades of grey, which was perhaps a reflection of her own flaws and weaknesses. She knew more than anyone that there had been moments when she'd wanted to commit her own crimes, when she was close to and witnessed what other people were capable of.

'So far this is all routine, and I just want to make sure we've covered all the angles. It's the age we live in I suppose. Jacquie Bell's story has added a bit of edge to it all, and of course the reference to Tommy McMartin in the weekend story makes it all the more important we can answer anything that comes our way.'

MacKay relaxed slightly and was even more convinced that this was a female who'd created a big reputation based on what she could take from other people's efforts. He was certain her move from investigation meant she was just another desk jockey dotting the *i*s and crossing the *t*s. He could control it, so there was probably nothing to fear.

She pulled out a notepad and laid it on the table as she scrabbled about in her bag for a pen. 'If it's okay, Charlie,' (they'd reached first names by this time, although there was little warmth developing between them) 'I'll take a few notes about the original investigation because, to be quite honest' – she paused and locked her eyes with his – 'we've had a suggestion that Tommy wasn't the person who killed Mickey Dalton!' Then Macallan did the smile, all eyes, teeth and warmth.

'I beg your pardon?' He'd been suckered by the timing, weight and delivery of the question; the measure of inner calm he'd almost regained while he was waiting for her was shattered. MacKay struggled for the right answer, knowing that straightforward anger would put him at a disadvantage.

Macallan watched as if she'd just delivered an unre-turnable shot right at the beginning of a game. She'd knocked him off balance, and in these kinds of mind games it was hard to recover if the first shot found its mark. 'Oh, it'll probably turn out to be a dead end, and as far as I'm aware the evidence was overwhelming. I take it you were satisfied with it?'

He tried to work out whether she was playing a game or genuinely covering the bases on something that was nothing. Normally he would have gone for the latter, but he was no fool. Thinking she might be more of a good actress than a detective had been plain wrong, and he already had that one registered. He reminded himself that this woman had been trained to fight against paramilitaries and would be skilled in all the dark arts. He tried to play it safe, doing the best he could with a returned smile plus the assurance that he'd do anything to help and that of course the evidence was watertight.

'I wish every case was that clear, Grace. If there had been any doubt I'd have been the first to consider it.' He tried to act relaxed but no one can when a lie is partially exposed. She saw it in the shape of his mouth, the eyes that didn't quite open enough and how he flicked his hand to his face. There was tension there, but she didn't want to overwork it so eased off and ran into some routine questions that would let him relax for a few minutes.

As they proceeded Macallan started to press again, asked him whether any lines had not been followed and watched him lie through his clenched teeth. It was all there in his face: something from the original investigation – maybe just some corners cut, maybe human error – but it was there, and she knew the bastard had thought it would never see the light of day again because the case was 'watertight'.

The atmosphere in the office had chilled, and any pretence that they were two senior officers trying to do the right thing for God and the law was dropped altogether. His phone went a couple of times and he'd had enough – he needed to think and get Macallan out of his office. But she stubbornly refused to move and did a neat line in Lieutenant Columbo quotes with several 'just one more thing' questions she was able to keep pulling out of a hat. His nerves had been barely holding and eventually unravelled completely.

'Look, Superintendent, unlike you I'm busy. That's enough of these questions that have wasted my time. And while we're at it, I wish you'd come through me to look at my HOLMES system for the Dalton murder.' He stood, trying to take control and dominate a situation he'd already lost.

Macallan sat back calmly and looked up at him for a moment. She could smell corruption even under the eighty-quid-a-bottle cologne. 'We haven't wasted a moment here, Charlie – quite the reverse. I've found it very revealing. Second point is that it's not your HOLMES system, and I don't need your permission to look at it. I thought you would have worked that one out for yourself. We both have friends at the top table.'

She was satisfied, realising that she was moving into those dark places again and wanted to see what was there in the past, concealed by lies. She stood up, gathered her papers and nodded to MacKay, whose colour had deep-ened. He knew he'd underestimated the woman opposite and that she wouldn't let it go; she'd sensed the lies and had an insatiable appetite to find the source.

'I'll see you again,' she told him. 'By the way, I'm going to see Slab McMartin at some point. Just to show that I'm being open about what I'm doing. The other thing is, if you happen to have an address for Big Brenda McMartin, do let me know.'

She watched a small flicker in his cheeks and wondered what it meant. The threads would come together – she was sure of it.

MacKay never answered and watched her walk calmly out of his office. He sat down, and for a man who tended to avoid company away from the job (indeed almost relished the lack of it), he felt lonely. It was one of those rare occasions he couldn't work out a plan, because he didn't quite know what Macallan would be coming back with the next time.

But there would be a next time – that was a no-brainer.

47

Jimmy Adams didn't want to go near Glasgow so had agreed to meet Macallan in Perth, and she'd arranged an office in the local station. The old HQ building looked like it had been designed as a celebration of unimaginative blandness and made of grey Lego. It would do the job though, and Macallan had time to think on the hour-plus drive from Glasgow. There was a lot to consider, and she called McGovern to see how he was faring.

'Good so far but a lot to do. As usual Felicity seems to know exactly where she's going. Think we'll stay overnight if that's okay, so we can work late and get an early start here again.'

'Any problems?' Her gut told her that MacKay would make some attempt to keep eyes and ears on what they were doing. Especially if the bastard was dirty.

'There's a DC who was on the original HOLMES team here to help us out if we need to know anything from the investigation. Apparently Charlie MacKay wanted to give us as much help as possible.'

Macallan paused for a moment and a grim smile tightened her lips. 'Watch that one. You were right about

277

MacKay, and there's something wrong with this one. We just need to find it.'

'We always just need to find it. But Felicity loves this stuff, and if it's there she'll do the business.' He said he'd get back to her if they hit something.

When Macallan arrived at Perth, Adams was waiting in the reception area. As far as the locals were concerned he was a routine witness and there to give a statement.

Adams stood up. He looked nervous and not the image of a man who'd worked as an enforcer for Slab in his day. His hair was razored, but what was visible was white, and although the face below was blurring with the years, she thought he'd probably been an attractive guy in his day, if you were into hard men. Even though he wasn't tall, his shoulders were wide, and he didn't carry any weight. When she stuck out her hand he looked down and seemed surprised that a detective would want to shake – the ones he'd met in the past had tended to batter his ribs, and that was on a good day.

They settled into the office and when Macallan asked him if he wanted anything he said no; his voice was quiet and again not what she would have expected. He'd asked for the meeting, but she had no idea what he wanted to say, so she tried to open it up.

'You asked for this meeting, Jimmy. Where do you want to start?'

'First things first, Superintendent. I want to make things right for Tommy McMartin. No way I give evidence in court though, doesn't matter what you do. I tell you this story then it's up to you.' Adams had found his confidence again – his voice had gained in strength and he began to talk like the man he'd once been.

Macallan considered his words and decided that if that's what he wanted then fair enough, and she sensed something in his tone that made her decide there was no way she would refuse the offer. She'd seen it so often: that need to unload the burden of guilt. Macallan had been in rooms with men who'd filled graveyards with bombs and guns, and watched them sob like children as they tried to undo terrible events with the truth.

'That's okay with me. There's no tape machine in here and my notebook's still in my bag, but you have to realise it depends what you have to say, and if there's something said that needs me to intervene then I'll do it. You understand?'

Adams thought for a moment and nodded. 'What happens if I tell you what really happened to Mickey Dalton?'

Macallan tried not to show the impact of his words, but it was impossible. She shifted in her seat, trying to suppress her interest, and wondered if this was the moment the lies would come out into the light. It happened every now and again, but often enough gangsters would come forward with what seemed like red-hot information only for it to dissolve when it was exposed to examination. They did it for all sorts of reasons – getting even, removing opposition, women, an endless array of petty grievances – and Macallan had seen many of them herself. She had to be careful, because she was in a room on her own with him, and if what he said was any form of admission she would have difficult choices to make. It was a gamble, but she needed the truth, and no one could prove or disprove what had gone on in the room.

'Why, Jimmy? Why do you want to tell me this? Why are you here? I need that first.'

'Truth is that there's a good chance someone might kill me. May be hard to believe but I need to clean the slate.' He stopped and waited for a reaction.

Macallan was experienced enough and had seen her share of liars to treat what he'd said with care, but the tears welling up in his eyes changed that, and again was something she'd seen only on rare occasions. Some old gangsters, like many old men, spent a lot of what was left of their lives looking back. After a life of crime and violence those retrospections could jolt the souls of the hardest men into confessing what poisoned their memories.

'Who wants to kill you?'

'Well, it can't be Psycho from what I've seen in the news. I was working with Big Brenda an' we've been rippin' off the other teams for months. We tried to take one of Frankie Logan's deliveries in Edinburgh but trouble was it was McManus carryin' the bag. It was a giant fuck-up.' He paused and looked embarrassed by his language.

'It's alright.' Macallan knew that by the book she should have stopped him, called in a second witness and started throwing cautions at him, but it wasn't going to happen, because when he'd said he would deny it later, she'd believed him, and every so often detectives were faced with the same problem. It was a matter of choice, and she wanted to hear his story.

The more he relaxed, the more he wanted to talk. She only interrupted him to ask if she could make some notes so she didn't lose anything. He was okay with that and couldn't stop even if she'd wanted him to. There was too much he didn't want to carry on into his last years without explaining himself. He wanted to go back to his sister some day and feel cleansed of his old life.

He started with the mess in Edinburgh and told her everything up to the point he'd left Brenda in the car park at the Braid Hills. When Macallan heard Woods' name she knew that the strands were drawing together. She was in the middle of a web of deceit and would have to face the men and women involved before it was finished.

'I want out of the life. The problem is Brenda's still out there, and the truth is I should have helped Woods. The boy's dead now an' I'm worried the Logans or Brenda will take Bobo. Boy's a numpty but I don't want to see him carved up. Brenda's lost it completely an' someone's bound to take her out of the game shortly. That's up to you.'

Macallan thought about it for a moment. On the plus side, he was talking about crimes where there would be no complainers, so in effect no crime. She was safe enough with that but knew there was more to come. 'Want some tea? I need a natural break and think we'll be here for a while, if that's okay?'

He managed a weak smile; he was warming to her. 'Sure could, mouth's dryin' up. Never made a confession to the polis in my natural.'

Macallan organised the brew, then called McGovern and gave him a brief summary of what had happened.

'Careful there. You could end up in a mess if he starts admitting and you've no corroboration.' He paused. 'But of course you know that.'

'I'll take the flak, but to be honest I think most of this is just going to tell us what happened rather than putting anyone away. Might be a history lesson at the end of the day, but it does sound like Big Brenda might be writing the invitations to her own funeral. Last thing: get the phone records from HOLMES for Mickey Dalton and let's see what they tell us. If there is another story about the murder, the phones are always the best start.'

'We're already on it and looking at them as we speak. Or rather Felicity is and I'm doing the easy stuff.'

'Anything, Jimmy ... Anything that doesn't make sense get right back to me. I guarantee that if there's a problem, we'll get the call to stick to the remit and back off. As it stands we're still doing the job but barely inside the lines.'

Macallan returned to the room and saw that some of the colour had been restored to Adams' face, and they both knew there was no going back. He couldn't have the life he wanted without revealing the darkest secret of all. The one he'd never been able to forget. His memory contained the faces of few of the men he'd hurt in his life, just blurred images and patches of red. Sometimes he remembered the sounds they'd made as they'd groaned and begged for relief, but not the faces, unless it was someone he'd known well. Occasionally it had been one of the team he'd worked with. It was just a fact of life that some of them fucked up or grassed to the law, and his job had been to hand out whatever sentence Slab came up with.

'Okay,' Macallan said, 'let's get back to work. If I'm being honest, it might be there's not much we can do about the other robberies but there you go.' She waited and watched Adams weigh everything like the old pro he was.

'Look, nothing changes. Goggsy's a goner, and I can't make a bit of difference now. I don't go in the box, and if anyone asks I still deny this. Nothin' the polis can do to me that'll hurt me now. I don't give a shit about the other dealers losin' gear – I'm here about Tommy and Brenda.'

Macallan sighed – she didn't want to lose whatever it was he had. She knew it might be the only chance to discover what had happened before Tommy McMartin's suicide.

'Go on, tell me the story about Mickey Dalton's death,' she said, careful to avoid the word murder in case it spooked him.

For a moment he said nothing, and she watched a small

tic start at the edge of his left eye. Breaking the habit of a lifetime was clearly putting him under enormous strain – grassing was easy once you'd done it a few times, but the first one was always hard.

'Tommy didn't kill Mickey Dalton.'

He let the words hang in the air before he spoke again. Macallan felt the muscles in her jaw tighten. Here it was, a small window into the events of the past. Danny Goldstein and Andy Holden had believed Tommy when there wasn't a shred of evidence to support his story, but it was those age-old instincts beyond explanation that had told them the truth. Given the nature of their positions both those men should have humoured Tommy but never believed a word.

'How do you know this?'

'I was there. Well, I drove Brenda to the job. She went in an' done the thing herself an' I stayed in the car. I was with Crazy Horse the few days before it an' we scouted the boy Dalton. No one told me why. "Just do the fuckin' job," was all I got. Watched him, an' I remember Crazy Horse nearly pissed himself when we seen the boy meetin' up wi' Tommy. It was a set-up but don't ask me why. I wasn't told, but they did it and set Tommy up for it. Seemed weird at the time because Tommy was a star, but in my game, you just never know.'

'Tell me more. If that's it then given Tommy and Crazy Horse are dead and Brenda's unlikely to admit anything, it remains just a story.'

Adams looked slightly annoyed. Like most criminals he thought sufficiency of evidence in their world was the same as the law of the land. Macallan saw it and worked to keep him going in the right direction.

'We need more. Something that I can investigate. Pain in the arse but it's the way the system works.'

'Your side were involved. Brenda made a call to Slab

when she came back to the car. I heard her talking, and it sounded like Slab was going to call some suit. Don't know who he was but she made the call that night. Told Slab to get the troops to go to the flat. I'll never forget it.'

Macallan tried to work the information quickly and decide where to go with Adams. It was hard to know if this would fly, and she could imagine trying to get anyone interested in what an unnamed source had told her would be difficult. Unnamed sources came up with theories every day, and almost all of them were a waste. The trouble with this one was that she believed every word. She rolled the dice.

'You sure you won't give evidence?'

'One hundred per cent. I've told you what happened. You do what you want with it.'

'What about registering you as a CHIS?'

'Not goin' to happen, Superintendent.'

Macallan leaned back and stretched her back, which felt like someone had turned her muscles into reef knots. 'Can I talk to you again if I need to?'

He nodded and seemed relieved.

'There's somethin' else I need to tell you,' he added. He didn't wait because it was what really burned inside him. In another life, he might have kept the story about Mickey Dalton's murder and taken it to his grave. After all, what difference did it make after Tommy's death? But this he needed to get off his chest.

'Big Brenda'll take a few with her before she gets her ticket stamped. Woman's a mess an' been fucked up since she was a kid. Years ago, when she was still in her teens, I got a call from Slab an' drove him to the river. He was pissed an' ravin' like he'd lost the plot. Know what I mean? We were gettin' rid of a bairn. It was wrapped up in a sheet, but there was blood. Picked up Slab and the wean at his place, but Brenda was there, moanin' an' greetin' when we took the thing away. Can't get away from that night. It was a fuckin' sin.'

Adams turned grey as he told the story and began to shake with emotion. Macallan leaned back in her chair, trying to absorb what had been said. Another horror story. Something that had happened on a dark night years ago and nearly lost in time, but it was something even a man like Adams couldn't handle, couldn't explain and couldn't carry any longer.

'Whose kid?'

'Don't know, Superintendent, but had to be in the family, if you know what I mean? Christ, maybe it was Slab's – these things happen. Slab never told me, an' I was his right-hand man back then. Truth is, I don't think he would've called me if he'd been sober. Only mentioned it once and said if I ever talked about it he'd pour a can of petrol over me and light it himself. He'd do it too. Anyway, he was the boss an' we'd been through a lot so I never needed a warnin'. After that he was never the same wi' me. Eventually he had the turn and then I was punted onto Brenda's team. He hardly ever spoke to her an' Crazy Horse unless it was work, but fuck knows what it was all about.'

Adams leaned forward, clasped his hands to his face and sobbed for the first time he could remember. Macallan felt weak and unable to make the right decision. Horror: it existed everywhere. People went about their lives and rarely came across it, but it was always there, just waiting in the shadows.

She leaned over and gripped the back of Adams' hand for a moment, told him she was taking a break and went outside where there was a cold weak sun trying to burn through the haar that had drifted over the old city of Perth.

She leaned back against a wall and tried deep breathing.

What had she said to McGovern? Routine. The job was routine. She shook her head and tried to look forward. If Adams refused to repeat a word it might all be useless, but she'd try and find out what she could.

She asked herself who the truth was for and wasn't sure she liked the answer. It was as much for herself as anyone else, because no one would really care if all she came up with was a history lesson, but Adams' story meant Big Brenda might be both a culprit and a victim.

It didn't matter – she had to try and find out. Along the way she might work out whether or not it was true that a suit was involved on the night of Mickey Dalton's murder.

She went back inside. Adams' colour was still ashen, but he'd composed himself.

'Have to go, Superintendent. Make sure Bobo's okay and that Brenda doesn't start her own wee war.'

'One last thing then. According to our intelligence no one knows where she is. Any ideas?'

'I'm the only one who does know that one, Superintendent. See, I was her driver until last week, and she treated me like a numpty. Trouble was she almost forgot who I really was until I decked her. Drove her there a few times and that would be her safe house. Think she liked to go there when she was down. That happened a few times. Can't remember the number but I can give you directions. When you get there, it stands on its own so no chance of missin' it.'

He gave Macallan the directions and then wrote them down for her in her notebook. She had to check them back with him because the writing was almost illegible.

'Don't suppose you have a phone number for her as well? We have a number, but it doesn't seem to be used that much. Seems like she has a spare safe one. No more than I'd expect.'

'No problem.' Adams looked pleased that the informa-tion he'd given had pushed her buttons. All he wanted was to stop Brenda before she did any more damage, and especially if it involved Bobo. 'There's only two or three people know this number so chances are she'll still have it.'

Adams scribbled the number into her notebook, and this time she could just about decipher it without help.

When Adams stood up, Macallan offered her hand, which he took briefly but avoided eye contact. It had dawned on him that he'd let her see too much of what he was carrying and he felt ashamed.

Macallan got back into the car, called McGovern and asked him how it was going. He said he'd put her on to Young, who wanted to speak to her.

'What've you got, Felicity?'

'Well, perhaps nothing, but you wanted to know if anything seemed to be missing that should be there. We started with the phone records and there might be something or nothing. The investigation team did the usual and got phone records for both Mickey Dalton and Tommy. The thing is they appear to have requested the subscribers for most numbers but not all. There seems to be a pattern, and one number in particular that Dalton was in touch with roughly once a month at first and then more often until about four weeks before the murder. Then the intel runs out. To be fair, it could be that they had their culprit straightaway so they maybe just cut some corners – there's nothing too unusual about that. I'm also tempted to say some sheets are missing, but again that may be nothing.'

Macallan didn't want to start charging down blind alleys but it felt worth following up. 'See how it compares to the stuff Danny Goldstein gave us. Keep at it and we'll have a meet first thing in the morning in Glasgow. See you then. Oh, and could you put Jimmy on?'

She gave McGovern the directions to Brenda McMartin's safe house and asked him to track down the full address and any information on the house. 'Make sure no one knows about this information till I decide how to play it. By the way, I think I have a phone number for Brenda. Do the necessary and see what comes back.'

She headed back to Edinburgh, her mind swimming with the options and possible bear traps she would have to navigate to get to the truth.

As Macallan made her way home, intelligence officers were analysing what had been recovered from the locus at Bellshill. They had the phones taken from Woods, McManus and Abe Logan. These numbers were always a rich source of intelligence, and the safe number for Brenda McMartin was in Woods' phone. They hadn't realised it yet, but it was only a matter of time.

48

Brenda McMartin had nearly chain-smoked her way through a packet of twenty watching the front gate of Slab's home. She'd never thought of him as her old man or plain old Dad, just Slab. That summed him up well enough as far as she was concerned. She didn't mind waiting, as there wasn't much else she could do now apart from sit in her own place and listen for the sound of intruders. She was even past caring about that and had started to put on her favourite band, The Proclaimers. *Pity the boys came from the east*, she often thought, but she forgave them given the pleasure she got from the music and particularly the lyrics, which she thought never got the cred they deserved.

'Bring it on,' she kept mumbling over and over again. She was holding conversations with herself about what was to come; her marbles were coming loose and scattering in all directions.

It was nearly 10 p.m. when a woman wearing a long dark coat left the house and closed the door behind her. She was Slab's sister-in-law, lived nearby and as far as Brenda was concerned she was the human equivalent of a starving vulture. She helped look after Slab between visits from his carers. It was her job to check him in the evenings, but Brenda was sure she was robbing the old gangster for everything she could get her hands on. She was supposed to sit with Slab till the next carer arrived but Brenda knew she fucked off for a couple of hours before the relief came.

'Fuckin' cow!' she snarled, thinking it would be good to set fire to her place when she was in it, but she had enough to deal with. 'Maybe in the next life, girl.' She hissed the words in a stream of tobacco smoke.

Slab had really pissed off the whole family by refusing to die year after year; in fact, all he'd done was make sure the organisation and family collapsed in on itself. Brenda hadn't seen him for weeks, but every so often she'd sit outside at night and watch the place for hours. Occasionally she would go in and visit because she knew seeing her really wound him up. Brenda had hoped that her just being there might bring on a fatal stroke, but no luck so far. For years the only time they'd talked was if he had a job for her, or Crazy Horse when he was alive, and they were no more than staff who excelled at violence as far as he was concerned. He would be pissed off if he knew it was her pulling the rip-offs and dragging the name McMartin through the sewers, but then again, she thought he might have already worked that one out. Where once they'd been feared and respected, there was nothing left but ruin and dead men.

She waited, had another smoke and took as much time as she needed to be sure that she could have some quality time with Slab. It was time to say goodbye to the man she despised more than any human being she'd ever met. That was saying something, but this was a special night for her and the man inside the beautiful old red-stone villa. He'd come a long way; she remembered the stories of how he had battled and knifed his way through the gangs to take their family to a style of living that was a universe away from the concrete disaster areas they'd been brought up in.

Nothing was moving in the street, and she figured that the neighbours should be pretty well settled in for the night. It didn't really matter because she didn't intend to cause a racket. For such a big woman, she was incredibly light on her feet, and like a true pro she inspected the perimeter of the house, just in case. Even though she knew he was on his own till the next carer came in or he pressed his alarm, she checked for problems.

When she was satisfied she stood at the back of the house and let the cool night air and sounds wash over her. Blend with the night before you make your move – that's what the old gangsters had taught her and Crazy Horse when they were learning the trade.

If necessary she would break in, but she wanted to check other possibilities first and knew the old bastard always insisted on having fresh air in the bedroom both in summer and the coldest of winters. He said it was how he'd lived as a boy and it had helped make him strong.

She managed to get onto the solid wooden roof of the conservatory and then climbed the few feet up to the balcony outside Slab's room. The French windows were slightly open, and Brenda smiled towards the dim light visible through the heavy curtains that puffed occasionally in the light night air.

She crouched down again and waited for a full two minutes. All her senses were searching for warnings, making sure he was really alone and that some unexpected visitor hadn't turned up in the wrong place at the wrong time.

After thirty seconds, she picked up the gentle rhythm of almost inaudible snoring. Not the full-blown snorting of a strong young beast but the weak old lungs of a man with little left to give. There were voices, but she had nothing to worry about – it was football pundits talking shite for ridiculous money. Old Slab loved the game and all that came with it.

She stood up, opened the French window wide enough to let her pass and pushed the curtains back so she could slip inside, pulling them behind her.

The bedroom seemed stuffy despite the open windows, and the smells hit the back of her olfactory nerves. The room was spotless because Slab had always been almost obsessive about hygiene, even when he was torturing someone, and he'd always insisted everything was disinfected after he was finished. She picked up the smell of bleach, which she hated. It was mixed in with all those other chemicals that abound where someone struggles with the end of their life.

Slab was propped up in the old recliner that had been his favourite chair since her mother had been alive. The bed was made up behind him, but he preferred his seat. The oxygen mask was on, and he looked peaceful enough for a man who should have had so much on his conscience. There was a tartan travelling blanket on his lap, and he was wearing a sweater with the sleeves pulled up to his elbows – another old habit that still hadn't died.

He'd been weak when she'd last seen him, but now there was even more evidence of decline. The forearms that had once been of Popeye proportions were thin, and his puffed blue veins stood out against the receding, almost yellow, muscles underneath. His hair was no more than wispy strands scattered around the dull skin on the top of his head, and the stubble across his chin and cheeks – which had caved in a long time ago – was rough and patchy. She looked almost in wonder at the man who had terrorised the city at one time, whose brute strength was legendary and who had even thought to punish a couple of assassins with a concrete slab.

'Wish they could all see you now.' She said it in no more than a whisper, but his eyes flickered for a moment as some deep instincts reacted to the subtle changes Brenda had brought into the room with her.

As Lionel Messi scored another wonder goal on the TV she slipped off her shoes at the door and took the five steps that put her right over her father. There was no great rush and his eyes half-opened, although the lower edge of his eyelid could not lift completely to expose the eyeball. She smiled down at the man she hated so much and it felt good; for the first time in a while she felt a true rush of pleasure. Alone with her father, no witnesses and neither of them with anything to live for. It was a special moment, and she wanted to make sure they both experienced it to the full.

'Daddy.'

She'd never called him Daddy in her life, but it suited the occasion. In any case she liked the irony.

There was a tiny spark behind the dull tone of Slab's eyes. He was coming out of a deep sleep, and the pills made him groggy for a few minutes as his brain struggled with the messages trying to leap across damaged circuits. He made a sound: 'Nnnngh,' and it was somewhere between a word and a pitiful groan of recognition.

'What's that, Daddy?' She got down on her knees and put her head on his lap as if she was a loving daughter trying to give peace to the man who'd helped make her.

'Nnnngh.' He lifted his hands off the rests and they trembled above her head before they settled back on the chair.

Brenda lifted her head, stood up and leaned over with her lips to her father's ear. 'Remember what happened? I remember, Daddy.' She leaned back and found he was sweating. Just the reaction she wanted to see and enjoy.

Slab's systems worked slowly now, but his mind had cleared and he was frightened. It hadn't happened much as a young man, but he wasn't young anymore. Brenda hadn't come to hold his hand. She was torturing him, although not the way he used to torture people. This was different: slow and easy. No one to help him and he couldn't fight back.

There was another replay of Messi scoring yet another superb goal and the crowd roared in appreciation of the little genius.

Brenda looked round at the screen. 'He's brilliant, that wee man. Wish he was fuckin' Scottish ... Daddy.'

'Brenda ... please.' Slab got words out but it was an effort. Then he noticed the look in her eyes and saw the future.

His daughter walked over to the bed and very carefully took one of the pillows, doing her best not to disturb the neatly made up order. She stood in front of him again and let him take in what was coming. 'Now I'll just slip off the mask for a minute.' She was almost gentle as she did it. 'There we are. Bye-bye, Daddy.' She leaned forward again and whispered in his ear. 'I wish there was a hell so you could fuckin' burn.'

It was pretty easy really. Slab's terrified expression disappeared underneath the pillow she pushed over his face. She held it there firmly but not so hard as to cause bruising, and if he tried to struggle she barely felt a thing.

When it was done she watched his face for a full minute, staring at the point in his neck that she'd seen pulsing earlier. Satisfied, she took the pillow back to the bed and carefully smoothed it down till it was impossible to tell it had been moved. When the oxygen mask was back on his face he looked quite normal for a dead gangster. No blade sticking out of his chest or half his face blown off with a shotgun, as was often the case when you played the game in Glasgow.

'That'll do nicely,' she said into the room because her father certainly couldn't hear her anymore.

Brenda checked everything thoroughly, put her shoes on, slipped back through the doors and a few minutes later she was back in the car. She smoked another cigarette and stared at the house. She was glad that bit of business was done. There was a good stock of booze in her house and enough food to keep her going till they came for her. She decided she would try and get the Messi goals on Sky when she got home. They really were fucking beauties.

49

The same night that Slab McMartin died under his daughter's hand, Macallan was struggling to relax given the ideas and images that were swimming round in her mind. She tried to read but couldn't concentrate on the book for more than a couple of minutes at a time.

Eventually she managed to sleep and drifted towards her fears. It was night-time, nothing but darkness, and she couldn't distinguish a line between the sky and the land. She was standing by the river, which stood out in the blackness as if the light came from below, red and fierce. It was more like lava: viscous and treacherous. It flowed without a sound, and she recoiled because there were bodies in the hot mass, struggling to live, gasping in the torturous heat. They stretched out their hands to her, but she was frozen, unable to move her legs as she saw a man walk a few feet in front of her, look round and mouth a question, but there was no sound. Nothing.

Macallan wanted to ask him what he wanted but nothing passed her lips. The man smiled, and as he lifted a small bundle up to shoulder height above the river his lips moved again. He waited for her answer then dropped the bundle into the churning river. She watched in horror as a small arm detached itself from the bloody rags before disappearing. She started calling for help over and over but no one could hear her.

Macallan opened her eyes and reached for Jack, but there was only a cool place where he should have slept.

The dream had passed, and when her eyes closed again, Macallan slept peacefully. She knew how to deal with the demons now: when they came she thought of Jack and the children.

When she awoke the next morning Macallan pulled herself out of bed and couldn't avoid thinking about the work she was doing, the wedding and trying to make sure Jack and the children didn't come back to find her stressed up to the eyeballs. She was going to press hard on the Tommy McMartin case. The answers were close, and she had McGovern and Young, which could make the difference on getting answers. She owed Elaine Tenant for getting Young on loan – that had to have taken a deal of some kind. She marvelled again at how they'd progressed from outright hostility to respect, and it seemed to be entirely due to the fact that they both had the ability to compromise.

Macallan stuffed down some porridge and was on the road to Glasgow before the M8 clogged up like a chiplover's arteries, which it did most days. On arriving at Pitt Street, she found McGovern and Young both looking as if they'd been on the batter. She knew the eye bags came from a late night poring over what documents they had and probably annoying intelligence officers with requests.

'You two look well – been ill lately?' she asked. It was an old joke but they managed a joint tired smile.

'What we do for God and Nicola is no one's business.' McGovern tried too hard to look like it had just been another long night for the detectives, but his voice wavered slightly, and although Young looked tired, he looked knackered. That was something different given McGovern's health problems.

Macallan wanted to say something but kept it shut till she'd worked out the right form for the words. She'd made a mistake, a bad one and cursed herself for forgetting what was really important. They'd barely got started on this case and already she'd let herself become absorbed in it, despite everything she'd discussed with Jack and everyone else who cared about her. One of them was McGovern, the man who had walked quietly at her side through the horrors and hardly ever complained unless it was to protect her. They'd obviously done an all-nighter, which was just par for the course in investigation, but he'd been pushed behind a desk because he'd suffered a heart attack. It had only been a mild one but that didn't matter: Macallan knew better than anyone how important it was that what McGovern did was reasonable, and his doctor would not have approved an all-nighter. She told them they were going for breakfast on her and no arguments.

'Felicity, I need to talk to Jimmy on his own about another job. Go splash some water on your face and catch you outside in five minutes.'

Young picked up her bag and headed for the bathroom but had already worked out what Macallan was doing. She'd watched the dark marks spread like warning signs under McGovern's eyes during the night and had even asked him a couple of times to call it a night but all in vain. He was old school, and an admission that he couldn't last the pace would have been too much for him.

When the door closed Macallan pulled a chair from behind the desk and sat directly opposite and close to McGovern, who looked surprised but only for a moment because, like Young, he knew what was coming. In investigation work partners have no secrets. They might try to conceal them, but there's no space to hide from the other guy. They pick up all the non-verbals and the confessions that well up sometimes for no other reason than you're locked up together in a small world where the only person you can trust is the man or woman trying to help you scrape the dirt away from some dreadful crime or secret. Half the time they're the only person who really cares, and both sets of emotions and drives almost merge into one.

Macallan leaned forward and forced him to look at her. She noticed the small blood vessels that had littered the whites of his eyes overnight, the loss of fresh colour that a night's sleep would have given him. It was her fault, and she thought of his wife Sheena, and what he meant to her.

'Question, Jimmy. Tell me, exactly how do you feel right now? No bullshit or I'll get Felicity to bring Mick in to give you an old-fashioned CID interview.'

McGovern was a proud man and had always detested DOs who complained of exhaustion, which wasn't in the rule book when he'd first joined the department. Even though he realised he was wasting his time, for a brief moment he tried to act surprised. 'Okay, I'm just a bit tired. A good night's sleep and I'll be raring to go. We've found something – you were right again.' He almost looked like a schoolboy trying to cover some minor felony, dropping good news in to divert attention from the main problem.

Macallan was the most loyal of people to her friends, but she had that tough edge that meant she could take the hard decisions when needed. She'd already made up her mind that she would not risk her friend and then have to explain to the family who adored him why he wasn't coming home. 'Now you promised me you'd say if there was a problem, even though both of us knew you wouldn't. I could boot myself in the arse because I knew that and carried on, because I rely on you so much just to be there for me. I hardly questioned it when Elaine said you were available. That was selfish and stupid, but sometimes I'm like that. As Jack just told me recently.'

She stood up and tried to look at a drab grey sky through the grime that had caked the window for years. It was the beginning of another day's rain in Glasgow. 'You're going back to Fettes. You can work the intelligence there. I need answers quickly, and you can do that from there. They won't give me another officer to work this, you know that. So this is the script: we go and have breakfast, you finish what you're doing here and tomorrow you get to work in Fettes. There's a lot to do on the HOLMES stuff. Felicity can work here and pass the intelligence requests to you. Okay?'

'Don't do this, Grace. I'm fine.' McGovern hoped their friendship would buy him the time to finish the job and hold his head up. He knew Macallan was going to face some awful truths, and she would need someone at her side to uncover those secrets and deal with what they meant. He knew exactly the price she'd paid already, and she'd rebuilt her life, but she carried the memories like a virus that could reappear anytime.

'No arguments, please. I said at the start that at the first sign of a problem we rein it back for you. I know this hurts, but I can't risk you. There are too many people who care what happens. You were never Mick "I don't give a shit" Harkins. Hurting your family's not an option, is it?'

She gripped his hand and he stared at the floor, trying to avoid the truth. She let the seconds flow by while he absorbed what she'd said. It was hard watching such a proud man accept his fallibility, and she could have wept for him, but she needed to do for him what he'd done so often for her.

He took a deep breath and looked up at her. 'Tell the truth, I'm glad. I just can't do it anymore and thought I was going to keel over a couple of times last night. Christ, I used to work round the clock and come back for more. How does that happen?' He grinned but there was no warmth in the expression. 'I never saw the time passing.'

His shoulders seemed to have dropped a couple of inches and he looked beaten. In a way Macallan felt almost relieved because she thought he might use anger to relieve the blow to his self-esteem. It happened, and sometimes men needed something or someone to blame rather than admit the truth.

'It's fine. There's absolutely no shame in this, and I still really need you on my team. But please go home after we've had breakfast, kiss Sheena and the kids and get some sleep. Be at your desk tomorrow morning and, trust me, there's plenty to do. Felicity probably has a pile of intelligence requests ready to go. Am I right?'

'You're right, boss. Just be careful where you go with this. I'm not the only one carrying an injury. Am I right?' He managed a smile that resembled the real thing.

She put her arms round him. McGovern was right – they were both wounded, and more than they could ever admit.

'What's the plan today, then?' He said it with just a trace of envy. It was there but Macallan accepted it.

'I'm going to get to the heart of this. It's close, I can feel it. I'm going to buy you guys breakfast and tell you about Jimmy Adams, and you're going to tell me about what you've been doing all night.'

They found a decent restaurant that did breakfast. Young didn't need any explanation, and when Macallan said that McGovern would be doing the intelligence requests she breathed a quiet sigh of relief. She liked him a lot and was glad that he was being taken care of. Since she'd got involved with Mick Harkins she'd become even more aware what detectives were prepared to endure to get results, and it never ceased to amaze her. Indeed, it fascinated her, and in Mick's case was one of the things she loved about him, though he was certainly an advert on how not to behave in a responsible job.

They found a table well away from the two office types who were engrossed in reading notes and probably dreading a day full of meetings. The detectives ordered everything with toast on the side, while Young went for muesli and a glass of water. Macallan was already attacking the second fried egg by the time she started to talk about what had happened with Jimmy Adams. She kept it brief but divulged enough for them to get the smell of what they might be looking at and to understand that he seemed like the genuine article.

McGovern and Young had heard and seen their share of horrors in the past but the implication of what Adams had suggested was written all over their faces and they paled when she told them what had been said about Slab getting rid of a baby's body. Like all investigators they could harden themselves to most things, but whenever a child was concerned they felt as sickened as anyone else. Every so often some new story would unfold and prove again that human beings were capable of almost anything. There were no borders, and the only saving grace was that the vast majority of people weren't confronted with the atrocities unless they were unfortunate enough to be the victim or a witness themselves.

'What in the name of God does that mean with the kid? Was Slab the father then?' McGovern was no stranger to investigating incest cases and had done his share over the years.

Macallan shrugged. 'It takes us nowhere at the moment because Adams will close up if he gets an official visit or a request to stand as a witness. You know what these old-timers are like. This stays between us at the moment, but I'll disclose to Elaine to see where we go with it. Let's move on. Felicity, tell us what you've got so far.'

Moving on after such a revelation was difficult but it was the only way to do the job.

'Really interesting, and it may be something or nothing, but probably something if I was asked my opinion.' That was how Felicity tended to answer questions. The listener needed patience to get to wherever she was taking them. 'As I explained to you, the murder squad did request Mickey Dalton's and Tommy McMartin's phone records, because of course that would always be a priority job and would have stuck out if they hadn't.' She spooned a minute portion of muesli into her mouth and chewed while she flicked through a couple of notes.

Macallan looked at McGovern and winked. He grinned back because it could be infuriating but this was part of what made Young the character she was and it was all just part of the show.

'The team did check some of the numbers and requested subscribers . . . but not all of them. I thought at first that it might just be that the murder was solved right away and so they thought: why bother when there's such a weight of evidence? I've told you this already.'

She stopped again, sipped the water and looked at Macallan for a response.

'Yes, okay . . . and?'

'As I said earlier, there's a pattern in the omissions. There's one number that either contacts Mickey Dalton roughly once a month or he contacts the number. It seems stable for a while and then there's an increase up to about a month before the murder and then nothing.

The sheets for the period in those next few weeks prior to the murder are definitely missing. Might have been a coincidence, but of course we have the material Danny Goldstein gave us, and we've now had a chance to look at those.'

She sipped her water again, waiting till Macallan realised it was time for another prompt.

'Right, got that.'

'The sheets that Goldstein gave us cover that final period. The thing is that in the couple of weeks before the murder there's a flurry of activity between Mickey Dalton and the subscriber.'

'Do we have the subscriber?' Macallan asked, hoping there'd be an affirmative that was a straight arrow pointing at the answer.

'No, we don't, but I think it's relevant. The missing sheet makes no sense.'

'Get onto that one as soon as, Jimmy, and see what we can come up with.' Macallan sat back slightly disappointed, because nine times out of ten what seemed like a clue was nothing of the sort and cost effort for no result.

'There's more,' McGovern said, interrupting her thoughts. 'Always save the best for last. Given what we thought we might be looking at, I had a look through the original intel from the murder. Most of it was okay, but there's something interesting in the train of events.'

'Go on.' Macallan let the remains of her breakfast congeal on the plate.

'The police attending the locus were responding to an anonymous call about a serious disturbance. That's why the cavalry piled in. Thing is that when I thought about it, well ... Mickey was potted and Tommy was out for the count, so where was the noise? And there's no record of them getting a story from a neighbour that there was a rammy in progress. I checked the origin of the call and it went straight to the CID, who got the uniforms to go along, and they weren't far behind.' He paused to let it make a picture in her mind.

'So what we need to flesh out is this question: why would the CID be interested in a rammy?' Macallan saw the direction of travel. 'Keep digging.'

'Exactly.' The colour was back in Jimmy's cheeks and he was enjoying himself again. 'They got the call, walked in behind the uniforms and got themselves a top skull. Thing is, the person who took the "anonymous" call was Charlie MacKay. I got in touch with an old mate in the rubber heels and the suspicion up to that point was that the McMartins were getting a free run from the suits. Tommy's arrest meant that theory was out of the window and everyone was a winner, except the boy himself.'

Macallan glanced at Young and noted her look – it said that they'd found the key. There hadn't just been a series of coincidences – the raw stink of corruption was there now, still in the shadows, but Macallan would shine a light on it and see what it all meant.

'Anything else?' she asked. She was excited and revolted by it at the same time; they heard it in her voice and felt exactly the same.

McGovern was worried because he knew there was no holding Macallan back now – she'd walk into those dark places, and do it alone if necessary. There was no point in arguing – she wouldn't change her position. He knew her well enough to know that this one wasn't up for further debate. In any case he'd had to slip a couple of tabs from his prescription to ease the tightness in his chest. He'd had the warning and it was enough. He was risking it all, and he couldn't do that to Sheena and the children. His wife had invested so much in the lonely years waiting for him to come home, and she deserved the pay-off, which meant crossing the line together. He finished his summing up. 'That's what there is at the moment. We've started the ball rolling on Brenda's safe phone, tracing the calls, but the problem is we can't say it's a priority, because it's an old case and we're not reinvestigating, just filling in some background to Tommy's suicide.'

'I know.' Macallan bit her bottom lip, recognising that the implied warning was fair, but there was something that needed exposure and she wouldn't be stopped. 'I'll take responsibility, and we need to keep it tight for the moment. I'm going to see Elaine Tenant tomorrow and put it in front of her. Let her chew it over.'

McGovern nodded. He didn't want to say anything more at that point in case they ran ahead of themselves. 'Only other thing is that we should have Brenda's exact address and any other intel sometime today. Shouldn't be too much of a problem if Jimmy Adams is on the money.'

'Good.' Macallan seemed to drift for a moment then said it again. 'Right, you guys finish your breakfast. I'm going to see Slab McMartin. Think I'm safe enough – from what I hear his fighting days are all in his dreams. Probably looks completely routine if I go there, take a few notes and leave. He's still next of kin so on safe ground.'

'Do you have to see him?' McGovern asked, though he already knew what her answer would be.

'This is for all intents and purposes still a review of Tommy's death, and he's the closest relative we can find. I'm not going to say or do anything to raise his blood pressure at this point, and from what we've been told he doesn't care about Tommy anyway. After that I really need to sit down with Elaine and run this stuff past her before the next move. Hopefully you guys will get me a bit more ammunition.'

She stood up and raised her coffee cup in a mock toast to what they done, before heading out the door.

Macallan got into her car, tapped Slab's address into

the satnav and waited for a couple of minutes till her mind settled down and she could concentrate on the road. The wedding was another day closer. She had to force the pace, all too aware that in other places people would know she was coming and be making their own plans. That was the game: moves were being made on the chessboard and someone would win and someone would lose, though half the time everyone lost something.

There was no answer but she decided to head Slab's way anyway. She expected nothing special from him, but at least she could say she'd tried.

That assumption was on the money, because he'd been dead for several hours and wouldn't be talking to anyone this side of heaven or hell.

50

Macallan almost enjoyed the drive to Slab's house and felt relieved that McGovern's situation had been taken care of without too much grief. Her only concern was that he'd gone almost too easily, and if nothing else that confirmed he must have felt pretty washed out. It had been a bad oversight on her part, and she vowed to check on her friend at every opportunity until the job was finished.

Her train of thought was interrupted by the phone and even though she had hands-free she ignored nine calls out of ten, but it was Jack's name on the screen and she needed to hear his voice.

'How's my girl?' He sounded good, happy and she'd been surprised how excited he was about the wedding, expecting him to do the man thing of being slightly bored of the whole drama and horrified by the expense. There was none of that, and if anything, he was the one who wanted it to be a special day with bells and whistles added on. It was Macallan who wanted everything low key; it was her nature.

'Busy but getting there. How's my babies and poor old dog?'

'All good. The builders finished up early so we're heading back today. We have the car so won't arrive till later this afternoon. Is that okay? And how's work?'

'Are you kidding? Just can't wait to get a hold of you guys. We're still pretty busy, but I think a few days will wrap it up one way or the other.' She stuck to their agreement to keep the details well away from the family.

'One way or the other can mean a lot of things,' he said. 'As long as it's all wrapped up before the wedding.'

'God, Jack! Still sounds strange when you say it. After the wedding we'll be married.'

'That's the general idea, or else the celebrant will have really messed up and we'll have spent a fortune for nothing.'

'Okay, big man, I'll see you later then. Kiss the weans and clap the dog for me in the meantime.'

She finished the call and was trying to get used to the idea of being married as she turned into the street she had as the address for Slab McMartin. When she saw the patrol car and unmarked wheels she felt a knot wind tight in her stomach. It was fated: the job she'd been given was poisoned, not remotely straightforward, like looking for a clear image in a hall of mirrors. All she could see was distortion – shapes of things that barely made sense and never would unless she could find the meeting points, the places where the truth could let her see into the past. She was forming ideas but knew they could all be wrong.

When the young PC stopped her at the gate she pulled out her card and asked him who was in charge. He explained there was a CID officer still there and called him on his radio. A couple of minutes later an old suit came out of the front door and pulled off a pair of gloves before offering his hand.

'I'm DS Mark Dunbar, boss. Sorry, I wasn't expecting

anyone else to attend. We're more or less finished here. Is there a problem?'

Dunbar had a warm smile for an old soldier, and she thought he must have been one of the lucky few who'd managed to survive without despising the world. Mick Harkins said that if you could still smile at the end of your service you were either very sick or God loved you. Dunbar looked fit for a guy clearly round the half-century mark, and his suit was immaculate, another good sign that he still cared. She liked him and just knew he'd be good at his job.

He told her to come into the hall area and she explained as far as she could why she was there.

'What happened here then?' she asked when she was done. She already knew it was going to cause her problems.

'Well, maybe saved you a bit of work, boss. Old Slab finally cashed out sometime last night. I've known him for years and had a few run-ins with the family so I'm not their favourite DO.'

Macallan saw he was exactly what she'd thought and liked him all the more.

'As far as we can see it was probably natural causes, and the doc seemed satisfied. In any case, he was on his own although his sister-in-law was supposed to be there, but that's another story and there'll be a PM. There was no sign of any disturbance or forced entry, although the balcony windows were open. But apparently he insisted on that. Have a look round if you want. We're finished examining the room.'

Macallan said she'd just have a quick look, walked up to the bedroom and stood inside the door for a couple of minutes. The room seemed to be holding back on what had happened within its four walls.

Moving to the middle of the room she remained

motionless for another few minutes, waiting for some inanimate object to speak to her, tell her that this wasn't just a sick old man going on his way. She'd expected nothing from the visit to Slab's home but here it was again – Sod's Law. Or was it no more than an illusion concealing something else?

The curtains moved with an almost imperceptible whooshing sound in the fresh wind that had been increasing all morning.

Out on the balcony Macallan looked round at the view Slab must have seen thousands of times. He would have planned his moves and sentenced men to death in that same spot.

She looked over the rail and saw a few ivy leaves scattered round the top of the conservatory roof and trapped just under the ledges. In her imagination, she watched a dark shape clamber onto the roof area then scrabble up the tough branches of the old ivy that had spent its life covering the back of the house. The intruder was careful but couldn't avoid dislodging those leaves. *Get a hold of yourself, Macallan*, she thought.

She shelved the images, acknowledging how easy it was to get carried away with conspiracy theories. Maybe it was Sod's Law. It happened.

Back in the hall Dunbar asked her if she wanted to see anything else. Macallan said no, thanked him and took a step towards the door before stopping.

'Do you mind if I go back to the room for another look?' She again imagined the dark silhouette scrabbling up the ivy to Slab's bedroom. Two areas of her mind were in conflict. Why kill an old, done man? Why not? Hadn't he spent his life creating enemies? There had to be people who wanted to look into his eyes and savour his fear. There were no signs of a struggle, but someone that old and sick is easy to kill. Her head swam with conflicting scenarios.

Macallan stood on the balcony again and looked over to the conservatory roof. She was over in a second, lowered herself down using the ivy to hold her weight but careful to be as quiet as possible and cause no obvious disturbance. There they were round her feet, the result of her short downward climb: four ivy leaves, one slightly torn and the others just dislodged at the base of their stems. There were some paper hankies in her bag; she put them under her knees and got down where she could look under the ledges. There was a mixture of old muck and another three still-fresh ivy leaves trapped under the edges of the roof. It was nothing or something. If she started stirring it up that Slab had been murdered, that would be laying her head on the block and inviting the death blow. The ivy leaves only meant something if you wanted them to, and she'd be dragged off a case she had no right questioning. She'd be set up as the classic case of an investigator obsessed with conspiracies and unable to do the job she'd been tasked for. Slab was dead so who really cared?

'Thanks, Sergeant. That was good of you to give me access. Not really my place but old habits and all that.'

'No problem. Notice anything I've missed?' the DS asked. He would have been annoyed if he had. He was a proud man and always tried to be as thorough as he possibly could. He would never have asked the question in the first place, but he realised she was interested in something and that bothered him. However, even though he liked what he'd seen of Macallan, there was a difference of three ranks and that meant he had no leverage.

Sometimes the dice have to be thrown. Invariably it happens suddenly, without time to engage the conscious mind and weigh up the risks. It tends to draw nothing but a blank; however, like every gamble, sometimes it just comes off. Not because the player is a genius, just a risk taker who'll take the game all the way because the prize is to draw the stones back and be God for a moment. The only person who sees it all and why it happened the way it did.

'You ever get the impression old Slab had any of our side in his pocket?'

As soon as Macallan said it she almost recoiled at the implications of what she'd just done. She was taking the DS at face value, and that had gone wrong in the past.

Dunbar was a hard man to surprise, but Macallan had managed it. He was old enough and wise enough not to come straight back to her.

'Take a seat, Superintendent. That's a big question you've just asked.'

His smile had gone and he wondered about taking his own gamble on what she'd said. He decided it was fine, because he could come back at her without saying something that would end up in a libel case.

Macallan sat down opposite him and tried not to chew the edge of her finger.

'Some people reckon, besides myself I might add, that I was one of the best DOs in Glasgow ... but look where it got me.' He pulled out a pack of chewing gum and offered Macallan a piece, which she refused. He was struggling with withdrawals from his lifelong tobacco habit. 'I don't know why you've asked me that question. I know you're not the rubber heels, and as far as I know I'm clean anyway. And I saw the article that said you're looking at Tommy's suicide. So I guess you have your reasons for asking that.'

Macallan nodded and wished she'd just left it alone. 'I have my reasons, Mark. No problem if you don't want to answer, but I just had to ask.' She scraped the ridge of hard skin on her finger with her nail rather than chewing it like someone ready for the happy pills.

'I hassled these bastards for years and it cost me promotions. Someone stuck the knife in, and although I can't prove it, that's where I point the finger. Enough about me. The question is, did he have a friendly on our side? You can take it from me that he did. The Tommy McMartin case was a strange one and seemed completely against the grain at the time. What it did do was take the heat out of the suspicions that Slab was getting a free pass from us, or Strathclyde as it was at the time. Does that answer your question, Superintendent?'

Macallan still regretted it but nodded and thanked the DS, who had a list of questions in the way he was looking at her.

'Would you mind if I came back to you at some point, Mark?' She held out her hand and he took it.

'Anytime – anytime at all.'

Macallan headed for the car with more to think about. She was running out of places to go for the job. She could easily sit down and write a report that would close the whole thing down and no one would call it into question. She called Elaine Tenant at Fettes and told her she needed to talk.

'That's excellent, Grace, and I was going to call you. There's someone else who'll sit in on the meet, and we can do it today if you're on your way back?'

How things change – Tenant seemed genuinely pleased to hear from her. The reference to 'someone else' in the meet was intriguing, but it was the nature of what she was doing. It was apparent that some other box was about to be opened in Fettes, but she explained that Jack was on his way back and so they agreed to make it the following morning.

She was passing Harthill services when McGovern called and told her they needed to meet as soon as she was back.

'See you before I sit down in the morning with the Chief Super if that's okay?'

'Perfect, and Felicity will be there as well. Can't speak on the blower.'

After she'd hung up, Macallan put on some music – she needed something to soothe her strained nerves. She put on a Roberta Flack CD and the beautiful voice that belonged in heaven did its thing as she drove the car on autopilot, shutting off the problems she faced. The singer had always been Macallan's favourite musical treatment when things got tough.

As she glanced at the edges of Livingston slipping by on her left, the phone rang again and she saw the number but no name came up on the screen with it. She usually gave it a miss if that happened, but it was the third time she'd seen that number in a couple of days. The temptation was too much this time so she took the call, expecting some poor soul in a call centre trying to sell her something she didn't need. She said hello a couple of times and turned up the volume. Someone was on the other end of the line, and she wondered whether it was some perv hoping for a quick thrill.

'You called the wrong police officer, my friend. Now go and play somewhere else before I take a day off and come and get you.'

She realised she wasn't concentrating on the road and snapped, 'Look, you're wasting your time trying to frighten me. Now piss off.'

'It's okay, Grace.'

The line clicked off and she stared at the screen, which told her nothing. She had to hit the brakes to avoid ramming the back end of an old lady crawling along the inside lane. 'Jesus Christ!'

Some bastard had her number and was playing a game. She ran her fingers through her hair and saw she

315

was trembling. The caller had spoken in no more than a whisper but there was still something familiar about his voice. The problem was that detectives spent their lives meeting people who they dealt with then never saw again. Witnesses, villains, lawyers and just about every section of society. There would be a thousand voices leaving traces in her circuits.

Steady, Grace – it's probably nothing, she thought, although she didn't believe it and wished Jack was there. She ached for him and the children but reassured herself they'd soon be home with her.

Shortly after, Jack called to say they were just past Ayr, which meant they'd be home in a couple of hours. When she heard the dog barking in the background as if he was delivering his own message, it made her grin and briefly forget the previous phone call. She decided to nip into the Waitrose next door to Fettes and grab something nice for dinner that wouldn't take too much effort.

51

It felt like home again with the noise of the two little ones and the general chaos that a young family and a dog can create after time away from base camp. Macallan was almost overwhelmed by it; she kept closing her eyes and making sure that it was no dream. This family was all hers and they were happy together. It still didn't seem possible: Macallan happy with life.

When they'd eaten they decided to head for Inverleith Park before the children had to go to bed, and they let the dog run mad because there was always a good selection of hounds there criss-crossing the green fields. Jack knew Macallan was under stress, and he struggled to keep to their deal that her work shouldn't come home. He did the lawyer's thing and decided that as they were in the park, it couldn't qualify as the marital home. 'Talk to me. Something's up.'

'Thought we weren't allowed. That was the deal.'

He explained his legal interpretation, which made her smile. How on earth would she cope without Jack Fraser?

'It's a strange case, and in a way shouldn't bother me, but you know what I'm like.' She left out almost all of the details but did tell him about the anonymous call.

Jack looked round at her but didn't speak for a minute as they trudged slowly past the pond. They took a seat and pulled the children in close. He was just glad the kids couldn't begin to understand what their mother had to deal with. The dog had almost run its short legs off and jumped up beside them to complete the team. 'Don't know what to think about that. What do you think?'

'Difficult to tell. The world is full of people with nothing to do but hate themselves so they turn it somewhere else. You know what it's like – lawyers sometimes have the same problem. It's hard to separate all this stuff out.' She patted his arm and decided it was time to lighten the conversation. 'Anyway, I'll have this one closed off soon. It won't drag on, and God knows what we'll get at the end of it because they all seem to be dead or likely to die.'

Jack wished that was true, but he was surprised to find he wasn't frustrated at her struggling with another problem that would cost her. He admired that she could wade in and face her demons again. The difference now was that they were a strong family and all she needed these days was to come home, put her arms round him and then everything was okay again – she could deal with the consequences. In the past, she'd struggled with her problems alone.

Jack knew that eventually she would move on to some new challenge. He had the feeling that she just needed this case to prove she could still do it. Their life was moving on regardless, and he just had to help steer her on that course.

'Right, let's go home, you cook your man a nice steak and once the kids are bye-byes I'll let you chase me round the settee.'

She snorted a laugh and gave him one of those rare smiles that could light up her face and eyes. 'Okay, big boy, and I'll even give you a start.'

They headed home as the man watched them from across the pond.

52

He'd watched them from the time they'd left the house, following them as they wandered through the park and talked beside the pond. They seemed totally engaged with each other as they headed back home through Stockbridge, stopping occasionally and peering into shop windows as they talked and tried to restrain the dog heaving against his lead.

When he'd first met Macallan he could see she was so like him, involved with other people's lives but utterly alone. It was something that had almost reassured him, seeing others like him who wandered among the population like little islands. He'd always believed they were closer to each other than people like Macallan would ever like to admit.

It chewed that since he'd been away from the city somehow or other she'd changed lives. That wasn't supposed to happen, and the raw truth was that he would have been incapable of making the same change. It made him shake with rage that she could be a different person from the one he was sure could have wanted him in another life.

As he watched her look up at the big man at her side and brush something off his shoulder, it occurred to him that no woman had ever made such a small personal gesture with him, because he would have hated that level of intimacy. He remembered the way his wife and children used to look at him, could still almost feel the cold empty atmosphere in his own home that at one time had the same composition as Grace Macallan's family: two adults, a girl and a boy. The difference was that they had all detested each other.

He felt something like a vice grip his abdomen so hard he doubled over and groaned. Sweat poured out over his body, which felt sticky and cold even in the warm sunshine that bathed the streets. An old man put his hand on his shoulder and asked him if he was alright. He detested being touched by another human being and sprang back up, shoving his face close to the startled man, who took half a step back at what he saw in the stranger's eyes.

'Fuck off and keep your filthy hands off me!' He grabbed the old man by the jacket collar and pushed him away. The few walkers who saw the little incident shook their heads but decided not to get involved. The would-be Samaritan walked off in the other direction and felt ashamed that his physical strength had disappeared with his youth.

He was heaving in air and scanned the street for Macallan. He saw her with her little family further along the pavement, but they were moving slowly, as if they had all the time in the world.

He forced his emotions under control and moved along the street, taking the opposite side from her but guessing correctly that they were heading back home.

When they closed the door behind them he felt lonely. It was as if Macallan and her family were all he had left. This was his last mission in life, and when he tried to think of another purpose for his existence there was nothing but a vast empty space in his mind.

He pulled out his hip flask and swigged a couple of gulps of raw vodka. There was no pleasure in drinking now – it burned its way into his gut and would kick off the chronic acid indigestion that plagued him every time he put alcohol to his lips. Drink had been all that had kept him from walking into the sea in the previous months, but now it was a trial of strength to force it down his throat and struggle with the consequences.

He headed back to the cheap and nasty little B&B he was staying at to rest up for a few hours and let the indigestion tablets settle his stomach. There wasn't much more he needed to discover about Macallan, although there was still a mild thrill in watching her and her family when they had no idea that he was there, and at the thought that he'd been in their home, relaxed and studied their intimate spaces. He'd stared at the bed and imagined. He still had power and would use it to make his statement.

Her voice had thrilled him – the little edge of nerves he'd heard when she'd told him to piss off. He was enjoying it now and there was no way she could get to him through the phone. That would have been just too basic a mistake for a man with his experience. He had made the calls from call boxes, even though the experience of standing in those filthy coffins that doubled as public conveniences made him feel sick. He despised people, and particularly the ones at the bottom of the social ladder.

53

When Macallan walked back into Fettes the next morning, she still hadn't shaken off her reaction to the anonymous caller. She wanted to put it away, because getting her number was no problem for anyone who wanted to wind her up for some past grievance. The world was full of people who wanted to pay back a cop or the whole service – that just went with the territory – but she couldn't help tying everything in with the McMartin case. She knew she might be making too much of it and debated whether she should take it further. McGovern would keep it quiet though, so she decided to get him to track down the phone and see what it told them, if anything.

McGovern was waiting for her, though Young was delayed by about ten minutes. Macallan was relieved to see that he looked so much better than he had in Glasgow. The colour was back in his cheeks, and the lines of stress around his eyes had softened back. He was relaxed and seemed happy to see her. She took the chance to tell him about the call and said she hoped she wasn't making a fuss about nothing.

'Don't be daft. There's a lot of people out there with no

reason to love you, and you never know when one of our dissatisfied customers are going to make a nuisance of themselves. I'll get it checked but take it you don't want it to go anywhere at the moment?'

'Exactly. If you need anything authorised then I'll speak to Elaine as well, but it goes no further. It's this case, I'm beginning to see bogeymen everywhere.'

Young came in and they settled down with some coffee. McGovern looked like he was struggling to hold on, clearly itching to tell her a story.

Macallan gave them a quick briefing on her visit to Slab's house and what she'd seen there. On the grounds that there was little or no evidence, she left out her instinct that someone could have entered the house and killed him. She knew that McGovern and Young were already worrying that she was running off-script and she didn't want to make that situation any worse. There would be a PM, and if there was something suspicious maybe it would turn up there.

'Okay guys,' Macallan said, 'tell me what you've got because I can't help feeling we have a story here, though God knows if we can get anyone in court at the end of the day.'

She sat back and let McGovern take over.

'The thing is that this might just be another piece that doesn't solve anything, but I have to put my hands up and say that at the very least I'm getting the same stink in my nostrils that you have.'

Macallan had been feeling slightly out on a limb about what they were struggling with so the news that McGovern was on board made a difference to her. 'We did more of the phone work and blended the phone records Danny Goldstein gave us with the incomplete ones we recovered from the murder squad system on HOLMES. There's an interesting pattern, and Felicity has

324

done another full night on this on top of her day job.'

Macallan looked at the analyst, who was tired but clearly pleased with herself. 'Big thanks. I owe you and that man of yours a meal at the end of this.'

'I worked overnight so I could keep on top of my other work. Thought it would keep my bosses off our backs. If they saw my other stuff piling up there might be a problem ... but then you know that.'

Macallan nodded and looked at McGovern again.

'I've run the subscribers through the system and, put it this way, there's a few VIPs through here who were obviously enjoying Mickey's professional skills. Of course that does nothing for us. Felicity mentioned one number in particular though, and this seemed to be a regular pattern.' McGovern looked to Young. 'If you'd like to explain this and then I'll do the intel next.'

'I could see straightaway that there was a regular pattern with this one number.' Young took off her glasses and cleaned them as she spoke. 'Obviously for someone in his game there was a lot of traffic on the phone, including Tommy McMartin, but this number I'm describing sticks out because of the absolutely regular pattern almost up to the month before the murder. I think there's a good chance that it was a regular punter and looks like they had an appointment nearly every Thursday night. In the month before the murder there are calls at all times of the day and night. Initially the calls would last for some time, but as it went on a lot of the calls would be cut off after a few seconds, and in this type of analysis it could well indicate problems between the callers – phone getting put down and that kind of thing. Jimmy can fill in the intel now.'

Macallan felt a mild rush because she could see that they were about to give her something that could be really useful, and she wanted them to lay it on the table. It was important for her to have a grasp of the detail before she saw Elaine Tenant, so she would be trying to sell her something that made sense instead of the gut feelings she was playing with.

McGovern looked at a sheet of prompts again before he spoke. 'I got this subscriber's details, and at first glance he's interesting but no more than the VIPs on this side of the country. Anyway, his name is Ian Moore and he was a senior figure in the planning department in Glasgow. Might have been nothing on its own, but there was substantial intel that Slab had a large property portfolio and seemed to be ahead of the game every time there was a new development somewhere.'

McGovern picked up a glass of water and checked his notes again. 'I got subscriber's details for Moore's phone, and this is where it gets interesting. First of all, when he was making regular calls to Mickey he would invariably call a nice four-star hotel near what was his office at the time. It's a reasonable guess that this hotel was where they'd meet. We can tie that one down if you need it. Okay so far?'

Macallan nodded and pulled out her notepad as McGovern continued.

'When we look at Moore's call traffic then the picture clears. He makes occasional calls and receives occasional calls from a number that at the time was just down as pay as you go. Get this though: about a year later intel came in that the phone was used by one of the McMartin team, and in fact the intel was that it was the safe phone used by Slab himself. There's an increase in traffic between this phone and Moore in the couple of weeks before the murder.'

McGovern paused to check his notes again. 'We also know that the phone called the CID office on the night of the murder. In other words, this was probably the anony-mous call reporting the disturbance at Mickey's flat.'

McGovern sat back. He was tired again, and Macallan saw it even though her friend was trying his best to hide the sudden change.

'That phone being Slab's ties in exactly with what Jimmy Adams told me. Where's Moore now?' Macallan asked.

'We don't know yet because he retired on ill health and we're still trying to find out what that was about.'

McGovern watched Macallan work the information and the possibilities.

'Charlie MacKay's dirty; has to be. But I wonder if we can get our hands on him. What do you think, Felicity?'

'Given what happened, my hypothesis is that a problem of some kind developed between Moore and Mickey Dalton. Moore had some relationship with Slab, and we have the intel that they were heavily involved in property development. We know the call is made on the night of the murder from a phone that at least is used by the McMartins if not by Slab himself. We can be sure of all this. Where it goes depends on what we do now. There are lines of investigation, but will we be able to follow them up?'

'I'll go and have this meet with the Chief Super and get back to you.'

Macallan walked slowly to Tenant's office and spun the options. The clues were there, but could she get to the answer before the players who were still alive were beyond her reach?

54

Macallan knocked and walked into Elaine Tenant's office bang on time because she knew the Chief Super was a stickler for punctuality. Tenant had gone the extra yard to support her, so she thought she deserved the courtesy, particularly if someone was sitting in. Punctuality, or rather the lack of it, was something that had always been a problem for Macallan, who Harkins used to refer to as 'the late Grace Macallan'. She always took it on the chin because it was true.

Tenant seemed genuinely pleased to see her, and it helped relax Macallan, who was worried that what she'd been doing was going to backfire on her. A uniformed chief superintendent stood up as she came into the room and Tenant introduced him as Grant Cosgrove from the Counter Corruption Unit. Macallan was clean but there was always something about a visit from those boys that made you just make sure your memory wasn't playing tricks about whether you were actually a bent bastard about to get the big message.

He stuck out his hand and on his feet he was an impressive character, although definitely way the wrong side of fifty. Well over six foot, wide shouldered and not carrying an extra pound, he was either a gym addict or at least a keen sportsman. His thinning grey hair was cut skin short and it suited him. There was serious scar tissue above his right eye, which just added to the package, and Macallan thought that if she'd been into older men then he would be worth a look.

His smiling blue eyes almost made her forget why she was there and it was Tenant who brought her back to earth with a mild stab at humour, which was unusual for her.

'Grant's not here for you, Grace, so you can relax.' Tenant was pouring the coffee as she spoke, and Macallan had already picked up a vibe that there might be someone in the room who did fancy an older man. Cosgrove wasn't wearing a wedding ring so it was fair enough, but it was the first time Macallan had even imagined Tenant being interested in men. Perhaps her Chief Super was more human than she'd ever imagined.

They took their seats and Tenant didn't waste time on small talk before telling Macallan that the CCU were interested in Charlie MacKay. Macallan stayed quiet but found it hard to disguise her surprise at the turn of events. She'd been worried that if MacKay was bent she would struggle to prove anything, given that it wasn't really what she was supposed to be looking at.

'Can you quickly go over what you've been doing and anything you've found? Please speak freely in front of Grant. He needs to know what you know.'

Macallan felt almost relief that a team with the clout of the CCU and all their facilities were in on the game. They were under pressure in the press over the hunt for a leak in Police Scotland, but that wasn't her problem. She'd already taken the decision that she would not reveal her gut feeling that Slab had been murdered; nothing had come back from the PM yet to change her mind.

'There's been a development since we last spoke, Elaine, and I've just come from a meeting with Jimmy and Felicity.' She watched Tenant's head tilt back – she had her attention. Cosgrove never batted an eyelid – he was a cool one. But then she hadn't expected anything else.

Macallan briefed them on her visit to the prison. She moved on to the interviews with Goldstein, Holden and Adams before filling them in on the work McGovern and Young had been carrying out on the people behind the various phone numbers that had been in contact with Mickey Dalton in the weeks before his death. When she revealed what Adams had said about the murder and disposal of a child's body, they both shifted uncomfortably in their seats. Cosgrove might have been cool but he wasn't inhuman. Macallan was holding back on a question for Cosgrove but decided she needed an answer before she said any more.

'With the greatest respect, sir, it's unusual for you guys to come out and disclose who you're after. May I ask why?' She watched Tenant twitch slightly at the question, but she never believed in one-way traffic on these things.

Cosgrove nodded and seemed almost pleased with the question.

'I'm glad you asked, and I respect what's behind it. Let's just say that we know that you're quite involved in matters not that far removed from Charlie MacKay and that we trust Elaine and you completely. Your records tell us that. More than that, the two of you have stood by principles that have cost you in different ways. Sometimes we have to come out and trust people, Grace, because the majority in this job are clean. Simple as that. Will that do for now?'

She nodded and looked at Tenant, who was staring at Cosgrove, before continuing. 'Adams won't go on the record and that's final. You're welcome to try, but he's one of a dying breed. Unlike almost everyone these days he believes in the old ways and sticks to the omertà code.' Macallan apologised immediately. 'Sorry, I know we're in Scotland but I love anything with the Mafia in it!'

'No problem; you aren't the only *Sopranos* addict in this room.' Cosgrove smiled easily, Tenant's eyes flickered and Macallan suppressed a grin as she noted her boss's non-verbals.

Macallan told them what had been said and went on to report her meeting with MacKay till Cosgrove interrupted politely.

'We heard you had a difficult meeting with him, but what did you think of him?' Cosgrove put his cup on Tenant's desk and leaned forward slightly. She knew she was under the microscope, but that was no more than she would expect if they were taking her into their confidence.

'Jimmy McGovern knew him and had a negative opinion but nothing that could be described as criminal. I try to make up my own mind, but sorry to say I just didn't like the man, and my gut tells me he's dirty. I know that we're not supposed to have gut feelings nowadays, but that's the truth.'

Cosgrove nodded slowly as Macallan fired a question back at him.

'If you heard we had a problem, I'm guessing that you have a source close to him, either human or technical?'

'You have more experience of the dark arts than I'll ever have, Grace, so you know I can't answer that.' His smile was back and she knew she could work with him.

'I'll take that as a yes then.' She was pushing a bit hard and noticed Tenant strumming her fingers on the desk. That was a common habit she had and signified that the dialogue was just a bit too cosy. It was time to get serious and back to business. Macallan moved on to giving an account of the locus of Slab's death, relating it as a routine incident and making no mention of any suspicions.

'So the problem is that we have some red flags for corruption, but if people keep dying on us then where does it go? As it stands now, the next of kin is Big Brenda, and I thought I'd speak to you first, Elaine, before we do anything further.'

Tenant finished making a note and asked Cosgrove to brief Macallan on what they were doing that involved MacKay.

'We've been interested in him for some time. What I should say is that, as we've discussed, it's unusual for us to make an approach to you like this, and I'm sure you understand that our conversation must not go any further than this room. It's a compliment to you both that we looked at your records and felt we could take you into our confidence. What I can tell you right at the start is that if there is corruption it's nothing to do with money, or else he's brilliant at laundering it. It can only be about the desire to succeed, or promotion, or whatever term you want to use.'

'Seen it before, sir, and I guess we all have,' Macallan said quietly.

'MacKay has an excellent CV by any standard, much of it built on source information – and when I say source, I mean CHIS jobs. When he was in the Source Handling Unit he cultivated some top-quality sources and has continued since he left it. However, some of those sources seem to have received preferential treatment over the years, although we haven't been able to prove a direct link to him.'

'Does that include the McMartins, sir?' Macallan asked the obvious question.

'Of course, and as you know the Tommy McMartin

case gave him a strong defence against that accusation. We still can't figure that one out, but we believe he was running an unregistered source at that time, for whatever reason. Our suspicion is that the unregistered source was Slab himself, but that's still only a theory.'

Macallan lifted her head at the term 'unregistered source'. The old bogeyman. The days when detectives ran their own sources was long gone, and with justification: the practice had led to endless abuses and scandals where criminals who were run as informants were given a pass on almost anything they did. SHUs had been set up, and the sources now belonged to the force rather than to the individual officer. It was a serious disciplinary offence to go off-message on this, but it still happened, and it didn't surprise her that a man like MacKay would do this. She'd seen it often enough before.

A text came in on her phone. She checked it and shook her head at the contents before looking up at Elaine. 'Ian Moore is alive but very ill and suffering from Alzheimer's. We're cursed every way we turn on this.'

'Where do you suggest we go with this now, Grant? We have serious allegations here, but as far as I can see there's only Brenda to focus on – and MacKay. He's outside Grace's remit by a mile, and in any case I presume that's something you want to keep control of. As for Brenda, I suppose you would want to see her anyway, but you have no authority to investigate an old murder. Now we have Tommy, who we could describe as the accused or perhaps even another victim. Christ, this is a mess.' It was almost unknown for Elaine to use anything close to a curse, but the occasion and problem warranted more than that.

'I would like to see Brenda,' Macallan replied, 'but she probably won't speak to me because we didn't exactly hit it off the last time we met. Apart from that, there's not much more I can do on the remit for looking at Tommy's suicide.'

Cosgrove was deep in thought and rubbed his chin as he searched for a way ahead.

'First things first. You have an address for Brenda. You have to get that intelligence into the system. If she attacks some poor sod, or another criminal for that matter, you'll be neck deep for not making the information available.'

Macallan's phone rang and she looked apologetically at Tenant, who told her to take it just in case it was relevant.

She said okay a few times and set her phone back down on the table. 'Sorry, that was Jimmy again. There's intel from the NCA that they've picked up source information down there that there's a contract out on Brenda and it's a Liverpool team that are doing the job. That backs up intel put on by MacKay's team that there was a contract being sorted with a Scouse team.'

Tenant rarely drank but for the first time in a while she could have murdered a glass of something. The case was a collection of fragments that were becoming harder and harder to pull together. It was out of her range of experience, and she hoped Cosgrove could take the strain on it. She didn't have the answers but trusted the other two people in the room.

'The other problem,' Macallan continued, 'or advantage for us as regards Brenda, is that no one on the police side is really spending a lot of time looking for her. There are no complaints because the robberies were against other criminals. We have Jimmy Adams' story and nothing else about the murder so we can wait and see where that goes. There's a contract on her, so let me see her as Tommy's relation and deliver the Osman warning.'

The Osman warning was an obligation on the police to warn someone, whether they were a criminal or not (and they almost always were), that they'd received information that a threat to their life existed. It happened all the time. Although in most cases the police would have been happy to see the sentences carried out, it was the law and they had to comply. 'Normally it would be Glasgow that would do it, in fact Charlie MacKay's people. They don't have her whereabouts, but if I put this information on they'll pick it up immediately. Can you fix it, sir?'

She looked at Cosgrove and waited while he ran over the issues.

He made a note and looked back up. 'Consider it done. I'll make the calls now. I'm going to arrange it so that because you're doing the Tommy McMartin investigation, you have to see Brenda, and it's appropriate that you deliver the Osman warning. MacKay will get a call shortly to say you're handling it. Let's keep him calm. I want you to call in and see MacKay on the way and appear to make peace with him. Make it look as routine as possible while we follow up the various lines your team have dug up. We can work together on this.'

He looked at Tenant as Macallan's boss and she looked delighted that there was a reason to keep up their liaison. 'We'll do anything we can do to help, Grant.'

Macallan hoped Cosgrove fancied the offer Elaine was telegraphing across the room.

'The only thing though, Grace, is that you need someone with you, and I believe Jimmy's back behind the desk. He spoke to me and told me what had happened; you did the right thing. Who do you want?'

'DS Mark Dunbar, a Weegie. Don't ask me why, but I met him at Slab's and think he's a man I can trust on this. And he knows the McMartins.'

'It's done; I'll make that happen. Just call him in about an hour and make your arrangements.'

Macallan nodded and felt they were moving towards some kind of truth, but whether there would be a reck-

335

oning with anyone was in the lap of the gods. 'It won't be easy pretending with Charlie MacKay, but I'm ex-RUC SB, sir, so know what needs to be done. I'm going to call Brenda and just go for it.'

'That's good.' Cosgrove stood up and shook her hand.

The wheels were turning quickly now, and after Macallan explained to McGovern and Young what had happened, without mentioning CCU's involvement, she went back to her office and called Brenda's number. It rang for a full minute and there was no voicemail so she put the phone on the table and felt her shoulders ache with tension. She chewed the side of her finger and worried that what had seemed clear in Tenant's office might be upset by just not being able to find Brenda. She tried again and this time the phone was picked up after the third ring.

'Brenda McMartin?' Macallan hadn't worked out what she would say so played it by instinct.

'Who the fuck is this?'

'Superintendent Grace Macallan. We need to speak.'

There was a long pause and Macallan heard a radio playing in the background.

'Saw your name in the paper. You're on Tommy's case. That fuckin' insult in the hospital was out of order by the way.' She was referring to their only meeting, which had ended up with Brenda on the floor next to her hospital bed.

'Okay, tell you the truth, I've hardly been out an' it's drivin' me fuckin' mental. Any chance you could buy me a few packets o' crisps on the way?'

Macallan shook her head in wonder; it was the last thing she'd expected to be asked. 'OK,' she agreed.

'Where?' Brenda asked.

'I can come to your place. I know where you are.' Macallan knew that information would have an impact and there was another long pause before she heard a quiet snigger down the line.

'Sounds like you've had a word wi' Fanny Adams. Grassin' wee bastard. Doesn't make much difference so come ahead.'

After she hung up, Macallan went into the bathroom and splashed cold water over her face. She stayed there for a few minutes and tried to gather her thoughts. When she went to pick up her jacket and case she sent a text to Jack with a line of five kisses and a picture of a wedding cake.

She climbed into the car, turned the ignition and flicked on the radio. Another high-profile politician was up to his arse in alligators, and politics was hot with the European issue still tearing the Tories apart. Macallan decided that she couldn't stand another report on politics and put on a music channel that she hardly listened to on the way through to Glasgow. Dunbar called her and didn't seem the least bit surprised at the request he'd received from on high to team up with her.

'No problem, boss. Had a feeling we'd be meeting again.'

They arranged a where and when and Macallan stared at the M8 sliding below her on the way to the truth.

55

When Macallan hit the traffic on the east side of the city she called MacKay's number, felt a tremor in her stomach and had to work hard to control her nerves. When he answered he was guarded and obviously being careful with a call he hadn't expected so soon after their previous meeting.

'Look, we got off to a bad start and I want to come over and fill you in on what I'm doing,' Macallan told him. 'You were involved in the original case so it's only fair. I take it you got the call that I'm seeing Big Brenda and have to hand out an Osman warning?' She waited for his reaction.

'Fair enough, drop in. As for Brenda, well, she's not a priority for us anyway. Intel on the rip-offs is all we have – not a single complainer. So you have an address for her?'

'Speak to you when I get there. I'm picking up the DS who was at Slab's and he's going to Brenda's with me.'

'Who's that then?'

'Mark Dunbar. Seems okay.'

'Not my cup of tea.' There was too long a pause before

he said it, and that proved Macallan's original assessment of Dunbar was on the money. If MacKay didn't like him it was probably an unintentional compliment.

When Macallan picked up Dunbar he seemed relaxed given he'd had almost no information about what he was supposed to be doing with her. He had all the experience in the world, however, and had already guessed that her actions and words at Slab's house meant it was something to do with the McMartins, so he wanted in. He'd gone up against them so many times and had nearly always failed to put one of them away. It didn't matter – he would always have another crack if the chance came along, and something told him Macallan might just give him that opportunity – so why not?

'I'm stopping at Charlie MacKay's office on the way, just be ten minutes with him. I'll do that on my own and then we're going to see Big Brenda. Were you told that?'

'Superintendent MacKay and I don't get on that well, boss, so better I'm not there anyway. As for Big Brenda ... are we wearing body armour for that one?' He smiled and Macallan was glad he was there.

'What's the problem with Charlie MacKay and you then?' Macallan didn't want to hang about. She was close to putting a lid on Tommy McMartin's suicide and there was no time for polite 'getting to know you' patter.

'It's simple really. I don't like or trust him, and the feeling's mutual. He tried to do my legs a couple of times for no other reason than that.'

'If you don't mind me saying, it's unusual for someone at your rank to be so candid about one super to another?'

'My feeling is you're of the same mind as me, and given what you said at Slab's place I think I'm in the right territory? As for Brenda, I haven't seen her in a long time. From what I hear that team's fallen off a cliff and there's an awful lot of villains out there would love to give her a red card.'

Macallan told him just enough but not too much. When it came to it, Dunbar was only there because if Macallan tried to see Brenda on her own and anything went wrong, there would be career-ending fallout.

'By the way, Mark, has anything turned up at the PM for Slab?' She knew there couldn't be because that would have been headline news, but she had to ask because the feeling was still there.

'Nothing as far as the pathologist is concerned. Natural causes. Christ, the man had an encyclopaedia full of medical problems. The thing is, I don't think you were convinced, boss. Just call it one of those old-fashioned feelings.'

He smiled when she looked sideways at him but ignored the observation. 'I get the picture.'

When Macallan walked into MacKay's office he hardly made any attempt at warmth but at least tried for cordial. She hoped that would do. It was all a sham anyway, an act to buy time so that Cosgrove and his team could try to find enough links to corruption to make a case, or at least a credible allegation.

He invited Macallan to sit down and she saw the tension flicker across the muscles in his face. He made a pretence at looking through some notes, but it was obviously just a way to avoid eye contact with her.

When MacKay finally ran out of diversions he looked up at her and put his palms on the desktop before speaking.

'So tell me, how is your review going? Is there anything I can help you with?' He was wound tight and Macallan wondered why that was; he seemed spooked. She couldn't know that he was only doing that human thing of running endless scenarios on what might go wrong. He was a man carrying more than his own share of sin, but up to that point he'd always believed he was fireproof.

The Tommy McMartin thing should have been straightforward. Mickey Dalton and Tommy were both doing the big sleep so what was the problem? It was Macallan and the suggestion that someone thought the murder was a fit-up. It was history, but it had come up out of the ground like the hand of a corpse in a far too shallow grave. Nothing substantial had been put to him, but he was human and had started to worry. Christ, even Slab was bye-byes and he'd been the man who'd made the call that night to go to Dalton's flat. It had been a strange one, finding Tommy, the young prince and Slab's favourite. He'd never made sense of it, and when he'd asked Slab about it later he'd been told to keep his fuckin' nose out of the business.

A smell had developed around MacKay and his team when people noticed they kept taking out Slab's rivals but no one with the name McMartin. Wrapping up young Tommy had put all the sanctimonious bastards out of the game, though, and got the rubber heels off his arse. He had no idea who'd actually killed Mickey Dalton, but it was a set-up, no doubt about it.

That would have been it had he not seen, weeks later, a routine intel report from a beat cop saying he'd spotted Big Brenda, Crazy Horse and an unidentified male driving in the area that night. It was nothing on its own, and those kinds of reports came in every day, but it clicked with MacKay. Big Brenda and her lunatic brother were more than capable, and he was aware that both she and the late and unlamented Crazy Horse hated Tommy. It made sense. Most of the links were dead, but Brenda was still alive, and if she'd been there that night and

Macallan was going to see her ... It was hard to believe that Brenda would talk to the police though, and she was as good as dead anyway: it was only a matter of time.

The other problem as MacKay saw it was that Macallan's team had been looking at the HOLMES system. His man had told him they were fishing among the phone records, which made his skin freeze because he knew he was exposed there. He could easily have explained it away before as just cutting down on the number of enquiries in a case that was already solved, but now there were just so many ifs and too many fucking buts.

'You okay?' he heard Macallan say and realised that his mind had drifted. She'd been talking to him and he'd been staring into the shadows as he struggled with his fears.

'You look pale. Look, I can come back – I just need to take a routine statement to wrap up the work I've been doing. I'm going to see Brenda, so we can do it next week if that's okay?'

He stared at her and the consequences of his past broke into his mind like flashlights going off. He was a senior cop, but senior cops could go to prison. The woman sitting opposite him had done it to another cop before.

'Where the fuck did you get Brenda's address?' He had no control over what he said and it burst through his lips as if he'd lost control of his breakfast. His breathing was unsteady, and there were dark stains under the armpits of his expensive Italian shirt.

Macallan was taken by surprise – she hadn't expected any of this. MacKay was regarded as Mr Cool and they were a long way off proving anything against him. In fact, she knew it might well go unresolved – it wouldn't be the first time some bent bastard kept climbing up the greasy pole despite their past. She tried to stay calm but she was watching a man come apart in front of her.

'I got the address and phone number from a new source.' It was only partly true but would do. 'Where's the problem? We've put it on the system.'

'The threat to Brenda. How did that come about?'

His face was heart-attack red and Macallan tried to think of a way to make a dignified exit, but her own emotions were taking over. She realised what was happening. Every good detective had seen it a hundred times. He was riven with guilt and couldn't control the fear of being caught.

'You know what? Just get the fuck out of here,' he said, no longer interested in her answer. 'I'm doing my job keeping a lid on all those scumbags out there while you fuck about with an open and shut case from years ago. Hassling me like some half-baked PC. Your problem is you don't know what it's like trying to keep it all under control!'

Macallan's anger began to rise because she no longer needed evidence. The bastard was dirty. 'What do you mean by control?' She was being confronted, and despite what Cosgrove had said she couldn't walk away from the challenge.

'It's people like me that stop it all going off.' There were white flecks of spit at the corners of MacKay's mouth. 'You just don't get it. We've got Triads, Yardies, Poles and horrible bastards from all over Europe. The old days are gone. We can't get into these gangs so we have to keep our own on top of the pile. We can work them, control them and that way we keep order.' He blinked a few times but the outburst had said so much.

Macallan looked at him and tried to grasp it. Cosgrove was right. It was about power – the classic case of villains controlling the story through people like MacKay.

'You think you're the only one who ever dealt with this stuff?' she asked him. 'RUC, my friend. The Troubles, that's where I learned my trade. Scraped up the pieces after bomb blasts, slept with a gun next to my pillow and lost some fine men and women along the way. Who the fuck do you think you are, the Glasgow branch of UKIP?' Macallan, struggling to keep a hold of her own feelings, almost matched MacKay's level of anger.

MacKay had to release the nervous energy flooding his system. He had to get her out of the office before he lost it completely. He stood up, strode round the desk, shoved his face too close and started jabbing her arm while he growled, 'Stay the fuck out of my way.'

It had gone too far, and he'd underestimated her once again. In the first meeting, he'd written her off as someone who'd made her name off other people's work; now he thought she was no more than a physically weak female, no match for a guy who did weights four times a week.

Macallan let her training take over and she acted instinctively. She was still seated but pushed her left hand up and gripped the inside of his wrist, twisting it against the joint. He hissed with pain – it felt like his elbow was cracking.

He took a half-step back and tried to push away from Macallan so he could extend his arm and relieve the pressure. It meant he was off balance for a moment and he stumbled back, the top half of his body hitting his desk so his legs were splayed, his toes just off the floor. If Macallan had had time to think she would never have done it, but she was still running on instinct so she drove her knee up into the exposed groin of the helpless superintendent. Then she let his wrist go, stood back and asked herself what she'd just done. She spent a moment heaving in air and then the doubt passed and she smiled. It reminded her of the moment Big Brenda had landed on the floor.

MacKay, who had made the same mistake of underestimating her, slid to the floor clutching his balls and the pain that had made him forget about his wrist.

'You fucking bitch,' he wheezed. It was all he got out before she turned for the door then stopped.

'You're done, Charlie boy. Just hope you know that.'

When she got outside Slaven was on his way in. 'He doesn't want to be disturbed for a bit,' she told him.

Slaven turned away and Macallan headed back to meet Mark Dunbar.

Once MacKay had managed to get himself together, he picked up his phone and called Jigsaw to tell him where Brenda McMartin was and that they'd need to hold back for a little while because she was getting a routine visit from the law. 'By the way, they know there's a contract so you'd better get your arse into gear.'

He put the phone down and stared at the qualifications, commendations and photographs on the walls of his office. A senior officer had once described his career as glittering, and it was only days and hours since it had seemed that nothing could touch him, that he had control over people inside the job and on the other side of the fence. It had all been an illusion. All the photographs and framed citations were no more than a testament to the fragility of what he thought he possessed.

He sat back behind his desk and ignored the phone ringing, hardly moving a muscle for several minutes. The receding pain was the least of his worries. Through his rage, humiliation and weakness as a human being he'd reacted to Macallan like a child. And he'd used his own phone to call Jigsaw. As a detective, he knew what that would mean if Macallan or anyone else looked at what had just taken place, or rather after what was planned for Big Brenda.

345

'God.' He only said the one word, but unfortunately for him God wasn't listening.

Jigsaw smiled quietly to himself, pleased with the call from MacKay. It always looked good when you could go to the boss with a nice piece of inside info. He'd claim it was from some bent DC who owed him money, because a relationship with someone in MacKay's position and rank would spook Frankie Logan.

Jigsaw had worked quietly in the background for MacKay for a couple of years and it was a good deal. The name Jigsaw only existed in the secret CHIS file and was only used by MacKay and his handlers, including Tony Slaven. To everyone else he was Alan, the Quiet Man and youngest of the three Logan brothers. A couple of years earlier he'd been pulled for a serious assault and MacKay had used the opportunity to recruit him. It was easier than he'd expected, and it had quickly become clear that Alan resented his elder siblings, who took him for granted. Sometimes it was just that simple.

'Play the long game with us, Alan,' MacKay had told him at that first meeting. 'You move up the ladder and we put you in control someday. First chance we get, we take out Abe when the time's right. How does that sound?'

Alan had liked the sound of that a lot, and MacKay loved it when they took the bait with so little effort. 'Sounds good to me, Mr MacKay, and this assault charge?'

'What assault charge, Alan? The fucker had it coming ... right?'

They'd shaken hands and laughed at the same time. As far as Alan had been concerned it was a good deal for him, and they'd parted ways with both of them thinking they were the one in control.

When Macallan stepped out onto the street and waved to

Dunbar, who was parked about a hundred yards away, she was still pumping high levels of adrenalin though her veins. She raked through her bag, grabbed her phone and got Jacquie Bell's number.

'Hi, gorgeous, how's things and do you have any inside info? I need a good story.' The reporter did nothing that was just plain and simply normal, and that included answering her phone.

Macallan couldn't find the humour button – she was wound up too tight, but she knew exactly what she was doing. 'You still working the prison story?'

'Definitely. And forgive me if I'm wrong, honey, but is Grace not a happy bunny today?'

'It's a long story. Sorry, but this McMartin thing is turning into a mess and heading in too many directions. I need you to do something for me.'

'Go ahead.' Bell put down her gin and tonic to pick up her pen.

'The next piece you put out, mention that the police are following definite lines of enquiry regarding police corruption in relation to the Tommy McMartin case. Okay? The only thing is, I need it out there as soon as.'

'You sure about this?'

'Definitely. I want someone to know I'm serious. Let him stew a bit.'

'Great. I thought I was going to have to make something up about the Sturgeonator being into devil worship or something. Lot of people who read the *Daily Terror* would love that one. It'll be in tomorrow.'

'Thanks, Jacquie. Drinks on me, and sorry if I sound a bit off, because I am.' She was about to put the phone down when Bell caught her.

'By the way, a couple of the dailies, but not mine, have mentioned your upcoming wedding. That's what comes

347

with celebrity: writer husband and famous ex-detective wife.'

'Christ, what next? And by the way: once a detective, always a detective.' Macallan had lightened up – Jacquie always managed to make her laugh at herself. She was just too serious, unlike Bell, who saw the world for what it was – a big mad pantomime and far too crazy to take seriously.

When Macallan jumped in the car, she did something almost unknown for her and pulled down the vanity mirror to check her face, which was red and blotchy.

Dunbar pulled away from the kerb and glanced a couple of times at Macallan, who'd said nothing. 'I'm a really experienced DO, boss, and with the greatest respect, my assessment is that you and Mr MacKay either suddenly discovered you were crazy about each other or' – he paused a moment – 'the exact opposite.'

Macallan looked round at Dunbar for a second, thinking he was out of order and had forgotten the rank difference, but then she realised there was a touch of Mick Harkins about him – minus the awful health regime and slightly bent morals. She saw his barely contained grin, heard Jacquie Bell's voice in her head and got the joke.

'Okay smart-arse, let's get something to eat then we go see Big Brenda.'

She leaned back in the seat, closed her eyes for a minute and concentrated on Jack and the children. His family were Ulster Scots and he was going to wear the kilt. He wouldn't let her see the fittings but she imagined that with such a large, powerful frame he would look a bit special on the day.

She wondered if she should call Elaine Tenant and tell her she'd just kneed a superintendent in the balls but decided it probably wasn't a good idea. MacKay couldn't make anything of it, and at the very least his credibility would have been down the toilet if he ever admitted what had just happened.

As Macallan and Dunbar headed south towards Brenda's safe house, Cue Ball Ross was starting up the engine on his hired car. He'd just taken the call with Big Brenda's address. He didn't like the reference to some police team visiting her, but it had been described as 'routine' so he'd just watch her place until it was dark and he was sure it was clear to do the job. Cue Ball had been thinking long and hard about the future and figured if the McMartins were out of the way there might be an opening back in Edinburgh for him. The Scousers had been good to him, but he wanted to go home.

He turned on his radio and pissed himself at the news that the mighty Glasgow Rangers had been gubbed again as Celtic continued to dominate. He knew the Scottish game was shite, but he missed it just the same. He'd been to a few of the big English matches, but the crowds sounded like they'd all been doped up on happy pills. He missed the venom of the Scottish league. It was crap football, but that wasn't everything.

56

They pulled up about a hundred yards from the address and stopped to have a look round. The old cottages were fairly well spread and had been built when people could still have space as well as a roof over their heads. The gardens were all tended, and it had that quietness and feel of a community that was rarely found in a city environment.

'Not what you'd expect for someone called The Bitch,' Dunbar said just as Macallan had exactly the same thought.

'What do you think? Inside has to be a tip.'

'Has to be. You can take the girl out of the scheme but you can't take the scheme . . .'

A hundred yards further back Cue Ball pushed himself up to get a better view and watched them head for Brenda's place. He'd arrived about fifteen minutes earlier. They were pigs, no doubt about it, and so far that proved the info had been on the money.

He pulled the ring on a can of Irn Bru and settled back in his seat. He was relaxed and thought that if this job went well it would give him big cred with Terry Norman down in the Pool. If Cue Ball went back to the business in Edinburgh then he could set things up with Norman as his main supplier and everyone would be a winner. It was as sweet as a nut, and he imagined himself in a flash pad down on the Shore in Leith.

When Macallan and Dunbar got to the front gate of the single-storey cottage they had their first surprise. The garden was cared for; it wasn't award-winning, but someone had obviously put time into it. There wasn't a single discarded crisp packet or pizza box to confirm what they'd imagined. The next surprise was that the heavy old front door was open, a glass-panelled vestibule door closed behind it. The two officers looked at each other, shrugged and pressed the bell. The curtains were all closed, and they watched the downstairs ones twitch for a moment before Brenda opened the door. Wearing her eye patch and a T-shirt that said 'fuck the polis', she seemed to fill the space, and it was one of those moments when her visitors wondered whether she was going to ask them in or attempt to eat them at the door. She nodded and turned back into the house. They took that as an invitation to go in.

'Shut and lock the door behind. Some bad people out there.' Brenda didn't realise how right she was, given that Cue Ball Ross was watching the house with a loaded shooter and a knife to keep him company.

The second surprise for Macallan and Dunbar was that the place had no unpleasant odour apart from the faint trace of booze trailing in Brenda's wake. There was a hint of tobacco smoke, but she must have kept the place aired and it felt clean enough. None of it made sense.

They followed her through to the lounge where they'd seen the curtains move. It was pleasing on the eye: full of old furniture that looked like someone had wandered slowly round second-hand furniture stores and antique shops picking each item with care. Like the garden, it wasn't *Country Life* standard; nevertheless, it was a world away from where this woman and violent criminal had been raised and trained.

'Sit down but I'm offering you fuck all to drink. I mean, you're filth, and I haven't forgotten you.' She pointed at Macallan. 'And where did you pick up that fuckin' has-been?' She winked at Dunbar, but there were traces of a grin on her lips and she couldn't hide a measure of respect for the man. 'Still never managed to get any of us, eh?'

'Nice to see you as well, Brenda, and it was good trying. Shut down a few of your businesses over the years so at least I cost you a few quid.' Dunbar said it as if he was catching up with an old friend. No trace of fear or tension. He was class and Macallan just kept on liking him.

'Okay, get to the point. You want to speak to me, so speak.'

Macallan tried to keep it as formal as possible. She had to issue the threat-to-life warning and any failure carried a heavy price for the force if it didn't take place. She told Brenda that they'd received information that there was a serious threat against her and that they believed it was credible. They offered support and all the other bollocks that Big Brenda wasn't the least bit interested in.

As Macallan worked through the formalities a smile spread across Brenda's blotchy face. She looked like she'd been hitting the sauce with a vengeance and her complexion, spotted by broken veins and traces of dry skin, had taken on a deep purple hue. Despite that, the smile was wide, and somehow the message that someone was intent on killing her was received like a fairly decent joke.

'Well, well. So some tosser wants to kill Big Brenda. Boo fuckin' hoo. Nothin' new there then, is there?' She shook her head as if the two cops were children saying something innocently amusing.

'We have to tell you this. It's serious this time. They're coming for you. We know you've been ripping people off. It's payback and you know it.' Macallan knew she was wasting her time but this had to be done by the book.

'Rippin' them off. Any complaints from anyone?'

'You know that's not likely.' Dunbar looked her straight in the eye. 'We're just the messengers, so do what you like with it.'

'I'll do fuck all then but wait. Any objections?'

Brenda got up and walked through to the kitchen then called back: 'Changed my mind. Want a drink?' She returned with a vodka bottle and three glasses.

Macallan and Dunbar said no and watched Brenda fill a glass almost to the brim. It made their eyes water when she tipped her head back and downed it in a oner. She smacked her lips and gave a long, satisfied sigh.

'Sure ye'll no have one for the road?'

'I need to ask you a couple of other questions, Brenda.' Macallan was fed up with play-acting. 'I've been looking at the circumstances of Tommy's suicide in Barlinnie.'

She hesitated; she hadn't rehearsed her lines and wondered whether she should just walk away and let the dead lie peacefully.

Macallan would never be able to explain what happened next but she tore up the script in a moment and went with her gut. 'I'll take that drink before I go on.'

That caught Dunbar off guard, and he looked round at her with a question in his eyes. Although he never voiced it, the question was definitely 'what the fuck are you doing?' Then he saw it, knew exactly where she was going and let it run.

It caught Brenda as well, and she stared at Macallan

before picking up the bottle and filling one of the spare glasses half full. 'That enough?'

Macallan nodded and Brenda filled her own glass to the top again.

'Tell me what happened at Mickey Dalton's, Brenda. This might be the last chance for any of us to know the truth.'

Brenda glanced towards the door and seemed lost in her own thoughts before looking back at Macallan. She nodded. 'Just you. I'll talk to you on your own. That's the deal.' She tipped back the glass again and emptied it.

Macallan looked round at Dunbar; they never spoke a word and didn't need to. He stood up and took a step towards Brenda. 'I'll be right outside. Do not take the piss.' He stared at her till he was sure she'd got the message then closed the door behind him.

'What do you want to know?' Brenda swallowed hard, and for the first time Macallan saw something else behind the mask of a cold bitter criminal who seemed to have almost no feelings when it came to other human beings.

'People have said that they didn't believe Tommy killed Mickey Dalton. We haven't a shred of evidence to prove that.' Macallan thought she'd throw the dice and see where they landed. 'One person said it was you. Said they didn't know why, but it was you. I'm not going to lie: they won't stand up in court, but that's what they said.'

She'd rarely touched spirits since the children had come along, but now was the time and she swigged the vodka back. The fiery liquid scorched the back of her throat and soon began to surge through her bloodstream, taking the edge off.

'Fair enough. I'm fucked anyway.'

Macallan sat mesmerised as the woman who had terrified so many in her time told it all.

'My old man was a bastard of the first order. He hated me and my brother Bobby – that's Crazy Horse to you but always Bobby for me.'

Macallan watched Brenda's nose start to run as she carried on.

'The old man was makin' a fortune in property deals and had the top man in plannin' right in his pocket. The inside info came straight into his lap.'

'Was that Ian Moore?' Macallan asked and lifted the glass again. It was as if they were locked in their own small confessional.

'That's the bastard. Thing is, he was a bender an' liked boys; in fact he couldn't get enough. Turned out he'd been doin' Mickey Dalton for months and fell in love with the boy.'

Brenda filled her glass again and for the first time Macallan noticed that she was starting to slur, although it was barely noticeable and most men would have been halfway to a coma the way she was packing it away.

'Turned out that Mickey boy was a greedy wee bastard and started to take Ian Moore for every penny he could lay his hands on. Next thing he threatens to tell the man's wife all the dirty stuff they've been into. So guess what?'

She emptied the last of the vodka into her glass as Macallan gave the obvious answer to the question.

'Moore went to Slab and asked for help?' Macallan saw it all becoming clear like a reflection settling on a disturbed pool.

'Exactly.' Brenda said it as if Macallan was a friend. The vodka was having a most unusual effect on her.

'The old man gave me an' Bobby the job to sort Mickey Dalton, and his exact words were: "Do whatever's required."' She laughed at some inside joke that Macallan couldn't make out in the picture that was still swirling, though she was almost there.

'Bobby tracked Mickey for a few days an' guess what?'

'They see him with Tommy.' Macallan saw it opening up like a stage play and everyone was in their places now.

'Exactly again.' Brenda wasn't going to stop now. 'Thing is we fuckin' hated Tommy. Swaggerin' bastard thought he was the dug's baws, an' the old man thought the sun shone from his sweet little arse. We didn't mention Tommy. Told the old man fuck all and followed orders. We did the job.'

'But according to the CCTV records no one was seen entering or leaving except Mickey and Tommy.' Macallan threw the question in because McGovern and Young had noticed it on the HOLMES system and it needed an answer.

'We were good at what we did. We'd looked at the place beforehand and deeked the camera. There was a back way in over a wall.'

'But how did you get in?'

'Still don't see it.' Brenda was giving a lesson now. 'We'd already decided on a way to take Tommy out of the game to pish in the old man's face. We pulled this boy Mickey an' terrorised the fucker wi' a chainsaw. Told him we were after Tommy an' wanted to set him up. The boy agreed to get Tommy off his skull an' leave him for us. Poor twat never saw it comin'. Fanny Adams drove me and Bobby to the job. Daft bastard opened the door, didn't he? We done him and let Tommy take the drive for Bar-L. Simple really, an' when we told the old man, Bobby spat in his gob. Honestly, right in his puss. You should've seen the bastard's face. Nothin' he could do but go along wi' it an' pretend he knew nothin' about Tommy's poofery.'

Brenda looked exhausted but pleased, and her face glowed with the excess of alcohol pounding through her

356

arteries. 'It was fuckin' payback for that auld bastard, an' he deserved what he got.'

Brenda got up and swayed slightly before heading for the kitchen and bringing in a fresh bottle.

'No more for me.' Macallan was joining the strands and the set-up was there, but so was something else. The hatred for Slab, his contempt for his own, and Jimmy Adams' story about a child being discarded in the Clyde.

'Whose child was it that Slab threw into the river?' Macallan threw back the dregs in her glass and watched Brenda's face struggle with the question.

'Jimmy Adams?'

Macallan nodded and waited for the final piece of the truth.

'Mine.' She looked back at Macallan, who saw her one eye fill. Brenda shuddered with the awful secrets that rose like bile in her throat.

'Was Slab the father?' Macallan held her breath after asking the question, as if the slightest movement might stop Brenda uncovering a secret that she'd kept buried all these years.

'Him?' Her chest heaved with emotion and distress. 'It was Bobby. Bobby was the only one who ever cared about me. The old man found out when I fell pregnant an' went mental so he killed the wean. That's why the bastard hated us. Tommy's suicide ... well, just lay that on the old bastard as well.'

Brenda sat back and fumbled at the pack of cigarettes beside her.

Macallan stared at Brenda, lost for words and reeling at the pictures flooding her imagination. She forced herself to see Kate and Adam at home, but they faded as quickly as she could bring them into her mind. It was too much.

'Gimme one of those.' Macallan pointed at the packet in Brenda's hand.

357

'Didn't take you for a smoker.' Brenda offered the packet and Macallan put her first cigarette in years to her mouth. She took the lighter Brenda offered her and tried to control the tremor in her hand. It tasted awful but the effect was immediate, and her head felt light as the nicotine hit the receptors in her brain and dopamine flooded into her system. They didn't say anything for the next couple of minutes as they both absorbed what the disclosure meant.

Brenda spoke first. 'What happens now?'

'What do you want to happen?'

'Leave me here.' Brenda looked weak and ill. The fight had gone from her – all her aggression had been left in the past.

Macallan knew exactly what it meant. With the exception of Jimmy Adams, who was never going to say anything to anybody else, she was the only person apart from Brenda McMartin who knew it all or nearly all.

She stood up and threw the remaining half of the cigarette into the fireplace.

'One last question. When did you last see your father?'

'I managed to see him before he died.' Brenda locked her one good eye onto Macallan and let the answer hang in the air.

'That's what I thought. I'll give it a few days but I'll probably have to come back once I've completed the enquiries.' Macallan picked up her bag, feeling sick.

'That'll do me, Superintendent. Won't get up 'cause I'm pished.'

Macallan let herself out and found Dunbar, who saw the grey pallor and strain carved into her face. 'Tough in there?'

'Hard going. Let's go.'

After about ten minutes Dunbar couldn't hold it any longer. 'Can I ask what happened in there, boss?'

Macallan stared ahead and he began to wonder whether she'd even heard him. She was lost somewhere in her head. He gave up and concentrated back on the road, but then she said, 'She denied everything. Refused to admit a thing.'

'Fair enough. I thought that might be the case.' He knew it wasn't true but something had clearly shocked her and she didn't need interrogating. He left her to go back to her thoughts.

A while later she took a call from McGovern that her anonymous call had come from a public phone box. It hardly registered with her.

When Macallan left the cottage, Brenda McMartin was feeling the effects of the booze but also a sense of relief. She was so tired it hurt. It was more than that – it was exhaustion that just made her want to lie down and close her eyes forever. However, there was something she needed to do first.

She went around the house and opened all the back windows, then the lounge window to clear the smoke and put The Proclaimers on a loop. That done, she swayed her way down the back garden, returning a couple of minutes later with the sawn-off she'd stashed.

She slugged back a couple of glasses of water, couldn't hold her eye open any longer and went to sleep in her favourite chair, confident that everything was in place.

57

He'd read the article several times. Each time his gut knotted and the anger rose in his chest, making his heart pound and ache. Sometimes his breathing became laboured and he wondered if he needed medical treatment. But then what was the point? There was no real purpose in his life anymore, and he could see nothing but a blank page for his future. His family were beyond his reach and his daughter was dead. If he ever tried to approach old friends they would turn their backs on him – he knew that without question.

'Old friends' – the term made him grind his teeth. He'd never really had someone who was close, someone he could share his troubles or joy with. All he'd ever had were human beings he could use or abuse. Recently he'd wandered through the old Lawnmarket where he'd spotted a couple of people he'd worked with in the past, and even though the years of abuse were catching up and he'd aged quickly, their eyes registered recognition. They passed him by without a second glance.

There was only one more thing to do and he looked at the paper again. Macallan was getting married. Her life was all success, distinguished career, a distinguished husband and a distinguished life. So many admirers and any comparison with his own life made him choke.

He looked at the name of the hotel where the wedding was to be held and waved down a taxi. It would be an idea to have a drink in the place and see where her big day was going to happen. He mumbled the word 'bitch' then pulled himself together before climbing into the taxi and giving the driver directions.

58

Cue Ball watched the pigs drive away and settled back down till it was dark. His great strength was that he always stayed focused and treated each job seriously. He never acted the cowboy, which was why he'd survived so long when nine times out of ten he was half the size of the opposition. When he was asked to do a bit of wet work he did it as a job, and he regarded himself as a professional. He still thought it was a strange quirk that he'd been hired to do Big Brenda as his first job back in Scotland. Just part of the business. People had to be wiped every so often or there would be chaos.

He hardly saw a soul all day apart from a few old sorts with their dogs. He was sure none of them would recognise the car, but he was in a good spot anyway, where he wouldn't attract too much attention. He sat in the back, which meant he couldn't be seen through the privacy glass. A plastic bottle took care of his bladder and he was patient. It was a great virtue in his game: the ability to pick the right moment to act.

Cue Ball hadn't meant to sleep but it happened. He woke with a start and found the sun had long gone.

There were a few lights on but the street was filled with shadows, and the back of the line of cottages would give him all the cover he needed. The shooter he stuffed into his belt had no silencer, and he would only use it as a last resort. The place was so quiet that gunfire would be heard a mile off, and if the bizzies got a call then he wouldn't have much time to get back into the city where he could lose himself.

A dog was spooked somewhere – no doubt it had sensed him creeping along the overgrown path at the back of the cottages. He kept calm because the place had to have regular visits from foxes, which meant the natives wouldn't get too fussed when their dogs got a bit excited about something out there in the night. The couple of dog walkers he'd seen earlier had nice cuddly pets, and there were no signs of Dobermans or Rottweilers in the area, so that gave him some peace of mind.

He stood motionless in the garden at the back of Brenda's address, puzzling over why he could hear The Proclaimers belting it out when there were no lights on in her house and no signs of movement. It was good practice to wait and get the feel of your surroundings before making a move, yet after twenty minutes still nothing had happened, and as his eyes adjusted to the light he could see that all the windows were slightly open. He was puzzled – she had to know there was a target on her back, and even in ordinary circumstances, why would she do this?

He decided to give it a bit more time. *Why is she listening to music in the dark?* he wondered. He considered it might be a trap, but it was all a bit obvious.

The minutes passed and still there was nothing moving, and apart from the music there was hee-haw from inside the house. He had to make his move or call the whole thing off, and that wasn't an option for someone with his attitude to dangerous situations.

He got in below the bedroom window and waited for a couple of minutes but still there was nothing. He looked in through the glass and saw the room was in near darkness, but a door to the hall was open and there was enough light coming in to see there was no one in the bed. He pushed the window up slowly, stopped to check the long knife in its sheath and patted the handle of the shooter. He already had his gloves on, but he was as aware as anyone of the problems of DNA, and falling hairs could be a particular hazard. When he was done he'd burn everything he was wearing.

He pulled the balaclava over his face before easing himself over the window ledge and into the room, still trying to hear through Craig and Charlie Reid singing a song about Jean. The room was cool, and from what he could see it was well decorated and seemed cared for. He couldn't connect it to the crazy woman he'd fought and pulverised in Leith way back when.

He moved soundlessly into the hall and looked round into the lounge.

Brenda was asleep in an old armchair so he waited again, making sure he had all his bearings in the house. He could see the front door, the stairs and that the curtains were almost closed in the front, but he could see the front window was open as well. He shook his head and his nose twitched with the reek of stale booze being exhaled from someone who'd taken far too much on board. He noticed the two bottles; if she was pissed that was a bonus.

Another couple of steps to the middle of the room and he drew the knife. The shooter was out of the question with every window in the place open, so he moved forward with the knife at the ready.

Brenda McMartin had brute strength in abundance and more than almost any man. She'd been pissed when she sat back in her favourite chair, but she'd known exactly what she was doing. She could handle drink like a true pro, and before she'd settled down she'd taken the sawn-off they'd used in Edinburgh and placed it back on the low stool beside her chair.

Brenda's eye snapped open and Cue Ball stopped for no more than a couple of seconds. It was his only mistake that night, but it gave Brenda the moment she needed. His surprise at seeing her awake bought her that precious time. All Brenda had hoped for was to look into the eyes of the man who came for her – and here he was. She grabbed the sawn-off at the same moment he realised he'd fucked it up and launched forward with the knife. It was too late for the shooter anyway so he just had to go for it.

The knife drove in hard just below Brenda's ribcage and she groaned with the shock. Cue Ball had pushed forward and downward hard because she was sitting. He ended up on top of Brenda, whose face was almost touching his. He caught the rank stink of her breath as she shoved the working end of the shotgun into his side and blew half his gut away. Cue Ball died almost instantly, and although Brenda was bleeding to death and hardly able to move, she had enough strength to drop the gun and pull his balaclava up.

'Fuck's sake,' was all she managed to say when she recognised the remains of the man sprawled on top of her. She died less than a minute later.

The noise of the shotgun was enough to alert a neighbour, who thought it might be a good idea to call the police.

That's how the local law found Big Brenda McMartin and Cue Ball Ross – still locked together in an awful blood-and-guts-covered embrace. It was a horror, but for the old

PC who was first on the scene it was a perfect opportunity to display to the young probationer accompanying him the black humour that keeps some cops sane when they have to clean up humanity's mess.

'Now I was with the CID at one stage, laddie,' he said, 'and my guess is that they shagged themselves to death and the man on top exploded with the intensity of it all.' He shook his head at the innocence of youth as the probationer rushed outside and threw up over the front garden, which in technical terms was part of a crime scene.

59

Two days after Brenda McMartin and Cue Ball Ross died together, Macallan walked into Elaine Tenant's office and took a seat. Grant Cosgrove was already there but Macallan could barely force a smile. She was tired, and she'd torn herself apart wondering if she could have done anything differently. She kept true to her deal with Jack and didn't discuss it at home, but he was annoyed because he knew she was on the same old roundabout of self-doubt that tended to be her way of responding to events that were usually out of her control anyway. She kept thinking about the look of disappointment on his face that she could be so unhappy such a short time before their wedding. Jack had gone quiet on her; it was the first time that had happened between them and it frightened her.

Cosgrove seemed okay, and Tenant was positively glowing. It wasn't what she'd expected, and if nothing else it helped to ease her own mood a little.

Tenant walked over to her with some fresh coffee and spoke while she was still on her feet. 'Grant wanted to sit in and have a quick run over things and see where we go. Do you want to say anything first, Grant?'

He had a mouthful of coffee and just shook his head. Tenant glanced at her notes for a moment. 'The forensic work has been more or less completed at the locus, and as far as we can tell the story is straightforward ... if that's the correct term in such circumstances. The boys are pretty sure that this man Cue Ball had been given the contract to kill Brenda McMartin. There's a pile of intel that he was working for a Liverpool villain, Terry Norman. As you know, the original information came from a source run by Charlie MacKay's team and was then followed by a source close to Terry Norman with the info that the Logans had asked him to take on the job – because there was too much attention on the Logans after the Bellshill situation. Okay so far?'

Cosgrove and Macallan nodded so Tenant carried on. 'As far as we're concerned the threat-to-life warning was delivered and, as usually happens with the villains, she didn't want anything to do with us. I've read your report, Grace, and that's about it. She said nothing else of importance.'

Tenant looked at Macallan and noted the dark shadows under her eyes, the tight lips and wondered again what was behind it. She knew the detective well enough to know that she had a habit of storing her troubles inside, but she'd never seen her like this before and could see no obvious reason for it. The events at Brenda McMartin's home were terrible but not of Macallan's making.

'That's it really,' Macallan said and glanced out of the window at a beautiful cloud-free sky. 'I asked Brenda about Mickey Dalton and she denied it all. There was nothing more I could do. She wouldn't speak to me about anything. It was a waste of time.' She looked directly at Tenant. 'Not much more we can do with this.'

Mickey Dalton, Slab, Tommy McMartin, Brenda and Crazy Horse were all dead. Macallan had decided that the truth could stay with the dead. Trying to make sense of it was impossible, and Macallan knew that Brenda McMartin had wanted to die. She'd wanted it to be over, so that was a resolution of sorts. The woman had received a death sentence that had been carried out. It was nothing to do with justice, but it made sense. Macallan had been tormented for years by her own demons; it made her wonder what Brenda had suffered in her own dreams and nightmares. Macallan knew she would carry her decision for the rest of her life, but it was enough that she knew what had happened. Nothing they could do now would make any difference.

Tenant took over again. 'So, Grant, it's over to you.'

'Well, first of all I want to thank you for the help you've given us. As for Charlie MacKay... well, there was circumstantial evidence but he had wiggle room if he'd been clever about it, and of course Slab's dead now.'

Macallan sat up and forgot about Brenda. She knew where this was going – a bad couple of days was about to get worse. 'But what about the failure to investigate the original case properly? The missing phone records?' Some colour had come back into her face.

Cosgrove put his cup down and nodded. 'Ian Moore can't talk to us and Mickey Dalton certainly can't help us. I know and you know exactly what happened, but if he played the plausible deniability card and stuck to his guns then we'd have toiled.'

Macallan was about to say something she'd regret, but Cosgrove was a real operator, saw it coming and put his hand up. 'If you wait a moment. Please note I've been using the past tense in relation to what our Charlie could have done to save his neck. I don't think you realise that your last visit to his office had unforeseen consequences, apart from the fact that he needed painkillers after the event.'

Tenant looked puzzled, but Cosgrove didn't let her in on that particular part of the story yet. Macallan blinked a couple of times and realised that there had to be some technical job on MacKay's office or phone and so the knee to the balls would have been picked up in all its glory. She watched the edges of Cosgrove's eyes crimp and a barely suppressed smile break out on his face. 'When you left him he lost it completely and made a call to a high-level source inside the Logan team. Gave the source Brenda's address, told him that the police had picked up the threat from the Liverpool team and that you were on your way there. He's hung, Grace. My team are on their way to his office as we speak. I don't know if kneeing a superintendent in the groin is recommended practice, but let's say that in this case it worked.'

Understanding gleamed in Tenant's eyes, but she looked pleased at the same time.

Macallan felt her shoulders ease off and she sat back in her chair with her mouth slightly open. 'We got him then?'

'We got him,' Cosgrove confirmed. 'Now I need to go. But one last thing – we've been looking at you for a while and there's a post coming up in our team. Why don't you apply? Anyway, think about it.'

He picked up his briefcase and offered his hand to Macallan, who hadn't replied. She took it, still not knowing what to say. 'See you at the wedding,' he said.

'The wedding?' Macallan had no idea what he meant.

'You gave me a partner's invitation, Grace,' Tenant said, looking ever so slightly embarrassed but more than ever so slightly pleased.

'Jesus,' was all Macallan managed to say before

Cosgrove smiled broadly, winked at Tenant and left the office.

'That'll be that then,' Tenant said and shrugged her shoulders innocently.

60

Macallan hardly slept the night before the wedding. They were in a lovely old room overlooking the beautiful undulating coastline of East Lothian. Jack and the children were still asleep. He'd taken one too many in the bar with his family and friends from Northern Ireland. Harkins and Young had arrived early on and by 9 p.m. the manager had had to warn him about his language and the nature of the jokes he insisted on telling anyone who'd listen. Young had managed to get him to his room by midnight but Mick being Mick ... he'd do it all again at the reception. She shook her head at the thought that Tenant and Cosgrove had hooked up so quickly. She was glad, and happy for Tenant, who'd turned into a human being.

Macallan stared out at a glorious morning and realised they would be able to get married in the gardens. She still couldn't get used to the idea that the day had actually arrived. Sometimes she worried that being married would change things and maybe for the worse. Life for them together had been good, and more than she ever could have hoped for in the years before she came to

Scotland. Darker images, however, kept intruding – the look on Big Brenda's face as she'd told Macallan about her child would stay with her for the rest of her life. Her depressed mood had passed quickly though, and she knew that sometimes the past was better left undisturbed.

Later, the piper led Macallan along the path through the gardens towards Jack, who looked like a male model the way he carried off the kilt. She gave one of her rare smiles when he turned to her, and although she felt a bit uncomfortable in the simple wedding dress, she was happy. The children, unusually quiet and a bit overawed by what their parents were up to, were in the safe hands of Jack's mother, who adored them. McGovern gave her a big thumbs-up as she passed the guests lining the route.

The celebrant kept it short and sweet. They'd spent a lot of time on the vows, and when Jack was saying his part a fat tear rolled down Macallan's cheek, which alarmed Adam, who started to cry for his mother. It got a laugh from the guests, and Macallan broke off from the ceremony, picked him up and resumed. Jack's mother brought Kate over to him and they completed the ceremony each with a child in their arms.

The sun baked the sheltered gardens at the back of the hotel, and it meant that as the day and alcohol wore on, more and more of the guests spilled out to sit in the late-afternoon heat. Macallan was happier than she had been in a long time, and for once she put all her cares to the side, because of all people Jack deserved this day more than anyone. He'd been all she could have asked for in a man: he was patient, kind and accepted all her sides – and there were a few.

She had a couple of glasses of champagne and the more she looked at him in his kilt, the more she realised what a prize he was. He looked fit, no doubt about it.

They were sitting round a wooden table strewn with

empty glasses, and Jack took off his dress jacket, which was just too warm in the heat of the day. Everyone was relaxed and laughing, and the children were away with their grandmother to play on the beach for an hour. Macallan closed her eyes and lifted her face to the sky. She prayed that the moment would last as long as possible, and she wondered if they could all be this happy again.

Harkins was standing at the doorway to the hotel, where there was a bit of shade, because like a true Scotsman he'd turned into a tomato after half an hour in the sun. He'd suffered a bit of a hangover that morning and was trying to be sensible, but after his second drink he'd felt the old magic returning and was now just getting into gear. He was leaning against the doorway while Young dropped strong hints about getting married, which he was batting away as diplomatically as possible.

Harkins saw it first – those old instincts that made him what he was. He looked over to the gardens and it was as if all other sound and movement had frozen apart from the man striding towards the huddle of guests. He turned away from Young, who was still talking, and for a brief second tried to work out if he was pissed or imagining it. It was real enough and it was trouble; he just hadn't worked out what kind. The man wouldn't have meant much to most of the guests besides Macallan and him. Harkins knew him better than anyone and had cause to curse their relationship. Jonathon Barclay looked a bit wasted now, but it was him, and he was definitely in the wrong place.

Barclay had been a leading Edinburgh QC and Mick's informant. He'd been wrongly accused of killing prostitutes when in fact it had been his loopy son who was the serial killer. The son had nearly killed Harkins, and the whole episode had cost him his career and full health.

Harkins looked over to Macallan, who was sitting next

to Jack with her face up to the sun and her eyes closed. He looked back again to find Barclay was closing on her. He moved towards Macallan as fast as he could and screamed, 'Grace!' It was loud enough to make an impact and every head turned.

Macallan snapped open her eyes and tried to adjust to the light again. She lost precious seconds as Barclay closed on her, and Harkins saw the knife ready in his hand and screamed again.

'Grace!'

She was too slow to react, but Jack was fit enough and quick enough to see the danger looming towards her. He acted instinctively and was close enough to Macallan to push up onto his feet and get between Barclay and his wife of a few hours. He wasn't quick enough to stop Barclay reacting and driving the knife up between his lower ribs and into his left lung. Jack didn't feel any instant pain – more like heat in his lower chest. He reacted only an instant after Barclay and hit him with a right hook that broke his jaw and left him twitching on the slabs in front of him. Jack turned to Macallan, who was on her feet.

'Grace.' He was gasping and saw Macallan put her hand to her mouth as she looked down. He dropped his head and saw the front of his shirt was turning red.

'Oh, Jack. Jack!'

He collapsed in front of her as she dropped to her knees and pleaded with him to live.

61

The cemetery and old kirk at Inveresk was one of the most scenic resting places in Scotland. An impressive site, it stood on the ridge that overlooked Musselburgh and a large part of the Forth shoreline. Any visitor could stand in the old part of the cemetery and see why the Romans had used it as a stronghold. Protected on one side by the River Esk, they'd built the ancient bridge that was the only route north and south for centuries in the east of Scotland. Invading and retreating armies had used it, and the doomed Scottish army had left their positions on the other side of the river to charge to their deaths at the Battle of Pinkie Cleugh, one of the darkest days of many in old Scotland's history.

This day, though, the sun shone again. It had been a brilliant period of weather, and men and women made their way to the graveside from all directions.

Macallan stared at the coffin, numb and cold despite the warmth of the day. She was afraid she might break down and dug her nails into the palms of her hands. She barely heard anything that was said, still in shock, but when she looked up and realised that her name had been called she stepped forward.

As the coffin was lowered into the ground the tears ran down her face and dropped onto the dry earth. The coffin settled and she stepped back from the grave. Jack put his arm round her and gripped tight. He was still weak but had recovered well and had been determined to make it to Jimmy McGovern's funeral.

Macallan put her head on his shoulder and thanked any God who was listening that he was alive. She'd prayed when it had looked like he wasn't going to make it, even though she was a confirmed atheist.

McGovern, that quiet rock of a man. He had only been in her life for a few years, but he had been her friend as well as a colleague. In Ulster she had lost more than one close colleague, but it never got any easier. She found it hard to imagine he would no longer be in her life. Too early, but that's what happened sometimes. His heart had been weaker than he'd admitted, and it had just given out one night when he'd been watching a match at home. McGovern had been a native of Musselburgh and he'd told Macallan a lot about it, proud of the Honest Toun's ancient history.

When they were finished Macallan walked round and took McGovern's wife in her arms and said something quietly to her. Jack watched and sighed. He was lucky to be alive, and he promised himself that they wouldn't waste a day of their lives. They'd love, spoil the children and make sure nothing would change that. McGovern had had that with his wife – he'd seen it every time he'd met him and his family and he knew it was worth all the effort.

He walked over to Macallan and Sheena McGovern, who were still holding hands. Macallan had explained to Sheena that Jack still wasn't strong enough to attend the gathering after the funeral much as she wanted to be there. Jack kissed Sheena on the cheek and took Macallan by the hand. 'Let's go home.'

Macallan looked at all those names on stones. So many stories. 'Let's do that, Jack.'

EPILOGUE

Later in the summer Jack's mother was in Edinburgh for a few days and convinced them to take some time off from the children and go away for a night. They decided on Glasgow, a swish hotel and a great show in the evening. Jack was fully recovered and writing full-time again.

The next day they wandered round the city centre and did some shopping, which Macallan never really enjoyed, but Jack had encouraged her to brighten up her wardrobe. He always wound her up by saying that she dressed like an undertaker half the time.

They stopped off for a coffee and as Jack browsed the paper she stared out of the large window and people watched. She was only vaguely aware of the music playing somewhere nearby.

'It's weird, Grace, but they're still running this story about Psycho McManus. It's turning into a real mystery and the conspiracy theories are starting.'

'What's the latest?' She was still staring out of the window and saw the source of the music just a few yards further along the road. It was a Salvation Army team giving it laldy for the Lord.

'They still can't find out where he came from before he was sixteen. No trace of him anywhere – no family, and no one claims to have known him. Jacquie Bell's done a bit today.' He read something from Jacquie's piece. '*It will remain one of gangland's great mysteries.*' He put the paper down and smiled. 'How about that?'

Macallan wasn't really listening. She was staring at one of the Salvation Army team who wasn't playing an instrument. It was Bobo McCartney, dressed up in a uniform, handing out leaflets and praising God. She shook her head and smiled. Life was strange indeed.

As Macallan and Jack relaxed and laughed as she told him the story about McCartney's arrest, his sister Wilma was on a train back home. She'd seen the reports on the web about McManus being killed by the police and just wanted to be back in Glasgow again.

Alan Logan was in a bar only a few hundred yards from them. He too was pleased with life. His brother Abe had been handed a heavy sentence and was cracking up in Bar-L. All he had to do was wait for his chance to take Frankie down and their empire would all be his.

Some things never change.

GLOSSARY

Bam	nutcase
Bar-L	HMP Barlinnie
Big Hoose	HMP Barlinnie (usually 'The Big Hoose')
Bizzies	detectives
Blues and twos	blue light and warning tones
Boracic	skint (rhyming slang, from boracic lint)
Bottle of B	Buckfast wine
Carly	Carlsberg beer
Ceramics	piles
Cocos	police (from Coco Pops rhyming with cops)
Crash bag	emergency medical response kit kept ready by prison officers
CROP	Covert Rural Observation Post
Dabs	fingerprints
Deek	a look
Denis Law	marijuana (rhyming slang for draw)
Dubbed up	locked up (in prison)
Dug's baws	the best (the dog's bollocks)

DO	Detective Officer
E Hall	the protection wing in Barlinnie prison
Gadgie	many different meanings, derived from a Romany word; tends to mean a male and probably close to a 'ned' or someone of low status or bad dress sense
Glasgow smile	a cut along the length of the mouth and into the cheeks
Goonie	Scots for nightdress
H	Heroin
Hee-haw	fuck all
HOLMES	Home Office Large Major Enquiry System
Howlin'	smelly
Inspectorate	Scottish Government body that reports to the Parliament and has responsibility for the inspection of the effectiveness and efficiency of the Police Service of Scotland
Jakey	addicted to class A drugs or, more likely, alcohol and regarded as a low life as a consequence
Jambos	Heart of Midlothian FC (from jam tarts rhyming with hearts)
Keech	excrement
Laldy	Glasgow slang meaning to do something with great gusto (could be anything from singing a song to attacking someone)
Locus	the place where a crime or other incident has occurred (legal term; Scottish alternative to the 'scene')
Malky	to attack or murder

382

Moody gear	a commodity that is fake or of poor quality
NCA	National Crime Agency
Neds	non-educated delinquents
On the batter	taking part in a drinking session
Osman warning	given by the police to someone when information has been received of a serious threat against that person (and required to be passed on even when the information has been obtained during a covert intelligence-gathering operation)
Plouk	a pimple/spot
PM	post-mortem
Pokey	prison
PSNI	Police Service of Northern Ireland
Radge	someone who is a bit deranged and gets into fights
Rammy	a brawl or fight
Rubber heels	anti-corruption/internal investigations squad
SB	Special Branch
Scooby	a clue (rhyming slang, from Scooby-Doo)
Scran	something to eat
Snash	aggravation or verbal abuse
Swanny	toilet
Wean	child

ACKNOWLEDGEMENTS

I'd just like to say a special thanks to the prison authorities and staff in Barlinnie prison for making me so welcome. It was a bit of a revelation. I've done a lot of prison visits in my time as an investigator, but I only realised during my research for this book that I had never been further than the interview rooms. It opened my eyes to the tremendously difficult job the men and women do in these institutions, and thank God they're there. The prison scenes in this novel are fiction and cannot come close to what life is like there, so for anyone who thinks that time inside is a holiday then please think again. In fact, what was going to be a short passage in the book became one of the most significant parts of the story.

Thanks also to the team at Black & White for all their support. I now realise it's a team effort. Of course, thanks to all the people who encouraged me to make Grace take on another case. I loved writing this one.

Detective Grace Macallan returns in ...

Our Little Secrets

1

Davy McGill, or 'Tonto' as he was better known, ran like fuck across Gorgie Road, his lungs burning with the combination of high intensity activity and the fact that Pete the Pole was chasing him with a large axe. He'd got the name Tonto from his love of Indian food and his almost encyclopaedic knowledge of the cuisine; it was the only thing apart from the Jambos that he'd studied in depth.

'I fucking slice you up!' Pete the Pole had screamed it a few times now and Tonto knew for certain that if the boy caught him that's exactly what he'd do. He was nuts and everyone had warned Tonto not to deal with the radge; he was built like Superman and consumed so many steroids that he was in serious danger of exploding one day.

They were hard times for Tonto, although it was never anything else, and he was dealing to anyone who could supplement his wages. The previous couple of years had been reasonable enough by his own shite standards, selling dope or stolen gear around the city or wherever he could punt it. At one time he'd done a bit of work and bought his gear from the Flemings in Leith, but they'd been sent to gangster heaven so he started working for the Graingers, who basically ran the west side of Edinburgh and were still expanding. A bit of part-time dealing supplemented his earnings with them, which never seemed to be enough. It wasn't that Tonto was any worse off than most of the guys in his position, and his spending habits were limited to a few bets on the nags, bevvies when he could, and following the Jambos. The truth was that working at the bottom end of a gangster's team didn't really pay that well, and all that stuff in the movies about the glamour, that was just shite. He wasn't exactly Prince Charming anyway, pish poor with the ladies and only tended to score when some inebriated female was in a worse state than him. And as for his flat . . . well, it was cold and barely furnished; it certainly didn't have a 'home sweet home' sign hanging anywhere. Apart from that, the stair he lived on was inhabited by drunks and bampots. However, as he was always staggering around the edge of the poverty line anyway, he spent most of his waking hours on the streets hunting for new ways to earn, so his domestic situation didn't really matter much to him. The Graingers paid him for the odd dope run and dealing, but he was way down the pecking order and he wondered if he'd ever get to be a real gangster, whatever the fuck that was.

The Graingers were OK as long as everything was hunky-dory, but seriously violent bastards if there was trouble. Their old man was Dublin Irish, a small-time gangster who'd come to Scotland to try and make a better life. It hadn't taken him long to discover he was just back in the old one with a slightly different view from the front door. To appease his second wife, who'd said she could not tolerate the idea of living off illegal income, he ended up in a shite job feeding the scaffie's lorry but determined his boys would do better. That had partly worked: his eldest son, Dominic, having noticed that his father looked old before his time, decided at an early age that he wanted success, and quickly. It just wasn't the kind of success his stepmother had envisaged. But as his generation had been told that greed was good, she tried to believe perhaps it wasn't all his fault.

He started to build his own gang and mini-empire in the concrete heroin fields of Broomhouse and Wester Hailes, and his stepmother only started to forgive him when he bought them a decent home in Inverleith. She got through life by pretending the boy wasn't what he was; his dad was secretly quite proud of him. And although the house was enough for his parents, Dominic wanted nothing less than it all, the result being that by the time he was in his twenties he was respected even by the bad bastards.

Something marked him out as a bit different, just a bit savvier than the normal career gangster. He'd realised that eventually even the best of them took a fall – they always got that little bit too greedy and stood under a big fuck-off light that shouted 'Arrest me!' He'd seen it and learned the lesson. As quickly as he could turn illegal wonga into legal wonga he invested in legit businesses, and he was good at it. Most of the investments thrived and he had a gift for negotiation with other businessmen, whether they were on the right or the wrong side of the law. On the surface he positioned himself squarely in the middle of the legit business and let his younger brothers carry on with the villainy. That way he spread the risks, and although his siblings always came to him for decisions, he'd put firewalls between him and the crime side of the business to keep himself reasonably safe. It didn't make him completely fireproof, just safer than most, and it would take pretty determined law to come after him. That was the secret – make yourself really fucking difficult to catch and most of the time it'll put the law off coming after you. He took care of the finances from the crime side for his brothers, and they were happy to leave it to his skills in washing their profits. At least that's how it should have worked.